DECLARE WAR

The Charlemagne Files Collection
Volume 1

Trinity Icon
Cetus Wedge
Brevet Wedge

K.A. Bachus

Copyright © 2015, 2020, 2022, 2024 K.A. Bachus
All rights reserved

The characters and events portrayed in this book are fictitious. Any similarity to real persons, living or dead, is coincidental and not intended by the author.

No artificial intelligence or machine learning technology was used in the creation of this book or its cover. No part of this work may be used in the creation of machine learning or artificial intelligence technology without the author's express permission.

No part of this book may be reproduced in any form or by any electronic or mechanical means, including information storage and retrieval systems, without permission in writing from the publisher, except by reviewers, who may quote brief passages in a review.

Published in Bangor, Maine, United States of America
Contact the publisher at info@charlemagnefiles.com

Library of Congress Control Number: 2024921724
ISBN: 979-8-9916011-0-8

Visit: https://www.charlemagnefiles.com

Cover by Marigold Faith

CHARLEMAGNE FILE TIMELINES

Volume One
Trinity Icon, early 1970s
Cetus Wedge, early 1980s
Brevet Wedge, nine months later
A Lighter Shade of Night,
mid to late 1960s

Volume Two
Lion Tamer, five months later
State of Nature, early 1990s
Vory, a year later

Volume Three
Swallow, five weeks later
Quiet Move, late 1990s
Goat Rope, 1999

CONTENTS

TRINITY ICON	1
PROLOGUE	1
ONE	4
TWO	6
THREE	8
FOUR	13
FIVE	16
SIX	20
SEVEN	25
EIGHT	28
NINE	33
TEN	39
ELEVEN	45
TWELVE	48
THIRTEEN	51
FOURTEEN	58
FIFTEEN	61
SIXTEEN	67
SEVENTEEN	72
EIGHTEEN	76
NINETEEN	79
TWENTY	82
TWENTY-ONE	88
TWENTY-TWO	92
TWENTY-THREE	98
TWENTY-FOUR	103

TWENTY-FIVE	107
TWENTY-SIX	110
EPILOGUE	114
CETUS WEDGE	**116**
PROLOGUE	116
ONE	118
TWO	123
THREE	128
FOUR	133
FIVE	139
SIX	145
SEVEN	154
EIGHT	161
NINE	166
TEN	171
ELEVEN	178
TWELVE	183
THIRTEEN	189
FOURTEEN	197
FIFTEEN	204
SIXTEEN	211
SEVENTEEN	218
EIGHTEEN	222
NINETEEN	229
TWENTY	234
TWENTY-ONE	239
TWENTY-TWO	245

TWENTY-THREE	250
TWENTY-FOUR	256
EPILOGUE	260
BREVET WEDGE	**263**
PROLOGUE	263
ONE	265
TWO	268
THREE	270
FOUR	276
FIVE	279
SIX	283
SEVEN	286
EIGHT	289
NINE	292
TEN	296
ELEVEN	301
TWELVE	305
THIRTEEN	309
FOURTEEN	313
FIFTEEN	316
SIXTEEN	320
SEVENTEEN	324
EIGHTEEN	329
NINETEEN	333
TWENTY	336
TWENTY-ONE	342
TWENTY-TWO	345

TWENTY-THREE	350
TWENTY-FOUR	354
TWENTY-FIVE	357
TWENTY-SIX	362
TWENTY-SEVEN	368
TWENTY-EIGHT	373
TWENTY-NINE	379
EPILOGUE	386
A LIGHTER SHADE OF NIGHT	**390**
INTUITION	390
COLD CUNNING	398
AVARICE	405
VASILY'S CARPET	410
THE SURVIVOR	416
PICTURE WINDOW	424
ON FIRST ACQUAINTANCE	431
BLACK SHEEP	437
THIRTY-EIGHT HOURS	445
COUNTING COSTS	451
QUENCHING THIRST	458
KEEPING SECRETS	465
PRIMER CHARGE	475
A LIGHTER SHADE OF NIGHT	490
TWO PAIR, ACE HIGH	498
CHARLEMAGNE AND THE SECTION	505
GLOSSARY OF USEFUL TERMS (GUT)	507
GLOSSARY OF GAME NAMES	510

TRINITY ICON

Early 1970s

PROLOGUE

Tsaritsa lingered in every breath. Sweet, aristocratic, it was Mara's favorite incense. She closed the church door behind her. Her left arm tingled, aching, warning her of death that day. She ignored it. She did not need that arm to cross herself as she kissed the icon of Saint Sergius. She would not need it for the dusting, or the polishing, or the sweeping. It was a little sore, that was all, and these old bones had known soreness before.

It took time to find where the Matushka had hidden the supplies. The woman was not very organized. Not that it is easy to be organized with four young children. Easy, no; necessary, yes. Mara offered to do this Monday's cleaning instead of watching those children for the Matushka. It was the least she could do—the very least. The very least she could get away with after seeing the unruly crowd of small bodies in the Matushka's living room.

Mara stood among the saints with a duster in her hand. They gathered around her, smiling at her from their windows to the Kingdom of God. She turned slowly and smiled back at them, at their places on the iconostasis before the altar and on the walls and stands around her.

What a life I have had, thought Mara. I would just as soon start over as to finish it. Is that possible, God? She shuffled to the Icon of Christ the Pantocrator, crossed herself in the prescribed manner, and kissed it before dusting it. All things are possible with God, but I doubt He will let me start over. And because I doubt, He certainly will not.

Mara did not often think deep thoughts. They were dangerous and useless and she had given up all attempts to understand such things long ago, on the death of her third child. Faith was her support and her only weapon, faith in God, distant and unknowable, faith in the Church, a haven, a comfort, a system of salvation, and faith in every mystical possibility ever presented to her. Superstition ruled her reason. It was rare for her to doubt. It was more rare to understand.

Her faith gave her great comfort through the years. It brought her through the purges. It brought her through the Great Patriotic War. It brought her through the searing pain of great loss, year after empty year. It did not, though, improve her discernment of either the finite or the infinite. She had seen enough of the finite to know she was not particularly interested in seeing it more clearly. But something nagged at the back of her awareness, telling her she was missing the mark in her search for the Almighty.

Missing Him or not, she continued her lifelong struggle to approach. She was as much a part of the Church of Saint Sergius as the icons and candles. She could be seen, at Vespers, during Royal Hours, throughout the Sunday Liturgy, lighting candles or crossing herself quickly, three times to everybody else's one. Straight, coarse streaks of grey hair escaped in thin tufts from under her black shawl and fluttered in the breeze created by her mobile right arm. Her thin lips moved soundlessly with the droning Slavonic chant of the choir —whether it was present or not. Today it was absent. It was Monday and she was alone with the saints.

As she reverently dusted the icons on the north wall, she stopped before the Trinity Icon, where another old woman, Sarah, laughed at the message three angels were giving her husband. She dusted Sarah and pondered the second coming.

I am becoming quite a thinker. I wonder if my children will be all grown up. If they are, they will be perfect, won't they? Then how will I know them? And how can it be heaven if I have missed them growing up? If they are little, how can I raise them as old as I am, or will I be young again? And Kolya, will he be young or old? How would he have looked in his old age?

She remembered a game they played before the children came. They had only an hour or so every day before his parents came home from work. The apartment was so small and crowded, it was difficult to get around obstacles. But after making love, they would arm themselves with two perfume aerators left to Mara by an ancient babushka who had known an easier time. There was no perfume in their corner of Stalin's Russia, even if they could have afforded it. Instead, they filled the fragile relics with icy water, and, naked and giggling, chased each other around that small space, hiding, seeking the advantage, spraying, and shrieking as the cold mist found its mark. When they had exhausted themselves and their bottles, they would collapse, damp and panting on their narrow bed for a last cuddle before polite tapping at the door announced that his parents were home.

Mara smiled at the memory. She replayed it in her mind, substituting her own now-aged body, and imagining Nickolai as he might have been in his old age: balding like his father, somewhat potbellied, but still vital, still laughing. The revised memory widened her smile. As her memory extended in time, she succeeded in misting her husband's narrow, hairy behind, and she broke a fifty-year silence.

Her cracked, cackling laugh sounded strange in her ears. Stranger still was the answering chuckle from just above her right shoulder.

ONE

Vasily's Carpet
3 September 1990

My Darling Daughter,
I know the recruiters have contacted you, and that you are considering entering the game. I know because of the questions you asked me this holiday. 'How did you meet Daddy?' was artless and cute when you were five. At eighteen, it takes on new meaning.

Of course, they want you for your education and your facility with languages, but there is also the matter of your pedigree. I don't think, in all these years of your training, that anybody has explained this to you. I will do so now, with more detail than my usual "I met Daddy in Chicago."

I tried to teach you what I know about the next world and the things that have been proved necessary for getting there. I have also given you basic skills for living in this world, in the civilized, sunlit world, where you have, for now, the privilege of going to school.

The others have taught you, and taught you well, all the necessary family survival skills for the black world, where secrets are both weapons and currency. Of course, these skills do not merely protect you in our world; they also draw you into it.

Heredity counts for nothing in the face of free will. Your inheritance is only another gift to be used or rejected. But the recruiters think they want you for it. Even if whatever genetic combination you are were immaterial to them, they would want you for your family connections. These remain, no matter what or who you are. There are people who love you, and, the recruiters believe, will do anything for you. I hope to give you some idea of what 'anything' can be—another subject where your training has been vague.

In writing this, I had to step back in time within myself. Memories tend to be two-dimensional—black and white newsreels without emotion—but what I have to tell you is about an event in my life that involved all of me. I've tried to tell it so that you will not only understand but also feel a little of what I felt then, which I think is the principal intent of any writing. I have the advantage of distance in time so I can be more objective than I could have been twenty years ago, but your father was my beloved, remember, and I miss him still.

No document can fully reveal the living man, despite the faith bureaucrats place in their reports. Still, your recruiters don't have any of this in their files, nor should they.

I did try not to, but I know I've allowed a few words of advice to creep in here and there—and one or two lectures. I am a mother. I cannot resist giving advice. Here's the first piece of it, no doubt unnecessary: Do destroy this when you've finished reading, won't you, dear?

Your loving mother,
Alexandra

TWO

I was born and brought up in Chicago, a first-generation American born to Russian immigrant parents. My father was a salesman or something and was gone most of the time until I was fifteen, when he had an accident that hurt his leg and forcing him to retire. His early retirement put us in a poor financial position, and I struggled to go to college.

We lived on the south side, near 87th Street and Cicero Avenue, in a plain brick box of a house built in the 1960s. It was different from the others on the block only because it had a chimney; my father insisted on having a fireplace in the living room. The neighborhood was on the very edge of the city; the south suburbs began across 87th Street. It was an urban residential place, missing both the dynamism of downtown Chicago and the serenity of rural Illinois.

For three years after high school, I lived at home and commuted to school. I majored in Chemistry at the Illinois Institute of Technology on 31st Street near the Dan Ryan Expressway. I earned a few small scholarships and worked every third semester to make up the gaps in tuition. Everything worked out until I began to concentrate on my major.

It seemed that as my coursework became more demanding, so did my mother. I finally came to a difficult decision, financially and otherwise, and left home on a Wednesday during the first semester of my third undergraduate year. I had to leave. Life in my parents' house was intolerable and I could not study. My mother, God rest her soul, was impossible to live with and we were having a blow-up on average once a day.

I remember my father standing in the doorway of my basement room, surveying the open suitcase and two cardboard boxes that held all my belongings.

"Anything I can carry up for you?" he asked.

I nodded, checked the closet again, and closed the suitcase. Papa left with a box, reappeared, and silently lifted the other box. The stairs creaked beneath him on the landing, echoing in the empty room, disturbing the silence of the house—a void silence, caused by the absence of noise, not the presence of peace. I took the suitcase off the bed and followed my father upstairs.

Outside, our goodbyes were sparse. "How about coming for dinner on Sunday," he said. "For your mother's sake."

"I thought she never wanted to see me again." I read the desperate warning look he gave me. "Okay, Papa, I'll be here."

He closed my car door, ignoring the rust chip that fell on his shoe. Stooping to look through the window, he said, "By the way, Father Paul wants to see you. He called while you were packing."

"Why?"

"He didn't say. Just stop by before you go... home."

Home. It lifted the tension a little to know that my father, at least, accepted my leaving as a natural progression, not a betrayal.

I drove an old Volkswagen Beetle at the time—very old. It ran well (when it ran), but it was not aesthetically pleasing to look at. People had a hard time deciding what color it was, and it had several nasty habits, like occasionally—make that frequently—refusing to start. I drove it out of love and poverty.

That day, the Volkswagen started on the third try. I ground it into an uncertain forward gear and lurched ahead, too busy trying to see the road through a scratched and dirty windshield to acknowledge Papa's melancholy wave.

THREE

My old bug tick-ticked up the steep driveway of the priest's house, shuddered, coughed, and died ten feet from where I wanted it to stop. I left it in gear, set the parking brake, and waited for it to finish rolling backward another five feet before stepping out.

Father Paul's wife, Erin, answered the door looking a little less harried than usual. She was a first-generation American like me but from a large Irish family. That she was now the Matushka of a Russian Orthodox Church was a testimony to love and the American melting pot.

"Hello," I said.

"Hello."

We stood at the front door looking at each other, locked in the kind of mutual unseeing stares that afflict people who are absorbed by their own affairs.

I forced myself to speak. "Papa said Father Paul wants to see me."

"Oh." Erin gave a rare smile and moved back from the door. "Come in."

Two red-headed bodies, three feet high and moving fast, hurtled past me as I stepped over an assortment of trucks and toy dishes.

Erin did not seem to notice them, nor did she make any attempt to stop them as they dashed screaming down a hallway to the left. She pointed toward the right, "He's in the dining room," she said. "Go on in."

The 'dining room' was the window end of a long, narrow kitchen. It doubled as Father Paul's office and was partitioned from the kitchen and open-plan living room by two patterned curtains. On the near curtain, rectangles in graduated sizes and shades of purple drew the eye toward the floor where an old green carpet in the living room met the yellow tile of the kitchen. The other curtain was either uncertain brown or faded purple, with only a hint of a former pattern. The arrangement did nothing for the room but proclaimed, rather loudly, a lack of taste and money.

The room would look much better without those awful curtains, I thought. I was more convinced of this when I stepped behind them and had to raise my voice over the din of the children to get Father Paul's attention. If this ugly partition was meant to offer privacy, it failed.

The priest looked up from a blank pad of lined paper. Several wadded balls of the same paper were strewn across the table. His expression, in contrast to his wife's, was more haggard and worried than usual.

"Alex! Thank you for coming so quickly. I need to talk to you."

"Good morning, Father." After kissing his hand, I sat down in an uncomfortable chair next to him. "She's called you then," I said.

"Who?"

"My mother."

We exchanged puzzled looks.

"Has she?" The priest seemed startled with sudden understanding. "Oh, yes, she has. But that's not why I asked to see you."

His expression turned inward again, and I was struck by the toll the struggle was taking. Paul Strukov was only in his thirties, but dark circles under his eyes and a permanently worried expression added ten years to his appearance. His struggle was not only financial, though money problems were real enough. I suspected that if this were the only problem, Father Paul would bear his poverty gladly, rejoicing in his weakness as did his eponym, the Apostle. But the gnawing sorrow came from the sad state of his congregation, not his bank balance. On the previous Sunday, I had realized suddenly that I was the only person between the ages of ten and forty who regularly attended the Divine Liturgy. Old women brought their grandchildren to church. No one else had time.

The priest picked his words carefully. "I want to ask your help. It's a little delicate. I mean, I don't want to accuse. It's...."

I said nothing, giving him time to think. With a sigh, he continued.

"The Trinity Icon has been stolen. It's gone, and I think I know who took it. I'm asking you to help me get it back."

"The what? Which one? Do you mean the one with Sarah and the three angels?" I briefly wondered if he was accusing me.

"That's the one," he said. "It's very valuable. Yesterday, someone offered me twenty thousand for it. It was written for Tsar Michael, you know."

"No, I didn't know. Did you sell it?"

"Oh no! I could never sell that icon."

"But it would solve a lot of problems. You could get the church roof repaired, fix up the house a bit...." I stopped for fear of implying I thought his house needed fixing, though it did.

"Yes, I know, but that's not important now. What's important is that when I walked the man to his car...."

"Which man?"

"The man who offered to buy it." Father Paul paused a moment as if he were finding his place in a rehearsed narrative. "Yesterday, when I walked him to his car, four or five boys suddenly scattered from the south wall of the church. They were spray painting it. With obscenities."

"And when you went back it was gone?"

"No, it disappeared later, sometime last night. But I've thought about it, and those boys must have been near the window when we were discussing it. I had opened it for some air, and well, they could have heard his offer. And when I turned him down, they may have thought..."

I waited, but when he didn't continue, I said, "What did the police say?"

"I haven't called them." He hurried to explain: "I don't want... I recognized one of the boys and I don't want to take a step that may damage him forever."

"Who?"

"Boris Nikitin."

"He's no boy."

"Well, he's young. He can change. He can't be twenty-one yet. A lot can happen to a man...." An inward look suggested the priest was speaking from experience.

"He's older than I am and I'm twenty. What do you want me to do, Father?"

"Talk to him."

"What?"

"Talk to him. Mention that I haven't called the police yet and that if it's returned, you know. No questions asked. That sort of thing."

"Why are you asking me?"

"You know him. You went to school with him."

"We went to the same high school, but I certainly don't know him."

"You're the only person I know who can approach him without it looking strange."

I did not tell him how mistaken he was. I looked at his anxious face, sighed, and said, "Okay, Father, I'll try."

"Great! I knew you would." Relief brightened his features for a moment.

The cloud returned, though, when I said, "So, what did my mother say?"

"When?"

"When she called."

"Oh, the usual. She asked me to tell you to go back home."

"Are you telling me to go home?"

"No. Do what you have to do. But be kind to her, won't you?"

"Of course." My voice rose in bewilderment. "Why do some women get that way, Father? I don't remember my mother being so bitter when I was a child."

The priest shrugged and changed to a more comfortable subject; he had had his fill of difficult topics that day. "How's school by the way?"

"It's fine." But I was not so easily put off. "I had to move out, Father. Finals are in three weeks and I can't study at home. You do understand, don't you?"

"I do, but your mother doesn't." He sighed and stood up, stretching his arms from the shoulders in the half-hearted manner of a weary man. "Are you sure Sizzle Burger will hire you again next term?"

"They always do. Two terms on, one term off. It's worked for three years now."

"Yes, but can you afford an apartment as well?" He pulled back a curtain. "It seems to be taking you long enough to finish school without adding this expense."

"I know what I'm doing." I immediately regretted my unthinking reply to the good man, especially because he was right and I knew it. In three years, I had barely completed two years of college.

We walked to the front door, picking our way around and over trucks, balls, books, and dolls. Erin was playing patta cake with her youngest. She did not notice that I was leaving.

The beetle started the first time. I let it roll backward down the drive, then began the struggle to find first gear. I noticed Father Paul saying something to me from the doorway. I shook my head. He repeated it, but I could not hear him. I cut the engine at the same moment he ran up to the car.

"Just wanted to say thank you again," he said.

"Oh. No problem, Father. I'll do my best."

The priest walked back up to the house, stooping to collect a toddler that had escaped through the open door. I sat, blocking two lanes of traffic until the bug started again on the fourth try. As it lurched into first gear, the traffic jam resolved itself in front of me, and several cars fell into line behind. Among them, though I didn't pay attention to it at the time, was a light blue Rambler car, slightly dented. I remembered it later when I had reason to. It followed me to my apartment, parked across the street, and did not leave again until the last of my boxes had been unloaded.

FOUR

It was Saturday afternoon before I could keep my promise to the priest. I knew where Boris would be. I found him where he spent most of his waking hours, in a rundown restaurant across the street from the high school. Two years after leaving (not graduating) school, he still sat in a corner booth, nursing cokes and pots of coffee, making each dollar last two hours, meeting a dwindling roster of his contemporary cronies, and coaching a growing number of younger admirers from the high school.

I approached his table, sat down opposite him, and was granted an audience. After explaining myself and asking a few questions, I was convinced of one thing: Boris was far too stupid to steal a twenty-thousand-dollar icon.

"You know," said Boris, "You're not as ugly as you were in school, man. I bet if you took off them glasses, you might even…" He reached across the table. "Naw. I guess not."

I retrieved my glasses from his dirty paw and wiped at the greasy thumbprint he had left. I succeeded only in smearing it, sighed, and put them back on. I had begun to slide out of the booth to get away from this bum as quickly as possible when I realized someone was standing at our table.

"Vasily, my man!" said Boris with what seemed forced enthusiasm.

"Hello, Nick," said the man. I detected an accent even in these two words, and for a moment wondered who Nick was.

"Hey, siddown, man," said Boris. "Don't mind the ugly broad. She's just leaving." To me, he said, "So I don't know nothing about no icon, okay? See ya."

Having resolved the origin of "Nick" in "Nikitin," Boris's last name, I turned my attention to this man, Vasily. He was, even through the haze of one greasy lens, magnificent. Everything Boris was not, this man was. He was muscular, well-dressed, and seemed intelligent.

"Icon?" He stared at me intently.

I melted.

"Yeah." Boris leaned toward me. "Scram, Sasha," he whispered.

"No, please, don't leave because of me," said the stranger. He sat on the booth seat next to me, effectively preventing me from going. He regarded me with penetrating light grey eyes. I noticed that two fingers were missing from his right hand. It seemed to be his only flaw. His jaw was firm, his features even, he was almost thirty. I was flustered and immediately infatuated. I struggled to maintain some dignity.

"Sasha," he said, "Are you Russian, then?"

"No," I managed to squeak. "I'm American. Please call me Alex." I immediately regretted the automatic response, registering his Slavic brow and accent and sensing that he might be offended. He did not seem to be, though, so I asked, "Are you Russian?"

"No." He did not elaborate.

"What icon is it that you know nothing about, Nick?" he asked Boris.

"Oh, I dunno. Some icon's gone missing at St. Sergius' Church. I told her I don't know nothing. I ain't even been in there in ages. Listen, about that guy you asked me about...."

"What icon is missing, Alex?" Vasily asked me.

I stumbled over every other word of explanation. I was puddled and incoherent under his gaze, wishing my intelligence would present itself and draw his attention away from my unruly hair and big nose, knowing it never would unless I could get hold of myself. I was in agony as I heard my voice screeching, tried to modulate it, forgot half of what I meant to say, said the other half stupidly, and finally gave up without saying much of anything.

"Is it valuable?" he asked.

"Yes. Someone offered Father twenty thousand for it the day before it was stolen."

"Twenty grand!" Boris was suddenly interested.

"Who?" asked Vasily.

"I don't know." I began to recover as it occurred to me that there was a lot I didn't know. The exercise of mentally listing the questions

I needed to ask Father Paul restored me to my usual distracted state and I did not immediately notice the intensity of Vasily's stare.

He made me notice it though, when he began asking me questions about myself. His gaze seemed to search me; his questions probed me. His apparent interest in me struck something deep inside that I had not known was there. This had never happened to me before and it deepened my first infatuation.

Vasily was soft-spoken, understated, but in a way that suggested tremendous power, as if he were accustomed to having his way. His spare conversation did not come from reticence; it came instead from an expectation of obedience and the self-assurance of a man with control over himself and others. He seemed to have a wry sense of humor as well. He spoke to Boris in circles, while he questioned me directly. He made Boris uncomfortable and appeared to be enjoying it, in the way a cat plays with a mouse before killing it, as an interest in life, a natural way to have fun before business begins.

When I told him I was a Chemistry major, Vasily became more animated, brought out an expensive pen, and began writing, left-handed, equations on a napkin. I was in my element now, and we had fun with combinations. He was an expert chemist.

He asked what my last name was, and I told him breathlessly hoping yet disbelieving that such a man could be interested in me. His reaction when I answered was striking. He seemed disturbed and uncomfortable and gave me a piercing stare as if I had insulted him in some way.

"I am sorry I have kept you," he said, rising abruptly. "It was nice meeting you, Alex, and I hope I will see you again."

I did not see how this was going to be possible. Although I had answered his questions about many things, I hadn't told him where I lived and he never asked me for my phone number. I didn't have a phone, but I was disappointed he didn't ask.

"I will talk to you later, Nick," he said to Boris.

"Sure." Boris watched him leave.

I wanted to watch Vasily, too, but Boris drew my attention instead. There was something in his expression, something I didn't understand, servility, certainly, nervousness, yes, and… fear?

FIVE

Immersed in the splendor of the Divine Liturgy at St. Sergius's on Sunday morning, I set aside all earthly cares, and thoughts of my mother, Vasily, Boris, and Boris's insults. For an hour and a half, I deliberately did not look at the conspicuously empty spot on the north wall where the Trinity Icon had been. I waited until after the final blessing to study it. My mother's continued refusal to speak to me gave me time to look at it closely. I was grateful.

I could picture the icon that was missing. It had been one of my childhood favorites. I remembered gazing at it during the long chants of the Liturgy. I could see it in the candlelight of the Liturgy of the Presanctified Gifts during Lent. It spoke to me of joy, humor, love, and the power of God.

Sarah stands in her tent, laughing, as three angels tell Abraham that Sarah, well into her nineties, will have a child. She laughs at the thought of an old woman pregnant and for the joy of having a son, for the love of her husband, and for the love of God who would bless them so. She is completely human in a divine circumstance, laughing at herself as she bows to the will of God.

The colors were still vivid after almost four hundred years, the gold more valuable than ever. The icon consisted of three pieces, two smaller sections hinged on either side of a large middle section so that the icon could be closed. Closed, it would be three feet square, too large to be inconspicuous. Opening it added another three feet to its width.

"I think your mother wants to talk to you," Erin said, interrupting my study of the blank wall.

"No, she doesn't. She's not speaking to me."

"She keeps staring at you." Erin tried to shake off the four-year-old tugging on her skirt. She did not succeed, and another child attached himself to the other side.

Erin reminded me of a walking beehive. Her children hovered around her, buzzing.

"I'll talk to Mom later, at dinner," I said. "You're looking rather happy today."

"Happy? Well, yes, I suppose. I'm always happy."

Maybe, but then you hide it well.

"It's a shame about poor old Mara, isn't it?" said Erin.

"Mara?" I searched the few remaining people gathered at the door, looking for the old woman who had been as much a fixture in that place as the icons. "Where is she? She wasn't here today. Is something wrong?"

"She's dead."

"Dead?"

"Died Monday."

Father Paul walked over and whispered something to his wife. She moved away with two in tow, scooped up a third, and told a fourth to follow her. The child complied by running around her as she made her way to the door, completing the beehive effect, and leaving the church behind in comparative silence.

"Did you talk to him?" asked Father Paul.

"Yes, Father."

"And?"

"I'm sure he doesn't know anything about it." I hesitated, looked at the worried priest, and asked, "Can I ask you a couple of questions, Father?"

"Sure." His word was open, but his expression had closed.

"How did the thief get in?"

He shrugged. "Picked the lock, I suppose."

"It was locked then?"

"Of course." He seemed distracted.

"And the windows?"

"No sign there."

"You have the only key?"

"No," he said with great patience. "The Parish Council president has one, but he's been in Florida for two weeks."

"One more question—no, three more. First, who offered to buy it?"

"I don't remember his name, but he gave me his card." Father Paul searched his pockets. He opened his wallet and handed me a business card. "Do you want it?"

On the one hand, though I had been asked to help, it wasn't any of my business. On the other, I was curious. I took the card. The name on it did not begin Vasily.

"Second question," I said, "Was his the first offer you've had?"

"For this icon? Yes. I'm negotiating several offers for others, but none of them are nearly as valuable."

"Others? You're selling others?"

"Yes, the Council decided it was the only way to raise the money to fix the roof before it falls in."

"But you turned down this..." I looked at the card, "this guy Brent Grayson. Surely the sale of one icon would have taken care of everything."

"Not that icon."

"Why not?"

"I can't. I won't sell that icon. Some things are more important to this church, to my work." His expression closed more than ever. "What's your third question?"

"My third? Oh, yes. Who else knows about the offer? Who have you told besides me?"

"Nobody." The priest thought for a moment. "I did mention it to the bishop's secretary that evening at my house. But he wouldn't have had time to tell anybody else before it went missing. He didn't leave my house until after ten, and the icon was gone by six in the morning."

"The bishop's secretary! Why was he here? Is the bishop coming?"

"You said three questions, Alex." He covered this evasion with a smile. "We'd better get some coffee before it's gone."

...

That afternoon, I had dinner at my parents' house. When I climbed into my old Volkswagen afterward, I hugged the wheel before trying to start it. Dinner had been a disaster. The first course consisted of a long sulk seasoned with sighs of martyrdom. Next came a rushing stream of hysterical accusations, half in Russian, half in English, covering every misdemeanor I had committed since the day I stopped wearing diapers. For dessert, there was a virulent curse topped by a violent door slam. I did not stay for coffee.

The street lights had just come on when I parked in front of my studio apartment. I walked upstairs, unlocked my door, and stepped from the bright hallway into the sepia gloom of the apartment, navigating by memory across the room to turn on a light. I had turned on the light and put the kettle, full and sizzling, on the tiny stove before I noticed Vasily sitting on the sofa bed in a shadowy corner, watching me silently.

SIX

My apartment was on the third floor of a block-style brick building near Pulaski Road. It consisted of one room and a bathroom. The room was divided by a short counter that created a kitchen nook with a two-burner stove, sink, and small refrigerator. This was the view as the door opened, and where I had first concentrated my attention when I came in, as there were two leftover slices of pizza in the fridge that could, maybe, erase an empty dinner.

I was not used to having strangers waiting for me on my sofa.

To the right of the door was the bathroom. To the left was part of my furniture, a stack of planks and cinder blocks that made a system of shelves to support my stereo and books. Across the room from the stereo was a sofa bed, where Vasily sat, one arm casually sprawled over the top while the other held a magazine in the fading light from the only window on his right. The window looked out onto the street. In front of Vasily was a small, plain coffee table Papa had found in the attic and let me have.

I stood with my mouth open, trying to find words to fill the space.

He said simply, "Hello."

When I was still mute after a long pause, he said, "I came to see you, knocked on the door, and it opened as I knocked." He stood and walked toward me. "I came in to see if everything was all right and decided to wait for you."

I recovered. I felt a cold shiver spread through me as I faced the intruder calmly, my initial infatuation dissolved by his lie. The door had not been open. My disordered appearance disguises an orderly mind. I have a system for everything, from putting books on a shelf to locking my door. I have never locked myself out of home or car, have never lost a document, and have never discovered a forgotten item in the bottom of a drawer. I catalogue, group, classify, and place each item in my life with unsparing precision. I do this without descending into obsession because my rationalism is simply a natural result of the way in which I think, and it causes problems only when I am forced to live with someone as chaotic as I am systematic. Like my mother.

I faced Vasily and for the first time understood that he was dangerous. The knowledge cleared my mind and allowed me to think and to watch him carefully.

"Did you find your icon?" he asked.

"No," I said. "Why? Did you?"

"I am not looking for it."

"But you're interested in some way."

Vasily looked at me with a different intensity. I watched his eyes move from my frazzled, unkempt hair, to my perpetually wrinkled wool skirt, and back to my face.

"You are not what you seem," he said.

The kettle whistled wildly, billowing steam. "Coffee?"

"Yes."

"Why are you here?"

He took a moment to reply, so I had time to look up from the stove to see his expression. He seemed to make a decision. "I came to ask you to have dinner with me."

Another great lie.

"I don't know you," I said.

"Nick introduced us."

"Who? Oh, Boris. He's hardly what I would call a reference. I don't even know your last name."

"Sobieski."

"What's a Pole doing with a Russian name?" I handed him a coffee mug.

"Sobieski is Polish."

"Vasily is Russian."

"Poles use it."

"Obviously."

"I did not know Americans worried about such things."

"I'm not worried. I'm curious."

"That appearss to be your biggest problem."

Our conversation continued this way until the coffee was gone. We answered questions obliquely or not at all and circled each other in a verbal contest for advantage. With difficulty, we agreed to meet at a restaurant of slightly better quality than Boris's hangout.

I was not sure how I should feel about this milestone in my life. On one hand, I had just made my first date. He was not just any date, either, but a handsome, apparently wealthy man who radiated power and self-assurance. I was uneasy though, because I could not believe such a man would be interested in me, and I knew instinctively that he was accustomed to having his way.

For some reason, he kept bringing the topic around to my parents. Where were they and who were they and did I know where they were from? I answered simply 'Leningrad' since this was what I had been told. I was on my guard with this man and unwilling to say more to him.

"Do you believe in coincidence?" he asked me, finally getting the hint that I did not want to talk about my family.

"It depends on what you mean," I said. "If you mean do I believe that coincidences happen, yes, I do. I think there is plenty of evidence. But if you are asking if I believe in pure chance, no, I don't."

"Precisely."

"Which?"

"There is no pure chance," he said. "A coincidence happens because someone causes it to happen."

"Yes."

"There is always an explanation."

I was not sure what he was getting at. "No," was my answer. "There is not always an explanation."

"There must be. If there is a cause, there is an explanation."

"Not necessarily," I said. "The cause can be the primary cause of all things, who requires no explanation. Even where there is a surface, or human, explanation, if you trace it back as far as it will go, you come to the primary cause."

"God?"

"Yes. Of course."

"Are you going to preach to me now, Alex?"

"No, why?"

"Are you devout?"

"What does that mean?"

"Even if one allows that God is the original cause, there is still a natural explanation. Don't you agree?"

"No, I don't," I said. "God is not bound by natural laws. He can do things directly, without using natural forces."

Vasily looked at me strangely. "If there is a God, and if He is interested enough," he said.

"There is, and He is."

Moses' tongue was loosened when he required it. Not mine. This was the best I could do. I can sit in an easy chair and conduct brilliant philosophical arguments with myself. But as I sat next to Vasily that day, engaged in a conversation I was having difficulty following, logical argument failed. Faith cannot be shared by logic.

"If He is interested," said Vasily, "then it is in a general way, not individually."

"I disagree," I said.

"What is your argument?"

"My argument lies in the word coincidence. To coincide means to exist or happen at the same time. Do you accept Einstein's theory of relativity?"

"Yes."

"Then you accept that time is relative."

"Yes."

"Then for events to coincide within the infinity of time, yet each within its own relative time, requires direction from outside of time."

"Or chance."

"No. Not chance. Coincidence is common to the human condition. Everyone experiences it. Its frequency suggests a cause greater than chance; its universality means it is individually directed."

"I don't agree," he said. "Universality cannot mean individuality."

"Then what is your argument?"

He seemed distracted and did not answer. Instead, he changed the subject and we had another cup of coffee. As we talked, I had the impression he distrusted me. He seemed forever trying to catch me at something, but I did not know what. Our conversation ranged over many things, his arguments always well defined, and his insight better than mine, especially regarding people. He avoided philosophy though, and kept the topics centered on the concrete.

After an hour, my infatuation returned; he was fascinating. But I did not forget how he must have come to be there. It sobered me and made me careful.

"Saturday, then," he said, draining his cup. He stood to leave. "I will pick you up."

"No," I said. "We said we would meet."

"Oh, yes. That's right. I will see you then." He walked to the door and seemed bothered by something.

I went with him to the door, hoping with everything in me that he would kiss me. He didn't. I was bitterly disappointed. He unlatched the deadbolt lock with some expertise and let himself out.

Once he was gone, my disappointment gave way to a desire for security. I attached the chain lock, knowing it was useless, and searched for something to put against the door. There was nothing heavy enough to hold it so I settled instead on an alarm and piled several pots precariously under the doorknob. Safety provided for, I rushed to the window to satisfy my curiosity. I reached it in time to see Vasily climb into the passenger side of a black Mercedes parked under a streetlamp.

SEVEN

On Monday afternoon, when I should have been attending a physics lecture, I approached instead a large glass building gleaming in the center of a crowded parking lot. I found Grayson's suite on the second floor, entered through a door labeled Grayson Antiquities, Inc., and stumbled gracelessly to a stop in front of a manicured, but vapid, receptionist.

"Is Mr. Grayson in?" I asked.

"Do you have an appointment?"

"Uh, no. I was in the area and thought he might see me. If I could just ask a question or two..." I glanced nervously at my reflection in the mirrored wall behind the receptionist. The image did nothing to encourage me.

"What is this regarding, please?" she said.

"An icon. At Saint Sergius."

"Just a moment."

I glanced at my reflection again and tugged at the front of my suit. I can take a designer suit and make it look like it came out of a garage sale. And this was no designer suit. Frump, I thought. That's me. What am I doing here?

"He'll see you now."

"He will?" Recovering from the surprise, I tried to assume a more dignified demeanor. The mirror showed me a frump trying to look dignified. I gave up the effort and rehearsed the questions I wanted to ask Grayson. The receptionist led me to the polished mahogany door of his office.

Grayson opened the door and held out his hand. "Mrs. Strukov. You found it!" he said. It was a statement, not a question.

This threw me off momentarily. "Uh, no. Sorry." I shook his hand. "My name is Alex Dolnikov. Father Strukov asked me to ask you a few questions."

"You're not Strukova?"

"No."

"What's the priest want to know?" He waved me into the room and indicated a chair across from his desk. "Come in; come in and sit down."

"I have just a couple of questions."

"You said that. What are they?"

I watched him as he walked to the window on my left. Balding, thin, with a large nose and a prominent Adam's apple, he reminded me of a vulture. He hung his predatory head over the sill and surveyed the parking lot below. He was very thin, almost emaciated, but his office was opulent, every item expensive and self-indulgent. Cut crystal jars of expensive candy graced every flat surface. He paced from one jar to the other taking liberal samples.

His nervousness must keep him thin.

He did not stop moving. With each mouthful of chocolate, he returned to the window. I had just cleared my throat to ask my first question when he stopped by the window and suddenly bent lower over the sill, staring at a point in the traffic below. He spun furiously and faced me, glaring.

"Who sent you?" he demanded.

"I...." I did not have an answer. I had sent myself, actually, after it was no longer my affair. I had done my part by talking to Boris, now I was being a busybody. But I couldn't stop. Too many questions tugged at me, demanding answers. I was nosy. I admit it.

"What do you want?" he demanded again.

"Just a question."

"So ask it!"

"You offered Father Strukov twenty thousand dollars for the Trinity Icon."

"That's not a question."

"Did you?"

"Yes."

"And he turned you down?"

"Yes, damn it."

"Were you expecting him to accept?"

"Of course I was. We were supposed to close the deal, weren't we? Look, you tell him," Grayson turned briefly from his minute study of the parking lot. "I'll go twenty-five, but that's it. That's as high as I'll go."

"He told you he'd sell it?"

Grayson looked at me suspiciously. "I thought you said he sent you?"

"He did. Sort of. Did he say he'd sell you the icon?"

"Yes."

"When?"

"Monday." He tore his eyes from the window again and gave me a narrow look. "What do you mean, sort of?"

I ignored the question and rose to leave. "So he said yes on Monday but no on Tuesday?" I asked, backing toward the door.

Grayson advanced a few steps, studying me. "That's right," he said. "It's Charlemagne, isn't it?"

"Who?"

"You know who. I know and you know and you tell those spooks not to worry. I'll have the money before tomorrow. Tell them. You got that? Tell them."

"Sure. I'll tell them." I hadn't the faintest idea what he was talking about, but I found his company unpleasant and was anxious to get out. I stumbled again on the doorstep, recovered, and walked away quickly. I was almost out of the building when I heard him calling behind me, "Tell them!" I turned and saw that he had followed me down the stairs from his office suite.

Once outside, I ran to my car, praying it would start the first time. It did and I lost sight of Grayson as I sped through the sprawling parking lot.

I reached the adjoining street and turned right, not noticing the light blue car turn behind me. It was small and innocuous and meant nothing to me. I did notice the black Mercedes behind it, though. It was distinctive, and I had seen it before.

EIGHT

Though I noticed and recognized the Mercedes, I did not seriously believe it could be following me. I knew Vasily was interested in the icon in some way, but I assumed he had come to see Grayson, and I expected the Mercedes to park in the lot. I was surprised, then, when it was still two cars behind me at the on-ramp to the Dan Ryan as I drove to school.

Surely there is no reason to follow me. He knew where I lived, and I told him where I went to school.

My exit was coming up. As an experiment, I drove past it, watching the rearview mirror. There was no hesitation from the Mercedes. On impulse, I crossed two lanes and took the next exit suddenly. The Mercedes was still one car behind me. I was so fixed on it that I continued to not notice the small blue car between us. I began to panic and did not register the anomaly of two cars following me through otherwise deserted streets in a rundown industrial area of the South Side.

The tame tick-tick of my Volkswagen's engine became a wild scream as I pushed the gas pedal to the floor. I tore my eyes from the mirror and found myself heading into an abandoned warehouse area. It was a desolate place, several blocks long, bounded by scrap yards and boarded-up buildings, the only deserted and wild space for miles. *You fool.*

The Mercedes moved up behind me. I took a gentle curve in the road without skill, skidding more than turning, but managing to stay on the pavement. As the road straightened, the Mercedes moved into the oncoming lane and accelerated.

The next curve defeated me, and my Volkswagen fishtailed from side to side as I struggled with the wheel, gripping it knuckle white, almost giving myself up to wholesale panic. A flash of blue passed by my left elbow. My wing mirror was filled with a black reflection bearing down on the left rear fender. A van appeared in the oncoming lane. As the Volkswagen's rear skidded toward the right shoulder, the Mercedes clipped the front left fender, hooking it and dragging it forward, and changing the direction of its spin.

The tearing metal and boom of contact were whispers compared to the roar of the van that screamed by me within centimeters of my nose, its horn blaring. It took another moment for my car to stop—on the sidewalk, facing the opposite direction. I wasted no time. Shaking hands ground the starter, forcing a spark. The Mercedes was not in sight as my beetle sputtered and whined back down the road in second gear.

I drove to school and decided to collect myself at the library, hiding between two rows of shelves containing the ancient philosophers. I took Plato from a shelf and sat down with him at a small table in a private corner. Opening the book in front of me for camouflage, I put my head in my hands and tried to stop shaking and organize my thinking.

Mental organization did not help the situation. My parents' home was severely uncomfortable and my apartment now felt unsafe. My car was badly damaged; the left front fender had peeled back as if iopened with by can opener, and the wheel shimmied strangely. Even if I could find the money to fix it, which I couldn't, it would take days in any shop, days I would have to skip class.

My grades so far that term were no better than my finances. This was the buckle-down part of the term, the latest point in which I could start paying attention and maintain my A average. I did this every term. I began by doing nothing, or as near to it as I could. I studied only enough to get a maintaining grade on the midterm, then three weeks before finals, scrambled to catch up. By finals week I was ready, having expended no more than four weeks of effort during twelve weeks of school. Of course, the last three weeks were intense, but for some reason, I had to flirt with failure to generate any ambition. I am not recommending this, you understand, and I hope you have more wisdom in this area than I had.

Finals were two weeks away. Father Paul's icon had already taken more time than I had to give, and I did not think my car's left front wheel would last to the end of term. The recent possibility of physical danger receded in the face of certain academic disaster.

"I'm in over my head this time," I muttered.

"Are you?"

He was sitting in the chair across the table from me, wearing a suit this time, with a tie and vest that made him oddly out of place in an academic environment. His coat bulged open as he leaned casually back in the chair, revealing to my angle of sight the edge of something underneath, a black strap of some kind, a bulky outline. I knew what it was.

Intellectually, I knew I was in danger. Emotionally, I did not feel it. I feared finals week more than the threat sitting across the table from me. Simple humility, a rare enough virtue in me, convinced me that I was not important enough to warrant the attention of anyone too dangerous. Vasily was either interested in me and harmless, which seemed unlikely, or dangerous but disinterested.

Either way, despite all I knew, despite my rational analysis and attempts to interest myself in the possibility of running, I could not move. Maybe my body was still moribund after the energy it had consumed on the road. Perhaps my will was sapped by the prospect of academic ruin. Whatever the reason, I did not run.

I also did not properly observe the man in front of me. I mistook the accusation in his expression for indifference. I thought the irony in his words came from boredom. I ignored the bulge under his coat and chose not to see the steadiness with which he stared at me.

I surprised myself with an angry, impatient response to his question. "What's it to you?"

"It depends," he said, "on how your mistakes affect me."

"My mistakes?" I struggled to keep my voice from shrieking. "Affect you? You have some nerve! You're responsible for it all and you have the nerve to…"

I was too enraged to notice his expression grow even colder. I was not pierced by his stare, nor did I appreciate the sneer with which he answered me.

"And how am I responsible for what you have done to yourself, little girl?"

"Done to myself?" *And don't call me little girl.*

I could not believe it. "I did not run into myself on the road, Mister. I did not chase myself and wreck my only means of transportation to school two weeks before finals. I did not do that, Mister!"

Vasily's sneer remained, but his brow furrowed, as though puzzled. Suspicion was still first in his tone, though, when he said, "Chase yourself? Are you accusing me? I did not chase you."

"I know perfectly well that you drive a black Mercedes. You nearly killed me."

"If I meant to kill you, Alex, it would not have been 'nearly'."

I shivered. His words, his attitude, were becoming clear to me. "Why did you chase me? What do you want?"

"I did not chase you."

"It must have been you."

"Where were you and your boss going?"

"My boss? What boss? I don't work during school terms."

"Your boss. Do not lie. You went to see him. You both came out of the building, and he followed you from the parking lot."

"Who followed me?"

"Do not act stupid with me, Alex."

I tried but failed to understand. "I don't have a boss this term. And you're the only person I know with a Mercedes."

Vasily put one hand to his forehead in a gesture of frustration. "Listen. I was in the Mercedes. Your boss was in the other car. Your boss, the man you are working for."

"What other car?"

"The blue car."

"There was a blue car?" I replayed my memory of the chase. I could not see a blue car but sensed the presence of other traffic. But my boss? Who?

"I'm not working for anybody. Honest."

"You are trying to find an icon." He said it slowly and distinctly, the way a teacher would explain a lab procedure to a dull student.

"Do you mean Father Paul? I'm not working for him. I...."

"You are very good, but now you are overdoing it."

"Overdoing what?"

"Pretending to be stupid."

"I'm not pretending. Believe me. I've never felt so stupid. I don't have the foggiest idea what you're talking about. I have six finals to take in two weeks, a car with a bent wheel and no fender, no money to fix it, and no vehicle to replace it, and you're going on about Father Paul in a blue car." I slammed the book down in front of me and began to get up. "I've had just about...."

Vasily's grip on my arm stopped me. It was a peculiar grasp, made with his right hand, the one that was missing the last two fingers. It should not have contained all the power of a whole hand. But it did, and it levered me irresistibly back into the chair. He leaned across the table and said, softly, carefully, "Whom did you see today?"

I saw the connection. I finally noticed the blue car in a mental replay of the afternoon jaunt about town. "Grayson? Brent Grayson? You were following him? He happened to be behind me, and you were following him! Well, that's a relief." I got up again to go. I was levered back down again into the seat.

"He did not 'happen' to be behind you." Vasily released my arm, leaned back in his seat, and studied me. "He was following you, or you were leading him."

"Leading him? Where?"

Vasily did not answer.

"Look. I'd like to understand it all, but I don't have time, and it looks like it would take a very long time to explain. I don't know when to butt out, that's all. Father Paul asked me to talk to one person. I got curious and talked to another one. I hereby officially declare that I am no longer curious about any icon. I quit. Leave me out of it, OKAY?"

Again, he did not answer.

I ran my fingernail down the corner of the book, making a ratchet sound. I looked at him again, noticing for the first time how cold he was, and that he did not seem to believe me.

He broke the silence. "I will take you home."

I did not like this idea, but he gave me no room to protest. He led me from the library with sure authority, swiftly through the front doors, down the steps, and across the now-darkened street. He opened the front passenger door of that black Mercedes, helped me in, and closed it behind me. I heard a lock catch. There was no light in the car when the door opened. Nor was there one when Vasily opened the back door and slid into the seat behind me. I could see the outlines of two other men in the car, one in back, the other beside me, driving, but I did not see their faces until they were illuminated by the bright lamps overhanging the northbound entrance ramp to the Dan Ryan.

"This is not the way to my apartment," I said.

NINE

"*Erstens essen wir,*" said the driver next to me.

I understood this. Four years of high school German left me competent in simple conversation. I almost replied in the same language, but something stopped me. Vasily knew so much about me, did he know this, too? Or was this something I could keep from him, possibly to my advantage? I knew I was going to need any advantage I could get. Thought and decision took only a moment. "I don't understand," I said.

He said we will eat first," said Vasily. He leaned forward from the back. "We know a quiet place where we can talk."

I hoped they did not notice my shudder. I did not want these men to know that I feared them because I had decided to base my defense on ignorance. 'Talking' did not sound like a pleasant prospect.

"Misha's English is not very good," said Vasily. "Is there another language you can use that we all know?"

"No. Sorry."

"What about Russian?"

"Sorry. I don't know Russian."

"You must know Russian. Your mother is an émigré. Surely, she taught you Russian."

I groped for a response. "I'm not fluent. My Russian is practically useless. My mother gave up on me years ago."

"Good. We'll use Russian." Vasily leaned back in his seat.

The decision had been made, but no language was used for another half hour. The car made its way across the city with silent occupants. Enveloped in a luxury I had never seen before, surrounded by men I instinctively knew were not safe, I felt small and insignificant, imprisoned in a fast-moving cage of power and wealth, in circumstances I did not understand.

After one of many turns, the car glided down a curving driveway in front of an older building, not as tall as the skyscrapers crowded around it, and stopped under a long awning that stretched from the front door of an exclusive restaurant. A uniformed footman reached for my door, but Vasily jumped out of the car and helped me out before the man could reach the handle. I thought of screaming but had no time to decide. I was marched into the building quickly, Vasily gripping my arm tightly, while the other man who had been in the back seat walked ahead to make arrangements.

We were shown to a table immediately. It was the only table in an elegant little room. *How nice. How private!* I debated the possibility of running out of the room. But I could be mistaken, imagining things. Wouldn't I look a fool running out of a posh restaurant in downtown Chicago? And then where would I go? How would I get back to the South Side at that hour? I didn't even have a dime for a phone call.

Our table was centered in a semicircular booth, very cozy. I was helped into the right side of it; Vasily sat on my left, his arm around my shoulder. The other two men blocked the left end of the booth to my right. I considered slinking under the table, but Vasily held me very close, so close that I could feel the gun under his coat, the one I had guessed at in the library. He was letting me know for sure. Threatening without speaking, smiling at me. I returned to ignorance as best defense and pretended not to notice. I smiled back at him.

The third man explained to me in passable Russian that this was his favorite restaurant in Chicago and would I please allow him to order for me. He introduced himself as Louis, said proudly that he was French, and treated me to a light conversation that I found easy to follow. He was gallant, jolly, and warm. He had dark curly hair and darker eyes that changed intensity according to the subjects we discussed, none of them important. I began to like him and to doubt I had any reason to be afraid. Then I glanced at the driver, the man Vasily called Misha. I noticed his expression as he filled my glass again with the incredible wine we were drinking. Chateau something, by Rothschild somebody. Like liquid candy. Not a hard, too sweet, obvious candy, but a subtle one, warm, enticing, and melting. Misha watched me carefully, and I remembered that I was afraid, there was reason to be, and I had decided to pretend that I wasn't. This was not difficult, since the wine was affecting me, making me warm and comfortable despite my grim situation.

But I did not like Misha. He had a polished and beautiful exterior that nonetheless suggested hidden menace. Like an iceberg, he seemed most dangerous beneath the surface. He was as handsome as the other two and maybe more, blond, blue-eyed, well built. Unlike them, there was nothing likable about him. His stillness was immediately chilling, his politeness clipped, form only, devoid of the human compassion that originally spawned all forms of etiquette. One would not forget such a man, but one would want to. He did not look at me, he looked inside me. Even more, he invaded me. My response was instinctive. The more he probed, the more I did my best to conceal. He gave me more than a few mental shudders.

A young guy in a suit came to the table and spoke to Misha in German. I pretended ignorance but was able to catch most of it.

"Who is the girl?" said the man.

"You tell us," replied Misha.

"Frank will want to know what you're up to. What should I tell him?"

"Tell him I sense a threat that I will take care of."

"I am not so sure," said Vasily. "She may be what she appears to be." (This was not very clear to me. My grasp of the conditional and subjunctive was, and still is, shaky at best.)

"Let's not be hasty," said the man. "Let me see what Frank has to say." He turned to me and asked in English, "May I ask your name, Miss?"

"Alexandra Dolnikov."

He repeated it and left.

The man's visit seemed to mark a change in the atmosphere of the little room. Louis's charm and the warmth of the wine receded before an onslaught of questions from Misha. His questions were politely phrased, in perfect Russian that was nonetheless not native to him, but each made me tremble. He knew much already, but I could not be sure how much. I did my best to appear thick, innocent, and uninvolved, without actually lying, since lies create a labyrinth that can be deadly to the liar.

"Vasily says you are looking for an icon," he said. "Have you found it?"

"No." I risked a few more words. "I'm not looking for it. I told Father Paul I would talk to Boris Nikitin about it. He thought Boris might know. That's all. Really."

"Have you known Grayson long?"

"I don't know him," I stammered. "I... Father Paul said he offered to buy the icon, so I asked Mr. Grayson some questions. That's all. Really."

"Why did the priest ask you for help?"

"Oh, I don't know. Because I went to school with Boris, I suppose."

"Why did he tell you about Grayson's offer?" I shook my head. I did not understand.

He put on his worst 'being patient' look. "You are twenty years old. Why are you, of all people, trusted with such things?"

I had no answer. Why does anybody tell somebody something, anything? What makes people drop bits of information, as though leaking them from a bucket, for others to pick up willy-nilly? And why do I pick up and keep all those bits that are dropped in front of me?

"What did Grayson tell you?" came the next salvo from cold corner.

I was still wondering how I had come to be young and trusted at the same time, so this question caught me off guard. I answered it automatically. "He said, 'Tell them I'll have the money tomorrow. Tell them.'"

Louis broke the tense silence after a few seconds. In German, he asked Misha, "What do you think?"

"She is lying," said Misha.

It sounded like a death sentence, and I involuntarily blanched. Misha, who was watching me carefully, noticed and raised his eyebrows in surprise and recognition. His meaning could not have been clearer if he shouted it in perfect English. He had not known I understood German, but he knew now. And he considered it proof I was lying.

Before I could further incriminate myself, a short, round man with bulging eyes came up to the table. He spoke to Misha. "She's clear."

"No, she is not."

"As far as we're concerned, she is."

"But it is my concern that counts most here."

"Yes, well, let me see if I can cool the situation, all right?"

Misha answered with an icy stare.

The new man was slightly nervous but seemed to know what he had to do and was determined to do it. He turned to me. I was comforted by the coffee stains on his shirt and tie; it reminded me of my dad.

"Miss Dolnikov, my name is Frank Cardova. I'm sure you'd like to be going, wouldn't you? May I take you home?"

"Yes, please." I whispered it.

Nobody moved. Frank Cardova stared back at Misha. The room seemed filled with explosive vapor, waiting for a spark. It was the moment of disaster when silence gives the boundary between peace and violence.

But the moment passed. Misha gave the slightest nod to Vasily, who left his place and extended his hand to me, helping me, almost pulling me out of that booth. Cardova propelled me out of the restaurant in much the same way that Vasily had dragged me in. After my initial relief, I wondered if I was wise to trust yet another man I had never met. I looked at his receding hairline. He would eventually be quite bald. Papa is certainly not bald, I thought, and he is older, so why does this guy remind me of him?

"What the hell were you doing in there, young lady?" he asked me when we were safely in what I guessed to be a rental car on the way to my apartment.

I wanted to say 'trying to stay alive', but I was still not sure about this man. "Having dinner," was all I could manage.

His googly eyes swiveled off the road and onto me. "I see," he said. "Bit of a daredevil, are we? Like taking risks? Why not get a burger and eat it on a subway track during rush hour?"

"Who are you?" I asked. "And who are those guys?"

"I told you my name and those guys are poison. Stay away from them."

"I know your name, but what are you? Are you one of them?"

And why are you so much like Papa?

"I'm their babysitter, so to speak. I'm not one of them, but I am beginning to wonder what, exactly, you are."

"You all seem to know everything. I don't know anything."

"That's a very good policy," he said. "I advise you to stick to it."

"I will. I'm through with this... whatever this is."

"Glad to hear it, now tell me all about it, my dear."

"I said I'm through."

And I'm not your dear.

"Just tell me everything—the truth."

His voice carried a note of authority, again like your grandfather, so I told him.

"So Grayson thinks it's him and he thinks it's the money," he said when I finished, more to himself than to me. "That one's a bad egg, young lady. Stupid move on your part, going over there. You drew a lot of attention to yourself."

"Grayson thinks what's the money?"

"Nothing. Don't worry about it."

I tried a different tack, curiosity and a sense of security momentarily pushing my earlier resolutions aside. "Is it money?"

"No, of course not." Cardova was again speaking more to himself. "He owes some people a lot of money and thinks he can save himself. He's wrong. They aren't the people and that's not the reason."

He drove and I watched the city slide by until we were parked in front of my apartment. I had not told him where it was. I was beginning to wonder if there was anybody who didn't know where I lived.

"Listen," said Cardova, "Those guys are hazardous to your health, eh? Especially Grayson. Don't go near him again."

This was a surprise. "I thought Grayson was pretty harmless. I mean, compared to Misha."

"It all depends on the circumstances. Grayson's are desperate and he knows it. That makes him dangerous and unpredictable. Nasty combination. Plus, you never want to stand around at the target end of a firing range, and that's what I'd call a twenty-five-foot circle around Grayson right now. Misha, as you call him, is just plain dangerous, but predictable. Everything he does has a reason. I'll do what I can to keep you out of his sights. You do your part and you'll be all right."

"So who is Charlemagne?" A sudden memory brought it to my mind; impulse asked the question.

In the light of the street lamp we were parked under, I could see Cardova's surprise. "Where did you hear that?"

"Grayson said it. Or he asked it. He said something about 'it' being Charlemagne."

"Did you tell them that?"

"No. I just now remembered it."

"Well, forget it. Completely. Wipe it away. Don't ever say the word again. Got it?"

"Got it."

TEN

I was feeling particularly secure the next morning as I sipped my coffee. There was no Mercedes outside. My pots and pans intruder alarm by the door was undisturbed. Frank, the dear, wonderful man, had solved things, and I was determined to take his very good advice. Safety was attractive today.

As I surveyed the pans by the door, I noticed for the first time a note lying on the floor. Father Paul had arranged a meeting at his house with my mother and could I please come over before going to class? No, I could not. No car. No phone. No finals. No future. Safety was suddenly not enough. There were other problems to solve.

I managed to call the priest from a pay phone down the street. He said he would pick me up and take me to school after our meeting. I dreaded this meeting and would have been glad of any excuse to get out of it. But his offer of a ride to school was a temporary fix to an immediate problem.

In Father's house, the ugly curtains were drawn back, combining the dining room with the living room and improving the look of the whole place considerably. Mama waited for us, having coffee with the Matushka. The two women sat at either end of the table, watching absently as a chaotic and noisy jumble of little bodies hurled themselves and their toys around the living room.

Erin stood and offered me her chair. Father Paul took a side chair while his wife made more coffee.

"Father, I know you mean well," said Yelena Dolnikova, "but this daughter of mine wants nothing to do with her own mother."

"Mama, I'm right here. You can talk directly to me."

"Why should I? You never listen."

"I do listen—when you have something to say."

"I always have something to say."

"No. You're always saying something. It's not the same thing."

Unsurprisingly, this infuriated Mama. She became temporarily speechless, a rare condition.

"Now then," said Father Paul. "Why don't we try to find some common ground, a starting point for understanding? You two cannot go on hurting each other this way."

"There is no common ground." Mama said this before I had a chance to say it.

"Yes, there is. We must find it." Turning to me, the priest asked, "Why did you move out, Alex?"

"I have explained that to her ad nauseam."

"Explain it again, Alex."

"I don't want to hear it," said Mama.

"Please, Yelena Alexeievna, just a little while. Please," said the priest.

I felt the bitterness rise in my throat as I remembered what it had been like at home. The priest's presence barely helped me resist the urge to list my mother's offenses and come directly to the point. "I can't study at home, Mama."

"Why?" It was not a question. It was a confrontation. "Tell me why."

"Because you won't leave me alone." I could not contain my exasperation any longer. My reserve faltered, and I spewed it all out, word after word, hurtful or not, not meaningful as a whole except in the emotions expended and the pain perceived.

"Because I can't go anywhere without you following me around. I can't sit with a book. I can't have silence and peace. It's one stupid conversation...."

"Stupid!"

"Yes, stupid. One after another. No proof of anything, but you accuse everybody of everything, and I'm tired of hearing it. But that's still not it. It never stops. I get up in the morning, and you're talking. I go to bed. You're talking. Same topics. Same people. Mara did this. Mara said that." My voice had risen considerably so that it did not have far to go to become a scream. "I don't care what Mara said."

"Well, she said it on her deathbed. I thought you would like to know. You never listen!" Mama was also shouting.

"I don't want to know! May her memory be eternal, she was a crazy old woman. I never believed a word of what she said."

"You have no respect for the dead or for your elders. You know nothing. She suffered much. She had real wisdom."

"What?" I accepted the cup of coffee Erin offered me. "She shut out everything new. She was mired in superstition."

"New is not always good."

"It's not always bad."

"True. But you are no judge."

"I'm a better judge than you think, Mama."

"She said what on her deathbed?" asked Father Paul. "When did you see her, Yelena?"

"Just before you came, Father. I saw you pull up to the hospital as I was leaving. I waved. Didn't you see me?"

"No. What did she say to you?"

"She told me about the icon."

I was suddenly interested. "What about the icon?"

"Now you're interested. You couldn't be bothered on Monday night, sitting there with your fancy notebooks and drawing numbers and letters like some secret language. It's that ancient alchemy is what it is. It will lead you to perdition! A wise old woman lies dying in a hospital and you don't want to know about a miracle."

I groaned. "Not the miracle again."

"Yes, again. No, not again, because you never listened the first time. You don't really believe."

"I do believe, Mama. I just don't trust Mara's interpretation. There's probably some explanation. What's the miracle?"

"Even when there is an explanation," interrupted the priest, "It can still be a miracle."

Erin refilled his cup. "I agree with Alex," she said. "There is always an explanation, usually somebody's imagination."

"I didn't say always," I said.

"You've given birth four times and you don't believe in miracles?" Mama asked Erin.

"No, I don't. I don't see that mess out there as a miracle." Erin pointed to the living room.

"Well, it is. You just don't know how to discipline your children, that's all."

I put my head in my hands and waited for the explosion set off by my mother's wayward mouth.

"You have your nerve telling me how to raise my children," shouted Erin above the din. "You don't know what I put up with!"

"I do know. I've been there. What you put up with is what you get."

"My children won't leave me."

"But you'll want them to!"

"Mama," I said, "What was the miracle?" It was the only thing I could think of to stop the shouting. Father Paul's "Now, now," was not working.

"What miracle?"

"Mara's miracle."

"Oh. The icon, the Trinity Icon, laughed. Sarah laughed. With Mara! Mara was thinking about her late husband—you know he died in the Gulag. Mara thought something funny about him—she wouldn't tell me what—and she laughed, and Sarah laughed with her. Imagine it! The icon laughed. We have a miraculous icon. Isn't it wonderful?"

"That's not entirely accurate."

"What? You don't believe it? Well, Mara heard it and I believe her."

"I'm sure she did. I find it easier to picture the icon laughing than Mara with a smile on her face. No, I mean it's not accurate because we don't have the icon, miraculous or not." Turning to Father and cutting off Mama's next comment, I said, "Did she tell you about her miracle, Father?"

"Yes."

"On Monday?"

He nodded.

"You believed her. Didn't you?" asked Mama.

The priest looked distinctly uncomfortable. He shifted in his chair and stared into his coffee. "No," he admitted. "I didn't."

Mama's eyes opened wide, shocked, horrified. Erin, who had been noisily shifting dishes between the sink and cabinets, became still.

Father Paul continued. "But I was in the church the next evening. I was to meet someone there, as I explained to you before, Alex," he said with a confidential look. "I was contemplating that icon when it struck me, just as you mentioned, that it must have been something to see Mara laughing. The thought made me chuckle." The priest looked into his coffee again. "Then Sarah chuckled, too."

"So you turned Grayson down."

"I had to. I couldn't let that icon go. Where would it wind up? No matter how many assurances he gave me that it would go to a private collector, what if it were placed in a museum? On a wall next to who knows what? Think of the people in this church, the people who should be in this church. I could not let go of a miracle."

A loud crash of a frying pan into the sink signaled a renewal of the Matushka's efforts to express herself without speaking.

"You told the bishop's secretary," I said.

"Yes. We drew up a plan to try to verify the miracle."

"You would have looked like a fool," said Erin.

"I would not have, Erin. I am no fool and the bishop knows it." He sighed and slumped in his chair. "But that's neither here nor there now that it's gone."

"Like my little girl," said Mama. "My little girl is gone, too. The icon will turn up, Father. You've mislaid it. But my little girl?" She gave me a pleading look.

"No, Mama. I'm not a little girl, and I have to make my own home."

"You will always be a little girl to me."

"I know. That is part of our problem. You don't see me as a person."

"I do see you as a person."

"If you do, it's a person you made up. Your idea of me has nothing to do with who I am."

"I know more about you than you think. You forget, I made you."

"God made me."

"He gave you to me to finish and polish. I do know you. If there's something I don't know, it's because you never bother to tell me. You keep your life away from me like you're afraid I might steal it."

"You don't give me any space. You want to know everything. Can't I have some privacy?"

"I don't want to know everything. I just want to protect you. I want to tell you what I know so you are not hurt. Don't you understand that? Where is your car? There is an example! What has happened to it? Do you have any idea how much it hurts not to know?"

"The car broke down, Mama. That's all."

"What will you do now?"

"I'll manage."

"How?"

"I'll think of something."

"That's it. You will think of something." Mama threw her hands in the air. "Don't ask for help. Don't relieve your poor mother's mind. You will probably hitchhike or something. Some nut will pick you up...."

"I won't hitchhike. But I have to make my own way."

"The way is a lot harder than you think." Mama stood up. She picked up her purse and walked to the door.

"I'm a lot stronger than you think, Mama."

"Yes. I know you think so. Goodbye, Father, Matushka." She let herself out, slamming the door as her goodbye to me.

...

I watched the traffic around us as Father Paul took me to school. There was no sign of a black Mercedes, but I realized I felt torn between regret for the absence of Vasily and relief at the absence of Misha.

ELEVEN

My last class that day was Physics. The book was ponderous but the professor made us bring the thing to class. So I was saddled with it all day, along with three notebooks, a lab book, a three-ring binder, and my purse, a large bag-like affair that, collapsed and mostly empty, hung on my shoulder. I left the physics building and took a shortcut to my car, walking behind the math building toward the library parking lot where my crippled beetle squatted, looking dejected. I hoped I could make it limp home, where I would make a decision about our futures.

It had been a grey day, with a drabness that dampened color and sound. In the late afternoon, the dim light faltered in an early sunset. Nothing was distinct. The lines of buildings, landmarks, trees, and signposts were smudged in a watercolor dusk. There had never actually been daylight that day, only a lighter shade of night. Full night was returning, creeping along the narrow lane I walked on. It hid the tall man until he was right in front of me so that I had no warning, and no opportunity to run.

"I have to talk to you," he said.

I could not, at first, remember who this was. I peered through the gloom trying to see his face. The voice was American. He was too tall to be Frank Cardova.

"Did you tell them?" he asked.

It was Brent Grayson.

"Tell who?"

"You know who."

"Tell them what?"

"The money." He dragged the word out, with forced patience, his teeth clenched.

"Oh. Yes. I did."

"What did they say?"

I tried to think, tried to remember every word said, every expression. My only distinct memory was my fear.

"Nothing," I told Grayson. "I don't think they said anything."

"Well, here. Give them this." He handed me a large brown paper bag.

I protested, not least because the bag was heavy and I had enough to carry.

"Take it. Give it to them. Give it to Charlemagne. See, here's the money. They can go back where they came from."

"Money?"

"Fifty thousand. No! Don't open it here. It's all there, don't worry. Tell them to go away."

"That's not the reason," I muttered.

"What?"

"Somebody told me you're wrong. Somebody said, 'They aren't the people and that's not the reason.' So take this back."

"What the hell are you talking about? Who said that?"

"I don't know, and I don't want any part of it. You take this back. I've had enough."

"Oh no you haven't," he hissed. "You'll take it to them or I'll find you. You got that? I don't care what the reason is. There's fifty thousand dollars in that bag. It ought to be enough to buy them off. Take it. Tell them if they want more, I'll double it. Got it?"

I shrank from the menace in his face and voice. "Got it," I whispered. I was saying this a lot lately, without getting anything more than a very uneasy feeling.

Grayson returned to the shadows; I could hear his footsteps on the pavement, walking quickly at first, then breaking into a run.

I walked a few steps, trying to balance the bag of money on top of my books. It slid to the left, threatening to fall. It slid to the right. "This is not going to work," I muttered. I dropped the lot and stuffed my books into my purse. One notebook had to be folded to fit. The others stuck out at odd angles, making the purse hang awkwardly on its one long strap. I put the strap on my shoulder. It slid off and the heavy bag thumped to the ground. I adjusted my balance, grabbed the paper sack, and was halfway to a standing position when I realized someone was standing in front of me again.

"Gimme the money," he said.

I looked up, still in a crouch, the heavy purse dangling from my left shoulder, the paper bag in my right hand. I saw a head silhouetted against the distant glow of the parking lot street lights. The hair was long and unkempt. A knife poked at me from the shadows, barely illuminated by the lights behind.

I shuffled slightly to the left, to make him turn his head so I could see his face. The knife followed me, coming closer.

"Gimme the money!" he insisted.

It was Boris. I could see him now. I could also see the parking lot to the left. There were no obstructions. I could run, but weighed down as I was, he would catch me. I could not bear the thought of giving way to him. He was so low. He was my ideal of the despicable. I did not fear him because he was so contemptible, a fawning braggart, no brains, no courage, but plenty of ambition. My mind worked for a way to disappoint him as if this were only a mildly interesting puzzle.

"Come on. Gimme it."

"I can't. It's for Vasily."

"I know that. I was watching Grayson for him. Gimme it and I'll give it to him."

"Will you?"

"Sure."

"I'm not so sure there is money in here, though," I said doubtfully. "I was just looking in the bag, and it looks like just some wrapped packages. Is that how they wrap money?"

"What? Lemme see." He stooped as I brought my left hand to the right to open the paper bag. The movement started the strap of my purse sliding toward my elbow. I moved my left hand as if to stop it, but instead grabbed the strap and changed the trajectory of the swinging purse so that it swung up toward his head. The edge of my physics book caught his right eye; his head snapped backward and he fell heavily.

I ran to my car without pausing to look back. I checked the mirror as I searched for my key. Nobody coming. I found the key, but it would not go in. Tearing my eyes from the mirror to look at what I was doing, I took the key out of the light switch and put it in the ignition, checked the mirror again. Still nothing. Turned the key. Nothing. Pumped the gas pedal and turned the key again. A reluctant cranking sound. A figure emerged from the side of the math building, staggering. I turned the key again; the Volkswagen started; it limped from the parking lot, making scraping noises and pulling stiffly to the left—with me chuckling at the wheel.

TWELVE

I made it to the 87th Street exit before the left front wheel fell off. Still several miles from my apartment, I started walking. After an hour, both shoulders ached from alternately carrying the book-filled purse. My feet hurt and I was hungry. I stopped on a busy street corner, well-lit and bustling, hoping for a sign of a bus stop. I found one, but the last bus had run fifteen minutes before.

My aching feet and shoulders did not concern me as much as the fact that I was about to enter an unwholesome neighborhood alone, at night, carrying fifty thousand dollars in a brown paper bag. When Vasily pulled up in front of me, then, I was not faced with a choice between safety and danger, but between dangers known and unknown.

I looked at him. He did not look sinister sitting alone in a small boxy red car. I looked past the street lights at the dark avenue stretching before me. He had never actually threatened me, had he? I was probably imagining things when I thought there was a gun under his coat. Frank's words receded in a hazy recollection of some marvelous wine. Didn't I still have a date with this guy for Saturday? He was my first date and I was afraid to get in a car with him?

"Get in," he said.

I got in.

The car was new. It smelled new. Everything on it glittered. There was a sticker in the window.

"New car?" I asked.

"Yes. Do you like it?"

"It's nice."

He looked at me as we waited for the traffic light to change. "You do not like it."

"I do," I insisted. "It's just, well, it's not you, is it?"

"Isn't it?"

"No. It's a girl's car." I glanced at him as the light changed and we began to roll forward. "Is it your girlfriend's?"

He did not answer for a moment. I could not tell if it was because he was deciding what to say or was too busy trying to find the next gear. He was unfamiliar with the car. "Look in the glove box," he said.

The temporary registration was in my name. My name, my address, my social security number, my driver's license number, my date of birth, my height, weight, color of hair and eyes, all typed in neatly, accurately, precisely.

"You forgot my hobbies, dreams, aspirations, and what I did in the second grade," I said as I put it away and turned off the map light.

"Pardon me?"

"Nothing."

"This is to replace the car you say I destroyed."

"Thank you. But I can't accept it, you know."

"It is your car. You must accept."

"I can't."

"Why?"

Because ladies do not accept expensive presents from men. Because it's a form of selling oneself. But he hadn't asked for me. It seemed a bit presumptuous to think that he would. He had wrecked my car, and this car was registered to me. It wasn't as if I could walk away from it without anyone noticing.

"How do you know so much about me?"

"I know only the surface things."

"Isn't that enough?"

"We'll see."

He was semi-communicative. I risked another question. "How did you get into my apartment the other day?"

"I told you."

"You told me a lie." I surprised myself with this little spark of courage.

He was surprised, too. "How did you know?"

"I don't forget things. I don't lose my keys, and I always lock my door. It's a talent of mine. So how did you get in?"

"Louis taught me how to open locks. Yours is ridiculously easy. I had no trouble."

"Louis opens locks?"
"He can open anything."
"Sounds like he's very talented."
"We are all very talented in some way, Alex."
"What's your talent, Vasily?"

I did not expect an answer to this question and I did not get one.

He pulled up in front of my apartment building and set the parking brake.

I could see his face in the street light and decided to risk one more question, to see his reaction. There are times I can't resist doing things like this. In school, I had a furious urge to pull the fire alarm, just to see what would happen. I finally pulled it one day in the fourth grade. I learned my lesson about fire alarms, but I still pull them figuratively now and then.

"What's Misha's talent?" I asked.
"That is not a name you are privileged to use," said Vasily.
"I don't know him by any other name," I answered.
"You do not know him."
"Then what should I call him when I refer to him?"
"You should not refer to him." He looked at me intently. "Or me, or Louis." He climbed out with difficulty and walked to my side of the small car, opening my door for me. He was such a gentleman.

I looked him in the eye defiantly.
"You are reckless," he said.
"You don't have to walk me to my door. I know the way."
"Don't be silly."

As we entered the building, I could smell somebody's dinner cooking. The aroma reminded me how hungry I was. I struggled up the stairs with my purse and bag of money, considering how to get rid of Vasily and the money quickly enough to attack the leftover pizza in the refrigerator. I turned to him at the door with my key in my hand and a rehearsed speech on my lips. He knocked softly. It opened, and he ushered (pushed) me in.

Vasily locked the door behind me as I stared mutely at my one-room apartment. Louis stood at the tiny stove, cooking. Misha sat on the sofa with a paperback. The stereo played Sibelius. Both men had their coats off, guns in full view. They looked very much at home.

THIRTEEN

"Why are you trembling, Miss Dolnikov?" Misha asked it, in German, as he set aside the book.

I tried to stop shaking. The heavy purse slid from my shoulder to the floor with a thump. "I'm not trembling."

"I do not like liars. Why are you trembling?"

I did not want to say, "Because I think you are going to shoot me." I was afraid it would become fact. Once uttered, the words could not come back. They would reach their destination and spark the act. It was, is, a superstition of mine, an automatic reluctance to say what I fear most. There was always a chance it had not entered his mind, and I wasn't about to put it there.

"I... You might rape me or something." To me, this was so implausible, it had no chance of becoming reality. At twenty, I had never been on a date, never kissed. No boy had ever expressed an interest in me. I was not ugly, but I thought I was and carried myself accordingly. I was slightly plain and my habits were far enough outside what was considered normal, that I was never in a position to learn differently. I preferred study to parties, books to boyfriends. My knowledge of sex was limited to common cliches and finding ovaries in laboratory nematodes. Mama was distinctly old-fashioned and guarded such information as if it were a state secret.

I expected an answer along the lines of 'those with least to guard, guard it most fiercely'. I was prepared to be insulted by the man sitting before me and preferred an insult to a bullet. I was surprised, then, by his answer.

He regarded me silently for a moment before speaking. His blue eyes brushed over me, my frizzy hair, the glasses sliding down my nose, my baggy sweater and loose blue jeans.

"When I want sex," he said, "I prefer the woman to be willing. Are you willing?"

I could not answer at first. I did not know what he meant by this, but I was suddenly aware that there was a prospect worse than being shot by this man. It was the thought of being touched by him.

"No," I croaked.

"Do you have a boyfriend?"

"No."

"Ever had a boyfriend?"

"No."

He stood up and walked over to me. I dropped the paper bag as he grabbed the front of my jeans and unbuttoned them. I grasped frantically at his hand, trying to pull it away. His other hand took the hair at the back of my head in a vise grip, pulled my head back, chin up. He kissed me then—if you can call it that. It was a violent, invasive, intimate investigation against my will. I was not accustomed to being helpless. It was an education. His right hand investigated, also roughly, with a savage precision that hurt more than my body.

He ended the kiss but kept his hold on me as he said. "Rape is not about sex. It is about power." He stared into my eyes; I barely saw him through my tears. "Do you need a lesson in power?"

"No," I sobbed.

He released me. I stood trembling in tears, grasping at my pants as if they were all I had (and they were, then).

"Now then," he said, "why are you shaking?"

"Because I am afraid you will shoot me."

"That is better. That is a reasonable answer. But I prefer to use a knife." He sat down again on the sofa. He spoke softly, in formal Russian. "I am more likely to cut your throat. Do you believe me, Alexandra Fyodorovna?"

"Yes."

"We are making progress. You are not Grayson's lover?"

"No!"

"And you do not work for him?"

"No."

"Who do you work for?"

"I've only ever had one job, at Sizzle Burger, but I don't think that is what you mean."

"Very good. Frank assures me that you are a typical American schoolgirl. I don't find you to be typical, and that bothers me. Stop shaking!"

I did my best, which was not very good. I stood, still stupidly holding my pants. He hadn't exactly done anything to put me at ease.

"I have taken into account your family background, but when you lie, it bothers me more."

"I haven't lied." As usual, my mouth ran off while my brain was occupied elsewhere, wondering what my family had to do with this.

He looked at me again and began to get up.

I corrected myself quickly. "Just the one time and my German is not that good."

He sat back down. "You conceal too much from me, Alexandra. Or you try to. It makes me wonder what you are up to."

Vasily opened a bottle of wine, poured some into a paper cup, and brought it to me. I was still holding my pants, unwilling to let them go. He put the cup down on the counter, gently pulled my hands away, and put me back together. I will never forget the look he gave me. It was not sympathetic or even compassionate, but a frank, knowing, look of regard. What Misha damaged, Vasily healed with one look. I loved him from that moment.

"What is in the bag?" he asked as he handed me the wine.

It was not the same wine as the night before, but it was nice and I took a long sip before I answered.

"Money."

"Money?"

"Money," I repeated. No one said a word. Nobody acted curious. Louis and Vasily set the coffee table with paper plates piled with coq au vin. They must have brought the ingredients with them. There certainly had been nothing more than cold pizza in my kitchen. The two men sat on the floor opposite Misha and all three began to eat. I stood there feeling ridiculous and hungry.

"Sit down," said Louis. "Eat." He pointed to a fourth plate on the little table.

I sat cautiously next to Misha and ate every scrap as if it were my last, a reasonable assumption given the circumstances. It was delicious. Louis is a wonderful cook.

It was Louis who finally asked about the money.

"So you carry your money in a sack?"

I looked at it. It was still on the floor where I dropped it, a few feet from the door.

"No. It isn't mine."

"Whose is it?"

"Yours?"

"Mine?"

"All of yours."

"All of ours?"

"I guess so. He said to give it to 'them,' and then he said to give it to Charlemagne, but I don't...." I realized my mistake when I saw the look on their faces.

"And who told you about Charlemagne?" asked Misha.

"Nobody." I struggled to gather my scrambled brain about me. "I mean, Grayson said it. I don't have any idea what it means."

"Somebody else said it, or you would not be so nervous."

"I'm nervous because you terrify me."

"Who else said it?" Misha persisted.

"Frank Cardova told me not to say it."

I still don't know how Misha reads me so accurately.

"He gave you good advice." Misha stood up. I shivered as he passed by me and picked up the bag. He looked inside it, then looked at me. "Charlemagne is our trade name. We," he gestured toward the other two, "are Charlemagne. Grayson told you to give this to us?"

"Yes."

"Why?"

"He said something about now that you have the money, you can go away."

"We want no money from him."

"I told him that."

Misha's puzzled expression narrowed. "And how did you know that?"

"Frank said it. He said something about it not being money."

"And you told Grayson that?"

"Yes."

"What did he say?"

"He said it didn't matter. That it should be enough to buy you off, and if you want more, he'll double it. There is fifty thousand dollars there, he said."

"Fifty thousand?"

All three men roared with laughter. I was not in on the joke. Not having ten dollars to spare, I did not find a bag of money particularly amusing. Misha threw the bag at me.

"Here," he said. "You keep it. Fifty thousand would not cover our expenses."

I knew I could not keep a bag full of cash of uncertain origin, but I was finally catching on and out of simple prudence did not argue with Misha.

Vasily was still chuckling. He sat on the floor, hands behind, legs stretched out before him. I tell you this because of what I saw in his laugh. I saw goodness. It lasted only a moment, but it was there, despite whatever other reality there might be, or that I would come to find out later, either in fact or in my imagination. There was a man there, who could laugh, not a monster.

We had coffee. Louis showed me how to pick a lock and gave me a few tools. Vasily and I discussed music. I thought his taste a little old-fashioned. I was beginning to relax when Misha sat next to me again.

He put one hand on my shoulder and turned me to face him. I feared the worst and tears started against my will. I bit my lip trying to hold them back.

"Stop that," he said. "I am not going to touch you."

I made an effort.

"We must make a decision about you." He said it rather gently—for Misha.

"If that's meant to make me feel better," I said, "it doesn't."

He ignored this and continued. "We live in a world with many secrets, Alex," he said. "Do you know that world?"

"No."

"Maybe not. You were born to it, but it seems, not brought up in it." He paused, watching me steadily. "We would like to meet your parents."

"My parents? Why?"

"Because then I will be sure you are what you say you are. Then I will know you are not working for Grayson or someone else. There have been too many coincidences that involve you. Is that plain enough?"

"Yes. But I don't see what my parents have to do with it."

"There is another reason." He paused and glanced over my shoulder at Vasily sitting behind me. "In our world, facts are very hard to determine. We can find anything in a file, but we rarely get the facts when something happens, because nobody will talk about it. Nobody. So we get only rumors."

He paused, considering his next words. "We want to talk to your parents for two reasons: to make sure of who you are, and to clear up a rumor."

I did not point out that he was being as obtuse as any rumor maker. But I did finally stop shaking.

"The question," he continued, "is which one of us should go with you to meet them. I do not think we should all go."

That was a relief. I thought for a moment. Louis was the most charming and seemed relatively harmless, compared to the other two.

"Louis," I said.

Louis laughed, Vasily chuckled, and Misha smiled.

"Louis," said Misha, suppressing a laugh, "is too dangerous."

I thought that was an odd statement coming from this man.

"He is very hot-headed," he explained, "and has no connection between his brain and his gun. I think I should go."

This was the last thing I wanted. "How about Vasily?" I asked.

"Vasily?" Misha rubbed his chin, then looked at Vasily. "Can you?"

"Yes."

"Are you sure?"

"Yes."

"Maybe you are right," he said to me. "It would be useless to have you next to me shaking all the time, and it is Vasily's business. Vasily will go in with you."

"Frank is here," said Louis.

I must mention here that Louis said this from the window. All three of them checked that window frequently. I don't think the street below was unobserved for more than a few seconds at a time. They also stopped talking whenever they heard my neighbors on the stairs. At times I fancied they acted more like the hunted than the hunters.

"I've been looking all over for you guys," said Frank when he came in.

"Then you are pretty stupid," said Misha.

"I love it when you flatter me, and it's nice to see the girl still in one piece. How are you doing, Alex?"

"Fine. Thank you." It wasn't a lie, but I have felt better.

"Fine? Good. Are we all through here? Satisfied? Ready to get on with it and leave the girl alone?" He emphasized 'alone'.

"Not quite," said Misha.

"What now?"

"Vasily is going to meet her parents."

"He is?" There was a note of panic in Frank's voice. "That's not safe, in my judgment."

"You have no judgment, Frank."

"Let's not be hasty. Tell you what; why don't I nip downtown and pull the file? I know I can get you authorization to read it."

"Your files mean nothing, Frank."

"But they are informative."

"Vasily will learn more this way."

"But let me have a minute with Alex, will you?"

"No. If you have anything to say to her, say it here."

Frank looked at me, biting his lower lip. He glanced at Vasily, then back at me. "Tell your Dad," he said, "that Buddy says 'Hi.' Tell him I'm on the all-star team now."

FOURTEEN

I led a simple life then. For example, going from one place to another posed problems only when the distance required a form of transportation I could not afford. When this was the case, I stayed put. I was never vexed with the paradox of Zeno. It did not bother me that I could never, logically, travel distance A because this would require me to first travel one half of A, then one half of the one half, and so on, ad infinitum, never starting out or ending up. When I was twenty and wanted to go somewhere, I either stayed put or I went. It was that simple.

Not so with Charlemagne. My parents lived three miles away. The discussion required to cover it took half an hour. First, should we take my new car or the Mercedes? I wondered how we would take the Mercedes when that was chosen because I had not seen it parked outside. Next came a conversation, no, a plan—yes, it was a carefully laid plan—of how we would leave the building, what route we would take to the car, and who would watch our backs.

Today, this procedure is second nature to me; then, I thought it silly. They took it seriously, though.

The Mercedes was parked on another street half a block away. Vasily and I made our way to it. I say 'made our way' and not walked because what we did to get there cannot be construed as walking. Skulking might be a better word, but still not entirely accurate. Skulking in an apparently natural way? Maybe. At any rate, we stayed in shadows, often with a wall on one side. Vasily seemed to prefer this and stopped frequently to listen.

At the car, he produced a small, powerful flashlight and inspected the Mercedes before he touched it. He looked underneath it and in the wheel wells. Satisfied, he unlocked the front passenger door and searched the interior, under the seats and the dashboard.

This took only a few moments, but he was so careful and so serious it frightened me.

"Is this car more like me?" he asked when we were safely on our way.

"Yes and no," I said. "It's not a girl's car, but it's not you, either."

"Do you like your new car?" he asked. "Does it suit you?"

"I like it very much. Thank you. But it doesn't fit me, either."

"Nothing fits for you tonight, does it?"

"I guess not."

"Why doesn't the car fit you?"

"It's too pretty. I'm more the old Volkswagen type."

He paused for a moment, then said with what sounded like anger, "Alex, you are not ugly. Stop talking that way. Stop thinking that way. It is not humility; it is foolishness, and it causes you problems in other areas, like sex. That was an incredibly stupid thing to say to Misha. You are hopelessly naive in some respects."

I was still working on 'You are not ugly'. Besides Papa, no man had ever said that to me. This was new. This was a revelation. "Are you saying I'm pretty?" I asked incredulously.

"A woman need not be pretty to be attractive, Alex."

"I'm not pretty."

"No. But you are not ugly."

"Plain, then."

"No. Definitely attractive."

How can I describe how those two words affected me, especially to you, a young woman who has never doubted her own extraordinary beauty?

I changed the subject so his compliment could not be changed, expanded, or depleted by further explanation. "Why do you take such pains to look inconspicuous," I asked, "and yet drive a distinctive car?"

"It is not distinctive in the places where we usually drive it," said Vasily. "We have this car for three reasons. Frank gave it to us; it is equipped with everything we need, and Misha likes it."

That made sense. "Misha likes things to be elegant and beautiful, doesn't he?"

"Don't insult yourself again."

"I'm not. I just get the impression Misha doesn't like me."

"You are insignificant to him. That is all."

"Who is significant?"

"His friends and his enemies."
"Who are his friends?"
"Louis, me, his family."
"He has a family?"
"Yes."
"A wife?"
"Yes. Stop acting surprised and do not say a word of this to Frank."

I could not help acting surprised. I could not imagine any of these men married. Another thought gave me a sudden pain. I approached the subject cautiously.

"Does Louis?"
"Does Louis what?"
"Does Louis have a wife?"
"No."

I could not ask. There was a long pause, during which we pulled up in front of my parents' house. Vasily turned off the engine.

"Neither do I," he said, "but in a few minutes, I think, that will not matter to you."

FIFTEEN

Mama answered the door.
"Mama, may I introduce Vasily Sobieski?"
She did not move but stood as if frozen in place and looked at him steadily. "I carried you out." She spoke Russian.
"Yes. I remember."
"You were four years old."
Papa called from another room.
Mama stepped aside and ushered us in. "It's Alex, Fyodor," she called. "She has brought... someone."
She looked again at Vasily. "You've grown tall and good-looking." She seemed to debate her next comment before saying it. "You favor your father—in looks."
"Yes," he said. "I favor my father."
"I brought you to an Austrian family. That was your mother's instruction. A well-to-do family. They had a son a year or two older, and a Polish housekeeper. Michael, I think they called him. The boy, I mean. Did you get on well?"
"We grew up like brothers."
"Good. Good. Please, sit down."
"No, thank you. I will stand."
He stood with his back to the fireplace, hands in his pockets. Papa's chair was in the corner on his right, another chair, the one my mother had indicated when inviting him to sit, was on his left, the front door behind it. In front of him was the sofa, where I sat down next to Mama, my jaw still dragging the floor. Behind me, a single hallway led to all the other rooms in the house. There had once been a separate entrance to the kitchen to the right of Papa's chair, but my father had closed it up. Having too many doors was only appropriate in certain buildings, he said, not in his home.

Papa came in from the hallway, paused, then sat in his chair.

"Please," he said to Vasily, "sit down."

Vasily stayed where he was.

"Papa," I said, "this is…"

"Yes, I know, Alex."

"Papa, I'm to tell you Buddy said 'Hi,' and…."

"Buddy?" He looked at Vasily, his jaw clenched. "Still your babysitter?"

"We know him as Frank," said Vasily.

"We? Are you still together then? Where are the others?"

"Elsewhere."

"You must be uncomfortable." Papa put his hand to his forehead. "Of course. My apologies. Here, take my seat. I'm well out of it; I'll sit with my back to the door." He got up and sat in the other chair.

Vasily sat in Papa's chair.

Papa turned to me and said, "You know Alex, there are some animals that cannot sleep unless they are touching a secure surface. These guys are like that."

I was still processing my mother's words and did not know what he was talking about. But he was about to tell me.

"I hear you're major league now," Papa said to Vasily. "Is that true?"

"I am not acquainted with American jargon," Vasily answered.

Frank's words seemed to fit here, so I interrupted. "Frank said to tell you he's on the all-star team."

My father's eyebrows arched. "Charlemagne is number one now, is it? Where's the team captain, the one with the knife?"

Vasily did not answer.

"And the wiz kid, the Frenchman? Listening in, I imagine." Papa stretched his neck and leaned over each side of the chair as if looking for something.

"I thought you said you were well out of it?" said Vasily.

"I keep up with the news. I assigned Frank to you guys, you know. Long ago, when you were trigger-happy brats and Frank showed some potential. I understand you're quite a weapons man. It fits, given your history. Next question is, what are you doing with my daughter?"

"We are not sure about her."

"Frank told you she's clear, surely."

"His information is not always accurate."

"It's as accurate as it gets."

"People are more informative than files."

Papa scratched his chin. "Whatever this is, it must be big, and it's going wrong."

"Yes."

"And my daughter?"

"She turns up every time it goes wrong."

"Well, I assure you, she's not in the game. Where is Frank, by the way? With the other two? What's he think he's doing?"

"He thinks he is doing his best."

"His best to stay alive, I imagine. Is my daughter the only reason you're here?"

"No."

"I thought not. Your father?"

There was a pause before Vasily answered, in a low, flat voice, staring at the carpet in front of him. "I was told he was shot with his own gun."

I looked at his face, wondering what was going on, what on earth these people, people I thought I knew, were talking about. Vasily looked up. His grey eyes held no expression, no emotion at all. They were two-way mirrors. He could look out, but I could see nothing inside. My parents had suddenly arrived from another planet.

"Don't look at me!" said Papa. "I was just his babysitter. I never touched his gun."

"What's a babysitter, Papa?" I was tired of ignorance.

"A babysitter controls a specialist, Alex. He provides the logistics support he needs: cars, safehouses, papers, that sort of thing, helps locate and isolate the target, and," with a pointed look at Vasily, "keeps him from contaminating the local populace. Something Frank's not managing too well."

Vasily shrugged. "There has been a question as to whether your daughter qualifies as a member of the local populace."

"That's all we have ever wanted her to be," said Mama. She leaned forward when she said this, treating Vasily to one of her more malevolent gazes.

"She has picked up some traits then, despite your efforts."

"Yes. Despite our best efforts."

I interrupted again quickly. "I have a right to know what's going on now, Papa. Tell me what a specialist is."

"You have no such right, young lady," said Papa. "But I suppose sometimes the lack of information can be as dangerous as the possession of it. Maybe you need to know."

He looked at Vasily briefly. Vasily was looking at the floor again, but he raised his clear eyes and watched my face as Papa explained.

"A specialist is someone who does what has to be done when no one else will do it. He hunts terrorists and solves strategic problems. Other words? Hunter. Killer. Assassin. Most of them work roughly along ideological lines, but they belong to no government. They are for hire."

Somehow, I had suspected this, but the spoken word hurt. I could not look at Vasily. I studied my hands in my lap as my father continued.

"Your friend here is the explosives expert for the best specialist team in the world. Their success record is one hundred percent. Never beaten."

I was beginning to cry, but Papa was not finished.

"The reason they are so successful is because they are very smart, very skilled, and ruthless. That is why Buddy is their babysitter. He is the best we have and it takes the best to keep such a weapon from exploding in our faces."

My tears were not entirely for Vasily. My father's involvement was an alien idea to me, though I finally understood some of his eccentricities.

"We?" I asked. "Do you mean the government? You weren't—Frank isn't—one of them?"

"No. I was not a specialist. I worked for Uncle Sam. But don't take relief from that, Alex. In any world where responsibility is understood and taken seriously, there are no grades of guilt, only levels of skill."

"Uncle Sam? But you were Russian."

"No, I wasn't."

"You were born in Leningrad."

"No. Cincinnati."

Vasily interrupted. "We are wasting time," he said impatiently. "Will you tell me about my father, or not?"

Papa did not answer him. He turned to me instead. I felt rather than saw Vasily's exasperation. I still could not bring myself to look at him.

"Alex," said Papa. "A specialist's greatest nightmare is to die by his own gun. It means treachery, betrayal. Usually, only one other person has access to it. Usually, that is his lover. A team is slightly different since they all have access—as do all their lovers. They take a bigger risk in treachery, but they have greater safety with someone to cover their backs, so they can sleep. Do you see?"

I saw, but I did not know why he was telling me this.

He turned to Vasily. "Your father was an ace. Only one person had access."

Mama spoke then, gently, so gently that I had to look at her to make sure it was her speaking. She spoke in Russian. "There was no choice," she said. "You were directly threatened. It was your father or you."

I finally managed a glance at Vasily. He sat like a stone.

"And my mother?"

"They took her before they knew he was dead," said Mama. "They knew who she was, knew she had access. You were on your way to Austria when she died."

She turned to me. "Help me make coffee, Alex."

I did not want to go, but the signals from both my parents were unmistakable and imperative. In the kitchen, I could hear the murmur of the two men in the other room. I wanted to listen, but Mama planted herself in front of me, took both my shoulders in her hands, and said, "Listen. That man in there, is he anything to you?"

I did not know what to say. Indeed, I did not know what to feel.

"If he is or if he isn't, I will tell you anyway. I saw his father dead, Alex, but more important, I saw him before he was dead, and he was already a corpse. Do you understand me, Alex? He was already a corpse, his soul murdered bit by bit with every killing. He was an animal; no human lived in that body. He was a collection of finely honed reflexes, nothing more. That man in there," she pointed to the living room, "is the same. He is empty. He is a corpse."

"All men can change, Mama. You have said it many times."

"No. Not this man. You don't understand. Even if he did turn, his enemies would kill him immediately. Don't you see? For him to quit, to really quit, he has to stop defending himself. He is hunted. He is always under attack. To stop means death, for him and anyone close to him. I give him five days, no more. Don't think you can do it, Alex. It is more likely he would turn you, make an animal of you. You are too young."

"But I am strong, Mama."

"You think you are."

"We must face all our choices with courage. You detest cowards, especially moral cowards, as much as I do."

"Yes, but there is a difference between a hero and a fool."

We made coffee and brought a tray to the living room, but Vasily was standing, ready to leave.

"Alex can stay here tonight," said Papa. "I will take her home in the morning."

Vasily looked at me. "I will take you home now," he said.

"It's no trouble," said my father. "I will take her."

Vasily's gaze was steady. I could not read it. "It is your choice, Alex," he said quietly.

I went home with Vasily.

SIXTEEN

We drove to my flat in silence. Vasily seemed preoccupied. So was I.

Frank, Louis, and Misha were waiting downstairs. Misha opened my car door. "Well?" he said to Vasily.

"She is clear."

"She had better stay that way."

Vasily did not answer. Misha addressed me. "I will walk upstairs with you."

"Please, don't bother."

"I'll walk her up," said Frank. He shifted on his feet from side to side, as if preparing to run. I knew he would not run. He was just nervous.

They had a discussion. Frank said he needed my signature on a form. Misha was impatient—with Frank and with me.

"Give me the paper," he said and grabbed it from Frank's hand. He pulled me out of the car and pushed me up the stairs in front of him, ushering me into my apartment in a hurry.

"I hope you are not so stupid that I must tell you to be discreet," he said.

"I'm not stupid." I was shaking again, but more from anger than fear. "And I don't like you at all."

He almost smiled. "Why don't you like me, Alex?"

"You are evil."

"I suppose you are a saint?"

"No. But at least I don't kill people."

"The difference between us, Alex, is not that I kill and you do not. It is that death surrounds me; it only puzzles you."

I scrunched up my eyebrows at him, confused, and he explained.

"When death is no longer only an idea in your philosophical little head, when you see it and smell it and are faced with only evil alternatives regarding it, perhaps you will have a claim to moral superiority. But I doubt it. Until then, I advise you to hate me less intensely, because hate is the next thing to murder and murder is not appropriate in an aspiring saint. Now sign this for Frank." He put the form on the counter and handed me a pen.

"What does it say?" I asked.

"Your government is informing you that if you say anything, the best thing that will happen to you is that you will go to jail."

"It says that?"

"It says some of that. I say the rest."

I understood him perfectly but took my time reading it anyway. I wanted to irritate him. He snatched the forms and pen from me as soon as I signed and let himself out without another word.

Good riddance.

...

Midnight is an odd time to run errands, I admit, but it was the best time for me—some things must be done without witnesses. After a check of the surrounding streets, I drove to the church and used Louis's tools to open the door. He had taught me well. I had no trouble. I quickly finished the two things I wanted to do and went home knowing the bag of money was safe but accessible.

...

I spent the next day expecting to see Vasily. I attended all my classes, a rare enough event, but it did me little good. My mind was on the cars driving by, looking for a black Mercedes. I concentrated on the people in the hallways, not my books, looking for a sandy-haired man of medium height with a solemn demeanor and a hint of exceptional strength. I was disappointed. I told myself I was being silly. I tried to convince myself that this was a foolish preoccupation with a man I was better off without.

When my last class ended, I avoided the narrow walkway I took the day before. I wanted no more surprises. I stayed on a well-lit path that wound around the biology building and was about midway down the walk when I heard steps running behind me. As I turned to see who it was, something hit me squarely in the chest and sent me sprawling backward to the ground, my books scattered under a path light. That light was my only company, and it did me precious little good.

"You think you're something," my attacker said. "I'll show you something."

Boris was on top of me, grabbing at my skirt, pulling it up, and tearing at my pantyhose. I struggled with everything in me. I fought him with a fury I never felt before. It was a question of power, all right, a struggle for power that I had to win. He was determined to show me and I was equally determined to prevent him.

I was winning until he cheated. He pulled out a knife and held it to my face, then moved it to my throat. I could see the bruise under his eye where I had hit him. I saw weakness and malice in his fleshy, unshaven face and I hated him intensely.

"I'll cut you," he said through his teeth.

"Cut her, and I cut you." It was a foreign voice, and it came at the same moment another knife flashed between our faces, razor edge toward Boris.

"Drop your knife and get up," said Misha's voice. I recognized it and was glad the edge of his knife faced away from me.

Boris got up and dropped his knife.

Louis pulled me up, helped to smooth my skirt, and brushed the dust from my clothes and hair. I saw Misha standing in the light, the point of that knife under Boris's chin. Boris babbled, hands raised, chin as high as he could hold it. Vasily stood to one side.

Louis led me away and Misha put the knife away and walked toward us. He walked on my left, Louis on my right. I heard Boris mumble something, then a dull thud. I turned to see where Vasily was, but Louis put his arm around my shoulder and led me firmly away.

"He won't kill him, will he?" I asked, not really wanting an answer.

"No," said Louis. "Nick will live."

We crossed a grassy area in the science quadrangle. The campus was emptying after the last class of the day. A steadily diminishing stream of cars left the surrounding parking lots. We sat on a bench and waited.

"I thought you didn't speak English," I said to Misha after a few minutes.

"I speak enough to know that is not a gracious thank you."
"Where is Vasily?" I asked.

He did not answer. We were silent for another minute until Vasily joined us. We walked to the parking lot, Misha and Louis in front, Vasily and I lagging behind.

"About Saturday," he said, "I will not be here and must break our date."

"Oh." I tried to act unconcerned. "Everything is going all right now?"

"No. It is still not right, but we should finish tomorrow and be gone quickly." He stopped, took my arm, and turned me to face him. "I never had any intention of being here on Saturday."

I waited for him to finish, not wanting him to say anything. I wanted him to leave right away so I could cry privately.

"But I would like to have dinner with you," he said. "Without Misha there to make you tremble, eh?"

He smiled and Humpty Dumpty was put back together.

"Yes."

"It may be some time before I can come back. Your government does not often welcome me. Will you have dinner with me when I come back?"

I nodded, and he kissed me. It was my first kiss. (I do not count the incident with Misha as a kiss for obvious reasons.) To dinner? I would have gone to Mars with him. What I knew about him, what he was, what he was about to do, what he could have done, disappeared in the joy of holding him and of being held by him. There were no other considerations, no other facts. There was only his kiss, his touch, and it was enough for me.

The Mercedes was already behind my car when we reached the parking lot. Vasily watched as I started it before he joined the others. Then the Mercedes turned onto the street, pulled over briefly for a passing ambulance, and left the campus, and me, for what I thought would be too long a time.

I settled down to wait for him, though, and spent the next day in a dream world of first love, attributing everything noble to my lover, blaming every nagging reminder of reality on the evil influence of Misha, and supplying the required miracle of righteous change in Vasily from my fertile imagination.

That evening, the evening of the day after my first kiss, at about six, my comfortable dream world of gentle miracles turned into a nightmare. In one of my nightmares, I am most terrified not by what happens to me, but by the part I play in it. If I am attacked in my dream, my inability to scream is what makes it a nightmare. If I fall from a great height, it is the last step I take before the fall that is most disturbing, because it is most regretted.

I was aglow with virtue and good intentions as I made a frugal supper in my tiny kitchen after school that evening. There was a knock at the door; it was Father Paul. In retrospect, I find it appropriate that it was a priest who broke my pious reverie and introduced me to a night of hell.

SEVENTEEN

"Are you busy?" Father Paul asked when I opened the door.
"No, Father, why?"
"Can you come with me? To the hospital? Boris Nikitin is very bad. He may die."

I remembered a voice from distant yesterday saying "Nick will live."

I shuddered.

"He wants to see you," continued the priest.

"Me? Why?"

"He won't say. But he desperately wants to see you. Can you come?"

I followed him to the hospital in my car because Father Paul was determined to stay with Boris until he was out of danger. Danger? When we arrived at the hospital, he told me he would wait outside the room.

"He's very bad," he said. "Don't stay too long."

I stood inside the door for a moment, staring at the thing before me. All my early virtue disappeared in the face of this reality I could not deny. The man I loathed was no longer a man; he was a pulp. The man I loved had never been a man. Only an animal could have done this. I could not pass this off conveniently to the evil Misha; he had been in my sight the whole time. Vasily had done this, was the only one who could have done this. He had done this without apparent effort, certainly without compunction, and then he kissed me.

Boris was difficult to pick out in the jungle of tubes and bandages. Every limb was encased in plaster.

His hands, suspended from a frame above him, were double their normal size with fingers spread by silver splints. His face, a blot of purple and red surrounded by hospital white, was swollen and unrecognizable. His nose was broken, his jaw wired together. He looked at me through one blood-filled eye; the other had been forced shut by the swelling.

I went to his side. He murmured something.

I bent closer to hear him.

"Forgive me," he said.

I don't know how long I knelt by that bed crying. It was a space of time outside of time. It ended when Father Paul came into the room.

"They think he will make it," he said gently. "Why don't you go home now, Alex?"

...

A mountain of stairs faced me at my apartment building. I climbed it one boulder at a time, watching my feet, and so I did not see Brent Grayson waiting on the landing by my door until it was too late. He grabbed me by my sweater and slammed me against the door, pushing the muzzle of a gun into my face so hard that it cut the inside of my cheek on a tooth.

"I'm going to die and you're going with me," he said.

I had no time to answer him. He was sweating, taut, heated by desperate fear, talking fast and without coherence.

"You didn't give it to them," he said.

"I did," I insisted, searching the stairwell for an escape.

"They're on me. They're dogging me. What did they say?"

"They laughed," I said with difficulty.

His color changed; he turned scarlet, convulsed with rage, fierce, and out of control. He hissed, "Laughed? Open your mouth so I can shoot you in your laughing throat."

I caught sight of a movement to my left, behind Grayson's shoulder. It was Louis. He held a finger to his lips in a gesture of silence. His other hand held a gun. He took aim.

"Open!" said Grayson.

"Wait," I said in desperation. "I know where the icon is."

He paused. There came a sharp pop from Louis's suppressed gun and Grayson was dead, slumping against me, then crumpling to the floor.

Louis was putting his gun away when Misha came up the stairs, two at a time.

"What the hell!" he said. "Open the door. Get that inside before someone comes along."

Louis had the door open before I could find my key. Vasily came upstairs and helped Misha pull the body inside. They put it in the bathtub. Louis escorted me in and bolted the door behind us all. The body did not frighten me as much as the wild look on Misha's face. It was a fury very much like Grayson's had been, but more controlled and therefore, to me, more surely deadly. He and Louis held a heated discussion in French that I did not understand.

Louis's temper flared. I was trying to edge away from the two of them when Louis said suddenly, in English, "She knows the location of the icon."

I did not like the attention I received then. Misha's gaze made the bones inside me sizzle. He said, "You know where the icon is?"

"Yes."

"Where?"

I was about to answer when Vasily said something in Polish. Another long and incomprehensible discussion followed. Vasily spoke quietly; Misha was more vehement. I did not speak Polish at the time, so I do not know exactly what was said, but Vasily told me later that it was an argument over my right to a free choice. He said I was the eventual loser, depending on one's point of view, but he never told me which way he argued.

Eventually, they decided something, because there came a flurry of questions. What was my dress size? Shoe size? Was there a store open? Where were my car keys? Louis and Vasily left, and I was alone in my apartment with Misha and a dead body.

Misha bolted the door, then went to the window. The curtains were closed and he stood by the far-right side of the window looking out through the narrow space where the curtain did not cover the side. He looked around the room and pulled the sofa away from the wall and slightly toward him. The side of the sofa was low, about two feet high. He rested one foot on it, leaned against the wall, and checked the street behind the curtain again.

I recognized it and remembered doing something similar—an alarm made from pots and pans. "You're afraid," I said to him, amazed.

He looked at me and I noticed other things. He was unshaven, his hair uncombed, his eyes puffy. He was tired.

"This place is not safe," he said. "Come here, so I can talk to you."

I approached warily.

"Ten days ago," he said, "we arrived to do a job that should take only two days. Everything was ready; then something went wrong. For ten days we have been living with only the protection Frank can give, and it is not enough. The entire black world knows we are here and exposed; our enemies are ready to exploit it. We are making too many mistakes."

"And you're afraid of dying," I said.

"No. Dying is nothing. Louis did Grayson a great favor by putting a bullet in his head. Much worse awaited him."

"Then why not quit now?"

"I don't know. Maybe you will tell me the answer to that tomorrow."

I wondered what he meant by this.

"Please describe the icon and tell me where it is." I told him, and he asked, "Then it can be taken apart? Into sections?"

"I suppose it can, but it is ancient. I am not sure it can be dismantled without damage."

"We will go get it. But first I will explain something to you. Sometimes people make choices for us, but even then, we can—we must—accept or reject the choice. That is unavoidable. Even by not choosing, we choose. Do you understand?"

"No."

"You will."

EIGHTEEN

We drove past the church and parked on an unlighted side street. Misha opened the fire exit door in the back and we slipped inside.

The moonlight glinted in sparks on the gold, on the candles, and on the icons. The iconostasis guarded the holiest place and hid the altar from our view, but the saints were here, in profusion, as witnesses. The prayers, of joy, despair—and sometimes boredom—clung to the walls, lingered under the ceiling, assaulted the senses in the same way the incense did, reminding out and breathing in devotion to God.

I knew the saints were furious with me for bringing this man into that holy place. I asked them to pray for me anyway.

We crossed behind the icon of Saint Sergius—oh, the look he must have given me at the sight of my companion!—and entered a little room to one side of the main entrance. The room, a closet really, was barely large enough to hold the two of us. Opposite the door, a tall cupboard took up one wall. It was filled with hanging vestments and boxes of candles. A sink and short counter stood against the wall on our left. There were no windows. Misha shut the door and turned on the light.

He stood above me as I knelt in front of the sink cabinet, searching for the opening I knew was there. I dug my fingers into the carpet, under the cabinet's baseboard. It pulled away easily. I reached in and slid the folded icon out from under the cabinet. Misha knelt beside me, regarding me curiously, as if he hadn't expected me to produce the icon.

"How did you find it?" he asked. "Did you hide it?"

"No. I just knew where to start looking."

"How?"

"Cleaning supplies. They're in the cabinet."

"Please, explain."

I tried to keep it simple. "The person who cleans the church hid the icon. It was logical for her to hide it in a place she knows well."

He was still puzzled, so I started from the beginning.

"Father Paul was about to sell the icon to Grayson, but something happened, and he backed out of the deal at the last minute. That night, the icon disappeared. Grayson wanted it badly, but he didn't have it. Boris was there because he was watching Grayson for Vasily. He didn't know anything about it, and anyway, there was no sign of forced entry. Boris would have broken a window or something. Not his style to forego malicious damage. Vasily didn't have it because he kept asking me about it. That eliminates just about everybody who doesn't have a key.

"That brought me to a dead end until Papa taught me something the night he met Vasily. It was the concept of access. One other person had access to the key. One person who knew about the proposed sale and knew the reason it fell through. One person who would have heard everything Father Paul told the bishop's secretary behind a useless dining room partition. That was Erin, the Matushka."

"She took the icon to sell it against her husband's wishes," said Misha.

"No." I looked at him, hoping he would understand what I was about to tell him. "It may have occurred to her to sell the icon. She even called Grayson. When I went to see him, he thought I was her. That's why he was so quick to let me in and that's how I knew he didn't have the icon. But somehow, she must have decided against it and told him it was missing. When I came, he thought she had found it and changed her mind. But Erin would not have sold it, because as much as they need the money, that wasn't why she took it."

"Why, then?"

"Because of the miracle."

His eyebrows went up, waiting for an explanation. I told him about Mara, and about the laughter Father Paul had heard. "Erin didn't take the icon to sell it. She took it to protect her husband from being called a fool."

"Do you mean there was no miracle?" he asked.

I could not tell if he was skeptical, or simply studying me, my words, and my expression. He was attentive, for sure.

"It doesn't matter if there was or was not a miracle," I said. "Don't you see?"

He shook his head.

I tried again. "Erin grew up in the western church. Her view is Western, and practical, based on the material, the visible, and the scientific. Miracles are explainable. They may be miracles, but there is always a natural explanation. Mara's, and then Father Paul's, miracle could not be explained. Erin did not believe it and was afraid it would open her otherwise sensible husband to ridicule and criticism. She couldn't bear this. She hid the icon. It was too big and awkward to move it far, and indeed, she didn't want to move it far. She only wanted it out of the way for a little while until her husband came to his senses."

"So was there a miracle?"

I remember his question so clearly, his insistence on an answer. I wonder now what answer he wanted.

I said, "I agree with Erin that Father Paul is too sensible to imagine such a thing. Mara, maybe, but Father Paul? Also, I'm an American, so my thinking is essentially Western. Unlike Erin, though, my heritage is Eastern. Some things need not be explained. Some things just are." I kept my eyes on the icon and continued in a whisper. "I believe there was a miracle."

I looked up to see Misha staring at me intently. He broke his gaze, took out his knife, and began prying a hinge off of one of the smaller panels. When the panel had been removed, he pushed the rest of the icon back under the sink and replaced the baseboard.

I held the icon panel on my lap as we drove back to the apartment. Misha asked me questions as we traveled, about many things, but said only one thing I found illuminating.

"Vasily is anxious that you should live."

NINETEEN

Vasily and Louis were waiting at my apartment. They had several packages of new clothing and were busy cutting the tags out of each piece, using razor-sharp knives that were not pocket knives. Louis's knife had a serrated edge. A pile of black clothing lay on the floor against the wall under the window.

The new clothing—the stuff they were sanitizing—was feminine. This bothered me because I expected them to leave now that they had the icon or part of it. I hoped they would take the body in the bathtub with them and I was ready to say goodbye. But Louis was undeniably holding a skirt, a short, aqua, jersey knit that I was sure could not possibly be for me.

"So long, then," I said, deciding on a direct approach.

"We are not leaving," said Louis.

"Yes, you are. You have the icon. Now go."

Misha leaned the icon against the wall and sat down on the sofa. "Come here, Alex," he said.

I went toward him, but not too close. He pointed to the coffee table in front of the sofa. "Sit down."

I sat on the table facing him. He looked at me for a long time before he began. He made me feel as if we were the only two people in the room. He had my attention.

"You must help us," he began.

"I can't possibly help you."

"You can, and you must. I will explain." He leaned forward. "There are two brothers. They are a team, like us, but they are not as skilled as we are, and they do not command the best prices. They have begun descending into terrorism for attention. And they are the worst of terrorists because they are indiscriminate. Do you remember the Paris metro bombing?"

"Yes."

"That was their work. Their trade name is Ill Wind. We call them Achim and Ahmed, for want of a better name."

I must have looked puzzled because he stopped and took more time to explain.

"We use trade names because other names are not permanent; they change with the identities we use. Some of us, like Vasily, have an advantage in people knowing our real names. His advantage comes from his father. But otherwise, we have no real names, except in police files or Interpol. So you see, it is pointless to tell you the real names of Achim and Ahmed. Those are the names they used with Grayson this time, their game names for this operation.

"I also cannot tell you what their alliance is, only that they kill. They use one cause after another as a cover for their demonstrations, but their purpose is to show what they are capable of and to advertise their skill. But they are too unstable and no one will hire or supply them. Several governments, yours included, have decided it is time for them to go, and we have the commission. It is a very large commission because no one else can or will take the risk."

"This is far beyond me," I said. "I'm just a college kid." I whispered this last because I was mesmerized by him and by his words. It was like an initiation, and I suspected that it was more than he had said on this subject for a long time, because he paused frequently, as if to form sentences around ideas that were not commonly spoken.

"I am getting to your place in this," he said. "Ill Wind is planning another operation. They will use the last of their explosive. But it is a very delicate operation and they need the newest technology to achieve it. They need a laser detonation system. Normally, no one will sell it to them, but one typically irresponsible government has agreed to give the system (which they stole from the Americans) to Ill Wind in return for something their prime minister can present in Moscow on a state visit next month. They hope to impress the Soviets with an important acquisition. Besides pleasing Moscow, they want to sink a hook into Ill Wind. There is always more than one motive, more than one plan, in any move of this game."

He shifted in his seat and sighed as if despairing of my ever catching on. I must have looked pretty unintelligent. I felt it. He leaned forward again, held me fast in that bright blue gaze, and continued.

"The hook was to be the icon. The plan was to blow up the Sears Tower. Completely. That was ten days ago. Achim and Ahmed arrived, with us on their heels. They met Grayson and he agreed to produce the icon. I do not know what his plan was, but he was desperate for money and I do not think he ever intended to pay your priest. But that is not important now. He was supposed to bring the icon, and Ill Wind would then trade it for the system. They would wire the building and make a very loud noise. Everything was supposed to be finished in twenty-four hours. But something went wrong. There was no icon.

"The brothers are well protected. We cannot get at them until they move. They will not move until they get the detonators. They cannot get the detonators until they have the icon. Do you see where I am leading?"

"Yes," I said.

"You have the icon."

"But now you have it. You can give it to them."

He smiled slightly, as much of a smile as one is likely to see on Misha. "They are prepared only for Grayson to give it to them," he said. "Tonight was to be his last chance to produce it. Now he is dead." He gave a side glance to Louis. "For a day or two we thought you worked for Grayson. Maybe they will think so, too."

"Maybe?" I did not like the sound of this.

"Listen carefully." He gave me a set of instructions, specific and simple. There were several important things that I had to remember, one of which was to forget everything he had just told me. I was more than willing to do that.

What is interesting, as I look back on it, is that he never asked me if I was willing to help in the first place. He assumed, and I never objected. I never thought to object to being an accomplice to a killing; I thought only about preventing another tragedy. I was part of a decision on who should die, but not in an affirmative way. My involvement was based on my circumstances, on the influence of the powerful man who sat opposite me, and on my own moral ambiguities. My subsequent actions were not heroic because I never decided. I never chose either side or no side.

But that absolves me of nothing. The *no* option was always open and I knew that. It would have meant death, but it was open all the same. Morality was a maze I could not negotiate. I did as I was told because I was not mentally prepared to object.

There was another area, though, where my moral training was explicit and indelible and we quickly came to it.

TWENTY

"Take off your clothes," said Misha.
"What?" I was horrified.
"You must wear these." He pointed to the aqua skirt and accessories.
"Take off your clothes."
I stood before him now, shaking again. I took off my jeans.
"The sweater. Hurry up," he said.
I complied.
He produced his knife and walked behind me as I stood trembling in my underwear. He tugged at my panties, cutting out the tag at the back. He stood in front of me again, reached behind, and slipped his fingers under the bottom elastic of my bra. He was looking for another tag, but it was too much for me. I broke down with a sob and pulled away.
"Scheisse!" He pulled me back by the arm, searched again roughly for the tag, found it, and cut it. "She is useless," he said to Vasily as he released me. "She will never survive. Look at her." Then he shouted at me, "Stop it!"
He was frightful. I shivered and sobbed. Louis handed me a checkered sweatshirt that matched the aqua skirt. I put it on quickly, anxious to put anything I could between me and all that venom.
Misha pointed at Vasily. "You must fix it," he said. "She cannot face Achim like this. He will know everything in five minutes."
Vasily crossed the room to where I stood half-dressed and miserable, put his arm around my shoulder, and led me to the sofa where we sat down together.

"Alex," he said gently, "please, listen to me."

My heart poured out gratitude with my tears. But my adoring look disturbed him. He looked away, then at Misha. I could not help but follow his eyes to Misha's grim, uncompromising face. When Vasily turned back to me, his expression had hardened; it was no longer gentle. I felt isolated again but made more of an effort to control the tears.

"Understand," said Vasily, "the operation comes first. Many lives depend on it, including ours, and you will not be allowed to jeopardize it."

I nodded. I understood.

"You are necessary to the operation because Ill Wind is not going to accept the icon from anyone else. We are not sure they will accept it from you. Their deal is with Grayson. If there is a variation, it must be logical."

He shifted uncomfortably, then spoke again without looking at me. He looked at my hands, in his hands. "There are always at least two ways to proceed in any situation. In this case, you can hand over the icon at once, be questioned briefly or not at all, and then shot, or you can hand over only part of the icon and be questioned at length."

Here was new information. I began to listen carefully. The word 'shot' was especially illuminating, and I wondered how many other revelations lurked in Vasily's next words. I lost the tears in a rush of fear.

"There are arguments for and against both plans," he said.

Mind if I add some of my own arguments? May I please state my druthers concerning the prospects of being shot? *And could I have a precise definition of 'questioned'?*

I was about to get that definition.

"It has been agreed that you should take only a part of the icon. It is a better plan operationally."

At this, Misha gave an exasperated sigh.

"It is," insisted Vasily.

"Yes, yes, sure," said Misha with his hands up in surrender.

"It is better operationally and it will give you a chance of survival," Vasily told me.

"So what does 'questioned at length' mean?" I asked.

Vasily's brow wrinkled, shading his colorless eyes.

"You said if I brought them only part of the icon, I would be questioned at length. What does that mean?"

"We are assuming that Ill Wind and their suppliers are as sick of this as we are," he said. "With part of the icon and you, Ill Wind should be able to negotiate for the detonators, on the understanding they will learn from you where the rest of it is. They will question you about this."

He paused, looked at me, then lowered his eyes. "They will hurt you." He stood and walked over to the window. "The longer you do not tell them anything, the better your chance of survival, but the more they will hurt you."

"But with your sexual problem," interrupted Misha, "I say you will not last two minutes."

"I do not have a sexual problem," I said.

"You do."

"Virginity is not a problem."

"Yours is."

"That's nonsense."

"It is reality, girl. When you meet Achim, you will find out. He will check you the way I did. He will discover where you are weakest, and he will tear you to pieces." He threw up his hands in disgust and walked away. "This is impossible. It will not work."

"It will work," said Vasily.

"How?"

"She must control her fear."

"And," said Louis, "she must not be a virgin."

Misha paused and looked at me.

God, no. Don't look at me that way. You're thinking too much.

"Choose," he said.

Here was an area where I was not lacking in conviction. I might compromise with murder, but never with sex. It was impossible. I would die first. I began to feel virtuous again. I was on firm ground here; I knew what was right and I would not deviate.

"No," I said.

"You must. Choose."

"I will not participate in any way. I'll die first. I will take the first option."

"You picked a fine time to develop a backbone, girl."

I felt Misha's contempt keenly, but not strongly enough to compromise my principles. I stood firm.

"Alex," said Louis. "This is not something to die for."

"There have been many sainted martyrs who died for it."

"You are no saint," said Misha.

"Your life and many others are at stake, Alex," said Louis. "Think of that. God will understand."

"We say that a lot, don't we?" I said. I looked at Louis. "Is that how you live with yourself?"

Louis answered with a glare, an unforgotten glare that has remained between us, separating and binding us at the same time, like a hyphen.

"Enough!" said Misha. "Alex, I will not allow you to jeopardize this operation, nor will I permit you to commit suicide over this trifle."

"Trifle!"

"Yes, trifle. Compared to what is at stake, it is a minor point. You cannot face Achim as a virgin. Choose one of us now or I will choose for you."

"No."

Misha looked to his left. I saw Vasily shake his head out of the corner of my eye, but I could not look at him. There was a very sharp exchange of words between them in Polish. Misha's vehemence bordered on rage, frightening me so that I looked at Vasily involuntarily. His gaze was locked with Misha's in a silent battle of wills, his face set in that expression I later came to know so well: total intransigence.

Misha looked away first, disgusted. "We will use chance," he said. "Do you have any playing cards?"

I would not answer him. The look he gave me sent a shudder through me.

"I saw some in the kitchen," said Louis. He retrieved a pinochle deck from the utensil drawer where I kept it and gave it to Misha.

Misha shuffled the cards and put them on the coffee table before me. "Cut them," he said.

"No."

Another freezing stare. "High card," he said finally. "Louis?"

Louis took the top card. It was a jack. He smiled and gave me a significant look, evidently not knowing it was a low card in a pinochle deck. Louis's jocularity can be deceptive; his true nature is often vengeful and he forgets nothing. The merest remark can lie buried in him, fertilizing his fury until it grows into a monstrous plant bearing fetid fruit. I know this too well.

Vasily took the next card. It was a king. I breathed a little easier. If it must happen, at least it would be with my love. It began to seem not so bad, compared to the alternatives. I calculated the probabilities. With eight aces available out of forty-six remaining cards, the chance of disaster was less than twenty-five percent. Misha took the next card.

It was the ace of diamonds.

"One more time," said Misha. "You choose, or we go by the cards."

Something inside me was screaming *Say Vasily, Come On Say It!* but I was paralyzed. I was entrenched in my cause, and having chosen, could not go back. That would be admitting defeat. I could not admit defeat, no matter how much I wanted to.

Vasily told me later how hurt he was. He said it would have hurt more to force me from my stupid stand though. But I think if it had worked out that way, I would have relented, and it would have been better for me. People who say they have no regrets amaze me. Have they never done something that hurt everyone and helped no one? Have they never been so sure they were right that they went to the wrong lengths to prove it? Or am I the only one who makes bad decisions when I am ignorant, scared, and confused? Good can come of evil by the grace of God, and eventually, it did even in this instance, but at the time, my ordeal was merely a shabby little drama that disgusted us all.

Vasily and Louis waited in the Mercedes outside.

"I do not understand how an intelligent girl can be so stupid," said Misha.

I suppose he was trying to put me at ease.

"I will do my best," he said, "but I am not gentle. It will help if you do not fight me."

I did not fight. There was no point. Neither did I cooperate. He was right. He was not gentle. I don't think there is anything gentle in him. Even the meticulous manners his aristocratic family took such pains to teach him do no more than muffle his natural abrasiveness. He is a stinging nettle in bloom: beautiful to look at but uncomfortable to brush up against.

Though I found out differently later that night, I thought at the time it was the worst pain I would ever bear. I maintained my composure, though, and when instructed, dressed myself calmly in the short blue skirt and checkered shirt that was to be my outfit for the evening. It made me look as I felt.

"Was that something to die for?" asked Misha.

"No." I hated to admit it.

"Was it worth hurting others for?"

"No," I whispered as my tears started again.

"There are many forms of selfishness, Alexandra. You and Vasily are perfect for each other."

TWENTY-ONE

By the time Louis and Vasily came back upstairs, I was well into a crying fit, a silent one, with wet cheeks and an occasional shoulder shudder. I felt, and probably looked, like a used mop. My hair was a disaster and I stood bare-legged straight because the damn skirt was too short to sit down in.

Vasily said something to Misha. I suppose he misunderstood my tears. If I briefly hoped for vengeance, it was a futile thought. I was new to the dynamics of the relationships within Charlemagne, but it did not take me long to see that there was a bond among these three men that I would not be allowed to disrupt. I began to understand where I stood with Vasily. This did not help my dwindling self-confidence, though it brought a little wisdom. I realized I was not important enough to cause Boris's beating, either. There had to be some other reason for that. Somehow this made me feel better, maybe because it relieved me of my share of the responsibility, however unintentional.

I was important to Vasily, but not in the way I thought at the time. Only many years later, when he began to thaw a bit and when I learned more about his horrific life, did I realize that when I first met him, he was incapable of loving me in the fairy tale way I had dreamed of. Love is an irresistible, selfless giving. Vasily loved me because he wanted me. It is not the same thing.

Hindsight can be comforting, but of course, at that moment, I had none of it. I simply stood, shattered and wretched, in the short blue skirt that made me feel like a whore. I had been violated, albeit with my tacit consent, and was being used ruthlessly, given a minimal chance of survival, a chance one of these men, at least, had argued I should not have. The worst was still to come, and I shivered at the thought of it.

Vasily made me sit down and then sat next to me, miserable heap that I was. He put his arm around me and drew me to him. At first, I resisted, could not bear to be touched, until I gradually understood that he meant to comfort me. I buried my face in his shoulder then, taking the comfort offered, momentary protection and safety in his arms.

He whispered in my ear, "Are you frightened?"

"Why?" I whispered looking up at him. "Do I look it?"

He smiled. "Can you never answer directly?"

"I'm terrified," I admitted. "I am more frightened than I've ever been."

His whisper became barely audible. "So am I. And so are Misha and Louis."

My eyes were wide open at this. "Oh great. Then what chance do I have?"

"Every chance. We are all scared, always. We survive because we do not let fear stop us. We keep thinking and we keep doing what must be done. Does that help you?"

"You're telling me not to panic. Is that it?"

"I suppose."

"So when does the fear stop?"

"In my world, never."

"Then I suppose, I have an advantage. I know a place without fear."

He looked at me with alarm, "Don't do anything foolish."

"I am not talking about death."

"What then?"

"Never mind."

"What?" he insisted. "Your God? I hope he gives you more help than he does me. Or your religion? It did you a great favor, giving you exactly the wrong thing to be prepared to die for."

"Virtue is not a wrong thing."

"Being stupid about sex is not virtue. Sex does not warrant death."

"Sex can feel like death in the wrong conditions."

He looked at me. Did I imagine a softer expression? "Assault is sin," he said. "Not sex."

"No time for theology," said Misha. He handed Vasily a folded pile of black clothing. "Get dressed."

Vasily got up and Misha sat in his place. It was like a wind change, and I shivered in a cold northerly as Misha opened a new make-up kit and began to transform my face.

"For all your piety, girl," he said, "you are no better than I am."

"I never said I was."

"Don't talk. You will smear the lipstick. You never said you were, but you think it. Your thoughtlessness can be as deadly as my knife. And can cause more pain."

"You are mired in evil." I said it through clenched teeth, as much in an attempt to keep my temper as to save the lipstick.

"We are all mired in it," he said. "Or did your Messiah come only for my sake and not for yours?"

"What do you mean?"

"Never mind. Philosophy is a luxury of the idle. We have work to do."

My face painted, it was time to do something with my hair. This fueled a debate. The hair was shoulder length with a blunt cut that made style more or less impossible. Louis solved the problem with a side ponytail that brought my mane under control, and a scarf that added color. I was rather pleased with it.

Misha did not like my skirt and used a stapler to tighten it and masking tape to shorten it. Shoes were last—high-heeled and painful.

The men wore black denim trousers, black boots, and black, long-sleeved cotton turtleneck shirts. Over these, sport jackets in different colors drew attention away from the uniform blackness of their clothes.

Why bother? I wondered.

Misha, as usual, read my mind, or my face, or whatever it is he does to know what I am thinking. I have only ever been able to conceal one thing from him in the twenty years I have known him.

He answered the question I had not spoken. "Black makes it difficult to judge," he said. "Achim and Ahmed are big men. We want them to judge our sizes without accuracy. We want to help them make mistakes."

Louis cleaned his gun, meticulously dismantling and rebuilding it. He rummaged through a small box of wires and gadgets and gave me a button-like object to swallow. "A precaution, so we can follow you," he said. "Do not lose it."

Misha gave me more instructions. "Do not lie to them. You do not know or you will not say, but do not lie. Allow them to think you are Grayson's lover, but do not tell them so. They will catch any lies, and from these, they will extract the truth. Make them work for anything you say. Keep the subject on the icon. Give us time."

"Alex," said Vasily slowly, as if uncomfortable with giving advice, "it will help to fix your attention on something you can see, a pattern in a ceiling, perhaps, and try to breathe in rhythm."

"Rest as much as you can," interrupted Louis. "And do not think ahead. Fear of pain is worse than pain itself."

"There are twenty-one distinct levels of pain," said Vasily. "Convince yourself that the last was the twenty-first, that the next will be no worse."

"No, no," disagreed Louis. "Do not think ahead at all."

TWENTY-TWO

Misha drove me in my car, while the others followed in the Mercedes. We spent most of the time in silence, but I ventured to ask a question or two of my own.

"You don't think they will hurt me badly, do you?"

"I know they will."

This took a moment to digest. "How badly?"

"I cannot explain it because you have never experienced it. You have no basis for understanding. That is why you are doing this because you do not know what you are doing."

"I don't understand."

"Exactly. It is the argument I gave Vasily, but he is adamant. He gave you advice. I give you a way out. If you tell them where the icon is, they will simply shoot you. There will be no more pain. It will help us if you wait as long as possible to tell them, but how long is up to you."

"You're not going to come and get me?"

"Yes, we will, but you are not our priority. When it becomes too much for you, you are free to get out."

He parked the car on a dark side street somewhere on the South Side, having driven the last half-mile slowly and without lights.

"Now listen," he said. "Go two blocks, then left. It is on the right. The place is called Rick's. Give me two minutes, then start walking."

"By myself?"

"Yes. There is no danger here. Rick's is a sovereign house. No killing, no exchanges, no secret work, only talk, at Rick's and within the approaches. These extend a little over half a kilometer all around the place. We are within that radius. You can walk to Rick's."

"What is a sovereign house?"

"It is a bar, and sometimes a restaurant, where everyone can go, in some safety, to talk. There are several of these places, in different cities around the world. Inside, it is usually divided into three or more sections. To the right is the West, and to the left, the East. In the center are the neutrals, true anarchists, and the indiscriminate. In countries with more factions, there are more sections. At Rick's, you will find Ill Wind in the center. Just ask the barman. When we come in, be sure you do not recognize us."

"But I'm hopeless. You know that. They will see it all over my face."

"No. They are not that good, and you are not a bad actress."

"Where will you sit?"

"We do not usually work for the East, for many reasons, not all of them ideological. We will sit on the right."

Rick's occupied more than one building. It was a collection of several small buildings, each built hard against the other. Any spaces between them had been walled up, making the place whole, but all the doors remained. They were painted the same color and matched the paint on the brick walls so well that the structure was a monotony of grey in the moonlight. There was what seemed to be a main entrance, lit by a small neon sign saying "RI_K'S," but this was the only distinguishing mark.

I entered through the lighted doorway, and after descending three steps, found myself facing a long bar that began in front of me and stretched away to my right. Clutching the section of icon hastily wrapped in two brown paper sacks under my arm, I asked a man behind the bar where I would find Ill Wind.

His answer was perfectly bland. He pointed to my right and said, "Third table, down the center."

At the end of the bar another step led down into a large room, filled with booths and tables, but clearly divided into three sections. The room was about two-thirds full. Only a few other women were sitting down, and none of us looked like ladies. The waitresses ran from tables to bar to kitchen, then back to tables.

Traffic between the sections was very free. Animated discussions in various languages took place at most tables, sometimes between tables, and I could even hear a few shouting matches between the sections.

I approached the third table in the very center. Two enormous and several smaller men sat at a table for six. I could not accurately count them because they kept coming and going.

The two big men were quite still. Misha had understated their size. These were giants. Whereas Louis was the only member of Charlemagne who even reached six feet, topping it by only an inch or two, these men were well over that. I estimated six foot four or more. And they had the bulk and the mass to match their height. I tried to convince myself that their girth was probably fat (they looked self-indulgent), but when one of them stood up and offered me a seat in a mock gesture of exaggerated politeness, I could not find evidence of even a spreading middle. He was as perfect and as muscular as Vasily or Misha or Louis, but much, much larger. Things were looking bleak. I began to doubt I was on the winning side.

And they had minions. They had countless nasty little men, little Borises, hangers-on who hovered around the table and eyed me with disgusting glee.

The one I came to know as Achim spoke to me first. "Buy you a drink?" he said.

"Yes, please. Vodka." This had been Misha's instruction. It would be good preparation, he said, without filling me up or making me too stupid.

Achim caught a passing waitress by the waist, pressed her to himself, and ordered my drink. I saw many things in his behavior and felt relieved.

He had straight black hair, an olive complexion, and a full mustache that would have given him a Latin look, but for the large, straight coptic nose that suggested an Egyptian origin. What I saw that relieved me was in his black predatory eyes. He was not much smarter than Boris. Or maybe he once had been, but now his mind was concerned with other things, comforts and excesses, and lacked the discipline to think clearly. He was a voluptuary without discernment and no match for the men of Charlemagne. I observed his brother and to my inexpressible joy found that he, too, was little more than a lesser man in tough-guy form.

"And what can we do for you, little girl," said the brother, Ahmed.

"Brent Grayson sent me."

There was immediate interest.

"Yes?"

"He said to give you this." I handed my package to Achim. He seemed to be in charge.

He tore a small section, then ripped the paper off completely. "Where is the rest of it?" he demanded.

"Brent said we should talk about it."

"Why isn't he here?"

"He's indisposed."

"Where is he?"

"At my place, taking a bath." I thought this was clever and was pleased with myself for one or two seconds.

"And where is your place?"

Payment for breaking Misha's rule, "Don't be clever." I was no longer in charge of the questioning. I had to get it back on track before they strayed into more questions I could not answer.

"That's not important," I said. "The icon is."

"And where is that?"

"I'll tell you when we come to an arrangement."

"What arrangement?"

"We, Brent and I, want a better price and some way to hand it over safely." I emphasized the word 'safely'.

"What price?"

"Seventy-five. It cost us more than we expected."

"Forget it."

I stood up. So did Achim. I started to leave, but he took my shoulder, covered it, in fact, with one enormous hand, and held me fast. He looked at me sharply and for a moment I saw the man he once had been or that he might have become, and it frightened me. He was formidable.

"You know where the icon is?" he asked.

This was the crucial question, the point from which I could not turn back. I had been strictly instructed to answer this question with what I thought to be the truth. The operation hinged on it. I had also been told the likely consequences of my answer.

"Yes," I said.

The two brothers spoke rapidly in a language I did not recognize. Achim told me to sit down, took the icon, and disappeared down one of eight shadowy corridors off the main room.

Ahmed began a conversation, obviously working his way to the subject of the icon. He tried several times to get me to reveal where it was, each attempt so clumsy and transparent that I found it hard not to smile as I evaded his question. Ahmed resembled his brother except that I could see no trace of the shrewd mind I had noticed in Achim. He was also in less perfect condition; his excesses had begun to show in his puffy face and swollen middle.

"Do you see those men over there?" he asked.

"Where?"

He pointed behind me and I turned. Vasily, Louis, and Misha were being shown to a table by a fawning waitress.

"Which men?" I asked.

"The ones just now sitting down. Do you see them?"

Yes, I see them you fool and I want to run over there and throw myself at Vasily and beg him to protect me from further contact with the likes of you except that would displease him and might even kill him so I will put up with you a little while longer.

"What about them?" I said, turning back to Ahmed.

"We are going to kill them—tonight."

That's what you think, you slug.

I pretended to be mildly surprised and impressed.

"You see...," he continued. "Do you see the blond one, the Austrian?"

I turned again and said, "How the hell do you tell who comes from where?"

"The blond one, the one on the right."

"What about him?"

"He thinks he is very good with a knife. We know differently."

You know nothing.

"Oh," I said. "And how's that?"

"Look at him! He is half Achim's size. Achim's arms are twice as long...."

Like a gorilla.

"...and he thinks he is smart." Ahmed was still talking. I had missed something. "But he will discover brains are shit against a mountain, eh?"

He roared at his joke. "Now the bomber..." He was suddenly serious.

"Bomber?"

"The one with the messed-up hand, the shortest one."

"They're all sitting down. I can't tell which is shortest, and I can't see their hands."

"The one with light brown hair, like yours."

"Yes?"

"He is the best. He is certainly the best." Ahmed's voice was lowered, his tone respectful. "He can blow up anything. He can place a charge in precisely the right place and in the perfect amount and detonate it at exactly the right time. He is incredible. Everyone agrees. He is the best. It is a pity he will die tonight, too. And the other one. They say he can listen to any conversation. Maybe he is listening now eh? Maybe he has a gadget that can pick up what we are saying right now. What do you want to say, eh?"

"What?"

"What do you want to say to them?"

Get me out of here.

"I think they're kinda good-looking." I took one more look at them.

Ahmed laughed loudly, drawing everybody's attention, including the three I was looking at. I turned away quickly.

"Their women, the ones who live, are high class. Way out of your league, little slut. They say," he leaned toward me like a conspirator, "that the Austrian can cut your throat before you know he's there."

I could see that he was trying to frighten me with the thing that most frightened him. I tried to look frightened. It was not hard to do under the circumstances.

"Why are you telling me this?"

"Because you will die tonight, too." His voice was still low, conspiratorial. "How badly you die depends on how soon you tell us where the icon is, eh? If you are a very good girl, we'll do you a favor and let the Austrian sharpen his knife on you. If he can find us, that is. They say there is little pain."

"I'm leaving." I got up to go.

Achim was suddenly behind me, speaking rapidly to his brother in their language. I was bundled down one of those corridors, protesting uselessly. Nobody paid the least attention.

So much for the safety of a sovereign house.

TWENTY-THREE

Besides pain, my memory holds only a few distinct images of that night. One is of a large cream-colored car in which we traveled and in which Achim pawed me roughly as a prelude to what would follow. He must have been satisfied that I was what I appeared to be because what followed was not sexual. Not that I cared much once it began. Still, I suppose Misha was right again. I doubt I could have withstood the psychological pain had it been otherwise. At twenty, my body held more strength than my mind.

I was taken to what I presumed was a basement in the Sears Tower. I had an impression of a very large building and I distinctly remember being forced down flights of stairs. Frankly, I did not care much where I was. My world had become centered on a grey metal case that covered humming ventilation machinery. It made a handy platform, six by six by three feet high, like an oversized, inverted double coffin, where they laid me out to hurt me. There were ducts, pipes, and valves above my head. Bare light bulbs scattered about this place gave light and shadows to more grey-cased machinery and ductwork and the faces of the men who gave me pain.

I saw these things in between the pain when I rested. When there was pain, I saw nothing but a red-painted valve handle above me that I concentrated on.

I came to know in the next few hours that life is not all that is and that losing it is not the worst thing that can happen. I had wondered why Misha said he feared pain more than death and after fifteen minutes in that cellar with Achim and company, I understood perfectly.

It was not just physical pain. It was a loss of everything else. While I hurt, I lost time, memory, mind, heart, and will. I was absorbed by myself. There was only me, a screaming, aching me I did not recognize. There was no time when there had not been pain, and there was no time when there would not be pain. Pain was now; there was only now, I could not escape it, and I could think of nothing else. A voice inside me counseled me, telling me this would end. Eventually, it must end; it could not go on. But I rejected this counsel because I had forgotten everything else. It would never end.

I did not pray. There were no prayers in me. Only pain. I looked down at a dark place within and did not like what I saw. Only the tiniest fraction of my will held onto the hope I had once foolishly boasted I would never lose. Yet that fraction was enough; I survived. More than that, I changed. It was a change that cannot be explained, only experienced.

During interruptions, I rested. I paid little attention to what was said. I did not answer any of the questions they shouted at me. The brothers left at various times and returned, carrying packs of explosives, timers, and detonators. Their suppliers had been satisfied with just the section of the icon and gave them what they needed. They no longer devoted their attention to me and allowed the leering henchmen much leeway in the way they treated me.

It had become pointless and I knew it. The pain was for nothing, and there was no sign of rescue. But I could not tell them where the icon was and end it. I longed for death. I knew it would release me, but I could not be the one to bring it about. I clung to life with white-knuckled determination. I would not let it go while it was in my power to keep it. Life was a pointless misery, but I hung onto it at any cost.

I had long since given up hope of rescue and was resting during an interruption when Achim came into the space where I was held. Ahmed had gone off somewhere—I don't know where—setting charges, I supposed. There were five or six odious henchmen scattered around me. It was a large space divided into sections by machinery cases, supporting pillars, and foundation work. It hummed and echoed.

In the echo, I heard a change in Achim's tone. I felt a change in his manner. I opened my eyes.

"Where the hell are they?" he said to one of the men who sat about ten feet from me watching something in a briefcase. Achim stepped behind him and peered into the case. "They should have been here by now," he said. "Any indications?"

"No. Nothing." The watcher shook his head.

"But everything is in place? All the sensors?"

"Everything." This time he nodded.

"There is no point to this thing if we do not get Charlemagne. Where the hell are they?"

Ahmed came in from a narrow space to my left. "They will be here," he said. "And even if they're not, it will be a nice big bang." He picked up more of what I assumed to be plastic explosives and began walking away to my right.

"The bang is secondary, fool," said Achim. "It will get us nowhere without the primary. Go on, finish, and let's get out of here. They are not coming. Somehow they know."

I felt his attention turn to me. I was careful not to look at him.

"Has she told you anything?"

"No," answered the man whose job it had been to apply pain for the last half hour. "Not a thing."

"Nothing?" Achim stood over me. "Look at me," he said.

I obeyed.

I could see very clearly. It was as if I were looking into his mind. I watched as he began to understand, even as I understood what his plan had been. What little hope I had left faded. This was a trap. Charlemagne knew it was a trap. They were not coming. Achim would shoot me now. Except that he would not shoot me now, I knew, because there was something else in his face.

"You should have told us by now," he said. "You have been coached." His face contorted with anger as he grabbed me by the shirt, pulling me toward him. "Who coached you?"

I had no opportunity to answer him as the man on my left slumped over the machine case I was sitting on, his blood splattered across my legs. The other men were falling also, but it was outside my experience, and I did not understand what was happening. Achim pulled me off the case by my hair and hooked his arm under mine from behind. I heard his knife open and felt it cold against my neck as he dragged me from that place. I did my best to stay on my feet and cooperate rather than test the edge of his knife, but my feet had been injured so he had to drag me as he ran through a maze of machinery and pillars.

I did not realize he was being chased until we came to a cul-de-sac formed by a large packing case, a pillar, and an outside wall. He turned, with me in front of him, and faced Misha.

"I will cut her. She is yours, isn't she?"

Misha's gun was pointed toward us. "She is not mine," he said. "Go on. Kill her."

Well, thank you very much, you bastard.

Achim hesitated, uncertain, and at that moment Misha crossed the ten feet between us. He kicked me squarely in the ribs of my left side. The force of that kick tore me from Achim's grasp and slammed me against the wall. I fell, breathless, and lay insensible for several seconds.

When I could look, I discovered that things were not going well for my side. It is true my side was only the lesser of two evils (depending upon perspective), and it is also true that I was not qualified to determine what constituted 'going well' or 'not going well'. But the point is that I would have been happier if Misha were the one on top with the knife. As it was, he was on bottom, the knife was in Achim's right hand, and Misha's left hand was around the larger man's wrist, straining to keep the edge from his own throat. I could not see Misha's right hand, nor Achim's left, but I could see the faces of both men. Their concentration was total. Only one would win.

I knew which one I wanted to win. I sat up, looked around, and tried to think. Misha's gun lay in the corner near where my head had been. I hadn't the faintest idea how to use it, but I picked it up. I considered trying to shoot Achim but knew I would never be able to do it accurately. The gun was heavy, so I held it by the barrel, crawled toward the two men, and swung the gun down on Achim's head with as much force as I could muster, which wasn't very much. It was so puny that nothing happened. There was only the briefest distraction.

But perhaps that distraction was enough for Misha. In the next moment, Achim grunted and heaved, spilling the bloody contents of his stomach over the right side of Misha's face and shoulder. There was a pause; then Misha levered the body away from him, and it fell face up, disemboweled, knife clattering from its right hand. Misha pushed himself to a sitting position, leaning against the wall, his knife in his right hand. There was blood everywhere, and he was wet with it. I felt sick but empty, and he waited a moment, panting to catch his breath, then held out his left hand as soon as my first bout of heaving had passed. I did not understand at first, then realized I still held his gun. I gave it to him.

"Don't ever touch my gun again," he said. His eyes were ice blue as he glared at me through the grime on his face.

I was too exhausted to be indignant.

I heard footsteps. Misha paid no attention and continued to glare.

It was Louis. "Ahmed is headed out. He has the laser control."

Misha looked up and nodded. He put his gun away and pushed himself up wearily, using the wall behind him for leverage.

"Cover Vasily," he said. "And take her with you."

TWENTY-FOUR

I hobbled, painfully, trying to keep up with Louis as he led me, and sometimes dragged me, through the cellar labyrinth. We found Vasily standing on a six-foot crate, calmly dismantling six small oblong packages of yellow plastic. He worked quickly, his face expressionless. He removed the detonator, the primer charge, and then the explosive, jumped off the crate, and stuffed the bomb into a sack that once belonged to Ahmed.

Louis lifted the sack and we followed Vasily to the next charge. This was in a more sheltered area where we surprised two building security guards who surrendered their guns to Louis immediately. When this bomb was safely in the sack, he and Vasily held a short discussion about the guards. Vasily glanced toward me. There seemed nothing available to tie them, but he dug into the sack and came up with two lengths of wire. Louis snorted derisively as he helped Vasily tie their hands and arms. He kept his gun on them and dragged them along on our quest. At each stop I slumped to the floor, trying to breathe without pain, not succeeding, and finally distracting myself by watching, fascinated, as Vasily worked. As did the guards.

Misha joined us eventually. He gave the laser control to Louis, who took it apart before putting it in his back pocket. In a short time, though it seemed long to me, Vasily announced that we had come to the last one.

This one was high on a wall behind a pair of crossed girders opposite a small space where the tied-up guards sat. The girders made an X halfway up the wall, each rising in the opposite direction at a twenty-degree angle. The bomb had been placed at the ceiling above the right-hand girder.

I was in a puddle on the floor, still trying to breathe, grateful that this was the final device.

"Hold this, please," said Vasily.

He stood over me, handing me the holster that held his gun. I guessed he had taken it off as a precaution. Unencumbered by the weapon, he easily pulled himself up to the last set of explosives and dismantled it. The immobile guards watched until Misha's sharp look made them turn their heads.

The last charge in hand, Vasily slid down, took his gun from me, and put it back on. He held his hand out, helped me to stand, and supported me on his right arm.

We stood under the girders, finished, but not relieved. Misha looked at me. "Will you be coming with us?"

I knew what he was asking, and I had an answer. He did not say, "Are you coming?" but "Will you?" He wanted to know if I would go with them to whatever lair they might slink to in whatever country that might harbor them.

I had seen enough death, felt enough pain, and shared enough guilt to last my lifetime. I loved Vasily, but I could not have just one part of him. If I wanted him, I must take all of him, as he was, and there was a great deal of him that I did not like. I remembered Boris. Vasily was made of the same fabric as the men who had hurt me that night.

Guilt was another problem. It was overtaking me. I had actively and willingly taken part in a killing. I could not console myself with the thought of the hundreds, maybe thousands, who would live that day. I could see only the awful reality of death in the bodies of those who died in that basement, evil though their intentions had been. I did not know if I had done the right thing. I knew only that I wanted no more decisions like it. Give me moral neutrality, no more questions I cannot answer, no more choices I cannot discern. I am a child of this world, and I am bound to it by chains I cannot break.

I said, "No."

Misha gestured with one hand, with just two fingers of one hand. A minimal gesture. Vasily raised his eyebrows, questioning, as his left hand reached for his gun. He shot the security guard on the right, just above the nose. Louis, who stood to our left, shot the man on the left. Both guards fell at the same time.

I was sick again. This completed the horror. My only comfort was that I would soon be rid of these men. We trudged to the exit, where we stepped over Ahmed's body, slipping in his blood.

The Mercedes had been parked some distance away. My condition slowed our progress. We had not gone far when I could go no further and collapsed on a green space, begging to rest against a tree. There was a brief discussion before Vasily and Misha left to get the car. Louis sat beside me.

"It was a trap for us, you know," said Louis.

"Yes. So I understand."

"We were lucky to have you."

"Pardon me?" I did not want to talk. It took too much breath.

"The sensor you swallowed picked up all their sensors. We knew every wire they used and had to find a way around them all to surprise them. That is why it took us so long." He looked at me. "I am sorry."

For what? For taking so long? Or for dragging me into this in the first place? Waste no apologies on me. Just take me home.

"You have been a very great help," said Louis. "Thank you."

Apologies and thank yous. Just take me home.

"Misha thinks they were greedy, but I think they were cowards."

I could only register my puzzlement in my expression. I had no breath to spare.

"They waited ten days for the lasers," Louis explained. "Misha thinks they were too intent on destroying the building as well as us, but he is wrong. Achim needed accuracy so that he could trap us and detonate at precisely the right moment. He did not want to fight Misha, just kill him. He was a coward."

He paused. "Misha won, anyway."

I nodded at the obvious.

"He did not win easily?"

I shook my head.

"It is always that way. It is always decided in a moment of chaos."

He paused again, then continued, picking his words carefully. "You are important to Vasily. This…"

That was all I heard before I fainted. I woke again in the back of the Mercedes, next to Misha, who stank with a vile odor. It was almost dawn, and we were heading south on the Dan Ryan Expressway. Louis drove, and Vasily sat next to him up front.

Misha's hand was under my shirt, exploring my bruised ribs. "I am sure I broke a few," he was saying.

I pulled away from him.

"You will be all right," he said. "We will take you to your parents' home. Your father will know a doctor to call."

I kept my eyes on the lightening sky outside, fighting the urge to be sick.

"Look at me," said Misha.

I did not. He took my chin and turned my face toward him. I glared at him, telling him exactly what I thought of him without wasting the breath to say it.

"Listen." He was glaring back at me. "Frank will ask you all about it. You must tell him nothing. Do you understand?"

I defied him.

"You will be in great danger if you tell him anything. Do you understand that?"

"What will you do to me?" I asked.

"I will do nothing," he answered. "Frank is a good man, but his organization is a sieve. Nothing is secure. You do not know what is dangerous to you and what is not, so say nothing."

"I don't know or I won't say, is that it?"

"They will not hurt you. Just say nothing."

Vasily turned and said something I did not catch.

"And burn these clothes before you see Frank," Misha said. "Do it immediately."

Gladly.

Vasily supported me as I struggled up the walk to the front door of my parents' house. We did not speak to each other. He picked the lock and I entered without looking at him. I shut the door between us, locking it with as much noise as possible.

I put on an old bathrobe and lit the fire my father always kept ready. I was watching the fire, watching the last bit of aqua turn to ash, when I realized my father stood next to me.

"Do you need a doctor?" he said.

"Yes, please."

TWENTY-FIVE

Mama fussed over me; the doctor bandaged me. I fell into a comfortable sleep for a few hours, warmly tucked into my old room. I delighted in this comfort and welcomed my mother's attention. I did not welcome Frank's visit, though. My father insisted on staying while Frank asked his questions. My only answer was silence. I was good at this; I had practiced.

"She's tired, Bud," said Papa. "Let her get some more rest before you debrief."

"She's not tired, Fred. She's been coached. She's been told not to say anything. Where's your brain been since you retired?"

"This is my kid, Bud. Leave her alone."

"I can't and you know it. You trained me." Turning to me, Frank said, "Alex, have you been threatened in any way?"

I did not answer.

"Okay. Let's try this. Look at me, Alex. We can pretty well piece together what happened. It's obvious you were there. There's just one thing we can't figure out. Please help us. There were two men, shot right between the eyes. They were unarmed, arms tied. Wearing security guard uniforms. Know anything about that?"

I turned away.

"No. Look at me and listen. This was no accident. Our friend Mack the Knife had to have authorized it, ordered it maybe. Any idea why, Alex?"

I was beginning to think. I did not like where my thoughts led.

"There's always a reason for what he does, Alex. Remember, I told you that a few days ago. Why'd he have them shot? Did they see something they shouldn't have? What could they have seen that would get them shot, eh?"

I remembered their surprised faces when Vasily climbed that girder. *No, not then, before then, before he climbed.*

"They were not what they seemed," I whispered.

"Very good. You're right. They were babysitters, controlling Ill Wind, and supervising the operation. They might have been useful alive. It's not like Charlemagne to waste a source of information. So what did they see that got them each a bullet between the eyes?"

I didn't tell him, but I knew. They saw me holding Vasily's gun. Misha knew who they were when he saw their surprise. But that still did not kill them. The order came after my decision to lead a 'normal' life, to tread the middle ground.

A word can kill. An omission can destroy as surely as a commission. I did not kill those men, but I was bound up in their deaths, and no matter how ignorant, my involvement was not entirely innocent. Until the week before, I had been firmly rooted in the belief of my righteousness. I had successfully avoided all the obvious sins. But now I was confronted with the fact that my silliest decisions could have consequences beyond me, beyond my intentions, and my control. I was not qualified to figure in so many questions of death. So who is? Misha? Vasily? The hot-headed Louis?

No. But at least they knew that. While I blithely made decisions based on my convenience, without regard to consequence, they saw consequence in every move.

My tears began when I thought about Vasily. What an awful place he lived in. I would not compromise with what he did, but I loved him, and I stopped judging him. I had a dismal record in judgment, anyhow.

Since then, I have always distrusted people who are convinced they are right. We are a confused and befuddled species, universally so, but too many of us depend on ourselves for answers to questions we have no business asking. We can pray for guidance and beg forgiveness, but we cannot depend on the righteousness of man. Earthly judgments should be made only by people who understand their fallibility.

I stopped asking myself questions and sobbed.

"Alex," said Frank softly. "You should have gone with them. If I can figure it out, others will, my dear. I'm not the smartest man around. There are bound to be others."

"What the hell are you talking about, Bud?" asked Papa.

"You know what I'm talking about, Fred. You just don't want to admit it to yourself. Your daughter has access to one of Charlemagne. It's the only explanation. She has access and she wants to stay home." He stood up to leave. "You can't stay home, Alex. When they come back for you, you'll have to go."

"No," said Papa. "She doesn't have to do anything she doesn't want to do."

Not true, I thought. On the whole, my wants and my have-to's were not matching up. But one want was overpowering: Vasily. I would have to live where that circumstance put me, pray for guidance, and beg forgiveness.

When Frank left, Papa brought a chair to my bedside, sat down, and took my hand. "Is it the one who was here? Is it Sobieski?"

"Yes, Papa."

I noticed tears in his eyes.

"Your mother's heart will break. She loves you dearly."

"I know. But I love him, Papa."

"Just like she loved his father."

"What!"

Papa looked at me intently, paused a moment, then decided I should know.

"I told him one lie, Alex," he said. "His mother was not the only one who had access. His lover, not his wife, chose the boy's life over his. I think she is going to regret it."

It took a moment for this to sink in.

"You let him think it was his mother?" I asked.

"I love my wife, Alex."

"But you…"

"Before you finish, listen to me. I will tell you what I told him when you were in the kitchen. His father was an ace, Alex, and he was the best. Nobody, not even an intimate, can sneak up on somebody that skilled."

"Are you saying he wanted to die—for his son?"

"I'm saying he was a light sleeper. That's all. And before you go explaining things to your lover, my girl, think about the consequences. I've told you this so you will understand it when your mother falls apart and I am left to put her back together."

TWENTY-SIX

Father Paul disagreed with my decision. He told me this many times in the next few weeks.

My physical recovery was quick. Papa's doctor called the school and had my finals postponed. Studying for them speeded my mental recovery, but I felt empty without Vasily. Father Paul assured me this was normal and would pass in time. I moved back to my parents' house and waited.

Frank gave me the entire icon I had taken to Rick's, though it was still in pieces. I don't know how he recovered it. When my feet healed sufficiently, I broke into the church and leaned the pieces against the northern wall. Another miracle. Father Paul did not ask me how I found it, but I could tell he knew I had. I also never told him who took it. I try, during confessions, not to confess other people's sins along with mine.

Father found the money also, where I had hidden it inside the stand that held the icon of St. Sergius. He moved the stand to make room for the ladder he used to replace the Trinity Icon, and there it was, all fifty thousand, in cash. Yet another miracle! The bishop was more skeptical, but after a careful and unsuccessful search for the owner of the money, he distributed it among the churches, giving the lion's share to St. Sergius.

Sarah disappointed Father Paul because, to my knowledge, she never laughed again. He seemed content, though, with the miraculous conversion of Boris, who even assisted in the Liturgy once he could walk again. This I know only second hand from Mama because I left while Boris was still confined to a wheelchair.

It was Boris's first Sunday out of the hospital when Vasily came back for me. That morning the papers were full of news about a fabulous shootout in St. Louis. Father Paul had just pronounced the final blessing when Vasily, Misha, and Louis entered the church.

They were grim-looking men, rather scruffy, unshaven, and disheveled. In contrast, Father Paul faced them calmly with splendor, strength, and power. Boris sniveled in his wheelchair. He had a long way to go yet. Mama began to cry. Papa wrinkled his brow and glowered with bitterness. I saw it all in a moment and ignored their faces from then on because my attention became fixed on my love as he crossed the room and stood beside me.

"Marry me?" he whispered.

"Yes."

"I have an announcement," began Father Paul. "This is Alex's last Sunday with us, and I think it is appropriate that we sing *Many Years*."

"Her last Sunday?" asked Erin. "Where are you going, Alex?"

I could not answer because I did not know.

Louis answered for me. "They are to be married and will live in Europe."

"Married!" This came from several people and was followed by hearty congratulations and questions and comments about my handsome fiancé (and unspoken but obvious surprise at my having landed him). There was a marked lack of enthusiasm among my parents, the priest, and the lump in the wheelchair, but nobody seemed to notice, least of all the Matushka, who was busy trying to welcome Misha and Louis into the church.

Misha gave her a sub-zero stare that could not be mistaken for anything other than active dislike. She was mystified, and I must admit so was I for many years, until Misha explained it to me at your father's funeral.

Misha did not like Erin because he believed she betrayed her husband by hiding the icon. It was tantamount to shooting him with his own gun, said Misha. She had access, and she misused it. I countered with the argument that she did so out of love for her husband. That made no difference to Misha.

Unfortunately, he and I had that discussion because he was accusing me of doing the same to Vasily. You see, both Mama and I were right. Vasily did turn, and when he did, he was dead within five days. Misha accused me of betraying Vasily by causing him to stop defending himself, but I told Misha that I never asked him to. Vasily's work was a No Man's Land that I did not enter after our marriage. It was his decision to leave his gun at home that day, his decision and his obsession. He did it as much for himself as he did for you or me.

He called you his miracle, and as you grew, entombed with the rest of us in the comfort and security of our prison estate, he wanted other things for you, things he knew about only vaguely, what he called a normal life. He was practicing, pretending, trying to experience life without fear, hoping to someday give you that kind of life, wishing it was his.

I miss him dearly.

I still tend to choose life at any cost, even this fearful, constricted life that we've tried so hard to help you escape. I was glad Misha did what had to be done when they tried to kill you with your father. I am only sorry you had to witness such a gruesome thing, especially when you were not yet twelve, and I fully understood your reluctance to go near Misha afterward.

But there is one other thing that I must tell you. I tried to tell your father, several times, but he always prevented me. You were his miracle, and he did not want to know the cause. He was your father in every sense except one, darling, because on that Sunday in Chicago when he came for me, I was already pregnant.

It always amused me that no one else saw the resemblance. I saw nothing but. Even Misha's wife, Katya, remarked on how closely you resembled Vasily, but then she had a talent for self-deception and maybe she was helping to maintain the fiction. I don't know. All I know is that your Slavic features came from me, dear one, but your exceptional beauty came from Misha.

As I look back on it, I think that everybody, Louis, Katya, and even Vasily, knew. Only Misha is truly in the dark about it. I know he is because he mentions marrying you off to his son. I suppose that night in my apartment is a non-event to him, as it can never be to me. Anyway, he has suggested a sponsalia, wanting me to agree to a marriage between you that is not a good idea for more reasons than he knows. I enjoy knowing something he doesn't. It does not happen often. But I thought to arm you with this knowledge just in case.

Your half-brother Michael is a chip off the old block, chiseled from stone, compelling, and doubly dangerous because he has inherited Katya's charm. He took Vasily's place in Charlemagne after his sister and mother were killed. I don't think he is particularly interested in you, but he is an obedient son, so do be careful and use this information if you have to.

It is because of Michael that the recruiters have contacted you. He has taken more responsibility within the team, and has a prejudice against Americans, after the loss of half his family. Frank has not yet retired and is highly placed in his organization, but his organization is still a leaky, loose collection of very smart men who can't keep secrets because they try to keep too many. Michael shuns them absolutely, and Frank wants you to help change Michael's mind. I'd say you have about as much chance of that as I have of converting Misha to Orthodoxy.

Still, there are miracles, and some cannot be explained. I remember something Misha said before we left the church that day, and I left home forever. Everyone else was crowded by the door. He was looking at Sarah, restored to her proper place on the northern wall. He motioned for me to stand near him.

"Do you think she will ever laugh again?" he asked.

"No," I said. "She has seen too many things that are not funny."

"I disagree," he said. "She will laugh again." He paused and looked at me. "But you and I will never hear it."

The End

EPILOGUE

Erin enjoyed this chore. It was quiet. Quiet was a precious commodity and there was comfort here in the empty church. The Saints, especially the women, commiserated with her as she dusted, polished, and vacuumed. It went quickly, sometimes too quickly, now that Yelena Dolnikova watched the children for her. It was odd that Yelena would offer to do that. No one else ever did, as much as Erin had longed for it, and Yelena had never been a particular friend.

I suppose she misses her grandchild, thought Erin. Strange that they should name the baby Mara. Too bad for Yelena that they live so far away. Still, the one time I met her daughter's husband and his friends! I have to admit I wouldn't want them to live too close. Alex always was a strange one. And I don't care what Paul thinks, that girl had something to do with the money, she and her creepy friends. No doubt. I owe her, though, for not telling Paul how she found the icon. Come to think of it, how did she find it?

Erin was not one to solve puzzles willingly and found a ready distraction in a new carpet burn that required treatment. Boris is hopeless, she thought. Paul insists that he is improving, but I don't see it. He nearly killed my husband when he set his vestments on fire with the incense. I suppose he tries hard, but I wish he'd start succeeding.

She said a short prayer for Boris's success.

She said another short prayer for her husband's rapid recovery.

Paul had suffered a second-degree burn over his lower left leg but did not take it well. Long-suffering was not his strong suit, he told her. She agreed.

"It's a good thing men don't have babies," she said.

"Ooh. Don't start telling me about labor and all that again. Ooh!" He groaned, moaned, and made himself a real nuisance.

"Why don't you try breathing exercises like we did when we had Peter? I'll coach you."

"You'll what? Don't be ridiculous."

"No. Really. It'll help. Come on."

Their concentration lasted almost two minutes as they stared into each other's eyes, breathing in rhythm. Until the laughter began. They accused each other of starting it but once started, it was mutual and simultaneous and overpowering, leaving them helpless in each other's arms, unable to speak, unable to do anything without laughing all over again.

Erin was dusting the Trinity Icon as she remembered this, gently rubbing a smudge from a shiny new hinge on the right side.

She did not realize she was laughing aloud again until she heard the answering chuckle from just above her left shoulder.

The End

CETUS WEDGE
Early 1980s

PROLOGUE

Disaster hung like a bottomland mist over the rented two-bedroom townhouse at the end of a city cul-de-sac. It hung down; it rose from the ground; it inhabited each room. It dripped from the mauve and teal Christmas wreath on the front door, making "Merry Christmas" a mournful greeting.

Mick and Stain sat in an old Buick across the street.

"What are you gonna do with your share, Mick?"

"I ain't fuckin' earned it yet so shut up about it. Just get ready." Mick tightened his ponytail by dividing it behind his head and pulling the two halves in opposite directions.

"Don't wave your arms around like that, Mick. Somebody'll notice. I'm gonna have a real blowout with my share. Party time!" Stain opened and spun the cylinder of the .357 revolver in his lap.

"There ain't nobody here to notice us. The targets ain't here neither, so don't go countin' all them chickens before they're even laid, man. And quit playin' with that piece before you blow your nuts off and then I gotta drive."

"Here comes somebody." Stain closed the cylinder.

A blue and silver minivan pulled up in front of the townhouse. A woman got out, opened the side door, and unlatched a toddler from a child seat. The child was in a bad mood. He whined and kicked her once, then settled into a whimper as she carried him inside.

"Now?" asked Stain. The townhouse front door was open.

"Wait," said Mick.

"I don't know if I can shoot no baby, Mick."

"I'll worry about that. You take care of her."

"I don't know."

"You don't gotta know. You just gotta do. That's the job. Think about the money and just do it."

The woman came back outside. She had brown hair, curly, shoulder-length, blowing wild in the cold wind. She pushed it out of her face, took some grocery bags out of the car, and went into the house. The front door was still open.

"Let's go," said Stain.

"Not yet."

The woman came back to her car a second time. She wore faded blue jeans and white walking shoes that absorbed the better part of a mud puddle as she stepped off the curb. She shook her foot like a kitten. One, two, mud is distasteful. She took the last of the groceries out of the car and slammed the car door. The heavy bags made her waddle a bit as she walked to the house.

"Okay. Come on. Let's do it." Mick opened his car door and stood in the street.

Stain pulled back the hammer on his revolver. He held it in his right hand and reached for his door handle with the left.

"Shit." Mick sat down again and closed his door, hunching down in his seat, trying to be inconspicuous.

Stain turned around. A black car pulled into the cul-de-sac. It was a Mercedes. Fan-cee. It parked behind the minivan. Three men got out, real dudes, suits and all, two blonds, one with dark hair. They all looked at Stain and Mick, then two of them followed the woman into her house. The one that was left stood on the curb to stare at them.

"I don't like this, Mick. That guy gives me the creeps. He ain't natural. He ain't real."

"He is too natural, Stain. He's a real, natural killer. I seen that look before, man. He's way out there, and we're gettin' the fuck outta here. Drive, man."

Stain started the car and reversed it all the way back out of the cul-de-sac. The man watched them go, then turned and walked into the woman's house.

ONE

My lawyer said I would be acquitted, and I was. That left resigning as the only honorable course, and I took it.

By accident, I met a gunship driver who had been in my pilot training class. He was still flying. I talked to him at a motel coffee shop and pretended I was in town on business like he was. I said I was looking for something better than I was in, not saying that what I was in was a load of the deepest kimchee, what with my unemployment run out, a new baby at home, and a wife who wouldn't even let me back in for my toothbrush last night.

He asked was I current. No. Was I the guy who...? Yes. He took a step backward. I might be contagious. What else had I flown? How long? How many hours? Told him all that. Could I get checked out again? Sure.

He said he knew some people and he'd put a word in for me. I wondered what kind of people he knew. Drop in the night special ops types, the kinds that fly unsafe airplanes into unsafe airspace under unsafe conditions. I got a real estate license while I waited. Didn't make a dime at it.

When the call came and there was no flying in it, I took it anyway because I'm not stupid. I know I'm not likely to fly again and, in the meantime, I've become attached to eating. It's my favorite hobby next to martial arts, and both joys cost money. Besides, Sally said something along the lines of Don't come back till you have a job, and even then, I went through training without her. After graduation, they put me behind a desk like some fucking shoe clerk.

My apologies to any ladies who may read this someday. But then, if you're cleared for WEDGE material, you've seen a lot worse so what the hell.

I kicked and screamed and they sent me upstairs to The Section. I was happy, apprenticed to number fifty-nine of a sixty-man unit. I saw some action at the lowest levels. Sally came to live with me and brought the baby.

I had just come back from a great success in Honduras, not even a reprimand for a change, and things were noisy in the ops room, with congratulations and explanations flying—within strict limits of need to know, of course. It was a Saturday night three days before Christmas. There was some cheer being passed around. I had some, and then some more, and developed a need for peace and coffee. These were in the hall, which was usually deserted because a lot of guys were convinced the coffee machine was just a home for bugs, the kinds that listen, that is, but I'm pretty sure it harbored a few of the other kind, too.

I was surprised to see a round, bald man pressing buttons randomly until the machine relented, dropped a cup, filled it halfway, then spat the rest out at him. He swore at it, took the cup, and looked at me.

"Merry Christmas, Bear."

I winced at the nickname. "Merry Christmas." I resisted the urge to say sir. I'm a civilian now.

"You don't like the name, eh? The Woman says she dubbed you that because your eyes are like a teddy bear's. Your record's more like a grizzly's, though."

The Woman was the only one in The Section. She wouldn't take a nickname, silly tradition she said, nor did she have a special ops coin. Too macho she said, but she gave nicknames to everybody else and never refused a drink when somebody forgot his coin and had to buy the bar. We called her The Woman behind her back. And if you believe that, you don't know us at all. This guy was a higher-up. It was good to know they called her that, too.

"Why don't you get yourself a cup of this…" He took a sip and scowled. "This is vile. They told me you drink this stuff, but I thought it must have been improved. It's still awful. Get some if you must and come to my office."

I fought the machine and won, stepping aside right before it spat at me, so it missed. Then I followed Buddy to his office. Long ago when he was a young hotshot agent there must have been meaning in the name, but now it was hard to think of the number two man in the organization and the number one man in everybody's estimation (everybody with any sense, that is), as a Buddy.

"What do you think of Jello?" he asked when we were in his office.

"I...."

"He's an idiot."

I kept my mouth shut. Jello was Chief of Section, Buddy's boss.

"How do you think he got his name?" he asked.

"He...."

"He melts in any degree of heat," said Buddy. "I know you heard it's because his face twitches like a bowl of gelatin or some similar nonsense that he's been putting out, but I know better. I was there when he got the name. He was an idiot then, too. He had WEDGE before me and got a lot of the wrong people killed, nearly including his own team. Fred Dolnikov was our boss at the time. He said to me, 'Buddy, I'm gonna save Jello's life. Hope it doesn't cost you yours. See if you can get a handle on these guys. If they live, they're going to be the best.' Sit down, Bear. Oh. Sorry! I won't use that name."

He waddled behind his desk and was silent for a minute as he sifted through piles of paper looking for something. "Sit down," he said again without looking up.

I obeyed. I sat in a worn easy chair in front of the desk, facing sideways toward the door. I looked around quickly. The man was the equivalent of a general and I was in his office. Even in the Air Force I never had this kind of attention without being in trouble, and here I was, the lowest, newest covert ops officer, in the same room with the man at the top, the man who handled WEDGE operations. I did not even know what WEDGE was, though I was getting an inkling. I knew that at some altitude far above my pay grade, we stopped using in-country operatives and began paying mercenaries and assassins. I also knew that way up in the ionosphere these mercenaries and assassins gave way to what were called specialists.

Buddy's was a pretty typical high-ranker's office, mahogany desk, stuffed chairs, credenzas, bookshelves, and all that. The picture behind his desk was unusual, though, not just because any pictures drove the counterintelligence sweepers crazy—one more place to hide things—but also because it was a picture of a window. No kidding. There was a sash, panes, sill and all, with a view of a park beyond it, complete with joggers and children, and even a mugging going on beneath the trees in the distance. There was a real curtain rod above it, and real curtains hung on either side. CI must have hated it.

"You like my picture?" asked Buddy.

"It's...."

"It's my snorkel, my ventilation, a lifeline to the surface world. I gotta have a window."

Strange statement from what amounted to a senior citizen in a world completely devoid of windows. The Section occupies an inner rectangle of corridors and offices, with a walk-in vault at its center for documents. It is surrounded by an outer rectangle of more offices, themselves without windows. The only windows in the entire building are on either side of the glass doors at the entrance to the lobby downstairs.

"No, really," he insisted, "what do you think about it?"

"I think I would be uncomfortable with my back to it."

He narrowed his eyes at me, which was not easy to do with eyes that bulge like that. "How long have you been here?" he asked.

"Six months."

There was an awkward pause as he stared at me and I stared back. "So soon," he muttered, then looked down at the paper he had in his hand. "Here's your game name. Stephen Donovan. Good Irish name. It has an honorable history in this business."

"I ain't Irish. I'm from Texas."

"Too bad. The computer calls the shots. You're Steve Donovan. This operation is designator NT, operation name CETUS, account WEDGE. I'm Frank Cardova, by the way. Call me Frank. Here's your legend." He handed me the computer-generated history of Steve Donovan.

I only glanced at it. I was trying to figure out how to explain this to Sally. Everything was classified, even the parts I understood, which were few. *Honey, I can't be here for Christmas because I'm needed for something important. They'll probably paint circles on my chest and call me Bull's Eye. Maybe I'm the test dummy for a new weapon.*

"Relax, Steve," said Buddy. "This is a promotion."

Was I that transparent or was Buddy's mind-reading the result of experience?

He started talking. "No doubt you know that WEDGE is our computer designation for the specialist team known to the rest of the covert world as Charlemagne. Have you heard of them?"

I shook my head.

He whistled. "You do know what a specialist is?"

"Not really."

"A babysitter?"

I shook my head.

He whistled again and closed the curtains over his picture. The room seemed darker. He came around his desk and sat in the easy chair across from me, his back to the door. He put one pudgy hand on each knee and took a full minute to think before he began.

"Steve, you are just now making the transition from a bubble cockpit to these concrete hallways. You're learning fast. After twenty-five years, I still have not adjusted to my room without windows. But there are men so immersed in the muck of our world—and you will learn how deep that is—they are so sucked down into it that they inhabit rooms that not only don't have windows but there are no doors, either. They're not just locked in, they're walled in. These are specialists, my boy. They take incredible risks and they do the impossible."

"Why?" I asked. "Do they do it for money?"

"They do it for buckets of money. Fantastic sums. But money is only another tool. Survival is their constant business."

"How, exactly are they different from regular mercenaries?"

"Besides the difference in price, they are far more effective. With a good babysitter, everything a specialist does is neat and tidy. There are NO repercussions."

"Babysitter?"

He bit his lower lip and thrust out his top chin. "You know that when you have to handle toxic chemicals, you're always careful to put on gloves, right? Well, a babysitter is like a pair of good heavy-duty gloves that the hierarchy puts on when national security requires them to use a specialist."

"And if there's a slip?"

"The glove takes the burn." He smiled. "I am about to be promoted. As Charlemagne's babysitter, I claim the right to choose my successor, and I have chosen you. Congratulations."

"What if I screw up?"

"You won't."

"What if I do?" I insisted.

The smile went away. "Oh, there's no doubt you'll burn, but I understand you're used to that."

TWO

I had a few questions. Closest to my heart: Why Me?

Frank got up, picked up the paper coffee cup on his desk, took a sip, and gagged. I had not touched mine, and now it was too cold anyway. Frank threw his, full, into a trashcan. It spattered across the wall on its way down.

"What is the first rule of deception, Steve?"

"Lead, don't feed."

"Very good. The best deceptions are thought of by the deceived. Now tell me the first rule of intelligence."

"Verify."

"Why?"

"Because of the first rule of deception."

"I find," said Frank with a sigh, "that I become more perspi... more perce... more brilliant with age. Of course, you know those two rules by heart. So does everybody else in The Section. The difference is that you live them. You have a pronounced problem following any other rules, my budding babysitter, Mr. Steve Donovan, but your performance so far shows a deep understanding of the principles of intelligence." He shook his round, nearly hairless head sadly. "Unfortunately, no one else does, least of all Jello, which is why we are here. A bureaucracy is like a septic tank, you see. The lightest material floats to the top, while the heavyweights decompose at the bottom. I think I'll stir the soup some and see what happens."

Frank hitched his belt up around his middle, clasped his hands behind his back, and began to pace, slowly, throwing his head up periodically when searching for a word.

"Let me see," he said. "About eight months ago, Jello sent me on a prodi... a ponder... a big wild goose chase. Something, somewhere, was going down and Charlemagne was needed and would I go get them please, verification would be forthcoming. I knew better, but orders are orders. I made contact and offered them the commission. They asked for verification, of course."

"So they don't end up killing somebody innocent?" I asked.

He stopped abruptly and tilted his head in my direction. "Nobody in our little windowless world is innocent, dear boy. Charlemagne wants verification so they are not deceived. It would be so easy for the Other Side to set somebody up and have us pay for it, and it would be just like them, too. They're such cheapskates. Where was I?"

"Verification."

"Oh yes." He started pacing again. "I told them I didn't have it, that my boss had it, and I would provide it before the start of the operation. They laughed. Then they walked out. I haven't been able to make contact with them since. That particular operation was a cata... a casta... a disaster. So was another one that came up in September. We could not find Charlemagne when we needed them. That was enough for the powers above me. I've already been told Jello is out and I'm in. Last week he went off on a pet project he thinks is going to get him promoted. When he comes back, he enters The Section History Book and I become Chief."

He stopped pacing and leaned toward me, hands on his desk. "The problem is, I can't do that job and this one at the same time. Who's to babysit Charlemagne? I think you're the best choice, the only choice. They'll eat you alive at first, of course, because you're so ignorant. What can you expect? But you're a natural intelligence officer, you speak German, you have me to train you—a considerable advantage—and you're a scrapper. I think you will survive. Close your mouth, Steve. It makes you look even more ignorant than we already know you are."

He stared at me with bulging eyes, like a frog deciding, is it dust or insect?

"I assume from what I know of you that you want the empl... the occu... the job. Stop me before I go any further if that's not the case." He tilted his head. "What's that?"

"I want the job," I said aloud.

"Good. Good. Be sure you have some reason ready that they'll accept. They will press you hard to find all your personal buttons. You won't want to give them too many of the real ones."

"Them?"

"Charlemagne."

Frank sat down again, this time behind his desk. Now he was the boss and I the subordinate, he the teacher, I the student. I listened, but without the real thing, without the actual people in front of me, I found it hard to remember more than the bald descriptions of the men he had known for more than fifteen years.

"I'll start with Sobieski," began Frank. "His is the famous name. His father was a solo specialist before him, one of the best, if not the best. My old boss, Fred Dolnikov, was his babysitter. The elder Sobieski died when this one was a youngster. I don't know how he took up with Charlemagne, but he's their weapons man, an explosives expert of the first rate, a fair marksman for a specialist, which means he's a helluva lot better than you or I will ever be but not the best in the biz as they say.

"He is considered the best at unarmed fighting, though. Like you, he has black belts in various styles. Also like you, he's medium to short, medium build, brown hair, but his is a little lighter than yours, almost blond. He has the prominent Slavic brow ridge over very, very light grey eyes, so light sometimes they seem colorless. He is missing the last two fingers of his right hand. He's almost forty by now."

"Forty?"

"Yes. Don't you start thinking that's old, Steve. With any luck, you'll get there yourself some not very far away day. Don't think these guys look like me, either." He patted his middle. "If anything, I've seen them become faster over the years. They had to, to survive this long.

"Where was I? That's right, Sobieski. Character? Hard to tell. I could sum the other two up pretty well, but this one is difficult. He seems to like Americans and everything American, whereas the others don't. His whole life is a long survival story, so he's more like a machine in some respects. He is quiet and difficult to know. I've never heard him say much and have always depended on Mack to keep him from killing me outright. The others call him Vasily and that's the name on his passport. He carries an Austrian passport, always in his real name, that lists him as a Polish refugee. His mother was Ukrainian, or so I understand.

"The Frenchman, on the other hand, never uses the same name twice, though his passport is always French. They call him Louis, pronounced the French way, but I have no way of knowing if that is his real name. He's fairly tall, about six-two, early forties, dark hair and eyes, slim build. He's the marksman. I don't know of anybody, east or west, who can beat him. He also picks locks and sets up pretty incredible surveillance. This guy is truly dangerous, vola... explo… unstable. He can be cruel, too. But he tells some pretty good jokes."

Frank leaned forward, put his arms on his desk, and played with a pencil for a minute before going on.

"The one who scares the bejesus out of most people, and I think with good reason—the longer I know him, the more reason I see—is Mack. I suppose you might call him the leader of the team. The others defer to him, anyway. While the Frenchman may be slightly insane, it's a human insanity, recognizable, almost familiar. Mack is perfectly sane. His judgment is flawless. If there is any question at all, any fork in the road, he will take the secure turn, even if it costs an extra life." Frank broke his pencil. "It is important never to be a security risk in Mack's eyes."

So far, I could see the wisdom in this.

He continued, "When I talk about him to other people, I call him Mack, because he uses a knife when silence is important. To his face, I say 'Sir.' The other two call him Misha. I don't know why, and frankly, I am less tempted to be curious every time we go out. From his accent, I gather that he is Austrian, though even for me, his accent holds more information than I can grasp. There is an odd quality to it that I can't figure out. He uses Austrian, German, and Swiss passports in various names."

There was a long pause.

"What does he look like?" I asked finally.

Frank played with his pencil pieces a little while longer. He shrugged. "Blond, very blue eyes, about forty. A little taller than you are, I suppose." He looked across the desk at me. "You'll know him the minute you meet him. He is unmistakable. He reads minds, too, by the way. It can become…."

He did not finish his thought. He did not even try leafing through the mental thesaurus he carried in his brain. He let the sentence, the topic, the training session, and the mission briefing, die on the spot.

"And CETUS?" I asked when he let go of his pencil pieces.

He looked up at me again. "The operation? It isn't properly called an operation, but I had the computer name it so we would have some way to charge expenses. I told you I haven't been able to contact them for eight months, didn't I?"

I nodded.

He stood up, took a paper from a stack on the left side of his desk, and handed it to me. "Imagine my surprise, then, when I saw this today. I hope you have a warm suit in that bag you brought back from Honduras. We'll take separate flights. Yours leaves first."

I was actually holding a WEDGE document. Since then, this has become routine, but at the time it was not just new, it was a revolution in my career, a coup d'état in a country heavily dominated by mercilessly suppressed rebellion. After Frank's weak description of Mack, I dimly understood the danger, but it could not dampen the thrill that went through me when I held that standard form message peppered with all the usual, mundane TSECRET/WNINTEL/NO-CONTRACT/SPECAT caveats and stamped at the top with the rare and almost magical word: WEDGE. I managed to read it; I devoured it, every computer jot, even the date-time group. It was from the FBI in Chicago. I was surprised. It had always been my impression that we did not speak, except during summits at the highest levels. Some people I knew ranked the FBI up there with the Other Side on their personal enemies list.

"Who is Eben Jared?" I asked. "Or, who was he?"

"None other than the Other Side's top solo specialist." Frank rubbed his hands together. "Eben Jared did his apprenticeship with the IRA, then attended all the top KGB schools for the particularly nasty, and finally set up on his own, freelance. He always gave them special rates. He was very, very good."

"But he's dead," I said. "So what's one more dead bad guy? Chalk one up for our side."

Frank whistled. "You are a cold one. Wet operations like this are not welcome in this country without our knowing about them. Who commissioned it? It is our job to find out."

"Not to mention who killed him," I said. I gave back the message and stood up, ready to go.

"Oh, we know who killed him," said Frank.

"I didn't see any mention."

"It's right here." Frank stabbed at a line of numbers with a fat index finger. The nail was bitten. The numbers meant nothing to me.

"Right here," Frank insisted. "The number of the ballistics match. That's Mack's gun."

I called Sally from the airport. She hung up on me.

THREE

"Can I help you?"

That's what she said, not what she wanted to do. Chicago's O'Hare Airport was largely deserted, of car rental companies at least. This little shrew had the only open counter.

I looked around. A man in front of me leaned on the counter, staring at her, his right hand clenched in a fist.

"Me?" I asked the woman. I don't butt in.

"Yeah, you." She said it to some point over my shoulder. She chewed gum noisily, like the desk clerk behind the counter in support section who issued my new shoes. He made me sign a form for the license, credit card, and passport that established my game name. He put a big X by the spot so I wouldn't miss it. I signed 'Steve Donovan'. Little things like that upset these bureaucratic types.

"So whaddayoo want?" She cracked her gum.

"Guess."

"We only got luxury cars left."

I did not want a conspicuous car. I looked around. Nobody else was open.

"It'll have to do," I said.

"It's a hundred and twenty-five bucks a day," she said, trying to talk me out of it.

The man in front of me pounded his fist on the counter. "You told me you didn't have any cars at all left."

"You don't want no luxury car." She popped the gum at him. It was not a pretty sight.

"I do so want a luxury car, you...." He closed his mouth with effort, but I didn't have any trouble figuring out the word he wanted to use.

With a noisy sigh, the woman drew a form from under the counter in slow motion. "Driver's license," she said to no one in particular.

The man produced an Iowa license from a slim black wallet and gave me an apologetic smile for interrupting.

I looked at him. He was young, blond, and not particularly well dressed. It was the smile that caught my attention. There was something hard in it, like a penny in a cake, only I couldn't be sure what value to place on the penny. I was probably making it up, fooling myself in the spirit of deception. Never give anything away, the schoolhouse had taught me, even a lie. Lies are better believed when the target makes them up. Just give him the ingredients. Here I was concocting nonsense like a fool.

I decided I was imagining the penny. This guy was all cake. The woman was right; he couldn't afford the car he was renting. He was a middle-class junior manager of some kind, probably a salesman on commission who would have to land a big one by Christmas just to pay for the car.

"You're twenty-four," the woman said to his license.

"You get a gold star for arithmetic," he replied.

Maybe there's a walnut shell or two in this cake.

"You can't rent one of our cars," the woman told him triumphantly.

"Why not?"

"Our insurance starts at twenty-five."

"I thought twenty-three was the standard."

"Ours starts at twenty-five."

"I have my own insurance."

"Company policy. I don't make the rules."

"No. But you revel in them."

If that got a sneer, I couldn't see it. Perpetual boredom and all that jaw work on the gum masked her expression as she held her hand out to me and said, "License."

I hesitated. Another counter was opening. The Iowan walked over there. "Sure," said the competitor, "we have midsized cars."

I defected without remorse, fell in behind the man from Iowa, and watched him fill out the form. He opened his wallet and pulled out a credit card with numbers so scraped and worn I could not read them. A picture fell out from behind the card. I picked it up from the floor and had a good look at it before giving it to him. An older couple, salt of the earth and apple pie, standing smiling in the snow in front of a shiny green and yellow tractor. There was a large red bow on the tractor's grill. The man in the picture held up a set of keys.

The woman behind this counter also held a set of keys. "Here you go, Mr. Taylor," she said as she handed them over. "It's a blue Ford Taurus, spot one four seven. There is a shuttle to the lot every ten minutes from just outside the door."

Though we did not take the same shuttle, I saw the Taurus pull out of the lot just ahead of me twenty minutes later. I saw it again as I took the exit for the Dan Ryan Expressway and headed south. And there it was in the underground lot at the hotel Frank told me to use. At the reception desk, I stood in line behind Charles Taylor of Iowa once more.

"Maybe it's under the name Peter Baker," he was saying to the reception clerk. "I'm a substitute for him. Peter Baker. From John Deere. Anything?"

"No, sir, I'm afraid...." The man studied a computer screen and clicked the keyboard a couple of times to make it look good.

"Any vacancies?" Taylor's expression was weary, his voice desperate.

"No. I'm afraid... wait, yes... yes, I do. We've had a couple of cancellations." He handed both of us registration cards to fill out.

"We're neighbors!" said Taylor when we were given the keys to rooms 632 and 634. "I'm Charlie Taylor." He held out his hand.

"Steve Donovan."

"How about a drink?" said Taylor. "There were no cars and no rooms until you showed up. You must be lucky. I'll need you around if there are any girls in the bar. I'll buy." He spoke quickly for a farm boy. "Are you married?" He asked it as we stepped out of the elevator but didn't wait for an answer. "You look married. Then again, I guess not. No ring. That's good. Neither am I. I'll meet you in the bar in fifteen minutes."

I spent most of that fifteen minutes studying my left hand. Of course, there was no ring. Marriage was not in Steve Donovan's legend. But the mark of the class-B bachelor was missing, too, because I never wore my wedding ring. It was dangerous in the cockpit and my wife had long ago locked it up to keep me from losing it. I pondered my unmarked hand for some time. This was such a small thing, insignificant, infinitesimal, as Frank would try to say, but Charlie's word 'lucky' ran through my brain again and again. My life had been a continual dogfight for so long that I was not accustomed to friendly airspace.

Charlie drank his scotch straight. I had mine watered down because I had to meet Frank at the morgue in just over an hour.

"What brings you to Chicago, Steve?"

I'm learning how to babysit a team of specialists.

Steve Donovan's half-page computer story did not satisfy the boy from Iowa, so I found myself filling in the gaps to defend against Charlie's carpet bombing of questions. I was pretty proud of myself, sticking to First Principles, Things I Know, and making them Steve's. I saw no reason why an FAA inspector should not have been an Air Force pilot in his previous life.

"What did you fly?"

I shrugged. "F-15s." It came out so smoothly, so convincingly, because it was true.

Charlie's blue eyes opened wide. "Really?" he said, with proper respect. "Did you ever shoot anybody down?"

Shit.

I suffered a century in the minute that it took me to come up with an answer. I finished my drink and chewed a piece of ice to buy time. "Air-to-air combat is a discipline, you see. Um… Orders are important, ah and ah, followed. Mostly."

Lame, I know.

Charlie nodded seriously, impressed by my sagacity. I felt my stomach turn.

"What's it feel like to fly a jet like that?" he asked.

"One of the best things about it is that it's the ultimate big picture," I said. "Before the gear is up, everything on the ground is small, smaller. Eventually, every stupid thing and every ugly thing is gone. What's left is perfect: perfect sea, perfect clouds, even perfect cities with straight, parallel streets and beautiful lights."

I sucked on another ice cube. Charlie didn't say anything.

"Another aspect of flying," I said when the ice was gone, "is that for me anyway, it's so natural. The airplane is part of me. Moving is like breathing—at Mach. There's life, freedom, power, joy, woven into a tendon that runs all through my body and out through the stick and back again at every response."

"You must miss it," Charlie said after a long pause.

I was looking at my empty glass. "Yes," I nodded. "Ah, No! I mean, I miss the F-15, of course, but I'm still flying BA-76s for the

FAA." *Did I cover that?* I could not remember if I had. Who the hell programmed the computer to put that airplane in Donovan's legend? I've never been in a BA-76. I'm not even sure I know what one looks like.

I told him I had to meet somebody and said so long before he could start another friendly inquisition. There are so many disgusting little details on the ground, like having to lie to likable people.

In the underground lot, I tripped over a bum who sat leaning against a pillar near my car. He was filthy, reeking, and drunk. In his fist, he held the neck of an open bottle wrapped in a brown paper bag. He wore one cracked sunglass lens; the other side of the frame was empty. It made him look like a pirate. Spilled booze, or something worse, glistened wetly on his greasy, grey-streaked beard. I found myself despising him. A ragged piece of cardboard taped to a box next to him said *homlees*. There were some coins in the box. I did not add to them.

"Bastard!" He screamed at me as I unlocked my car.

FOUR

"How do you do? I'm Nelson Hunsecker. FBI."

He looked like a banker: three-piece suit, greying temples, smug like a vault. He ignored my boss and held his hand out to me.

I shook it saying, "Steve Donovan," and introduced Buddy as "my boss, Frank Cardova."

Hunsecker had a subordinate with him that he did not introduce. The subordinate seemed vaguely familiar.

We were standing in a small, private room at the morgue. A dozen body-sized drawers were stacked in three rows of four along one wall. A small desk stood in the opposite corner. On the desk were a phone and a phone book open to a Yellow Pages listing of funeral directors. Otherwise, the room was empty, except for the echo of our voices and the shuffle and click of our footsteps on the flecked linoleum floor. Cold does not affect me, but I felt it this time, though I did not know if the room was cold, or if I only thought it was.

"I want you to know that we are at your disposal," said Hunsecker. "Anything you need, any support at all, just say the word." The man was still talking to me.

Frank answered him. "Thank you. Can we get down to business? Where's Jared?"

"Right here." It was the subordinate who answered and led us to the wall of drawers.

This guy was younger than Hunsecker, short, muscular, and black, with an enormous head and heavy features. Uncomfortably familiar. He opened the first drawer on the left in the upper row. We crowded around the body of a red-haired man, about forty years old, apparently undamaged.

"You verified the ballistic match?" Frank asked Hunsecker.

"Twice." It was the subordinate who spoke.

"Mack's gun." Frank reminded me.

"Where did you find the body?" he asked Hunsecker.

The younger man answered again. "In an apartment on the South Side. I'll take you there tomorrow."

"Who are you?" asked Frank.

"Sorry. I'm Jay Turner."

I wracked my brain but the name didn't mean anything to me.

"Jay here is a very fine member of our anti-terror squad," said Hunsecker.

Frank ignored him and asked Turner, "Time?"

"Eleven-thirty this, excuse me, Saturday, morning."

"You know exactly?"

"There are witnesses."

"Lovely." Frank did a mental calculation. "You must have been on the scene almost immediately. Who notified you?"

"The police."

"How did they know?"

"One of the witnesses kept telling them that the deceased was her husband, named Eben Jared, but he was carrying an Algerian passport in another name. The cops thought that was odd and called us right away."

"Nice to know somebody has a brain," said Frank looking at Hunsecker. To Turner, he said: "One of the witnesses said she was his wife? And the other one?"

"The other is a twelve-year-old girl. Seems to be his daughter."

"Daughter? Named Jared? And his wife called herself Mrs. Eben Jared?"

"Yes." Turner squirmed under the frog stare.

Frank turned to Hunsecker. "How long has the Jared family lived in your fair city, may I inq... ask?"

"Inkask? We don't have that infor...."

"All their lives," interrupted Turner. "The woman and child were both born here. As far as we can tell, they have always resided here."

"And at that address?"

"Ten years."

"Ten years? And when did you first learn all of this?" Frank's voice was rising.

"This afternoon."

"Nice work." Hunsecker bestowed a condescending smile on Turner.

"Nice work?" Frank's voice was tinged with hysteria, his face red. The redness spread upward to the bare dome at the top. "Tell me," he said to Turner through clenched teeth. "Tell me that they were an estranged couple and he rarely visited. Tell me she is an inconspicuous, homely little woman who is active in the church down the street. You can tell me this, can't you?"

"I am afraid I cannot." Turner hesitated, embarrassed.

Hunsecker tapped his foot on the linoleum impatiently.

"Actually," Turner managed to say under the heat of Frank's stare, "they were happily married. He lived there for about four months of each year, in total."

"And Mrs. Jared?"

"Reporter for the Daily Proletariat."

"Which is?"

"A rag funded by the Other Side."

Hunsecker interrupted: "Can we get back to the matter at hand? I have a meeting."

"This is the matter at hand," said Frank.

"What is?" Hunsecker gave Frank one of the condescending, patient looks he had been bestowing on his assistant. "Come, come now. We can save our condolences to the widow for some other time. Right now we need to clear this little matter up. She is demanding release of the body and we can't guarantee she won't go to the press behind our backs."

I knew that any minute now, Frank's eyes would pop out of his head and bounce on the linoleum.

"Doesn't it bother you, Hunsecker," Frank said slowly, "that the top solo specialist in the Eastern Block has been living more or less openly in your city for the last ten years, with a woman who holds a position in a KGB propaganda organization, and you only found out about it this afternoon? By God!" Frank lit the afterburner and ran to the desk in the corner. "I'll bet he's in the phone book! How much do you wanna bet he's in the phone book?"

"I don't think..."

"That's obvious." Frank picked up the white pages. "J. J-A. Ah hah! What street is this apartment on, where you found the body?" he asked Turner.

"Edbrooke."

"With an 'e'?"

"Yes."

Frank read the entry, "Jared comma, E period comma, Edbrooke Avenue." He looked up. "He's in the fucking phone book for heaven's sake!"

Hunsecker shrugged. "Yes, but he's dead now."

And then Frank gave up.

"You know, Mr. Hunsecker...." He forced the 'mister' through his teeth. "I don't want to take any more of your valuable time. You're right. We need to release the body as soon as possible, and I'll get right on it, but I think an underling will suit my needs just fine." He pointed at Turner. "Is this one any good?"

Hunsecker scratched his chin. "I guess he's all right."

"Then he'll do nicely. Good night, Sir."

Hunsecker started at this dismissal, gave Frank a narrow look, turned on an expensive Italian heel, and left the room.

Frank played connect the dot with his toe on the speckled floor. "Now then, you've got a lot to tell me," he said.

"Yes, I do," said Turner. "But first, allow me to assure you that we are not fools."

"Try."

"Hunsecker compartmentalized everything. The Daily Proletariat was CI's bailiwick. They noticed Mrs. Jared but had no way to connect the name with our files in Anti-Terror. They cleared her early on because she is a true believer. She is unaware that the paper is KGB-funded, and she still thinks her husband was a salesman. CI has been performing regular semiannual checks on her that, of course, the husband has managed to avoid, but in any case, his face would have meant nothing to them."

"But it meant something to you," I said. "Don't you have watchers at the airport? Wouldn't they have picked him up? I mean, a man with red hair and freckles carrying an Algerian passport?"

"Thanks, pal," said Turner. "They did. This morning. They tailed him for twenty minutes and lost him. They're good watchers." He looked at Frank. "When they lost him, I knew we had somebody big in the city."

"Make no mistake, my friend," said Frank. "You had somebody bigger. Let's go on. Give me an outline of the scenario and we'll go back over the details."

"Not here," said the FBI man. "I managed to secure a room here in the building where we can talk. I have already put up other information there. But before we go, I have something else to show you."

Turner walked over to the wall of drawers and pulled open the one next to Jared's.

"Sister-in-law to Jared," he said. "Killed by Jared's gun."

We looked at the waxen face of a beautiful black woman.

Jay opened the next drawer. "Neighbor of the Jareds, across the hall. A part-time whore killed, we believe, a few minutes before Jared. The bullet used was an odd one, a 7.65 French long, which matches number 17665Y on your watch list."

"The Frenchman," Frank told me.

"He is French then?" asked Turner. "I wondered. The report I received was that he was a Cajun and this woman's lover. If he is one of yours, why would he use such a weak charge?"

"Because it's French."

Turner's heavy brow wrinkled.

"If bubblegum were French, he would use it. Don't worry. His accuracy more than makes up for it."

"We noticed." Turner opened the last drawer in the row. "Now we reach the more interesting facts of the case. Those three were on the scene and we had them immediately. But as I investigated the incident and my investigation kept me on the premises here, I noticed some others. I have them all impounded."

We looked at the man in the drawer. He had been badly beaten, but the cause of death was most likely the hole at the top of his nose.

"The weapon is not on any list," said Turner, "but I believe these corpses are connected. This one is Nikolai Kolnichkov, a mid-level spook of the Other Side who, interestingly enough, has been on our missing list for the past six months." He paused. "We are convinced he has been on their missing list, too."

"Your source?" asked Frank.

"I cannot say."

"Verified?"

"No."

"When did he die?"

"About twelve hours before Jared."

"Why was he beaten? To teach or to learn?"

"I am sorry. I do not follow you."

"I like an honest man." Frank smiled. "Was Ivan here neatly pulverized to teach him a lesson or to learn something from him?"

Turner thought for a moment. "I would have to say to learn. Of what use is teaching someone a lesson only to put a bullet in his brain?"

"Bless you, my son."

Turner raised his eyebrows and threw a questioning glance in my direction. I shrugged. I was not quite used to Frank, either.

"And in what caliber did death come to our pickled Russian?" asked Frank.

"Ordinary nine-millimeter parabellum."

"From whence?"

"We think from Austria."

"Interesting. Any ideas on the weapon?"

"Glock 17. Is it one of yours?"

Frank did not answer.

"Is this the last body?" I asked.

"No." Turner closed the drawer. "There are five more."

"Same three guns?"

"In four of them. One of each in three, and an extra French bullet in the fourth."

"And the fifth?" asked Frank.

Turner drew his next breath through his teeth, looked at the floor, and said quietly. "This may not fit. It may be a simple murder, but I don't think so, and I'll tell you why when we're in the secure room. Right now, we'll just take a look at him so we all have a picture of what we're talking about."

He opened a lower drawer. An older man lay there, muscular and tanned. His hair was cut short, yet one sideburn ended in a Hasidic lock. "I made sure they left one sidelock," said Turner, "to give you an idea of how we found him. It is glued to his face. We found him in a complete Hasidic costume, all of it fake but well used."

"So you think he was a spook dressed up to look like a Hasid?" asked Frank.

I could not resist. "Or maybe," I said, "it's Halloween at the Chicago FBI and he was looking for a treat."

As they say, if looks could kill.

FIVE

"That remark was unnecessary and tasteless," Turner said to me when we got to his secure room, "but I will consider the source."

"Anybody with half a brain should be able to recognize a joke."

"Anyone without a brain should recognize a stupid one."

"Your problem is you take yourself too seriously," I said.

"I do not require advice from an adolescent flyboy."

"Boys! Boys!" Frank put himself between us. Just in time, for Turner's sake. "The problem before us all is that we have work to do, and when I say we, I don't have a turd in my pocket."

"A what?" said Turner.

Frank ignored him and walked to a large street map of the city covering the far wall. There were pins with little numbers on paper flags stuck into the map. To the right, a table was pushed against another wall, clean except for an empty folder and four or five stray sheets of paper.

Frank studied the map. "Tell me about the old trick-or-treater first."

After a sullen pause, Turner shrugged, walked to the table, and sat on it, his feet dangling. He yawned and rubbed his face.

"Allow me to begin, as they say, at the beginning," he said. "We impounded the body along with all the others we discovered today, make that Saturday, as we must be well advanced into tomorrow by now, at two o'clock thi… Saturday afternoon."

Turner's voice trailed off. He scrunched up his face, moved his jaw around in a circle, and forced his eyes open, big eyes, even bigger than Frank's, though not as prominent. He's very tired, I thought. I'm very tired, I thought. Why shouldn't I be? Up early, the trip back from Honduras, only to turn around and fly out here. *At least I still know what day it is.* He's very tired. He's more tired than he should be. And so on, until my tired thinking was arrested by that deep, official voice of his.

"At first, I doubted he was connected," Turner was saying. "It looked like a common mugging, but the costume bothered me so I ran a check."

He paused. Frank turned away from the map to look at him. "And?"

"And nothing." Turner shrugged. "Nothing in any U.S. File. So I checked Interpol, and what do you know, his name is Avrim Ben Hazi, Mossad, retired. Under a cloud."

Frank's eyebrows raised in surprise. "What's he doing in Interpol's files?"

"That was the very question I asked."

"Whooooom did you ask?"

"That I cannot tell you."

"That's twice now. Is this a good source? The same source?"

"Different source and an excellent one."

"Does your boss know about these private sources of yours?" Frank studied him with a skeptical squint.

"You have met my boss," said Turner. "He does not speak. He blithers. I cannot reveal my sources to him."

"Private networks are dangerous things. Your boss may be a blitherer and hard to live with, but your network will get you killed."

"My boss is not just hard to live with," Turner insisted. "He will get me killed. I have been unable to establish his bona fides as a blitherer."

"That is a very serious charge, my friend," said Frank, "I trust you do not make it lightly. And I wonder why you trust us."

"Twice correct," said Turner. "I do not make it lightly and I do not trust you. Still, I must work with you. Let us just say that Nelson Hunsecker is not consistently stupid. The malady comes out of remission only when it can do maximum damage, usually to my best agents. Someday, I shall catch Mr. Hunsecker being smart."

"That's your reason for the network? To trap one idiot? Will you invite me to your funeral?"

"I said, I do not believe he is a genuine idiot."

"Yeah? He seemed pretty bona fide to me." Frank turned back to the map. "So what did your network tell you about Avrim Ben Hazi?"

"He was in Interpol's files because he was a renegade agent of the Wrath of God."

"I thought that kind of information came only from the Mossad itself," I interrupted. "Is it verified?"

Turner glared at me.

"So," said Frank, "we have the following corpses gathered in the morgue on a Saturday evening: a pretty young woman, a two-bit whore, the top solo East Block specialist, an uncontrolled KGB agent, a renegade Israeli assassin, and four others who are...?"

"Two Americans, unknown, and two others, completely unknown," said Turner. "Maybe you should take a look at them. You may be able to identify one or two."

"Maybe, but I doubt I could beat your network," said Frank. "I will look later. It is already one o'clock and you're about to fall off that table, son. Give me the scenario now, from the beginning, so Dr. Watson and I can get our beauty rest."

"Who?" Turner shook himself from a near drowse, jumped off the table, and paced the room to keep himself awake while he told us what he knew.

"According to the pathologist," he began, "the earliest to die was one of the four you haven't seen. We found him at Midway Airport on the South Side, pin number one. The round that killed him matches the lethal one in Jared."

"That would be Mack," Frank said to me. Turner stopped pacing and stared at him. Frank waved him on.

"Next came your Ivan, Nickolai Kolnichkov," said Turner. "He died in an empty garage just outside the approaches to Rick's sovereign house, pin number two on the map. The time of death was approximately midnight last night. The cause was a nine-millimeter parabellum bullet to the head, not on your watch list."

Frank looked at me and shrugged.

Turner continued in his deep, fancy voice: "Ivan was severely beaten, reasons unknown, probably to provide information of some sort."

"He provided verification," said Frank.

"Pin number three," Turner continued, "marks an apartment on the near North side where three were found, each killed by one of the weapons already mentioned."

"No new weapons? No other weapons?" interrupted Frank.

Turner stopped, rubbed his chin, and gave a negative shake of his head. "Two were shot in the heart," he said, "the third in the head, execution style. The two unknown Americans and the other mystery man were in this group. Time of death is estimated at between two and four Saturday morning.

"Finally, the Israeli was found in an alley on the north side of the city, in full Hasidic dress, dead from loss of blood stemming from a knife wound to the carotid. He died at about breakfast time. Pin number four."

Frank swiveled around like a top to look at me, making sure I understood that this was Mack's.

"Next we come to the apartment on Edbrooke, number five on the map." The FBI man stopped pacing to sweep his arm through the air in the general direction of the map. The overhead fluorescent light seemed to bother him. He rubbed his eyes.

The official tone lowered slightly. Was this emotion? I watched Turner's face. It was grim and the eyes streamed with fatigue, but there was no sign of any change since we met an hour before. *Such a familiar face.*

"A few minutes before eleven twenty-five Saturday morning," he said. "Mrs. Jared, first name Cordelia, came home from the store with groceries for the evening meal. She discovered that her sister, Concordia Stewart, aged twenty, who lived with them, was, ah, entertaining a guest in her room. Mrs. Jared reacted angrily when her twelve-year-old daughter, Janey, told her Concordia's boyfriend was in the house.

"We have been able to ascertain that the reason this upset Mrs. Jared is because her husband was due at any moment and he always insisted that no other person be allowed in the house when he was there. This edict included repairmen.

"The boyfriend was a white American male, about five feet, ten inches tall, long blond hair worn to the shoulders, blue eyes, muscular build. He worked as a stock boy at the local Jewel supermarket and went by the name of Jerome Wajinsky. They called him Jerry."

Turner looked at us with swimmy eyes. He shook himself awake again. "Before Mrs. Jared could do anything about the guest, her husband, Eben Jared, burst through the apartment door. That is precisely the word she used, 'burst'. This door enters the living-slash-dining room. Concordia's room also opens to the living room, opposite diagonally to the front door."

Turner gestured ineffectively, trying to make us see the layout of the room he was describing. I nodded as if I understood, and he continued, "Jared shouted to his wife, who was standing to his left, and to his child, seated further left at the dining table doing her homework, 'Let's go now. We have to go now. Hurry up.'"

In Turner's low, official voice, Jared's words came over in equal, melodic pieces, scrubbed clean of the terror that had made the man shout.

Turner rubbed his temples and looked down at his feet. He took a deep breath, dropped his hands, and began to pace again.

"At that moment," he said, "the sister's bedroom door opened and several things occurred more or less simultaneously. A male voice in her room shouted 'No!' Jared drew and fired his weapon, killing the sister in the now open doorway. The boyfriend appeared partly in the right half of the doorway and fired at Jared, who was diving to his own right. A round hit Jared in the right arm and shoulder. His gun landed several feet behind him against the wall.

"At that moment, Mrs. Jared heard the front door close. She saw two men inside, both holding semi-auto handguns. One of these men bolted the door. There was a pause. The boyfriend, Jerry, now out of the sister's room, stood to Jared's right, the other two men to his left. The other two men were as follows: one was a blond man of about forty, with a mustache, wearing greasy blue jeans and a plaid flannel jacket. The other had long dark hair, greying and tied back in a ponytail, dark eyes, and a beard. Mrs. Jared and her daughter both recognized him as a Cajun from Louisiana who worked in a pizza parlor across the street. The little girl also knew him as the boyfriend of the woman across the hall.

"There ensued a brief discussion in what Mrs. Jared insists was Russian, between her husband and the older blond man. At some point in the argument, the younger man, Jerry, pointed his weapon at the little girl and prepared to fire. The Frenchman formed a sight picture on Jared's wife. Eben Jared then made a sudden move, reaching into his coat with his wounded right arm. The older blond man fired, killing Jared instantly. The ballistics match number 1656Y on your watch list."

Frank nodded politely.

Turner continued rapidly with no trace of his earlier solemnity. "There was now a brief, heated discussion in German among the three assailants. It was, perhaps, a disagreement. The older man ordered the other two out of the apartment. They complied and he followed. This concludes my briefing. Are there any questions?"

"Did Jared have a backup?" asked Frank.

"No. There were no other weapons on his person."

"Thank you. You have told me volumes in a few short sentences. But you will have to spell out your little joke to Steve. He didn't notice it."

"What joke?" I asked.

"The conclusion of my briefing. Did not you recognize it?" said Turner.

"Did not you?"

"Sorry. I read a great deal of early nineteenth-century literature."

"In the Air Force?"

"Pardon me?"

I had a hard time seeing him; my eyes watered in the bright light. Was he swaying? "It was the standard Air Force briefing, " I said. "Were you in the Air Force, Mr. Turner?" *And during which century?*

"Please, call me Jay."

Frank interrupted. "I hate to break up this rapproch... this reconcil... your making up like this, but we must be going now. Shall we say, until eight tomorrow, or rather this, morning?"

"Yes, of course," said Jay. "Where?"

"Let's meet on Edbrooke, but let's not all drive right up to the door. We can walk the approaches and meet across the street, in front of the pizza place."

"Very good." Jay walked to the door, but before he opened it, he turned back to Frank and said, "I must warn you about one thing. I will be required to introduce you to Cordelia Jared, and she may not cooperate with you because of me. The interrogation this afternoon took several hours, and she made it quite clear that she despised me at every minute."

"Why was that, do you suppose?" I asked.

"I am a tool of the police state in her eyes."

"So you don't think her dislike has anything to do with your unmistakable charm?"

"What is that supposed to mean?"

"Nothing. Nothing. Keep your sense of humor—if you have one."

"I have one, MIG Fodder. I simply will not waste it on such a poltroon."

Frank dragged me down the hallway.

"What's a poltroon?" I asked him.

"Let's go," he said. "We'll talk."

SIX

Frank fiddled with the heater. He started the engine of his rental car but did not put it in gear. The heater spewed cold air at us. Frank warmed his hands over it; they were that cold, that cold air could warm them, mottled pink, grey, and yellow, with little blue veins bulging from the backs.

"Let's go over what we know," he said.

"Why here?" I asked. "Wouldn't the secure room with the map be better?" *Read, warmer.*

"It's not secure."

"Jay seemed pretty competent." And the room was heated.

"He's very competent. Super competent. And the room is secure in the sense that nobody would be able to listen to us except Jay."

"Do you think he would?"

"I know he would."

"Why?"

"A man who sets up and runs a personal network is no longer obedient to orders. He's in the game for something else. This is what can happen when a smart man works for a stupid one."

I looked at the sheet of ice on the windshield making halos out of street lamps. The heater blew a degree warmer, but it didn't matter to me. I wasn't minding the cold. Hunger now.... Frank's teeth clicked until he forced his jaw shut.

I said, "I wonder how Handsome Hunsecker manages to get promoted, let alone stay alive."

Frank revved the engine. "How? Look at him! He looks like a movie star and talks like a diplomat. It doesn't matter that he's got shit for brains. Then there's Jay Turner, with a mind like a steel trap and an understanding that flows with the Colorado down the Grand Canyon. But he looks like Godzilla and he's a pure pain in the ass.

He'll never be promoted. And he's smart enough to know that. He's dangerous."

"So you think Hunsecker's a bona fide incompetent?"

"Yes."

"What about Jello? Have you ever thought...?"

"What about Jello? You mean, has he turned?" Frank laughed for a long time. "Jello's got twenty-five years' worth of bona fides, Steve. In all the time I have known him, he's crept along the edge of disaster, with only luck as a guide. He is completely consistent: if he touches an operation, he screws it up."

"How did Turner know I was an Air Force pilot, Frank?"

"Good question. He seems to know you."

"He is familiar, but I can't place him. Does that mean I'm blown?"

"No. You're blown when Charlemagne knows about you. From then on you'll be under their scrutiny at every operational moment, and maybe some other times."

I have to admit I had a short case of the willies when I heard the words 'under their scrutiny' and remembered the Israeli killer and his extra smile.

"So what's going on, Frank? Who are all those dead people in there?"

"That, my friend, is a network of some kind. All these guys have their own networks, Steve. That one in there was Jared's. I've never seen a whole network go like that before. But then, I've never seen Charlemagne use a new weapon before. What did Turner say, a Glock? Remind me to ask him how he figured that out." He laid his head back against the seat, opened one button of his shapeless overcoat, and closed his eyes. "You tell me now, my beamish boy, everything we know about this case."

I began to repeat Jay's briefing. Frank opened his right eye and swiveled it at me, like a knowledgeable fish looking at a hook. He was not looking for facts, he wanted mental gymnastics. I was to do those flips and somersaults needed to solve a logic puzzle. If Mary, Jane, and Sue are married to John, Ted, and Bill, but not in that order, and Mary is married to the baker and Ted is not the policeman, who is married to whom, and what are their occupations? I hate those puzzles.

I made a minor leap. "Sobieski is missing."

"Right," said Frank. "Where is he? He uses a Makarov. There is no sign of the Makarov. And who is the Glock?"

"Maybe the Glock was the babysitter."

Frank swung his head slowly, like the clapper of a bell striking negatives at the top of each arc. "No. No. No. No," he said. "Babysitters do not kill, Steve. Get that through your scrappy skull right now. Babysitters do not fight. They do not engage in operations. They protect their governments by maintaining a respectful distance from the nasty little details. Get that, get that now. You will be Charlemagne's social secretary and no more. You book their hotels and safehouses. You arrange for Mack to have his favorite Mercedes or whatever else may be appropriate. You scrub the area before operations begin. You protect the populace. You clean up afterward. You arrange payment. That's it. Ipso facto exacto."

He took a deep breath after the exertion. "The Glock was not the babysitter. The Glock is new. And Sobieski is dead."

"Not retired?"

"No. These guys do not have that option. They hunt and are hunted till they die."

"What about the life expectancy of babysitters, Frank? Do they retire?"

"I'm still around."

"Maybe Sobieski sat this one out."

Frank shook his head.

"Maybe Sobieski bought himself a new nine-millimeter."

"Come on, Steve. We have a description of the Glock shooter. Jerry is too young, too blond, and has too many fingers."

"Jay could have missed that detail." I rested my forehead on the dash. "No. Jay doesn't miss anything," I said through a yawn.

I sat up and saw Frank smile for the second time that night. "You have a long way to go, my boy," he said, "but at least you have transport for the journey. Now let's find time for sleep before our dance card fills up in less than six hours. I'll think aloud; you stay awake and listen.

"My guess is that Sobieski is dead. Retirement is simply not an option for a specialist. It's a technical impossibility. They need to gather intelligence to guard against attack, and they need to keep working to gather intelligence. Sobieski is not retired.

"Is he elsewhere?" Frank asked himself rhetorically. "Possibly, but I doubt it. It is not Charlemagne's style to split forces. Many elements in this operation are alien to them, but I think if Sobieski were alive, he would have been here."

A thought jerked me awake. I interrupted. "Frank, could they have split up? Had a fight? Disagreed?"

He considered it for a minute, or maybe he was considering how he would answer me, how he would convey what he knew, the way I know, I just know, where the runway is. Don't ask me to put it in words; only let me point to it until you see.

He opened his hand, palm flat at the top of the steering wheel, and he did point, at nothing at all, or at the dark and cold, or at the morgue. "They..." he began and trailed off. "This isn't in the file because I have no proof, but I think these guys go way back, grew up together maybe." He looked at me. "I think a break-up like that would mean treachery of enormous magnitude, enough to kill them all, not just one." He flared his fingers again and pointed at the foggy halo around a parking lot light.

I looked up and said, "I see."

Frank gripped the wheel again, then let go. He stepped on the gas again and fiddled with the heat. Sighing, he sank back into his seat and looking at the ceiling, said, "What else do we know?" His voice sounded much more tired. "We know that whoever commissioned this operation provided an incompetent babysitter or no babysitter at all. That leaves out the Brits, at least, and the French and the Thais. I know the men who handle the Charlemagne account for those countries, and they are all very capable. Nor would any of them allow an operation to go on without a babysitter, even if they were so bold as to commission it on US soil."

"Excuse me," I said. "But how do you know there was no babysitter?"

"Or the babysitter was incompetent," Frank repeated. "I know because of the woman across the hall. A competent babysitter would have had her out of danger well before the operation began. She was not necessary by that time and should have been held somewhere else until the danger was past. She did not have to die."

"Then why did the Frenchman kill her?"

Frank shrugged. "I don't know. I suspect she irritated him or got in the way somehow. The operation began shortly before eleven the night before and did not finish until after eleven the next morning. After twelve hours, it would not take much to make the Frenchman pull the trigger. One of the little things you will learn to do is remove the innocents from the scene before it starts. Remove yourself, too."

"I'm not supposed to stay with them?"

"Hell no. You'll get yourself killed!"

"But...."

"No but. We've been over this. Respectful distance. Don't forget. You're such a scrapper, I know you love a good fight, BUT THAT'S NOT YOUR JOB."

"What about Jared's sister-in-law, the pretty girl?" I asked. "Shouldn't she have been out of there too?"

"Concordia? No. She was necessary. She was the new guy's ticket into the apartment."

"So she had to die?" I remembered the pretty face in the drawer and ached a little.

"I didn't say that. I don't know what happened. She may have moved when she shouldn't have."

"You don't think the new guy pushed her out in front of him?"

"And then shouted 'no' like a rookie?" said Frank. "No."

"He was a rookie then," I said. I could identify. "That's why he missed." *God, don't let me miss.*

"Missed!" Frank gave me the frog-eyed stare. "He didn't miss, my dear boy. How could you think that? Where is your brain?" He searched the car for it, bobbing his head around the seat like a pinball on a bumper.

"Okay, okay, I'm fucking thick. Tell me why he didn't miss."

"They wanted to talk to Jared. The only way to do that was to disarm him. The new guy fired around a left corner disarming an experienced specialist in the process of a left-hand dive for cover. Brilliant shot."

"Why do you say they wanted to talk to Jared?"

"Because they did talk to him."

"Oh. Is that why you do this job, Frank? Do you do it to save an occasional bystander's life?"

"What are you getting at?"

"You seemed sorry about the death of the whore."

"Yes, I am. It was unnecessary."

"Then she was important enough to try saving."

"She was alive and human," said Frank. "Two attributes I find very important. I rather prize them in myself. Now, what is the problem?"

"What good is saving a life like that? I mean, where, exactly, do you draw the line."

My boss, the frog, metamorphosed into a crocodile. Of course, this business is predatory, but this was my first glimpse of the reptile in him.

"We do not draw any lines, Steve. We may wrestle with 'guilty' and 'not guilty' as verifiable facts of the shadow world, and these words may be equivalent to 'dead' and 'not dead' when we're through, but we do not place preferences on any lives but our own."

He looked at me like I was lunch, so I tested the water. I always do. I can't resist, especially in the presence of a dangerous animal.

"So if her life was so meaningful," I said, "why not spend Charlemagne's next fee on her? And now that she's dead, there is a bum in my hotel parking lot who could use the money."

He glared at me so I kept going.

"I just don't know if I'd spend a whole lot of energy saving the life of somebody like that bum. He begs. He reeks of booze. I can't see myself worrying about him unless...."

"Unless he's like you? Unless he agrees with you and looks like you and dresses like you or one of yours? Think about it, Steve. You want to define a life worth living. Did you put any money in his box?"

"No."

"Why?"

"He'd only drink it."

"Are you his momma now, Steve? Like hell you are. First, you want to give him Charlemagne's fee, then you want to tell him how to spend it. The truth is you hate him and you know that's not a noble thing, so you make excuses to assuage your conscience. You don't know shit about who he is, but you know who you want him to be, no matter how shitty he may find it."

I grinned at the crocodile. "Here's the extent of my heavy thinking, Frank: If he's my friend, I help him. If he's my enemy, I fight him. If he's neither, I leave him alone and expect him to do the same. Why did you pick me for this job, Frank?"

The croc withdrew and the frog returned, heavy-lidded. "You're a natural, my boy," he said softly. He sighed and looked out the windscreen. The engine labored in idle and produced only cold air through the heater vents. A hundred yards away the morgue was busy. A disaster somewhere spawned a stream of red, yellow, and blue lights, trucks, police cars, and grieving survivors.

I broke in on Frank's thoughts. "I'm getting close, aren't I?"

He did not answer. I was, in fact, very close. Frank was the rarest of government bureaucrats: he felt responsible. He treasured life because he saw so much death. He did not wield Mack's knife, but he wielded Mack and to him, it was the same thing. Like the ancient headsman, he needed absolution. Even this early in the operation, the hooker's death was a personal reproach, a disaster in the realm of responsibility.

"There is still so much we don't know," he said wearily. "We don't know who this new guy is. We don't know how or when Sobieski died. He was very much alive when I saw him eight months ago. And we don't know what they wanted Jared to tell them. We have work to do."

"And when you say we...."

He cheered up a little. "Right. We'll use your car tomorrow. Check your back and stick to your legend. Once I park this car at my hotel tonight it will no longer be secure and I won't have time to trade it in. Yours should be all right for a little longer. I hope."

"How do you know yours is secure? Jay's pretty sharp."

"All the alarms I set were in place when we opened it. Turner's people did not get in."

"Why won't your alarms work tomorrow morning?" I wondered what signals he set to tell him if the car had been disturbed.

"Because by then, Stevie boy, Charlemagne will know what hotel I'm in, what car I'm driving, and what I'm having for breakfast."

"But as long as the alarms are in place, the car will be secure."

"Not from the Frenchman. You have a lot to learn. The Frenchman can get in anywhere."

"The alarms?"

"He knows all my alarms."

"He's that good?"

"Even better. He's incredible. He has a gadget for every occasion, a tool for every lock."

"But why would they even care? I mean, they're gone, aren't they? All in a day's work; let's mop up and that sort of thing, right? Body count complete. Time to go."

Frank interrupted: "Are they, Steve? Did they wave to you at the airport? Did you throw them a kiss from me?"

"All right, all right. It's late. I'm fucking tired. I'm not thinking. I assumed they were finished."

"If they were finished, if Jared was the final hit, why bother to talk to him? What did they want him to tell them?"

"So you think they are still here?"

"I know they are."

"Verify," I told my boss. "What's your source? There have been no more bodies since this afternoon. They're gone."

Frank swiveled his round, hairless head so that it reflected the parking lot light above us. He kept his voice low; it was almost a whisper. "It's instinct, Steve. That's all. I have known them for almost twenty years. Something is very, very wrong here, and Charlemagne will not leave until it is finished." He paused. "I don't know why it isn't finished. I just know it's not. They are here. I can feel it."

...

It was past three when I parked my rental car in the underground lot at the hotel and walked to the elevator. The bum was there, asleep sitting up, snoring. The bottle lay empty at his side. I dropped a dollar bill and watched it float into the box.

"Thank ye kindly, suh!" It was a loud, exaggerated Southern screech that sent a shiver through me as I stepped into the elevator. I heard him laughing as the door closed.

On the sixth floor, I relaxed a little. Sleep was so close—on just the other side of my door—that it fuddled me and I could not get the fucking piece of plastic with the holes in it to work in the lock. As I fought with it, the elevator behind me opened. I was immediately awake, straining my eyes sideways, turning slightly to see who walked the sixth-floor hallway at three a.m. A man stepped off the elevator and crossed the hall. I remembered Frank's intuition as I slipped a hand in my coat to pat my Smith & Wesson. Did he pause? Business suit. Maybe forty. Maybe blond. Hard to tell in the dim light. Could be Mack. *But I'm not marked yet.* Frank had reassured me. The man entered the room next door to Charlie's, on the other side. My key finally worked.

I don't usually mind hotels, except the times when I'm kicked out of the house, but by six that morning, my room was a torture chamber. For three hours, I didn't dream, I nightmared. Stupid dreams woke me every few minutes and then refused to be remembered. I became obsessed with the locks on the doors, both the one to the hallway and the one that connected to Charlie's room, and couldn't sleep without having my back to one of them so that I had to check six every gigasecond or else grow eyes in the back of my head.

After another vague terror trance at six o'clock, I gave up and got up. I went to the window and opened the curtains. Street lamps below showed a street already busy with people moving around, walking, riding, running, making deliveries of newspapers, milk, and express packages, relieving another shift at work, or going home after being relieved. There was traffic forming streams of paired light beams, two-directional, and dancing on wheels, as if the conductor were live, and not just a set of colored lights on a street corner pole. I saw three near accidents right below my window. I imagined two drivers flipping each other the bird and a lady, a pedestrian, crossing herself as the cars swerved around her. I felt better. I left the curtains open because I needed to stay connected to the outside.

While I showered and shaved, I tried to figure out why I was so uncomfortable. It was the man in the room next to Charlie, I decided. He bothered me.

I had a good breakfast in the hotel coffee shop. The waitress was friendly and gave me a free newspaper. I read the funnies. The bum was not in the parking lot. No doubt he had embarked upon an entirely new life made possible by my dollar bill. In another year, he would be one of those remarkable success stories—all thanks to me.

All my alarms were in place when I opened the car. Sally might forgive me if I made it home by Christmas. Life was good even with a low ceiling over the killer expressway that led me south. I wished I could enjoy it more, but that guy in the hallway bothered me. There was something, some connection, something important, that I had in the crosshairs, but could not get a lock on.

SEVEN

We stood on a street corner and looked at the apartment building where Eben Jared hid his family for a decade right under the noses of his enemies. It was an older three-story building of dark brown brick with a common front entrance on the ground floor. Rusted metal fire escapes hung on the sides, as ugly as barnacles but not as secure. An eight-foot wall ran behind this and all the other houses on the block. Behind the wall was an alley.

"He had a perfect view of two streets," said Frank. "It's not actually on Edbrooke, is it?"

It wasn't. It was at the top of the "T" where 105th Street crossed the end of Edbrooke. The building was offset so that the east-side apartments looked down both streets. The Jareds lived on the top floor, eastern side, front apartment.

"Tell me, Steve, where would you start if you wanted access to that apartment?"

We stood in front of the pizza parlor across the street, looking at the right, or eastern, corner of the building.

"I'd start by trying to get into the apartment behind it," I said.

"Why?"

"They share a fire escape. It looks like the kitchen windows are connected."

"Good. Where else?"

"Across the hall, of course; the western apartment."

"Of course. And where would you position yourself to watch?"

"Right here, " I pointed to the pizza parlor. "Or from one of these houses on this side of 105th Street, east and west of Edbrooke."

"Good. How would you do this without alerting Jared's watchers?"

"By blending with the neighborhood." I thought for a moment. "I'd move in slowly, one at a time, and establish my bona fides over several weeks or even months before the operation."

"Excellent," said Frank. "Make it months. Jared was very good. He would have noticed any flaws." He looked past me down the street. "Here comes Turner."

Jay was still two blocks away, walking toward us. I thought I would fill the time and impress my boss by telling him about the marks left by wedding rings. I had opened my mouth to speak when I glanced at his hand. No sign of a ring. I would sound like a rookie, which I was, or worse, like a fucking fool, which I like to think I'm not. My throat was already making a sound though, and I had attracted Frank's attention, so I said, "I sure could use a cup of coffee."

He stared at me for a minute before saying, "That's not what you were going to say."

"How do you know what I'm thinking?"

"Get used to it," he said. "Mack would have told you exactly what you were going to say and why you changed your mind. I only know it had something to do with hands."

"What about hands?" Jay asked as he walked up.

"Nothing. Good morning." Frank was abrupt. "Let's go. I want to see the apartment across the hall first, then if you will introduce us to the bereaved Mrs. Jared?"

"How should I introduce you?" asked the FBI man.

"With our names, sweetheart."

"Was that supposed to be a Bogie impression?" said Jay. "Frank Cardova and Steve Donovan of what, sweetheart?"

I must admit, Jay's Bogie was better.

"Of the government," said Frank.

"She will wish to know which government. She will want to see identification."

"Show her yours."

"She will want to see yours."

"We don't carry any. You'll have to vouch for us."

"She is not going to tell you anything."

"On the contrary, she will tell me much, no matter how little she says."

Turner took a key from his pocket and led us across the street and into the building.

Two pairs of doors faced each other across the third-floor landing. A small, dirty window provided light and gave a view of the street below.

"Convenient," Frank said when he caught his breath after the climb. "No back entrance. Where is the access to the alley?"

"Around the sides," said Jay. "Behind the building is a lean-to that covers concrete trash bins set into the alley wall. The shed is accessible from either side of the building. The bins open to the alley for garbage pick up. There are access doors through the wall every hundred yards, and a few holes."

"Any holes near here?" asked Frank.

"None."

"Doors?"

"At the front and on the West side of the building. Both secured with good locks."

"Perfect. First, let's see the apartment where the Frenchman's unfortunate lover lived."

Jay opened the door to apartment 3C. We were greeted first by a stench, then by a horde of surly cockroaches that scattered reluctantly from the cushions of a filthy sofa as we invaded their room. Plates and utensils still crusted with decayed food were stacked like a cockroach condominium on a sticky kitchen table at the end of the room. Torn and skimpy curtains tried and failed to lend modesty to a dirty window overlooking the street. The rest of the apartment was in the same state as the front room. The bathroom was a nightmare.

From Jay's explanation of the body's position and attitude, Frank concluded that the woman died, needlessly, for some minor interference.

"What I find hard to fathom," Frank said as he turned slowly in the muck, "is that Louis spent months making himself at home here. Who could pay him enough to eat at that table?" He looked at me, then at Jay.

"Run across the hall," he told Jay. "And arrange for us to meet the tenant in 3A."

"Which?"

"In 3A, the one that shares a fire escape with the Jareds."

"I already checked. She wasn't home and doesn't know a thing."

"Just do as I say," Frank said with some heat.

He stood in the front room of that filthy apartment staring at a cockroach on a wall. I cleared my throat, but he did not move.

"Frank," I said, "is it possible there was no commission?"

"What?" He broke his long stare and looked at me. "There has to be a commission."

"Why? Maybe there was no babysitter because there was no commission. Maybe this was something else. Have you ever known them to work without being paid?"

"Only if it is vital to their survival."

"If Sobieski is dead, maybe something happened that was vital to their survival."

"Maybe," admitted Frank, "but on this scale? There's an entire network in that morgue. Why? Why so many?"

"Could they be avenging Sobieski?"

"That is an emotional response."

"They are men."

"I have never witnessed an emotion in any of them, even the more volatile Frenchman, that was strong enough to sustain an operation for months in these conditions."

"If not money and not emotion, what then?" I asked. "Ideology?"

"No. You're right. It is not ideology. Their working philosophy runs pretty much along your lines: friends, enemies, and others. This has to be money or emotion. But if it is emotion, it's more than revenge for Sobieski or even their survival. And if it's more than that, my knowledge of them is next to useless. I have never known them to risk so much for so long. For any money."

"She'll see you now," said Jay formally.

Apartment 3A was barren and cold, but clean. There were a few cushions scattered on the empty floor and after Jay's introduction, Sarah Tisdale invited us to sit down. Our FBI guy declined the invitation and stood leaning against the wall near the door, hands in his pockets, with a bored, irritated look on his face. Frank and I sat down, cross-legged on the cushions. Frank folded himself carefully. It took a while.

"Thank you for agreeing to talk to us, Miss Tisdale," Frank said finally. He tugged on a pant leg that had twisted around his knee.

"Oh please, call me Sarah." She smiled at me.

Sarah was a young woman, pretty in a way, with long, blonde hair parted down the middle and worn straight. She wore blue jeans and a sweatshirt and reminded me of a girl I dated in high school. She reserved her smile for me. To Frank, she was respectful and distant. She ignored Jay except for an occasional malevolent glance.

"You're not cops, are you?" she asked.
"No," I said.
"But he is." She tossed her head in Jay's direction.
"Not exactly," said Frank.
"Well, he's got that cop look. I told him I wasn't even home yesterday. Do you want a cup of coffee or something?"
"No, thank you," said Frank. "Sarah, did you know the lady in 3C?"
"Who? Dottie? Not really. I thought she was kind of a pig, personally."
"You never associated with her socially then?"
"No."
"Or her boyfriend?"
Sarah looked puzzled. "Do you mean the guy from the pizza parlor?"
"Yes."
She took a moment to answer. "There was one time."
"One time? When was that?"
"About three months ago. September, maybe."
"Please, tell me about it."
"There isn't anything to tell. Dottie came over right after I moved in. She was real nice to me like she wanted something and asked me if I wanted to meet this guy her boyfriend knew. She said we should all go out together and have a good time."
"What did you say?"
"I said no. I wasn't sure our definitions of a good time matched. Then a couple days later, she came over again with her boyfriend, and he talked me into going out with his friend."
"What was he like? Dottie's boyfriend, I mean."
She hesitated a long time. "I liked him, and I wouldn't have minded him at all," she said frankly. "But Dottie was insanely jealous. I couldn't blame her. I don't know why he stayed with her. I don't think she knew why, either."
"And his friend? The guy you went out with, what was he like?"
"He was gorgeous!"
"Can you describe him?" asked Frank.
"He was just gorgeous. Blue eyes. Great body."
"Was he older, like Dottie's boyfriend?"
"No. He was like about my age."
"What color was his hair? How tall was he?"

"He was taller than you guys, but not too tall. He had an orange mohawk."

"A what?" I asked.

She smiled at me again. "You know, a mohawk. His head was shaved, like, on the sides." She ran her palms along the sides of her head, front to back. "And he had a huge mohawk spiked up in the middle, orange, like. He was gorgeous."

"With orange hair?" I wondered how I was getting all these smiles with a short brown haircut.

"Well, it wasn't him, was it?"

"I don't know, was it?" I knew I sounded a little irritated. Frank interrupted.

"Why do you say it wasn't him, Sarah?" he asked. "What do you mean?"

"There was this guy a couple of years ago."

"A couple of years!" I stopped at Frank's signal.

"Go on, Sarah," he said. "What about this guy?"

"Well, there was this guy. I went out with him once and he could really play the guitar. I couldn't believe it when he played, like, it was so beautiful. It made me cry sometimes. Anyway, he wore this black leather stuff with chains and spikes and all that and my dad had a fit. I couldn't get him to see that it was just because of the band the guy was in. He had to dress like that, but it wasn't him. He played the guitar and he wore that stuff so he could play the guitar."

"And the guy Dottie's boyfriend introduced you to?"

"Same thing. I thought maybe he was a musician. He liked music. We talked about it a little." Her voice trailed off as if she were tired of the subject.

"But you didn't hit it off?" said Frank.

"No."

Frank waited. When she didn't explain, he asked why.

"Neither one of us wanted to."

We waited again, for what seemed a long time. Sarah looked at Frank and explained. "He scared me. They both scared me. Something else was going on. It was like they were disagreeing about something without even talking about it. Dottie's boyfriend kept giving my date these looks, and...."

"And your date?"

"He was like, defiant, or something. Anyway, he didn't want anything to do with me. It was mutual, really."

We thanked her and unfolded ourselves from her cushions.

At the door, Frank asked her one more question: "Did you ever see him again? Your date, I mean."

"Yes." She said it steadily, as if she expected the question. "I saw him at Gately's. He was with the girl next door. I don't know her name. He bought her a tape. His hair was down, tied in back, and it wasn't orange anymore, but I'm sure it was him."

She gave me another smile before she closed the door.

"Time, gentlemen," said Frank in the hallway. He seemed to be in a better mood. "Time is the critical element here. And now it is time to impose our obnoxious presence on the family of the lately deceased. Lead the way, my beamish boy!" He pushed a reluctant Jay Turner none too gently toward the door of apartment 3B.

EIGHT

Chilly, frozen, sub-zero, outside on a December day, and inside apartment 3B. The flat was warmly decorated for Christmas, an orderly, comfortable home, but its mistress, the breathtaking Cordelia Jared, was neither warm nor genial. She frankly hated us and said so with perfect brown eyes. She was more a chiseled sculpture of an aristocrat than a real woman, with a long, graceful neck held stiffly defiant.

She singled out Frank as the major bad guy in her life, evicting Jay from that special loathsome place in her granite heart. Many things were said at first, none of them fruitful, not printable, either. We managed to seat ourselves, without invitation, around a dining table standing a few feet from the entrance. The living room stretched before us, with a decorated Christmas tree at the far end in front of the window. There were lights on it; I could see the wires dangling from the lowest branches, but the lights were not turned on. The carpet was light grey with damp, pink patches where the nap had been rubbed up, one near the tree, the other across from the entrance at the door of a bedroom. The kitchen was open to our left. I could see the fire escape past a little white valance with a lace fringe.

After a series of monosyllabic answers from the magnificent statue, Frank seemed to make a decision. "Listen, Ma'am," he said, leaning forward in his chair to throw the words at her. "We are enemies. Make no mistake. We are as opposed as ever two people can be. You are right. I do a nasty, secret job to stop your money backers from ever getting into a position to tell me what sort of shampoo I must use on my hairy head. Your husband did a nastier secret job for your benefactors' side, and if you didn't know that, I'm telling you now. For the first, and probably only, time in our diametrically opposed lives, we have a common purpose: to find out why your husband is dead. Now answer my questions, Ma'am, and if I discover any truth in this matter, we might strike a deal along the lines of I'll Show You Mine If You Show Me Yours."

He opened his coat and showed her his gun. "Your late husband and I were in the same secret business, different companies, same ID cards, and we had no trouble recognizing each other. The fact is, I am the only one on either side with the expertise to unravel this thing. Whether you get any answers when I do unravel it will depend on the answers you give me now."

He buttoned his coat and leaned forward again. "When did you know your husband would be home yesterday morning?"

"Friday." She was cold and reluctant, but cooperating.

"Who else knew?"

"Janey, my daughter, and Concordia, my sister."

"Did your husband know about Concordia's boyfriend Jerry?"

"Yes. Eben asked a lot of questions about him."

"Did he meet him?"

"No."

"What exactly did your husband want to know about him?"

"He wanted to know if he had an accent of any kind, and how old he was."

"He was satisfied with the answers?"

"Yes," she said bitterly.

A young girl came into the room. She was a copy of her mother, with skin perhaps a shade lighter. Her hair fell in soft brown clouds around her shoulders, and she moved with surprising grace despite the long, ungainly limbs that marked her preadolescence.

"You must be Janey. Please, sit down." Frank stood up and pulled out a chair for the child.

"No," said the mother. "She's been through enough."

"Sit down, Janey. We were discussing your father," said Frank. "Can you tell me what his job was?"

The girl glanced at her mother, received a tired nod, then looked at Frank. Her eyes were swollen and her voice had a nasal tone. "He was a salesman," she said. She looked again at her mother but could not catch her eye. "He did something secret," she said softly.

I caught the shock on Cordelia Jared's face before she masked it.

"How do you know?" asked Frank.

"I helped him sometimes," said Janey.

"That's enough. Leave her alone," said her mother.

"Tell me about your Aunt Concordia, Janey," said Frank, ignoring the mother.

"Concordia was a saint," Mrs. Jared interrupted. "She was sweet and trusting, never...." Tears intruded. She put her face in her hands to stop them.

"She sure was a saint," said Janey. "Jerry said so, too."

"What did Jerry say?" Frank asked gently.

"He said she was like his sister. So was I, he said. Except Concordia acted like her, and I looked like her. That's what he said. I asked him if his sister was black then, and he said no, but she was a princess just like me."

"He has a sister?" asked Frank.

"He had a sister," the girl said. "She's dead."

"Did he say when she died?"

"No."

"Did he say how she died?"

"No."

"Do you remember when Jerry and Concordia started going out together?"

"In October," said Janey's mother.

"When in October?"

"I don't know. About the middle of the month, I guess."

"Were they serious?"

"Very," said the widow. "At least Concordia was. She was in love. She thought he was, too."

I could almost taste the bitterness in her words.

We spent the next hour reconstructing the three-minute episode of the day before. Frank stood in each position as Janey and her mother remembered it. As Mack, he pointed his gun at an imaginary Jared; as Louis, he stood by the door.

"The Frenchman never moved from here?"

"He didn't stay there, but I did not see him move," said Mrs. Jared. "I was watching Jerry. He was going to shoot my baby."

"Try to remember where he moved to, Mrs. Jared."

She concentrated for a minute. "He was next to the table by the time Jerry put his gun away."

Frank stepped to the table and crawled under it. He pulled something from underneath, stood up, cracked a small square wafer-like object in two, and tossed the pieces to me.

"A souvenir," he said. "An insect of the genus spiesmus lissenus. Let's hope we can continue in privacy."

He turned to the girl. "Was Jerry going to shoot you, Janey?"

She swallowed before answering. "Yes."

"What stopped him?"

"The other man."

"Which one?"

"The blond one. The one who looked like him."

"Looked like him?" Frank seemed surprised.

"Yes," agreed Mrs. Jared. "They did resemble each other. I would say they were related."

"It was Jerry's dad," said the girl.

"Why do you say that?"

Janey squirmed and threw an embarrassed glance at her mother. "When Jerry tried to argue," she said, "he got that look that says don't argue. He stopped talking back and put his gun away."

"What look is that?"

"You know. That look. My mom knows how to do it, too." She did not look at her mother.

"Yes, Janey, I know," said Frank. "It was a parent look, wasn't it?"

She nodded.

"But the other man argued, too, the one whose gun was pointing at your mom?"

"Yes. But that was different."

"When Jerry put his gun away, was he angry?"

"No. He looked relieved."

"And the other man?"

"A little angry, maybe, but more..." she wrinkled her nose in an adorable expression as she searched for the word.

Mrs. Jared supplied it. "Puzzled," she said. "He didn't seem to understand."

"Did you understand anything that was said?"

"No. I think it was all in German," said Jared's widow.

"I remember a word, though," Janey volunteered. "All three of them said it when they argued."

"What was that?" asked Frank.

"It sounded like 'rocka.'"

"Rocka?" Frank thought for a minute. "Do you mean *Rache*?" He pronounced the German 'ch' from the back of his throat.

"Yes, that's it."

There was a pause in which no one spoke or moved.

"Mrs. Jared," Frank said finally, "to your knowledge, did your husband ever carry more than one gun?"

"No."

Another pause. We all stood as still as the Christmas tree by the window. Frank was looking at it. I watched Cordelia Jared. Her eyes strayed to the tree and began to fill again with tears. Frank broke the silence.

"I thank you for your cooperation," he said quietly. "We will go now. I cannot tell you much, but I give you this. Your husband died to save you and your daughter. By reaching for a gun he did not have, he forced them to kill him. Once he was dead, there was no longer any point in threatening you. Whatever else he was, he was a brave man, and he loved you."

"So what the hell does 'rocka' mean?" Jay asked in the hallway.

I answered, "Revenge."

NINE

"That's interesting," said Frank.

We stood in the front doorway of the apartment building, bundled against the cold with overcoats, scarves, and gloves in various shades of black or grey. Jay and I stamped our feet in a not very subtle attempt to get Frank to stop standing there and do something, or at least say something. It struck me that we resembled the three blind mice, and I suspected Mack was around the corner with a carving knife, waiting to cut off our tails—or worse. When Frank finally spoke, Jay and I frowned at each other.

"What's interesting?" I asked.

"That gas station, down the street," said Frank. "From the window upstairs, all you see is the canopy over the pumps, but from here, you can look right into the shop."

Jay looked at the station to our right. "I checked it out myself," he said. "Nobody's been there." He stamped his feet impatiently. "What do you want to do next?"

"I don't know. What do you want to do, Mr. Turner?" said Frank.

"I want to show you the other four bodies in the morgue and then take you to the apartment where we found three of them."

"What about you, Steve?" Frank asked me.

"I want lunch."

"Good plan. It's only eleven. Let's do the apartment first and save the morgue for after lunch. We'll take Turner's car."

It took us an hour to get to the apartment on the city's north side. It was on the top floor of a white brick building on a tree-lined street. The apartment itself was in perfect order and nothing seemed disturbed or missing. The only sign that three men had died there the day before was a small blood stain on the carpet, not rubbed pink, where one had been found with an execution-style bullet in his brain.

We walked through each room. All the fixtures, furniture, and even the kitchen utensils had a generic quality. It reminded me of a safehouse. There were two bedrooms furnished as bedrooms and a third, smaller room that had been turned into a darkroom.

"Any photos?" Frank asked Jay.

"None."

"None? No films?"

"Nope."

"Negatives?"

"No."

Frank looked at me. "I don't suppose there is a restaurant around here where we can have lunch?" he asked.

"I noticed a place around the corner," I said.

"Thought you might've."

At the restaurant, there were bread sticks in a jar on the table. I helped myself.

"Mrs. Jared is a beautiful woman," I said before starting on a second stick.

"And rich," said Jay.

"You mean all the money he must have left her in Swiss accounts?"

"No. I don't think she is aware of that yet. I mean that she comes from a wealthy family. Her father was a banker."

"A banker?"

"Yes. And I don't mean that he was a teller. He owned the bank. I grew up in Cabrini Green."

"What's that?"

"A housing project on the south side of the city. My mother cleaned windows for the city for twenty years to get me out."

"I sense some animosity toward Mrs. Jared."

"I had a scholarship to the University of Chicago," he said, "until she spoke to the scholarship committee. Irregularities with my essay, she said. Not the content. No, her concern was that I could not cite my sources. What sources? It was a personal essay, an original composition. No, it could not be, she said. No one writes or speaks that way."

"Speaks what way?"

"The way I speak. People think I am pompous, or that I put it on to impress, but it is natural to me. I grew up reading English literature. Most of the alternatives in my neighborhood were deadly."

"But you did get your degree?" I asked.

"Yes, of course. I attended an out of state university."

I swallowed quickly in order to make a sympathetic noise and gave myself the hiccups.

Frank said, "Try holding your breath, Steve."

The waitress brought our food. Jay and Frank dug in; I was too full of breadsticks.

"So this is personal, not political. Am I right?" I asked Jay. "More of an in-house, a family feud, not some political struggle? Between you and Cordelia, I mean."

Jay's frown was almost a relief after a brief smile. Ancient stone idols should not smile. The gods are invariably angry. I was used to life that way and had no use for a joker in the heavens.

"All politics is personal, Steve," he said. "It is a trade in personal power."

"You fixed-wing flyers are all the same," said Frank. "You think politics is an airplane with two static wings, left and right."

"Isn't it?" I said.

"No."

"Then what is it?"

He swallowed his last French fry. "It's a helicopter, Stevie, my boy. There's just one wing that's moving all the time, and when you look at it, you see shadows of where it's been and where it's going." He took a French fry off my plate and twirled it to illustrate. "You see, there is no left or right. There is only the center and the edge. If you sit on the center, you get dizzy." He rolled his eyeballs around; I could have sworn in different directions. "If you sit on the edge, you get flung off. And if you try sitting somewhere in between, it cuts you to pieces."

He ate my French fry.

"There's another rotor behind," said Jay. "Spinning perpendicular to the main one. It keeps the torque of the engine from destroying the aircraft."

Frank looked at him and pushed my plate toward him. "Have a French fry," he said.

"So where are you on the chopper?" I asked Frank.

"I'm on the edge, holding on."

"Jay?"

"Ditto."

"And WEDGE?"

Frank shrugged. "Maybe they're somewhere on that back rotor."

"Aren't they Nazis or something?"

Frank choked on a fry. "Good god, no. Where'd you get that idea?"

"You said they never work for the Soviets."

"I didn't say never. But that WEDGE is not one or the other, I can testify. We've had a commission or two against Nazis. WEDGE has always taken the paper, at great personal risk, I might add, since they top a few Nazi hit lists."

"Then WEDGE is not left or right?"

"Use the chopper, Steve. Maybe they're on that back rotor." He shrugged again. "I don't know. In the day-to-day mess of this business, everybody on the chopper bleeds red."

"And everybody," Jay tried to swallow a mouthful of my French fries. "Everybody is trying to get into the pilot's seat."

"Not everybody," said Frank. "Some of us are content to keep certain people out of it."

"Sometimes to keep them out, you have to occupy it yourself." Jay was not joking.

...

Eben Jared and company were in their assigned places at the morgue. Frank did not recognize any of the three that were found in the apartment, but when Jay opened the last drawer on the bottom right, he flushed red to the top of his hairless dome.

"You know him." The FBI man was not asking.

"Yes," admitted Frank.

"Who is he?"

"I'll tell you later. I need to think."

"I need to know now."

"No. You don't."

"If you want any further help from me...."

"Don't you threaten me, my friend. I will tell you who this is when I'm damn good and ready."

It was my turn to pull Frank shouting through the echoing hallway, out of the building, and into the grey day where I hoped the air would cool his temper. We waited for Jay in the parking lot. I wanted them both to calm down before I had to ride back with them to Edbrooke.

"So who was it?" I asked Frank.

He looked afraid. He later denied it, but he was afraid.

"So much for your no-commission theory," he said.
"Why? Who was it?"
"Anatoly Lupin."
"That tells me a lot. Who?"
"He was a babysitter. A high-ranking babysitter."
"Whose?"
"The Bulgarians'"
"Jared's?"
"No."
"Part of Jared's network, then?"

Frank shook his head. "With all due respect for a dead babysitter, Lupin was not somebody I would include in a private network. Jared certainly would not have."

"Bit of a Jello, was he?" I asked. "Why are you so sure it was a private network?"

"Everybody else is outside established control, and the connections are unlikely, especially the Mossad killer. Only personal connections can explain it."

"But Lupin?"

"He had to be assigned. Neither Jared nor Charlemagne would have consciously chosen to work with him."

"He could have been assigned to Jared."

"No. Jared had a very competent babysitter of his own."

"Are you telling me the Bulgarians commissioned Charlemagne?"

"No, the Soviets. Sometimes the Bulgarians act as their cutouts on wet operations."

"Disturbing," I said. "But I can handle it now that the world is a chopper. Why does it bother you so much?"

"It doesn't. I just don't like unexplained, unexpected developments, that's all, especially when one of them affects me—and you, I might add—personally."

"What's that?"

"Lupin was the first to die. It seems Mack has lost what little tolerance he once had for incompetent babysitters."

TEN

"But you're not incompetent!" *And I won't be incompetent.* "You think so, do you?" Frank's breath made a fog around his chin.

For a minute I wondered what he was answering, my words or my thoughts. I said, "Yes, I think so."

"Define incompetent."

I thought about it. I thought about every bureaucrat I've ever been tempted to throttle. "People who are incompetent," I said cautiously, "take shortcuts or make long detours at the wrong places and don't even know they're lost."

"I think Mack's definition is anybody who makes a mistake," said Frank.

"But that's everybody."

"Right you are. I like your definition better, but you're not the guy with the knife."

"Speaking about the guy with the knife," Jay said as he stepped over a cement parking marker and rubbed the frost off an old car. He walked toward us. "It seems he met my boss last night. I just received word. I have been promoted. Do you think this investigation will take much longer? I have quite a lot to do."

Frank stared at him incredulously. "Are you saying Hunsecker is dead?"

"Yes."

"How?"

"It appears his throat was cut." Jay shrugged, as though such a thing could be in question. "They found him in an alley a few blocks from here, dead since about one o'clock this morning according to the pathologist. I had him impounded along with the others. Hunsecker, that is, not the pathologist."

Frank handed him a wadded-up piece of tissue from his pocket. "Here. Wipe the tears out of your eyes and get a hold of yourself."

We didn't say much on the way to Edbrooke. At first, I thought Frank was quiet because he considered Jay's car unsecure. But Jay couldn't even get him to make small talk.

So how come Frank, of all people, wouldn't talk? Was he still mad about their argument over the Bulgarian? No. The look on his round face was grim, not angry. Did he think Jay Turner killed Hunsecker? Impossible. Jay was with us until after two that morning. This new mood in Frank was a puzzle.

Something occurred to me. I dismissed it before it had a chance to fully form in my mind, but it intruded again, and I remembered a few details that seemed to support it.

One of the details I remembered was Jay and his mysterious sources. Frank said Jay was running his own network; he had stepped outside of control. I suddenly knew better, because I remembered where I had seen him before—at the Academy. Jay Turner was cadet Wing Commander during my first, my doolie, year. He was a zoomie, and not just any zoomie, but a successful, distinguished, disciplined graduate who knew how to wend his way through the moral labyrinth of any hierarchy, no matter how imperfect it might be.

Jay Turner was under orders. The question was, whose orders? As we drove south, only two minutes from our destination, my thoughts followed each other like an elephant walk, nose to tail, so closely that I had the answer before the FBI man turned off the engine.

Jay was dedicated to two things: personal success and ideological victory. He wanted to be in the pilot's seat for a combination of reasons, like his mother and his scholarship. Were there more? Hunsecker blocked the way. Chances were also good that Jay was right about the man's allegiance. He was not wrong about much. Cooperating with Charlemagne was a perfect solution, from his point of view. They were ideologically close (or so I thought); his cooperation would not compromise his patriotism (or so he thought—he did not yet know about the Bulgarian), and payment? Hunsecker. Jay Turner was not interested in money.

"Do you know who the watchers are?" Frank did not move his jaw much. It reminded me of Bogie again, but Frank was not playing this time. I squirmed in the back seat.

"We know two of them," Jay answered.

"Any foreigners living on the block?"

"Yes. An old Czech woman next door to the pizza parlor."

"Convenient," said Frank. "You're sure she is not a watcher."

"Yes. At least not for Jared."

I bounced a little in my seat, trying to get Frank's attention. He ignored me.

"Did you find the Frenchman's apartment?" he asked Jay.

"Yes. It is next to the gas station. Jerry's flat is two blocks further down Edbrooke."

"All clean?"

"Very."

"No sign of the third man?"

"None."

"Would you introduce me to the Czech woman, please?"

Frank was at his most formal, chopping up his words into little pieces so they would fit through the spaces between his teeth.

"Certainly," Jay said politely. "Please lock the door as you get out."

I bored holes in the back of Frank's head with a laser stare, willing him to turn around.

We got out of the car and locked the doors in slow motion. Turner began walking across the street. I tugged at Frank's coat. He shrugged me off. A car came by and I yanked him back to the curb.

"We're being led," I whispered to him.

His eyes opened in mild surprise. "Very good".

"But it's a trap," I insisted.

"Most likely, but for whom?"

"For us. Let's get out."

"No. Never take your work home with you, I always say. You're not yet at risk. You can go."

"I'm staying."

"Then shall we see where we're being led?"

Jay stood on the front porch of a dilapidated little house with white lace curtains closed behind vertical burglar bars across the front window. There were two deadbolt locks on the door.

"Nobody's home," he said.

"Try again," said Frank.

There was no answer.

"Move." Frank stepped up to the door and pounded it with both fists and forearms six or seven times so that the door shook on its hinges.

We heard a timid voice from the other side. "Who is it?"

Frank pushed Jay forward.

"FBI," said Jay, holding his open wallet up to the spy hole in the door. "We would be pleased to ask you a few questions if you do not mind."

There were more locks than the two we could see. We heard each one slide aside in the full freezing minute it took for all of them to be drawn. When the door finally opened, no more than three inches, a small, wrinkled face peered at us wide-eyed with fear from a height of less than five feet.

"I have not done something wrong," she said with a thick East European accent.

"That's right," said Frank. "We just want to ask a question. May we come in?"

"Ask what?"

"It's cold out here. Please, let us in."

She stepped back reluctantly, her distrust and fear forming another, unseen doorway on the threshold. Frank crossed it boldly. Jay and I followed after a momentary hesitation.

"May we sit down?" Frank asked when the old woman did not offer us a seat.

She nodded. Jay and I sat on a worn sofa with lacy crocheted arm covers and a knitted afghan on the back. Frank sat in an armchair. A ceramic Christmas tree with tiny lights on each branch stood unlit on the window sill. On the wall next to the window, an old-fashioned pendulum clock tick-ticked in the silence.

"Won't you sit down?" said Frank, pointing to an empty rocking chair across from us.

The old woman sat down slowly on the edge of it, glancing at each of us furtively as if she were unsure which was most dangerous.

"Mrs?"

"Cgagny."

"Mrs. Cgagny," began Frank, "do you have a tenant in your upstairs apartment?"

She seemed alarmed at the question. "Yes," she said.

"Is he an American?"

"Yes. Of course." Too quick to not be a lie.

"And did you tell the watchers that?"

Her veined and spotted hands gripped the arms of her chair.

Frank prodded, "Was Czech his native language?"

"No."

"But he always spoke Czech?"

She froze again.

"Did he always speak Czech?" Frank insisted.

The woman shook. "Except once," she managed to whisper.

"When?"

"When he first came. When he told me not to tell the watchers."

"What language did he use then?"

"German."

"And what did his use of German tell you, Mrs. Cgagny?"

There were tears in the old woman's eyes.

"I only want to know his nationality. I don't care what else you heard in his accent, just his nationality."

Her face registered almost instant relief.

"He was Austrian," she said.

"Blond? About forty?"

She nodded twice.

"We'd like to see the upstairs flat now, please."

She did not move immediately.

"He won't be back. You can relet the flat. Please show it to us."

Upstairs there was not much to see, except a good view of the Jared apartment across the street from the front room window.

"Did you make his meals?" Frank asked the woman while he stared out the window.

"Yes."

"And you did the cleaning?"

She nodded.

We walked through the other rooms. A chest of drawers in the bedroom was empty. Frank opened the closet. Two plaid flannel shirts hung there, and a pair of blue jeans, clean and pressed but stained with oil. He took one of the shirts off its hangar and showed me the label. It said 'Made in USA'.

"There you go," he said grinning. "Now you know what size shirt to get him for Christmas."

"You did his laundry, too?" he asked the old woman.

"Yes."

"It's in character, anyway," he muttered. "You can give these away or use them as rags," he said to the woman as he handed her the shirt. "Like I said, he won't be back."

...

"What was she afraid of?" I asked when we were back outside. "Mack?"

"Somewhat, of course," said Frank. "It's the ordinary reaction to being in the same room with him. There are many fears in this world, Steve. I don't know which is her particular fear, but you can bet Mack knows, and he used it to keep her quiet."

He shrugged his shoulders and slapped his sides. "That was a nice waste of time, confirming what I already knew, wasn't it?" He looked at Jay. "Where next?"

Jay shrugged.

"Okay. I'll pick." Frank pivoted his round body on one toe and turned in a slow circle. "I pick... the gas station." He pointed down the block and smiled at Jay.

We began walking. Frank allowed the agent to get well ahead of us and said in a low voice, "Does Turner know what car you're driving?"

"No. I don't think so."

"Good. Keep it that way. We'll talk later."

Jay waited for us. We caught up to him saying nothing. We slowed again as he walked on.

"I forgot to ask her if Mack ever left for any length of time," Frank said when Turner was a safe distance ahead.

"Should we go back?"

"No time. The game's afoot, my dear Watson, and perhaps we will make up the mistake in the next interview."

"No doubt," I said. "It's not that important anyway, is it?"

Jay stopped and we repeated our speed up, slow down maneuver.

"It could be," said Frank when Jay went on ahead again. "The information could confirm if this operation is commissioned or private. As a point of instruction, I might add that Mack would not waste this opportunity to tell me what he thought of my mistake."

"Pleasant to work with, is he?"

"He is abrasive and insulting."

I stopped when Jay did. I had more to ask and we were only a few yards from the gas station. I tugged at Frank's sleeve.

"Why are we being led?"

He shrugged.

"If they're still here, if there is something else," I said, my mind spinning, "then there is another target."

"Indub... undoubt... certainly."

"So what are they waiting for?"

"Who knows? Timing? Verification? Any number of things."

"And what part are we playing in this?"

Frank looked at me steadily for a moment, then walked away without answering.

ELEVEN

George Douglas owned and operated the rundown service station on the corner one block west of Edbrooke. He was an older man, a little rundown like his business. But what hit me right away was that he looked just like Frank, only with dark skin and a magnificent mustache, maybe to make up for the lack of hair on his head.

Jay watched Frank and George curiously as they shook hands. He grinned at me. "The sun was shining on the sea," he said.

I didn't get it.

He rolled his eyes to the ceiling, frustrated with me.

"Excuse me, gentlemen," he said, sending me the eyeball signal You'd Better Get It This Time. "The time has come, the Walrus said…"

I got it. "…to talk of many things."

Frank and George stared at us. There were no mirrors handy to tell them they looked like each other and reminded us of Tweedledum and Tweedledee.

"Right," said Frank. "Mr. Douglas, do you mind if I ask you a few questions?"

"Go right ahead. Call me George. Can I call you Frank? That was your name, wasn't it? Frank?"

"Cardova."

"Right. Samantha!"

A tiny woman entered from the shop floor to the left of us. In a forest, I would have thought she was a wood sprite—light, compact, and mahogany brown. I found it impossible to guess her age, though she was not young. She exchanged many words with her husband that were largely unnecessary but which fascinated me, because of the way she spoke them. Her elfin face animated every word, bringing it to life. She shooed us into a room the size of a closet near the cash register and told us to keep the door open so we could breathe and she could listen in.

The room was a box, ten by ten, filled with a huge old grey metal desk. George squeezed into a chair behind it. Frank took the only seat in front. I wound up stuffed in a corner behind Frank, trying to face the door. Jay had the door position, making Frank and me uncomfortable, but we had no room to maneuver.

"Look at this mess," said George pointing to a pile of coffee-stained receipts and orders. "I don't know what I'm going to do now."

"Can you tell me," said Frank with undisguised impatience, "if you've noticed any foreigners in the neighborhood?"

George laughed. "You want to know about Mack?" he asked. "Go on. Ask. What do you want to know?"

A lot of significant glances bounced around that little room.

"When did he come here?" asked Frank.

"In August. He started in August."

"What did he tell you?"

"He said he was an illegal immigrant, but he was a good mechanic, and if I gave him a job, he'd make me a lot of money."

"What did you say?"

"I said I couldn't afford no trouble. He said he couldn't either, and that if trouble came close, he'd leave and I'd be in the clear."

"And you gave him the job?"

"Yep."

"And?"

"And he was a great mechanic. More than that. He didn't deal too much with customers, but he organized all the paperwork around here, did the ordering, and paid the bills. Like I said, I don't know what I'm going to do now."

"Do you mean he's gone?"

"Yes."

"You said his name was Mack?" said Frank.

"He said I should call him that," said George. "He said I reminded him of somebody who called him Mack, so that name would do."

Jay and I looked at each other.

"Can you describe him?" asked Frank.

"He was medium, I'd say, blond, mustache—not as good as mine, though. I gave him some grief for that. Got him to smile once in a while."

Samantha leaned through the doorway. "He was very handsome," she said. "I have half a dozen friends at church who would have gone out with him. Did you tell them how he learned to fix cars, George?" She supplied the answer without waiting for her husband. "His father's foreman taught him how to fix farm machinery when he was a kid."

She kept going. "I kept trying to fix him up with Roberta. She's a lovely woman. Blonde like he is, but I don't think hers is real. It suits her though. Anyway, he didn't seem interested so I decided on Chrissy Jones, but I didn't have any luck there, either. I was about to suggest a lovely woman in the choir—the traditional choir, not the Gospel choir. She's a soprano. Her name's Nancy. I didn't get a chance, though, because that was when he went away and before he came back, Nancy said she was moving, so I didn't see any point in fixing them up. Tell them about when he went away, George. They'll want to know that."

George was able to tell us because a car drove up to the pumps and Samantha went outside.

"One day," George began, "Mack was in his usual spot. He always pulled the cars in a certain way and had his tools laid out just so. He was working on a car that day, and I was sitting on a stack of tires trying to get him into some kind of conversation—not easy, mind you. This car drives up, nothing special, but newish, and out jumps this young man with the strangest haircut you ever saw."

"What was that?" asked Frank.

"It was short on the sides and long on top, and the long part was parted in the middle, combed down, and pulled back in a ponytail. Nice looking young man, though. Reminded me of Mack."

"What happened?"

"Mack dropped the wrench he had and looked like he'd seen a ghost. The kid comes up to him, and they couldn't have said more than three words to each other, but I don't know what they were. They weren't English. Mack wiped his hands on a rag and told me he had to leave right then, but he'd be back in a few days. I was worried there might be trouble or something, but he said not to worry, the trouble was all his and he would be back. I had a hell of a time with all the job orders he left behind, but he was back in three days."

Frank looked steadily at Jay for a minute, then back at George. "When was this?" he asked.

"October. In the beginning of October some time. I remember because it was the second Sunday in October when we finally got him to come over for dinner, and...."

"And we got him to come over because of my foolishness," interrupted Samantha, once again in the doorway. "When he came back, I was desperate to get him to go out with somebody. I was really afraid for him. He was so silent and withdrawn. Before then, he would watch everything going on. You wouldn't believe how sharp he was, but after that time he went away and came back, he did a lot of staring. His work was slower."

"It was," her husband agreed.

"After a week with no more than five syllables out of him, I was gonna make a match for him, and I didn't care who with, so I came right out and asked him if he preferred men. I didn't know any like that, I said, but you never know when one might turn up."

I thought at first that Frank was crying. He had his face in his hands and his shoulders were shaking. "Good Lord," he said, gaining control of himself, "I wish I could have seen his face."

George chuckled. "Sam can put her foot in it sometimes."

There was an uncharacteristic pause from her before Samantha launched again, this time in a lower voice. "He put down his tools and looked at me and said with that heavy, 'Cherman' accent of his. It was really heavy, but he understood everything, well, except once. He said 'Look Zamantha, I know you mean well, but I had a wife and recently lost her. Please do not suggest anything else.' I felt so bad. How could I have been so stupid?"

"I don't know," said George. "How?"

"Oh, stop it, George Douglas." She turned to Frank. "I wanted to crawl under a rock, but I managed to tell him that if that was the case, then he needed people while he was grieving and he better come to dinner that Sunday for his own good. He said he didn't like being around a lot of people, and I told him it would be just us. 'Please, please, come to dinner; I'm so embarrassed,' I said."

"He came?" asked Frank.

"Yes," said George. "He came and we had—an interesting time."

"I can imagine."

"We watched a football game and we talked a little. He talked a little. Sam talked a lot."

"You did your share," said Samantha.

"What did you talk about?" asked Frank.

"Our kids, mostly," George replied. "I asked him if the young man who came for him that day was his son. He said yes. We started talking about what we wanted for our kids. I told him how I managed to get three out of five of mine to college and the other two in good jobs. He said he'd been able to get his son to go to a university, but events were working against what he wanted for him. I didn't quite understand what he meant, but I got the impression there was a disagreement going on or his son was doing something he didn't like."

Samantha started to talk again, and I tried to understand how this tiny acorn of a woman could have produced five children, now grown. She was interrupted by Frank.

"Excuse me, but did he say how his wife died or when?"

"No. I didn't ask," said Samantha. "I figured if he wanted me to know, he'd tell me. I did ask him if he had any other kids."

"What did he say?"

"No. But he kind of choked on it. He was a lot more relaxed at dinner after he'd had a beer or two. But his table manners were dreadful."

Frank leaned over in his chair, looking for an explanation.

"He kept his knife in his left hand the whole time," said Samantha, appalled. "We had a pot roast, carrots, and potatoes, and he pushed everything onto the back side of his fork with the knife, then put it in his mouth upside down. I couldn't believe it. I told him that when he judged he was ready to meet one of my friends, I'd be happy to introduce him, but he'd be better off not taking her out to dinner until I could have a chance to show him some table manners. All five of my children have good manners."

I knew this time that Frank was not crying. He covered his mouth to muffle a guffaw.

"What did he say?" he asked through his fingers.

"He didn't say anything. He just stared at me like he was bewildered. It was the only time he couldn't understand plain English. I was going to explain it again, but George gave me the 'shut up' signal and I never got another chance."

"Was that the only time Mack came to dinner?"

"Yes. I invited him again a couple weeks later, but he said he was busy. I was getting ready to invite him for Thanksgiving, but then it happened, and... well...." Samantha ran out of words. She looked to her husband for help.

"It happened? What happened?" asked Frank.

"Things changed," said George.

TWELVE

George sat forward in his chair, put both hands in front of him, gnarled fingers flat against the beaten grey surface of the desk, and looked steadily at Frank.

"Back in September," he said, "we started getting robbed. It happened about every week or ten days. About the third time, Mack was at the register; I was in here, watching through that door. This guy comes in with a pistol, points it at Mack, and tells him to cough up the money in the register."

George's pause at this point seemed significant. Frank asked him what happened next.

"Mack laughed," said George. "The guy with the gun started gettin' mad and I told Mack to give him the money. He did, and the robber ran out, and Mack went back to work. He worked on that car that night until we closed at midnight. I heard him chuckle every so often. I thought it was a little strange."

We waited for George to continue. He drummed his fingers on the desktop in a rat-tat rhythm, as if deciding how to tell the rest.

"I kept getting robbed," he said, "but I got smart and stopped keeping more than a few bucks in cash on hand. Mack didn't usually work nights, so he wasn't here when it happened until about a week before Thanksgiving. That night, he was working later than usual, and six or seven of these guys come in. They're a pack of big, mean thugs, like them hyenas that steal and scavenge a lion's kill and act tough like it's their own. They want my money—as usual. I give 'em twenty bucks. They said it's not good enough. I better come up with more the next day, or I'm gonna get hurt. If I call the cops, they said, they'll burn the place down. They want a thousand bucks—for fire insurance.

"Mack heard the whole thing from the shop floor. I asked him what he thought I oughta do. I was kind of hoping he'd stand with me, but then, I was between a rock and a hard place. I needed Mack to help me and I needed the police, too, but the two were sort of mutually exclusive if you know what I mean."

We all nodded.

"Mack said I should give them the money. I said no way. He told me to be patient, give them the money now and things might get better later. There was no way I'd ever give that scum my money, I told him. He said he'd give me the money to give them. I said there was no way I'd give them any money whatsoever. I would fight them, I said, by myself if I had to. I was talking like a fool, but I was so mad it made me brave.

"The next night, Mack stays late. Everything is pretty quiet. I got a baseball bat in the corner, ready. The guy who works at the pizza parlor drives up and starts pumping his gas. The young man who came to get Mack back in October comes in and asks for change to use the candy machine. I see the gang that's trying to muscle me start crossing the street toward the station and I pick up the baseball bat from the corner. Mack tells me to put it down and go to the office and stay there. I say I'm staying. He says stay out of the way and let him handle it.

"So the gang comes in. One's got a big chain; two got pipes; another one carries this hammer. There's seven of them. I counted them later when they were on the floor. The guy from the pizza parlor comes in behind them, throws the bolt on the door, and pulls the shade. Then all hell breaks loose."

George looked at Frank steadily. "I've seen some fights, but I've never seen anybody fight like that. In about a minute, all seven are on the floor, groaning, bleeding, or both. Mack picks up the guy who was sorta their spokesman and throws him against the wall. He holds him there with one hand and the other hand's holding a knife against the side of his neck. I gotta tell you about this knife. I don't know where he got it from, and when it was over, I don't know where it went to. But from then on, I always knew he had it and it separated us some more."

George leaned back in his chair again and sighed.

"It wasn't all that big a knife, but you could see it was sharp, of course. Why wouldn't it be? It was the way Mack held it there like he was used to it. He was... comfortable. 'Course, the guy against the wall weren't comfortable.

"Everything gets real quiet except for a groan or two from the floor. Mack's son, the young one I saw in October, says in a low voice, 'You're out of your league, guys. We'll let you walk out of here now, but if you come back, you won't walk again.'

"The guy from the pizza parlor takes all the weapons these kids are carrying, breaks the blades on half a dozen knives, and does something to two guns. Then Mack, and the kid, and him, all set the bums on their feet and shove them out the door. The gang scatters. Some run, others limp. I ain't seen any of them since."

"Was anything else said?" Frank asked after a long pause.

"No. Mack's boy bought a candy bar and left. The pizza man paid for his gas. Mack took the money and put it in the till. Nobody said a word."

"What did you do then?"

"Nothing. I said thanks and left it at that. Mack went back to work."

"Mack's son," said Frank, "his English was perfect? No accent?"

"No accent."

"You said there was a change after this. Did Mack change?"

"No," said George. "I did. After that, every time I looked at Mack, I saw his knife. When I looked in his eyes, I saw somebody who could use that knife. He was no cowardly punk. He was a professional. I ain't no fool. And I figured he was here for professional reasons that I was better off staying out of. I stopped trying to draw him out about things. We didn't have anymore what you'd call conversations, just comments about work, the weather, that sort of thing."

"You seem disappointed."

"We were... well, I thought we were becoming friends," said George. He put his hands on the desk again and stared at them. "Sort of." He spoke mostly to himself, then looked up at Frank. "After that night, I knew that would never be possible, but then I suppose you gotta take it like it comes. We're acquainted. I don't know who or what he is or how much was a lie. We're acquainted; that's all."

"You haven't seen him since...?"

"Friday." George lifted his hands, slapped his palms on the desk, and stood up in one dismissive motion. He looked at Jay. "You look tired young man. Why don't you go home? I'll walk you to the door."

Jay scowled, and looked around, confused. Frank stood to go but was waved back into his seat by his twin. "Stay another minute," said George, "and we'll have a cup of coffee. Is this your man?" he asked, pointing at me.

"Yes," said Frank.

"He can stay, too." He took Jay's arm and pulled him through the door, saying, "You look too tired to go on."

"Wait a minute." Jay shook him off and looked at Frank. "What about tomorrow?"

"Same as today, I suppose," Frank said with a shrug. It occurred to me that he was not expecting a tomorrow.

Jay held out his hand to Frank, who ignored it. "Just in case," said Jay, "it has been a pleasure to work with you."

Frank stared ahead in silence.

"It will work out," Jay insisted, dropping his hand. "I will see you tomorrow." Was he trying to convince himself?

Frank said nothing.

George pushed the FBI man out of the room none too gently.

"I'm not very good at this," he said when he returned to his seat behind the desk. "Sam!"

"What?"

"Coffee!"

"Don't you start that!"

"Please!"

"That's better." She stood in the doorway. She had three cups of black coffee with her.

"What do you have to tell me?" asked Frank, still staring ahead, not seeing the cup in front of him on the desk.

"I'm a live drop, you know," said George. "He told me that. He said to get rid of the FBI man and give you a message. This stuff is all new to me, but Mack said I wouldn't get nobody hurt. We had one more conversation before he left on Friday night."

"Tell me."

"I told him about my boy."

Frank's brow wrinkled.

"Mack was tense. Real still," George explained. "That was one of the peculiar things about him, the way he could be still, even when he was walking. He told me he was leaving. I asked if it was because of something going on with his son. He said no. But he was even more tense when he said that, so I jumped in the way Sam would."

"Thank you very much, George," said Samantha from behind the register.

George ignored her and continued. "I remembered how that young man fought those hoods in my shop one night, and I said, 'Is your boy turning out just like his old man?' I'll never forget the look on his face. I didn't need an answer and he didn't give me one. So I told him about my oldest son. I had so many plans for that kid. He was gonna be an astronaut. The first black president. He'd play for the Bears."

George took a sip of his coffee and cradled it in both hands. Samantha appeared in the doorway, silent.

"We did okay in fits and starts until he was fifteen," George continued. "Then I lost my job. Again. And we had nothing left. Sam and I weren't getting along and we had five kids to feed. I decided to leave. I was packing. My son came in and I saw his future. I could see him repeating every struggle I ever had, every stupid mistake, every misery. When he was born, it was like this new life had so many possibilities. He could do anything, be anything. But when I was packing that bag, I saw him surrounded by the same old shit. The poverty was the same; the fights were the same. Same. Same. Same.

"I put a shirt in the suitcase and remembered watching my dad do the same thing. All the changes I planned. I couldn't change nothing—nothing. I was sick of it. I was disgusted and trapped and so was my kid. I tried to say goodbye. He was sitting on the bed next to the suitcase, looking at me, and I thought how stupid I was for thinking he could ever play for the Bears. He was little like his mother, for chrissake. The same things that made me were making him and there was nothing I could do about it."

He took a slow sip from his cup. "Except stay," he said quietly. "I could stay. No, I thought. Impossible. And it won't do no good. All the other problems will still be here. He'll be shaped by them with or without me. I could only change one thing. I could stay. So I unpacked.

"Mack didn't say anything when I told him all this. 'I know it's not the same with you and your son,' I said. 'I don't know what your circumstances are, or his, and I suspect they're a lot different from mine, but the point is that if you can change just one detail in his history, do it. My boy's not an astronaut; he's not the president, and he's still too puny to play football, but he didn't go to jail when he was twenty like I did. He's working; he's happy, and he's got three fine sons. And I know his youngest will be president. The kid's a politician."

George looked at Samantha standing in the doorway and back again at Frank. "We know some people died yesterday in that building down the block that Mack was always watching. Sam and I are asking you to tell us one thing before we give you his message."

"Go ahead," said Frank. "I'll do my best."

"Did Mack's son kill somebody there?"

"No."

Both sighed and Sam bowed her head.

"But Mack did," said George.

"Yes."

Samantha moved first after the long silence and picked up the empty coffee cups from the desk.

"What did Mack tell you to tell me?" asked Frank.

"He said not to say anything to anybody except a man named Frank Cardova," said George. "I could make sure it was you, he said, by checking your gun. I said I don't know nothing about guns, so he told me to ask you what kind of gun you carry."

Frank opened his coat and showed his gun in its holster. "It's a Walther PPK."

Did I detect a hint of pride in Frank's voice?

"Yep. That's the one," said George. "Mack said, 'Frank looks like Elmer Fudd, but he thinks he is James Bond.'"

"I do not think I'm James Bond," said Frank tautly.

"Don't look at me."

"I wonder how he knows about Elmer Fudd?" I said.

"I asked him if Bugs Bunny was big where he comes from. He said he didn't know; he just had a lot of American cartoon tapes at home."

I tried to imagine Mack watching Bugs Bunny.

"Let's get to the message, George," Frank said wearily.

"You have an appointment with some guy named Slavin tonight at nine-thirty at Rick's."

I stood abruptly straight in the corner where I had been slouched against the wall. Slavin. Number three, Executive Action Department, First Chief Directorate, KGB. More than that, Slavin stayed in Moscow. He was an inner circle spook, with real information. They did not let his kind out very often.

THIRTEEN

I checked my back as I walked to my car. Frank said he would meet me there in ten minutes. After fifteen minutes it began to snow and I began to worry. After seventeen minutes, I became aware of a black Mercedes parked on the other side of the street fifty yards behind me. Mack's favorite car, I remembered. I watched it in the mirror, through the back window. It didn't move; I didn't move. My back window was a painting, with a car as center subject; a car watching my car, I thought; I didn't know. I suspected.

My senses were trained entirely on that Mercedes so that when the passenger door of my car opened suddenly, my elbow came down on the horn, sending a long blast of noise down the quiet street.

"Lovely," said Frank climbing in. "You might consider locking your doors and paying attention. Just a suggestion."

"I was looking at that Mercedes."

"Yes, I saw it."

"Is it them?"

"No. It belongs to the people in the house where it's parked."

I looked at the house, a battered two-story, like the others on the block, with a boarded-up window and dead weeds poking through the snow. There were houses in better condition, but this was not the worst. The cars parked on the street and in a few driveways were similar to the houses. The Mercedes did not belong. I stared at Frank in alarm.

"The question, Stevie," said Frank, "is not whether, but when. When did it arrive?"

"I don't know."

"You didn't see it arrive? It didn't drive past you?" He shivered. "Turn on the heat, please. I'm freezing."

"I didn't notice it until about fifteen minutes after I got here."

"Did you check this car? You did have it locked, didn't you?"

"Yes. I unlocked the door for you."

"Don't do that again. Wait until I get here. Did you notice the Mercedes while you were checking?"

"No."

"So it drove up from behind you after you arrived."

"Probably."

"It's important, Steve. If it was here waiting for you, that means this car is already blown. If it came later, they simply followed you here and we can get one more use out of it before they touch it."

I thought for a moment, picturing the street as it was when I first unlocked the car. "It came later," I said.

"Let's go somewhere," said Frank.

"Where?"

"I don't care. Stick to busy streets. I want to see movement, traffic, activity. Where's the deck?"

"The what?"

"The tape deck. You said there was a tape deck in this car."

"There." I pointed in front of him.

He pulled a cassette from his coat pocket. "I need to think before we talk. Just drive and be quiet."

The snow became heavier, darkening the dusk and making unlit buildings into silhouettes of black on dark grey. Occasional yellow lights haloed a few windows and added a brown tone to the buildings. I turned on the headlights and wipers and watched the mirror as I pulled away from the curb.

"Well?" said Frank. "Have we grown a tail?"

"Yep."

"Turn left up here." He pushed the rewind button on the tape deck.

I turned left. The headlights behind me turned left.

"Turn left again on State Street, right at the next light, and keep going. Do you like Rachmaninov?"

"Who?"

"Never mind. Do you like music?"

"Of course."

"Who is your favorite composer?"

I thought maybe Frank wanted light conversation, a relief from the pressure that pursued us with the Mercedes.

"I like Dire Straits' new album," I said, "but my favorite is U2."

"Me too? Sweet of you Stevie."

"No. U2. The group, U2."

"That's an airplane. Must be why you like it."

"It's a rock group."

"I know. I'm trying to be funny. Not an easy thing to do right now. What was that other group you mentioned?"

"Dire Straits."

"Appropriate. Do you have any of that with you?"

"No. I didn't bring anything like that."

"Sometimes I need music; it tells me a story. Other times it helps me think. Is it okay if we listen to Rachmaninov's second piano concerto?"

"Sure." I had never heard of it.

"Is the tail still back there?"

"I can't tell anymore with all this traffic."

"Funny. I haven't even noticed the traffic." He pushed play.

I did not hear a story, nor did Frank's music help me think. It did what all classical music does to me; it threatened to knock me out, especially after a sleepless night and a full day. I fought to stay awake and on the road.

Maybe Frank hears a story, but I'm hearing just bare chords on a piano. I forced my eyes open

The chords gave way to a dark symphonic melody that rolled along strongly while the piano became more complicated behind it. The melody lightened, became less sad, and receded, allowing the piano to develop its melody, clear, different, but related. There was a light period when I thought I could not fight sleep, but new notes and chords began to sound a doom that shook me into a kind of half alertness. My eyes stayed open but my mind rested on the sound of that piano. It flowed like a light stream, going underground while something else developed. The stream surfaced again and quickened. Spurred into a rush by the crescendo around it, the piano became a torrent threatening its banks. It broke. The original melody began again, only stronger and yet overshadowed by the piano, no longer simple, nor light, but pounding an insistent melody of its own. A melody that complemented, was related to, was a logical outcome of the original, but was nonetheless different, new, a bit raw and discordant, but a necessary and inevitable addition.

"There he is," said Frank, stopping the tape.

"Where?" I slammed on the brakes, looking ahead and all around. Wheels screamed on the street around us as we skidded left, then right. Horns blared their opinions of my maneuver. We came to a stop under a large neon sign that blinked yellow and red. I looked at Frank. He was holding his forehead with one hand. The shining top of his hairless head changed colors with the neon sign.

"What the hell?" he said. "You nearly put me through the dashboard. What's going on?"

"You said he was there!"

"Where?"

"I don't know."

"Who?"

I didn't answer. I could not trust myself to be civil.

"You nitwit," said Frank. He leaned back in his seat. "Not out there, there, on the tape—the music. Listen."

He leaned forward and rewound the tape a short way. I heard the crescendo again, and the break, then the two melodies, one older, one new, and more insistent.

"That's Jerry," said Frank. "Mack's son. He's operational now, and I think I understand some things."

"I'm glad you do."

"Let's go. We're blocking traffic. Turn right at the next light."

"Where are we going now, Elmer?"

"I do not look like Elmer Fudd."

"But you think you're James Bond."

"I prefer to model myself on Sydney Reilly. He broke the Trust."

I stopped in mid-chuckle when I remembered Reilly's fate.

"I will not get myself shot," said Frank.

"How do you do that?" I demanded. "How do you read my mind?"

"Logic. You'll catch on pretty soon. By the way, there is some question as to whether old Felix had Reilly executed or managed to turn him."

"I heard that theory," I said. "Which is worse?"

Frank did not answer me. Instead, he laughed.

"I'm sorry," I said, "but I can't follow this. I thought the subject was pretty grim."

He waved at me as he fought to catch his breath. "Turn left on 87th," he said. "I suddenly had a vision of what Mack must have looked like when Samantha asked him if he was gay. And then...."

He laughed again, louder. "Then he's offered lessons in etiquette by this little bourgeois American." His chuckle died down. "It's nice to know there are still a few things to laugh about."

He pointed me around the corner onto 87th Street. "Character is the key, my friend," he said. "I've spent more than a decade learning everything I could about them. So I can predict what they'll do and when. I can prevent tragedy. I can get them to work for us. I can manipulate them. Now they are manipulating me and it's hard to take, especially since I'm not sure what's at the end of it."

"I thought you told me we don't control them; we just babysit."

"Not control, manipulate. There's a big difference. Manipulation is more subtle and depends on information. It requires a thorough knowledge of the subject. After fifteen years, it seems they know me better than I know them."

"You seem to know them pretty well," I said. "You've accurately uncovered every move they made, even the details, including who did Mack's laundry. You said that was in character. How did you know to ask?"

"I know him. What have I told you about him so far?"

"That he is abrasive and insulting."

"Did I forget arrogant?"

"Yes, but I figured it out."

"Well, add that to the list. He's insufferably arrogant. I would expect him to have that little old lady waiting on him hand and foot."

"He's thoroughly reprehensible, is he?"

"Thoroughly."

"Then why do you like him?"

When he answered, he formed the words slowly. "I don't know." We rolled down 87th in silence until he said, "Turn right at the next street."

I turned the car down a dark residential street, lined on both sides by neat, boxlike brick houses. A thin layer of wet snow covered the short lawns. Most of the front windows showcased Christmas trees with lights. More lights blinked from eaves and trees, some multicolored, some bright white. I pulled over where Frank pointed.

"A couple of things bother me," he said.

"Only a couple? What are they?"

"First, of course, is Jerry. I don't know him, so I can't tell when he's acting differently. You see, it's the differences that reveal what's going on. The puzzles make me discover reasons. Reasons help me predict what's going to happen next. There are a lot of changes in this operation, and Jerry is a major one."

"But you know the other two men."

"Yes."

"Are there differences?"

"Several important ones." He paused as a car passed us. It was not a Mercedes. We both sighed.

"Mack is taking some massive risks," Frank continued. "To be unsafe for so long is not like him. They must be dead tired, spending the bulk of the past few months alone and exposed. The reason has to be compelling. If they are working for the Soviets, as I suspect we will find out tonight at Rick's, the reason must truly be a whopper. Mack's hatred of communists is almost pathological. I suspect it may be personal."

"You said they were on the back rotor."

"The what?"

"The back rotor of the chopper."

"Did I? Oh. Yeah."

"But you don't know their ideology?"

"No. After all these years, I still don't know."

"So you don't know if they're enemies or allies?"

"I suppose you can call them allies," he said, "but don't confuse it with friends the way Turner has. People who share the same enemies are not necessarily friends. They are our allies for the time being. We'd be foolish not to use them in our interests, and even more foolish to trust them more than that."

I waited for him to go on. The car was getting cold. I did not know where the Mercedes was and I was hungry. I thought we should move. Frank started talking again.

"The Frenchman bothers me," he said. "What could have compelled him to spend even one night in that filthy apartment? And why there, when there was a pretty girl in the more strategic flat? Especially after Jerry's half-hearted attempt failed. And why did that fail? That's another question. But let's stick to Louis. Why did he leave the pretty girl alone? I assure you, it's not like him."

"You want some brainstorming?" I asked.

"Yes. I'm weathered out."

"Maybe she was a watcher."

"No way. They'd have taken her out. She would have blown the whole operation."

"Maybe he didn't leave her alone."

Frank was silent.

"Maybe she lied to us," I continued. "Or, no, not lied, but just didn't tell us. He might have made her promise not to say anything, or...."

"Brilliant," Frank interrupted. "Brilliant. Pardon me while I pat myself on the back for my superb judgment in picking you for this job. You're quite right. She didn't tell us. We've been pointed in one direction and we've trundled along, waiting for somebody to turn us down the right road instead of reading the signposts for ourselves."

"Let's go back and talk to her," I said. I was thinking about hot coffee.

"We can't. No time."

"She may know something."

"Of course, she knows something, or Louis would not have bothered to keep it from us. But it can't be too critical, or they would have killed her or scared her into leaving."

"So they put a temporary stop on the information, knowing you'd figure it out?" I asked.

"It looks that way."

"Then what?"

"Then what what?" He blew on his frozen fingers. "Turn the heat back on. It's cold in here."

"Then what do they expect you to do now that you know?"

"What do you mean?"

I couldn't keep the irritation out of my voice. "If you can predict what they will do based on your knowledge of them," I said slowly, "surely they can do the same. What do they expect from you?"

Frank took a minute to answer. "They expect me to leave it at that."

"Why?"

"Because the information she has is a minor puzzle piece. It's probably only a pillow talk revelation of some sort they don't want me to know. I am pressured by time and fear not to seek it out. I could go back later. If there is a later."

"But not now?"

"No."

"Then they are manipulating you. The babysitter is being babysat."

"Yes. Damn it."

"There's no way we have time?" I wanted badly to get out of there. I checked my door lock again, and the mirrors.

"Only if we skip dinner."

This was a subject near and dear to my heart. The breadsticks at lunch were long gone.

"Would they expect you to skip dinner?" I asked.

"I don't miss many meals."

I remembered passing a restaurant on 87th Street.

"I'm not going to let Mack think he can read my mind every time," said Frank vehemently. "Let's go talk to the girl. To hell with dinner."

The only welcome part of this news was that we were leaving. I put the car in gear.

Frank put his hand on the wheel. "Wait. Not yet. We're here for a reason. I have something to tell you. Turn off the engine."

I did as I was told and waited, not with much patience.

"Are you absolutely sure," he said, "That they did not mark this car until after you got to it?"

"Yes."

"And nothing has been out of place at your hotel?"

"Nothing." I remembered the man next door to Charlie, but the thought was driven out of my head by the Mercedes that drove by slowly.

My misery was complete when the Mercedes parked down the street and no one got out.

"You're sure, Steve?" said Frank softly. "They must not hear what I have to tell you. Are you absolutely sure?"

FOURTEEN

It was like flying in weather. I had to rely on instruments, not instinct. There was no Mercedes on that street when I got there. "Yes," I said. "I'm sure. This car is secure."

"Any theories?" he asked.

"No." I was not interested in theories, only flight, of the save my skin variety, not the soar my soul.

"Then I will tell you my theory." Frank took a breath, puffed out his cheeks, and began, "I base it on the one person I know best."

"Mack?"

"No. Me. I have to ask myself, what makes me do the things I do? There are many reasons. Sometimes fear is one of them, but as uncomfortable as I am with the knowledge that our friends are sitting with possibly unfriendly intentions a few yards up the road from us, my fear at this moment is not the laser-burning kind that sears the heart. As much as I hate to see that car here, there is another place where its appearance would make me crazy."

I understood what he was talking about. Portraits of his wife, seven children, and two grandchildren adorned a bookcase in his office. I thought of my own family and shuddered.

"Exactly," he said, registering my shiver.

"But they don't have families," I said without thinking.

"On the contrary, my friend. They do. Jerry is one."

"He's grown."

"He mentioned a younger sister."

"Dead."

"My point exactly."

I picked up the line of Frank's reasoning. "Mack said he had a wife but lost her."

"And if you were to fail to prevent the unthinkable, what would move you to act then?"

"Rache," I said. "Revenge."

Frank nodded. "Now I will tell you a story. Look at the house on our right."

I looked. There was a light in the window. The curtains were drawn. No decorations.

"The light is on a timer," Frank explained. "No one lives there. The man who used to live there died eight months ago and his daughter has not yet disposed of the property. The man was known to us as Fred."

I had heard the name. "Fred from our office? Your old boss? Babysitter for the elder Sobieski?"

"Right, right, and triple right. And his daughter Alex married the younger Sobieski."

"In Chicago?"

"My question exactly. Not the marriage. I was here; it's a fact. They met on an operation. Very romantic. No, since we got the FBI message yesterday, my question has been, 'Why Chicago?' I think there must be a connection. It's not pure coincidence. They could have cleaned up Jared's network one at a time in different cities. They could have set the trap for him anywhere. Why here?"

"Because Jared's family is here," I answered.

"Precisely."

"How could anyone kill a child like Janey?"

"How indeed? I don't know the answer to that, but I know the answer to why. Children grow up to be like their parents. Some people have enemies who hate them not only for what they do but for who they are. Some people live in a room with no windows. Others don't even have any doors. I told you that once, didn't I?"

"Yes."

"I told Jello that once, too. Right here on this street, I explained that to him and I told him that I had no intention of entering that room. I have a hard enough time living without windows."

He paused and shivered. The car was getting cold again.

"Eight months ago, Fred died unexpectedly," he continued. "He had given me the means to contact his daughter, Alex, in an emergency. His wife died a few years ago and there was no one else. I prepared the message to Alex, but Stupid Directive of the Month à la Jello was that he was the only one who could sign messages, so I was forced to show it to him. He wanted to delay sending it so we could go through the house. I told him that wouldn't be necessary; I had a crew in the house already, and they would be out of there well before Alex arrived. That was not good enough. He insisted we come out here and see it for ourselves. We sent the message before we left for Chicago, but we put a delay on the visas to hold them up."

"They all came?" I asked.

"No. Just her."

"But didn't you say she was an American?"

"No, I didn't. She was, or is, but you've fallen into the trap of making assumptions without verification. The visas were for her bodyguards. She had six of them to protect her when she finally arrived, mad as a wet hen over the delay. Before she got here, we managed to spend two days in that house. We went through everything twice, tore out suspect walls, and used x-ray equipment. There were no letters, no addresses, no contacts. Nothing. Fred knew better. He was a professional and never wrote anything down. We put the house back together and prepared to leave."

"Another Jello-inspired rat screw?" I said.

"No," said Frank. His voice had become quiet. "He was right. There was something there and we would not have found it if I had not gone personally to take a look. I noticed something about the little bar Fred had in the living room. There were three kinds of vodka, which fit because Fred's favorite drink was vodka tonic. I am perhaps the only one still around who could remember that. Anyway, there was a refrigerator in the bar, one of those little square jobs that hold a couple of six-packs and some ice. I opened it again, just as the searchers had done. It was turned off and had been off for some time because it was dry and empty. I looked inside carefully, no sign of anything, but why was it empty? I looked in the main refrigerator in the kitchen. There were three bottles of tonic water."

"Maybe the little one in the bar was broken."

"Maybe. I took it apart to see if I could fix it."

"And you found?"

"A photo album." Frank's voice was now completely hushed, his manner subdued. "It was a slim album about eight by nine inches that slipped perfectly between the inner lining and outer casing where the insulation had been removed. The door seal buttoned over it."

I wiped the fog off the windshield so I could see out. Nothing moved.

"The photos featured the same little girl at different ages," continued Frank, "starting when she was a baby until about age eleven. One picture, though, had more people in it. It had a date of a few years ago written on the back. The people were grouped in front of a Christmas tree. There was a fireplace to their right, open boxes, and torn wrappings on the floor around them. The little girl was about two and she sat in the lap of a woman that it broke my heart to know I'd never meet. She was beautiful, and so was the other little girl of about four who sat on her right, obviously her daughter. There was an adolescent boy on the woman's left, with his arm around her shoulder. He held a guitar with a ribbon around it."

"Who were they?" I asked.

Frank looked ahead where there was nothing to see but the frost on the windshield. I think he forgot I was there. He went on talking. "I knew what I was looking at. The main subject of the album had to be Fred's granddaughter, Sobieski's daughter. The others I couldn't be sure about. The woman was not Alex, but the boy with the guitar reminded me of Mack. Jello noticed the resemblance, too, and decided we would keep a couple of pictures. I told him that was dangerous and unnecessary. I would remember their faces. He said we were required to keep records. I told him that if Charlemagne ever found out we had these...."

He paused and I wiped the windshield again. "I explained to Jello," he began again after a deep breath, "as patiently as I could, that while Charlemagne's families were probably protected by a fortress of expensive security, their ultimate defense was also the only thing that protected my own family—their anonymity. I never wanted to enter Charlemagne's room without doors. I do not have the skill to survive in their world."

"What did Jello say then?" I asked after a long pause.

"He said if I didn't want Charlemagne to find out we had the pictures, I damn-well better not tell them. We took the group photo and one recent picture of the little girl. That was when Jello restricted access to the file to just the two of us. I haven't touched it since. I don't want my fingerprints on it, to tell you the truth."

"How old would the boy be now?" I asked, doing a few calculations of my own.

"In his early twenties."

I started the engine and turned on the heat. "Is that all? Can we get out of here?" I asked.

"Yes."

We drove slowly past the Mercedes. Its windows were fogged. I wanted to pound on one of them and scream "What do you want?" I was hungry and tired and afraid, and to tell the truth, Charlemagne was the least of my fears.

"Jerry must have been taught English by Sobieski's wife," I said after I negotiated a left turn across three lanes of traffic on 87th Street.

"Yes," said Frank. "It sounds like he speaks flawless American English. He must have a better ear than his father."

"Mack isn't good with languages?"

"That depends on what you call good. He's fluent in six or seven languages. Besides his native German, his best is Russian, but pronunciation is a struggle for him; it's always accented."

"It's nice to know there's something he doesn't do well."

"Oh, he's human. He makes a mistake from time to time, but when he does, it's on the side of caution. When you meet him, assuming we all come out of this healthy—let's be optimists—he will probably insult you and then grill you on every detail of the commission you're offering, the most critical being the verification."

"I wonder if we went through a drive-through," I said, to hide the growling from my stomach, "if the Mercedes would follow us through."

"It's still there, eh?"

He wasn't taking the hint. I was going to go hungry.

"Frank," I said after a few minutes.

"Yes."

"I think you should give back the photos."

"I can't."

"Why not?"

"Unlike Jay Turner, I know who I work for. Uncle Sam signs my paycheck, not Charlemagne."

"It isn't right, Frank."

"Now hold on, Steve," said Frank heatedly. "Don't start deciding right and wrong again. Choose between allowed and not allowed, feasible and infeasible, expedient and inexpedient, but never right and wrong. That is a moral labyrinth you'll never leave."

"Okay, Frank," I said. "But give them back the photos. It is allowed because Jello is away, leaving you in charge. You make the rules now. It is feasible because it will be no problem contacting them since they are right behind us. Finally, it is, in my junior, amateur, unschooled opinion, expedient because my junior, amateur, unschooled instinct tells me they know you have them and they want them back."

"Instinct is not verifiable in this case, my dear chap. Give me some other basis. If they want the pictures, why don't they ask?"

"Your revenge theory is one basis for my instinct," I said. "And two minor facts that I think are suggestive. As for asking you for them, how would you answer?"

"No," said Frank. "It would be disloyal. I can't be disloyal."

"Disloyal to what, Frank?"

He did not answer. I pulled over in front of the pizza parlor on 105th Street.

"Disloyal to Jello?" I asked, turning off the engine. "You can fire me right now, Frank, but I am loyal to the Constitution, not to Jello."

"Your superiors have access to a wider range of information than you do, my friend," said Frank. "Be careful about the standards you decide to change at your whim."

"Yes. I know that argument," I said. "You're right: I don't have the fucking big picture, only a small piece of it. In that piece I see an idiot, or worse, making an idiotic decision that may have killed four innocent people and almost killed two more. I know how to fucking follow orders. I have learned that's no excuse."

"Steve, to fight these people...."

"I will not become one of them, Frank."

During the long silence that followed, I waited for Frank to send me home.

"So what are the facts that make you so sure they know about the photos?" Frank said finally.

"I'm not all that sure," I answered, still prepared for unemployment. "I said it's only a theory. But I'm thinking of the dark room in the apartment where the three were killed."

"There were no pictures there."

"Exactly."

"And the second fact?"

"No matter how secure the section vault may be, no matter how thick the walls, no matter how often the combination is changed, it is still administered by people. Access to that file may be limited to two, but it's controlled by dozens."

We spent another few minutes with our own thoughts until Frank broke the silence.

"Drive back down Michigan Avenue," he said, "and stop at the first gas station you see with a phone booth. I need to make a couple of calls."

I waited in the car, watching Frank on the phone, watching the traffic for signs of Charlemagne. One of Frank's calls seemed animated. He was arguing. The argument resolved, he hung up looking satisfied. When he came back to the car, he pointed out to me that the Mercedes was parked in a vacant lot across the street.

"The minute we leave this car," he said, "we'll have to assume it's compromised. Tomorrow morning, before we start, I want you to turn this one in and get another one. Make sure you pick out the new one. Don't let the rental agency pick it for you."

He leaned back in his seat as we returned to Edbrooke Avenue and parked again in front of the pizza parlor. "You know," he said, talking to the ceiling, "the revenge theory doesn't take into account the Soviet connection. And as for your photo theory, there may be some pictures involved somewhere, but it cannot be the ones Jello and I took. He and I were the only people who knew we had them until I told you just now."

"He may have told somebody."

"No. Jello never tells anybody anything—I take that back. He never tells them what they need to know. He always keeps the wrong secrets, but he always keeps them."

"What about his special project?" I asked. "The one he bragged about to you?"

Frank didn't say anything, so I pursued the subject.

"When you contacted Charlemagne eight months ago and they laughed at you and walked out, did you tell them Jello had the verification, or that your boss had it?"

"I said my boss had it."

"How did they know Jello was your boss?"

Frank remained silent.

"I have another question, Frank."

"Go ahead, I'm listening."

"Does Jello know you're getting his job?"

"I don't think so. Why?"

"If he knew, would he be happy for you, or would he hate you?"

"He already hates me, Steve. What are you getting at?" He sat up abruptly. "No. You're wrong. If Jello set me up and I'm the target, then what the hell are they waiting for? Answer me that, eh?"

I answered: "Verification."

FIFTEEN

We parked in front of the pizza parlor. I wanted pizza; Frank wanted information. I suspected only one of us would get what he wanted, and since Frank was the boss.... I followed him into the shop like a puppy follows a stranger hoping for a biscuit.

The proprietor of Geno's Real Italian Pizzas was a solemn, harried man of about forty, very much in charge and not interested in fools. He introduced himself as Joshua Atkinson and wiped off pizza dough onto a towel tucked in his belt before shaking hands with us. He was very tall, well over six feet, and looked like he worked out. A lot. I wondered what his style was and decided it was Aikido because he moved like a tiger. Two scars, keloid and yellow, snaked over otherwise regular features on his brown face, like warrior lines. It made him look fierce.

"Go ahead and ask," he said in response to Frank's polite request, "but I have to keep working. The guy who helps me disappeared again and I'm on my own."

"Again? He's disappeared before?"

"Yeah. Undependable S.O.B."

"Do you remember when that was?"

Frank did not get an answer right away. Atkinson pulled a pizza from the oven, boxed it, and marked it.

"Is he the guy you're asking about? The Cajun?"

Frank nodded. "Can you tell me when he disappeared on you the first time?"

"In October." He spread dough over an empty pan. "His girlfriend across the street can tell you. The day after he left, his old girlfriend went after her with acid. Naass-tee. I imagine she'll know the exact day."

"Old girlfriend?"

"Yeah. The one they pulled out feet first yesterday." He pointed a floured finger at the building across the street and then at Frank. "You cops? You think Emile killed her?"

"No, we're not cops," said Frank.

"But you think he killed her." Atkinson put the new pizza in the oven.

I found it strange the way he did it, like a shrug standing in for passion. Slide pizza into oven, slide corpse out of building, natural partners to conversation.

"I wouldn't be surprised if he did kill her," he said matter-of-factly. "He had plenty of reason. She was gross, and nothin' but trouble."

Plenty of reason. I kept my mouth shut and tried to shake off this infectious indifference to a life.

"I threw her out of here a couple of times," Atkinson continued. "I don't know why Emile ever took up with her in the first place, but it didn't surprise me when he dumped her as soon as the new girl came."

Frank winced. He covered it with another question.

"Tell me, Mr. Atkinson, have you ever been robbed?"

The man grinned. "I don't have much trouble with that. If you mean has anybody been stupid enough to try it, the answer's yeah. Once. Back in August."

"What happened?"

He pulled a pizza, round, gold, steaming, born to be eaten, from the oven. Not that I cared. I listened to the interview. Of course.

"Emile had just pulled one out of the oven," Atkinson was saying. "Like this one." He swayed slightly and with him the pizza on its long-handled spatula, threatening to hypnotize me. "A guy came in." He grinned. "He said gimme all you got and Emile...."

He swung the pizza sideways through the air, swiftly, deftly, so that it did not slide off the spatula. I ducked involuntarily. I had been closest to the simulated line of fire.

Atkinson's expression turned grim. "The guy ran out screaming. I guess the cheese burned his face pretty bad. I met somebody like that once." He pointed at the scar across his face.

Frank opened his mouth to ask another question, but he was talking again. "Emile went around the counter and picked up the weapon the guy dropped. He took it to pieces, put it back together, and put it in the cash drawer. He figured it wasn't registered and might come in handy—just in case. It's still there; you want it?"

"No. Thanks." Frank looked at that pizza. So did I. "Is there anything else about him you can tell us?" he asked.

Atkinson weighed his response. "What's to know? The girls liked him. He made good pizzas, and when he showed up, he worked hard. What else?"

"What did you think of him?"

The huge man looked Frank directly in the eye while he answered. "I think if he's a Cajun, I'm a Swede. I don't know who he was, but I know what he was, and if you're not a cop, I know what you are, too. I was in the game in Southeast Asia. I ain't stupid. I know when to mind my own business, which is what I did when he was here, and what I'm gonna continue to do. Any more questions?"

"No. Thank you for your time, Mr. Atkinson."

"My pleasure, Mr. Cardova." The phone rang. He answered it, "Yeah?" as we walked out the door.

We slipped across the street. I don't mean we made our way unobtrusively to the apartment building like good secret squirrels. I mean we slipped. The temperature had dropped quickly after sunset, freezing the wet snow on the old humpback side street, where layers of asphalt were piled on top of each other for so many years that the middle, where the paving was thickest, was two feet higher than the gutters. Getting to the middle was not easy, an uphill climb without purchase on solid ice. Coming down the other side was quicker and sportier. I slid to the curb. Frank followed, his arms waving wildly for balance, shouting "Whoa!" and a few other words.

"Now that I've provided the entertainment for the evening," he said when he was safely in the doorway, "I wish they'd pack up and go home."

"Where are they?" I searched the street.

"To your left on the other side of the street, about fifty yards down. It's just outside the circle of light from the street lamp."

"I see it."

Frank's face was pinched and scowling. "I hate it," he said, "when there are no windows. I can't see out, and I don't know who's looking in."

"But without windows," I said, "they can't look in."

"You think so?"

This time, it was a slower, harder climb to the third floor than it had been first thing in the morning. We were rewarded, though, by a cup of hot coffee from Sarah Tisdale.

Frank and I sipped reverently, hunching over and around the steaming mugs, selfishly trying to consume every vapor, every warm, overactive molecule. Sarah sat on a cushion opposite us, pulling tissues from a box labeled generically, black on white. She blew her nose and dried a fresh tear, then smiled at me—us.

"Sarah, why are you crying?" Frank asked when he had thawed.

She didn't answer.

"Is it because he's gone?" he persisted.

"Yes!"

We waited for the end of another crying fit.

"Did he tell you to be out of the apartment yesterday?" Frank asked. "Or did somebody else tell you?"

"He said not to tell you anything." There was more doubt than fear in her expression, though there was plenty of that, too.

"I know he told you that, Sarah. I've worked with him for a long time and I know him very well. You can tell me."

"Have you seen him?"

"In a manner of speaking, yes."

"I miss him so bad!" She sobbed again.

"Did he tell you to stay away from here yesterday?"

"Yes."

Frank's smile was a little self-satisfied.

"Can you tell me how you met him?" he asked.

"I told you this morning," she said. "That was the truth. He said to stick to the truth. 'Keep it simple,' he said. 'And let him draw his own conclusions.'"

"Yes, well, you did that very well, Sarah. Now tell me when and how you two, uh, formed a relationship."

She blew her nose. "It was the night we all went out together when Jerry and I didn't hit it off. I came home and went to bed. Emile must have gone to work. I don't know how he got in. I once asked him if he had a key, but he didn't answer me. I know I never gave him a key."

"That night," Frank prodded.

"That night I was asleep. He sat down on my bed and woke me up. It was after midnight. I wasn't really surprised to see him; I had a feeling all during dinner. I even thought Emile was glad Jerry and I didn't get along."

Sarah paused again when she noticed my cup was empty. I ignored the impatient look Frank gave me and accepted the offer of a refill. She offered Frank a cup of chamomile tea, telling him it would help him relax. He managed to convince her that coffee would suit him better and sat fidgeting on his cushion until she came back with two coffees and a chamomile tea. She made him taste the tea and smiled at me.

"You were telling us about when you and Emile...," he said.

"Yes. Emile said, 'Mind if I join you?' and I said, 'You smell like pizza.'" Sarah smiled into her tea cup. "And he said, 'You smell like a woman.'"

After a short, smiling silence, she looked up at Frank and said: "Did you want details?"

"Uh, no." The question seemed to startle him. "What about the last time you saw him?" he asked, collecting himself.

"Friday night." She paused as new tears appeared in her eyes. "He told me he was leaving and wouldn't be back. That's when he told me not to be here yesterday. I begged him not to go. He was always straight with me. Told me in the beginning this wasn't permanent or anything, but you always agree to these things before you get attached, you know. So I told him about Dottie, and like, he was furious with me for not telling him before. I never seen him so mad."

"What about Dottie?"

"Well, I told you how jealous she was didn't I?"

We nodded.

"In October, Emile left for a few days. I didn't know if he'd be back or not, but Dottie must have figured he was gone for good. The day after he left, I came out my door to go to the store. I needed something sweet—I get this incredible, like, sweet tooth sometimes—and she was waiting for me in the hall, holding this bottle. She like, threw it right at my face. I ducked, but it went all over my shoulder, up my neck and it was acid. It hurt like hell. See?" She stretched the neck of her sweatshirt and showed us what once must have been a lovely shoulder, now badly scarred and still partly bandaged.

"Then Emile came back," she continued, "and he had a fit. He must have said some things to Dottie that scared her pretty bad because she stayed away from me for a while. But about November, I started getting these phone calls. At first, she called about once a week and didn't say who she was, just screamed hateful stuff. But by the beginning of this month, she came right out with it."

Sarah took a long sip of tea. I noticed her hand was shaking.

"What did she say?" Frank asked.

"She said she was going to kill me as soon as Emile left. She called every day and told me that. I was scared. But I didn't tell him because I was scared of her. I wanted him to stay. Do you understand?"

"Yes," said Frank softly. "What did Emile say when you told him about the phone calls?"

"When he cooled off, he said not to worry; he'd take care of it." Sarah looked at Frank. "I didn't know he was going to kill her. Honest."

"I believe you. Did you ever notice his gun?"

She stared at Frank wide-eyed. "You are cops. I don't want to get him in trouble."

"We're not cops. If anybody's in trouble, it's me."

Frank put his mug down on the floor beside him and leaned forward. "I'm trying to understand why he went to the trouble to tell you not to talk to me. Nobody else was briefed that way. What do you know that was important enough to keep from me?" He asked the next question before she had a chance to answer. "Did you ever touch his gun?"

"Oh no! He warned me again and again never to go near it."

"That's a first," muttered Frank.

"Excuse me?"

"Try to remember, Sarah." Frank seemed to be trying to remember something himself. He squinted, pulling thin lids over his round eyes. "Did he say anything unusual or puzzling? Did he talk about his family? His friends?"

"He was always unusual," she said smiling. "He never mentioned any family. Once I asked him what happened to Jerry, and he said he'd gone home, if that's any help?"

"When was that?"

"Shortly after we started going out. Jerry came back though. I saw him. I told you that, didn't I?"

Frank nodded and stared at the floor in front of him, still squinting, willing her memory to work.

"Emile had a best friend," Sarah said after a long pause.

Frank's eyes opened, popping, as his head came up. "He did?"

"Yes. He said he had a best friend. I never met him though."

"What did he say about his best friend?"

Sarah seemed reluctant to answer and took another slow sip of tea before speaking. "I told him once that I love him. It must have been sometime after he came back in October because I still had all the bandages." She spoke slowly. "I knew better. He was always real honest about it being temporary, but I had to tell him. He didn't look at me, only at the ceiling, and told me not to talk nonsense. I put my head on his shoulder and pulled his arm around me tighter, and I told him love was not nonsense. He argued it was, and still wouldn't look at me. He'd seen his best friend crying over a coffin, he said, and that was never going to happen to him. He was so serious. It kinda broke the spell that morning. He got dressed and left without saying anything else. I kept things the way he wanted after that—temporary and fun."

"Bingo," whispered Frank. He looked at me sideways.

"I'm sorry I couldn't help you," she said.

"You've been a great help, Sarah," said Frank. "Thank you."

"You're welcome. Are you out of trouble now?"

...

I did not ask him the same question when we walked out into the cold. The Mercedes was still across the street, beyond the light.

SIXTEEN

"So why is it about time Louis told Sarah to stay away from his gun?" I asked Frank as I drove us to Rick's for the appointment with Slavin.

"What?" Frank shook himself and straightened up a bit in his seat. "Oh, Louis has a nasty habit of not warning women and then shooting them when they reach toward his gun in the heat of the moment."

"He does what?"

"He shoots them."

I waited for more explanation. The puny portion of confidence I had built in the last few hours was gone. Frank crumpled back into his corner, not interested in talking. I was interested, though.

"Is this fact?" I asked. "I mean, do you know of it actually happening? How many times?"

"Twice that I know of." Frank yawned, wide and noisy.

"That you know? It happened on your watch?"

"Once. The other time it happened to somebody else. I don't have any details of that one. Not verified."

"But what happened? Don't you think this is something I should know about?" The last word reached an octave over my normal speaking voice.

Frank did not hide the irritation in his voice. He spoke quickly, demanding with his tone, if not with the actual words, that I drop the subject.

"Operations are usually short and uncomplicated, Steve, but when they go on for more than a couple of days, the Frenchman, and maybe the others, but definitely the Frenchman, will find a little amusement along the way. Your job will be to check her bona fides and make sure she is warned not to get too curious. On my fourth operation with them, I failed to do both. She was on her own operation. I don't know who she was working for. These guys have too many enemies to count anyway. She was well-equipped to do the job but got dramatic about it and reached for his gun. He got to it first. Simple. They've never taken my word about the bona fides of a girl since."

"But this time?"

"This time he warned Sarah. I suppose it's not surprising since if he lost her, he'd be back across the hall. I've never known him to be so careful with a girl before, though."

"What do you do when...?"

"Turn left at the next light and let me think for a while."

He gave directions for parking the car, not for dealing with disaster. We walked to our meeting at Rick's.

"Any sign of the Mercedes?" he asked, blowing on his hands as if his breath would somehow make all the difference against the insidious cold.

"None." I tried to watch the cloud my breath made in the cold air under a street light overhead, but Frank was setting such a fast pace that it was behind me almost as soon as I spoke. It was like leaving a word behind on that empty street, first warm and living, then frozen, now dissolved.

"The car's probably wired by now," Frank said to me over his shoulder. "They don't need to follow us anymore."

"I didn't think what we talked about would be anything new to them," I said defensively, trotting three steps to keep up. I never understood how such a short, round man could move so quickly without actually running.

"I agree," he said. "I just needed time to think about your picture theory. Sarah's bit of information reinforces it, don't you think? I mean, if Mack is Louis' best friend, and if the coffin he cried over held the woman in that picture Jello and I kept, then if the picture had anything to do with her death, anybody who had anything to do with the picture is in deep trouble. I can see that. But I didn't do anything with it but lock it in a vault. The only other person who would know what to do with it and have access to it at the same time is such a blithering idiot that it blows your whole theory."

"How's that?" I squeezed the words out in frozen gasps.

"Setting me up is far too subtle a move for Jello. He could never think of it, let alone pull it off."

"But if he did?"

"He didn't."

"But if he did, Frank," I insisted. "If he did then he's not such an idiot."

"That is not worth considering."

"It is worth considering, Frank. It's always a possibility."

"I refuse to believe it. I told you before; it's impossible."

At that time I knew only the popular history of Frank and Jello, the stories told in the section of political maneuvers and dogmatic wrangling and loud, public arguments in vehement words that left them both red and shaking. If I had any sense, I would have realized such emotional hatreds have emotional beginnings.

Only recently somebody told me about their exploits as advisors in Southeast Asia, when they were brothers in arms, friends depending on each other for survival. It took me more serious thought, several months too late, to realize what my smug little theory meant to Frank. For Jello to turn would be a betrayal of his country that Frank could never understand. To arrange Frank's death was treachery of the first magnitude, even after twenty-five years of backstabbing competition.

I walked into Rick's without knowing any of this. Puzzled and preoccupied by Frank's blindness, I stumbled over the doorstep into a tray of empty glasses carried by a waitress. The tray flew from her hand over the bar and crashed into a row of bottles along a mirrored wall, announcing our arrival to the roomful of assorted spooks and assassins there gathered.

"Nice touch," Frank said sarcastically.

The waitress didn't care. She smiled and asked for my order. As we stepped into the large room to the right of the bar, I noticed half a dozen men in all three sections putting away their weapons.

"The rules against violence in a sovereign house are enforced by the clientele," Frank explained as we surveyed the left side of the room. "Making too much noise here can be unhealthy; I wouldn't make a habit of it if I were you."

I kept my mouth shut.

"There's Slavin," said Frank nodding toward the second table along the left wall.

"How do you know?"

"He's got a bag from Just Jeans."

"For the black market back home?"

"Of course not. He's a member of the Soviet aristocracy—the nomenklatura—central committee, inner circle KGB. He doesn't need the black market. But he can't go home to his wife and kids without some American blue jeans any more than I could come home from Hong Kong without a string of freshwater pearls and assorted jade earrings."

"Just like us, is he?" I asked.

"No way," Frank whispered through his teeth. "Don't ever make that mistake. Anything we have in common with these people is on the most basic human level only. Don't let that confuse you. They do not think like us. They speak the same words, like peace and freedom, but their definitions are something else, something appalling and terrifying. Their privileges are built on those definitions. Make no mistake, my friend. This man is the enemy. Don't let the blue jeans give him a benign camouflage."

I watched Frank, shocked by his intensity. He stared at the Russian on the left.

"Us Against Them?" I asked, not knowing what it was I wanted to know.

He nodded, scowling. It was an answer of sorts. To Frank, this was war, a personal battle where the stakes were bigger than the lives of the combatants. He was locked into it, hating perfectly, for a higher reason I didn't quite grasp.

But he held it tight and prepared to meet his enemy face to face. He tensed each limb and released, like an athlete at a meet. The muscles over his cheeks and around his mouth were pulled tight. He looked grim and strangely young and oddly exuberant. This was his moment. This was THE battle.

"And when you've defeated him, Frank? What will you do then?"

He shuddered, shook himself, and looked at me. "Go on to the next one. There will never be a shortage, my boy. Don't you worry. They're everywhere. I told you that before. Over here we call 'em the Mob. Over there, the Party." He grinned or tried to, but the scowl would not let go of his face; it only retreated behind a jolly mask.

"Another reason I know that's Slavin," Frank said, still stretching that odd grin, "is by the way all the local bad guys are fawning all over him trying to get close. Look at them. I wonder why they don't bow."

I was watching Frank, but I knew Slavin had noticed us. I could feel his stare.

"And finally, I know it's him," said Frank, "because I recognize him from a picture on file in the vault. Let's go say hi."

I didn't smile back at the joke. I didn't have that much control.

Ignaty Mikhailovich Slavin did not shake hands with us. He dismissed his hangers-on with an impatient gesture, cleared the tables around us with another gesture, and pointed to the two seats in front of him. After unsuccessful attempts to communicate in English and Russian, we settled on German, the only language all three of us knew.

"What's your brief and who gave it to you?" Frank began.

"Charlemagne gave it, but there is a price." The Russian's face was stretched in a sneer.

"Name it," said Frank.

"Verification that Jared is dead." The sneer seemed permanent.

"Saw him myself last night, in a drawer at the morgue. He didn't even complain about the cold—must have been acclimated by all those Moscow winters."

"I do not have time to listen to your infamous jokes," said Slavin. "Ask your questions and I will see if I can answer them."

The waitress brought the drinks Frank and I had ordered. Slavin asked for another vodka.

Frank did not touch his drink. "Who commissioned it?"

"We did."

Though he was surely bursting with questions, Frank was cautious, pausing between each one, trying to gather as much information as he could without giving away his own line of reasoning.

The first question was simply, "Why?"

"He was out of control," said Slavin. "Seriously out of control. He was involved in something that is a threat to Soviet state security."

"What?"

"I cannot tell you. But I can say that it is not important to this case."

"It resulted in his death," said Frank.

"But it has nothing to do with your own," replied Slavin.

Frank's pause was longer than usual. "Why are you telling me this?" he asked finally.

"This is part of the price. I cannot believe you Americans pay such extortionist fees. Surely a few simple revolutionaries cannot be worth so much money."

"They are when they threaten millions, you bastard, not to mention civilization itself." Frank hunched his shoulders over the table, still not touching his drink.

"Can we refrain from name-calling?" Slavin said. The waitress placed his vodka in front of him. He drank it in one gulp. "Or is that too difficult for such a civilized bourgeois shithead?"

Everybody felt better after that and we entered round two.

"Let's get back to the price," said Frank, finally sipping his drink. "What else did they charge you?"

"Too much hard currency and a couple of sacrifices."

"Am I part of the commission?"

"Would I spend a ruble on you?"

"Your babysitter's dead, too, you know," said Frank after another, longer sip.

"No, I did not know." Slavin shrugged. "Not much of a loss."

"Not one of your best men?"

"Of course not. I could not compromise one of my best. This entire operation has put me in a difficult position. My only consolation is that yours is worse."

"I'm overwhelmed by your concern," said Frank, leaning forward again. "What, exactly, do you know about my position?"

Slavin stared at Frank for a long time, then looked at the wall on his right. He peeled back a loose piece of wallpaper distractedly and seemed to have no intention of answering, so we were both surprised when he finally spoke. "Not much, I am afraid," he said. "I know I would not like to be Charlemagne's enemy right now, and my intuition tells me that you are considered one."

I dared to break the long pause that followed with a question of my own, not that I had any business doing so, but I could feel Frank's discomfort. I sensed it in his silence. I thought I could distract Slavin while gaining some more information in the bargain. What these two found obvious was still a mystery to me.

"When did you offer them the commission?" I asked.

Slavin examined me before answering. His voice was mechanical. "In January."

"They took it?"

"They refused."

"Why? Did they say?"

"They did not like my verification."

"What did you finally do to convince them?" This was a shot in the dark. I was not sure he would answer.

He stared at me, trying to read my thoughts. He decided (wrongly) that I did not know what I was asking, because, to my surprise, he answered.

"I allowed subsequent events to carry them to their own verification."

"How?"

Slavin accepted my stupid look and put on a patient air as he said, "I gave Jared what he always wanted. The rest followed naturally."

"You gave...." I didn't finish the question, because Frank interrupted.

"And what was it Jared always wanted?" he asked.

"Rache."

SEVENTEEN

The parking lot at my hotel was not as full as it had been. People were going home for Christmas. Other people. The wino begging for loose change sat propped against the same pillar, grimy fingers grasping the neck of another bottle in a paper sack.

"Merry Christmas," I said, dropping the change from my pockets into the box in front of him. The bum grinned at me, gap-toothed. I shuddered.

The lobby was perfectly silent. The management had spared me even the insipid wilted-leaf holiday music over the intercom system. Blinking lights on the Christmas tree in a corner by the reception desk left a pattern of colored streaks in my streaming eyes. I could barely keep them open. Sleep would be a cinch. I was on my way.

"I owe you, Steve," came a voice behind me. "Let me buy you a drink."

A hand clamped onto my shoulder, making me pull away instinctively. "I've had a drink," I said. "Thanks anyway, Charlie." I blinked at him, trying to focus. His suit was wrinkled, his tie uneven. There was a coffee stain on his shirt. I wondered if I looked as bad.

"You look awful," he said. "I insist. We'll go to the piano bar."

"How about a rain check?" I mumbled. "I'm beat."

"No rain checks. I leave tomorrow. Let's go."

I was too exhausted to resist and followed him meekly into the deserted bar. We sat at a low counter surrounding a white grand piano. A bartender took our order and brought our drinks. Three or four people sat at a table against a far wall. Charlie lifted my spirits but also pestered me. It was tough keeping up with his questions and almost impossible to stick to my legend without contradicting myself. I say almost because somehow, I managed it.

"My dad's a little disappointed with me," he said when the subject had worked its way around to our families. "What about yours?"

"My what?" I took a sip of my gin and tonic, convinced that one more drop of alcohol would surely make me unconscious. It didn't though.

"Your dad," said Charlie. "Is he happy with what you're doing?"

"He's dead. Died a few years ago."

"I think sometimes parents make unrealistic plans for their kids, don't you?"

"Huh?"

"What did your dad want you to do?"

"He wanted me to be a pilot," I said, studying the lemon in my glass.

"And you are one. Was he pleased?"

"I was one. And yes, he was pleased."

"Was? What happened?"

"I had an accident. So why is your dad disappointed with you?" I was desperate to change the subject.

"He sent me to very good music schools and finds it hard to accept that I'll never be a professional musician."

"Why?" I asked. "Don't you want to?"

"I can't."

"Why not?"

"I just can't."

"So you sell tractors instead? You don't look like a musician." I studied his conservative haircut and rumpled business suit.

"What's a musician supposed to look like?"

"Can you play an instrument?"

"Several."

"What about this one?" I had noticed him eyeing the piano.

His face brightened. "No, I couldn't."

"Come on. Let's hear something. What can you play?"

"What do you want to hear?"

"Do you know any of that classical stuff?"

"Some." Was there irony in that half-smile?

I tried to remember the name of the composer Frank made me listen to in the car. I couldn't. I knew the name sounded like a word that echoed in my head, though, bouncing off the walls of my skull like a blip on a computer screen, looking for brain matter to settle down on and be solved by, to be thought of and processed, sifted and stored, if it weren't for the alcohol.

"The guy I'm thinking of sounds like *Rache*," I said. "I heard a piano concerto by him today. You wouldn't know who I'm talking about, would you?"

Charlie said nothing. He studied me. Then he grinned—a boyish, mischievous, teasing grin that made me forget the penny popping up in the cake. "Rachmaninov," he said. "Is that it?"

"That's it."

"His second?"

"I think so."

"I'll play the first movement."

"Do you know it?"

What a stupid question. He played the first ominous chords and looked at me once to see me nod, yes, this is it. His concentration deepened so that he moved to another planet where communication is based on discreet bits arranged in octaves.

Maybe I was fascinated because I was hearing it live, not from a tape deck. How can any man control his coordination in such an intricate operation as playing a piano? It occurred to me that Charlie was very, very good. Of course, I'm no expert. But this music moved me strangely. There was no question of sleep.

It didn't matter that there was no orchestra. The same power rushed in a torrent to a crescendo that broke out on top with more insistence and distinction than it had on the tape. At that point—the one where I slammed on the brakes and almost broke Frank's bald head—at that point, Charlie looked up at me and grinned, then retreated to his planet and finished the movement.

"I don't understand why you think you can't do that professionally," I said when the spell had broken and the unanimous applause in the little room died down.

"I don't like being on stage." He gulped the last of his Scotch.

"Why not?"

He shrugged. "Too public; too one-sided. Makes me uncomfortable. I like to see who's looking at me."

Me too. I didn't say it, but he heard it anyway. We were empathic, as they say, and I began to wonder if he was telepathic, the way he spoke my mind.

It was after midnight when Charlie and I said good night in the hallway outside our rooms. By then, sleep should have waited on the other side of my door and jumped out at me when I opened it. It wasn't even at home. Or maybe it was at home, my home, checked out of the hotel because of the poor service and the holidays and the fact that I wasn't paying any attention to it. Reminded me of Sally.

I settled in a chair next to the dresser in front of the bed. From here I could see both doors, the hall door, and the one to Charlie's room. The dresser protected me on the left, solid pressboard with two real drawers and two fake ones. It had no legs because it was bolted to the wall. The window was on my right, sealed against unconditioned night air and the noise of life six stories down. I was a rat trapped in a corner from which I could fight, but never escape. I sat and waited for morning.

I must have dozed because I dreamed. Charlie came through the connecting door, sat down at the dresser on my left, and played it. I did not recognize the song. He asked me what a musician looks like and I said a musician wears an orange mohawk. He grinned and disappeared. There was a scratching at the door. The bum from the parking garage came in, offering help. I declined, politely. He said if I did not shoot down the chopper his best friend would cut my throat and cry over my coffin. Then, Frank came in, hung his big picture over the window, and drew the curtains on it. Even Jello was in this dream, nailing boards over the doors, but before he finished, Frank shot him and slipped through to the hall, bolting the door behind him—to keep me safe, he said. Charlie's next-door neighbor, the one I kept forgetting and remembering, unbolted it and walked across the carpet toward me. I could not see his face clearly, but he still bothered me. It was in the way he walked. He opened his wallet and took out a picture of two people in front of a house in Iowa. I looked closely and recognized my wife and son.

I woke drenched in sweat, opened the curtains over the window, and stood with my forehead pressed to the cold glass, straining to see the street six stories below. Nothing moved. My eyes searched for movement along the walls of the skyscraper canyon in front of me. Nothing. I studied the buildings I could see, some taller than others, dotted with light and dark windows like random pattern checkerboards. I wondered if there might be a man standing in one of those windows, his forehead pressed against the glass, watching me. I imagined there was. I stepped back and closed the curtain. It seemed definitive. I felt relieved.

I did not expect to see Charlie again; he said he was leaving early on Christmas Eve. It was a surprise, then, to meet him in the rental car parking lot when I picked up the new car that morning. I gave him a lift around the airport circuit and dropped him off at the domestic terminal. He was flying back to Iowa to sell tractors. I drove to Edbrooke Avenue to see if Frank was still alive.

EIGHTEEN

On Christmas Eve morning, Jay and I stood next to my car in front of the pizza parlor on Edbrooke. Our stamping feet made the only sound in the frozen air, echoing down the street unanswered. We waited for, and I worried about, Frank. He was late.

I was miserable. This was the low point in this job for me. Other times would be bad, physically even worse, but this was plain misery. The uncertainty about Frank, about what the hell was going on. I was in a bad fifties horror movie, groping in a fog, knowing I'd end up as dinner for some shapeless monster rising out of the steaming muck in front of me any minute now. I was tired, to the point I thought I would die soon, hungry, and I had the shakes from too much coffee. And right then, I knew there was no other job for me.

The misery was almost part of the attraction. It was like early week in pilot training, when the flight commander would read an emergency scenario and study the faces of instructors and students in assorted stages of coffee high. "What will you do, Lieutenant…" he would say, and every student would tense, waiting to hear his name. Sometimes it was my name. I would stand, the clock over my shoulder reading just after four a.m. A Styrofoam cup with an inch of cold coffee stood next to my open dash one, and I would pick up the book carefully so as not to spill the last bit of vile, black, necessary liquid. My mind would work. The right answer would come, and I could sit down. More than that, I could fly. For one more day, I could fly. Euphoria at dawn.

Frank's voice set the speed brakes on the memory. I landed back at Edbrooke.

"I'm still here," he said, "hale and hearty. No sign of a Mercedes. What about you?" He was asking me.

"Nothing. Maybe they've gone away."

"Not a chance. Maybe Mr. Turner can tell us where his buddies are lurking."

Jay scowled.

"What's your brief for today?" Frank asked him.

"I have no brief. I am released and at your service alone."

"When did that happen?"

"Last night."

"Did you see them?" asked Frank swinging his arms from front to back. It was cold that morning.

"Yes." There was a reluctant pause in Jay's voice. He was admitting compromise. I suppose I would pause, too.

"Well, how'd they look?" asked Frank. "Fresh, alert, and healthy?"

"No. Exhausted and rumpled."

"Poor dears." Frank clucked like a hen. "Did they happen to discuss their plans for me? Or maybe you already know their plans. Maybe it was a super-saver package deal, eh? Me and Hunsecker?"

"I did what I had to do to defend the Constitution of the United States." Jay poked his finger at Frank's chest. "You would have done the same in my shoes. You would if you had any balls."

"Sure, sure I would. I agree." Frank pushed Jay's hand away. "The only way to deal with incompetence is to snuff the incompetent. Good plan. Vladimir Ilyich and Uncle Joe would be proud. Which constitution did you say you were defending?"

"He was dirty, Frank," said Jay quietly. "I guarantee it."

Frank chuckled, stamped his feet, and looked at the sky.

"He was," insisted Jay. "Look. When have you known Charlemagne to work without verification?"

Frank's chin came down abruptly and he stared at Jay for a long minute. "Everybody makes mistakes. They're making one with me."

"I'm sorry to hear that," said Jay. "There was no mistake in Hunsecker's case and so far, you seem to be walking and talking all right. If there's anything I can do to help you stay that way, let me know. Charlemagne's jet landed at O'Hare this morning. Do you want me to put a hold on it?"

"No. Not yet." Frank turned to me. "You haven't left your new car alone, I hope?"

"No. It's right here." I pointed in front of me, then put my hand back in my pocket to prevent frostbite.

"Good. Let's go." Frank held up his hand in a signal to stop Jay from moving toward the car. "We'll see you later, Mr. Turner. Merry Christmas."

The two men stood in the cold in a long mutual glare. Jay broke the silence with what I thought was remarkable professional dignity. "You know how to reach me if you need me," he said. "Merry Christmas."

"You seem pretty cheerful this morning, Frank," I said after I started the car.

He did not answer me immediately because he was busy with the heater.

"Give it some gas, Steve. Let's get some heat in here."

"I said you're looking pretty cheerful, Frank. Why?"

"Head for 87th Street again," he said. Lukewarm air blew into the car. He adjusted the vent so it did not blow in his face. He fiddled with his seat and sat back with a sigh.

I gave up on an answer to my question.

"I am cheerful this morning, my brilliant lad," he said suddenly, "because, as Jay noticed, I am walking and talking, and the sun is shining—well, it is behind the clouds—and again like Jay said, Charlemagne rarely kills without verification. In my case, they aren't going to get verification, because there isn't any. By noon today, you and I will be winging our way home to Christmas dinner. Life is good. I feel good."

He sighed again and closed his eyes.

"You were happy and chipper before Jay said one word about verification." I pointed out. "Did you have sweet dreams or something?"

"I had a vision. Unfortunately, it was more of the nightmare variety. But I woke to two messages that made it all better."

"And what were they?"

"Answers to the two calls I made last night."

I waited. There was no point in pressing him, and the street demanded all my attention.

"The first message was from Alexandra Sobieski," he said. "I was pleased to learn that she is still alive."

"You called her?"

"I called a contact and have been rewarded with a message at my hotel this morning asking me to meet Alex at her father's house at nine o'clock. No doubt she's the one who brought the jet in. They must be getting ready to wind things up. You'd better step on it."

I did my best, but traffic was heavy.

"And the other message?" I asked.

"Was from Inch. He did what I told him to do, for a change. Of course, I had to use every dire threat in my vocabulary."

"You called Inch? The librarian? The man with the flaming sword who stands in the door of the vault guarding his precious documents from us infidels? You got him to do something for you?"

"I sure did." Frank was smug. "He's here and he brought the Charlemagne file. He also brought one of the heavy boys from the courier service to guard him and the file. I told him he could. He's such a nervous, suspicious little twit."

"That's magic, Frank. To get Inch to budge from his vault, on Christmas Eve, with a document, is just plain magic. I salute you." I saluted him and nearly hit the car in front of us.

"Just drive, Steve. I told Inch to meet us at Alex's father's house at nine-thirty. I'd like to have at least half an hour to talk to her first, so come on, step on it."

"I'm trying to. What are you planning to do with Inch's file?" I found a clear lane and made some progress.

"I'm going to give Alex those pictures."

I looked at him quickly. "Does Inch know that?"

"Of course not. I can't wait to see his face."

We had a good laugh at the thought.

Alexandra Sobieski was ordinary. I guess. She was in her early thirties, short, with glasses and curly brown hair. She wore a black suit with a straight skirt and black pumps. Absolutely ordinary, with an attraction, not beauty, that was equally absolutely compelling.

She sat in a corner of the living room of her late father's house, in the kind of chair that was popular in the sixties, hard, pseudo-modern, uncomfortable. Dust sheets had been piled in a corner, leaving a sofa and another chair uncovered. There was a cheerful fire in the fireplace, but otherwise the room was as ordinary as Alex.

Until then, I had confused the ordinary with the mediocre. Until then. Alexandra Sobieski was anything but mediocre.

Frank took a seat in the chair opposite Alex. I stood behind him by the front window, keeping a reluctant eye on our car parked on the street. There were two other men in the room, Alex's 'pilots' who would never have squeezed into the cockpit of a fighter. One stood a few feet to my left by the front door. He covered the front door. Literally. The other stood in the opening of a hallway that led to the rest of the house.

Frank expressed his sympathy. Alex told him to get on with it.

"Thank you for coming all this way on Christmas Eve," he said. He didn't seem willing to get on with it.

"We will not celebrate Christmas for two more weeks," said Alex. "I never could convince Misha's wife that it was Peter the Great, not God, who put Russia on the Julian calendar."

"She is Russian, then?" asked Frank.

"Was." Flat and hostile.

"I am sorry. When?"

"You know when. In October."

"Can you tell me anything?"

Frank shook his head as if to answer for her.

"Anything you want to know. My brief is easy."

It took Frank a while to get over the shock and form a question. While he rubbed his chin, Alex signaled the pilots to leave the room.

"Do you know anything about the operation?" asked Frank.

"Some."

"Was it commissioned or personal?"

"Both. I know very little about the commission, other than it was distasteful."

"But the personal?"

"Ask."

"Was it revenge?"

She nodded. "I know the story only second-hand, and it's an old one. Do you want to hear it?"

"Please."

"Misha came from a political family, not a specialist family like Vasily's. Misha's father was considered a nuisance in certain political circles. He angered quite a few people, mostly the extreme. When Misha was nineteen, the family drove to Vienna for a political convention. They made a holiday of it. It was Misha, his parents, his seventeen-year-old sister, and a six-year-old brother, in the car, with their chauffeur driving. They passed through a village where an ice cream vendor had a little cart on the street. Misha's little brother campaigned for an ice cream, and Misha got out of the car to buy one. As he paid the man, the car blew up behind him. The person who told me this worked in a bakery behind the ice cream cart. She said the heat from the flames melted the plastic umbrella on the cart. She also said that despite the noise of the fire, she could hear screaming from the car, even through the window of the shop, for almost a full minute after the explosion.

"Atrocities multiply themselves, I think. The person who bombed the car was a specialist named Jared. After the funeral—symbolic since there was almost nothing left—Louis and Misha went to Poland and pulled Vasily out of a prison. Vasily spent most of his adolescence in Polish jails, you see. The three of them paid Jared back the debt in vengeance—with interest. It was their first operation, not counting the prison break, and a complete success, if you want to call it that, except that one member of the Jared family, Eben, was in an English boarding school."

She stopped and looked at her hands in her lap.

"In January this year," she said, "a man named Slavin offered the team a commission on Eben Jared. Misha told him no. He was sure that Slavin was up to something. Besides, Vasily told me, Slavin's verification was useless.

"In July, Vasily drove to a city near our home for a business meeting. Our daughter begged him to let her go with him, but it was too dangerous. We said no. She disobeyed, as usual, and took her bicycle to follow him. I told Misha when I discovered her gone and he went after her. Mara caught up to her father in the parking lot of an office building. Right behind her was a man with a gun. Vasily pushed her out of the way. Misha's knife is very fast, but it was not fast enough this time. Vasily died in Mara's arms."

Alex closed her eyes and took a deep breath. She was grim, but dry-eyed when she looked again at Frank.

"Misha's son, Michael, came home from university and was allowed to help investigate. He was well trained for it." The sound of her voice scratched as though catching on painfully spicy food.

"During Vasily's funeral, Misha and I blamed each other every chance we had. Afterward, he came to my office with the most insufferably triumphant look on his face. He handed me a picture. He said Michael had found it in the apartment of the man who killed my husband. It was a picture of Mara, taken last Christmas, a picture I had given my father."

She looked at her hands, then at the fire, then at the ceiling, without fixing on anything. She rubbed her temples and I noticed her hands were shaking. "I won't tell you what that interview was like. I understand now that it is a serious crime to give a lonely old man a few pictures of his granddaughter." She said this loudly, with defiance.

"I thought my dad had burned them all," she said more quietly. "I had no idea any were missing, nor how many."

She put her face in her hands, dropped them, and stared at them in her lap.

"I had to tell Misha that there were other pictures, and that one would be valuable to the kind of person who would follow a little girl to shoot her father. I gave it to Papa because it was such a happy picture. I thought it would reassure him that his granddaughter was not growing up in a thieves' den."

She looked up at Frank. "I am sure you can imagine what I had to listen to when I warned Misha. I thought it was the worst day of my life. But it wasn't. In October, Misha and Louis were here, in Chicago, on Slavin's commission looking for that damned picture and trying to stop Jared."

She sighed and wiped at the corner of an eye with one fingertip. "Katya was my best friend, as sweet and mild as her husband is caustic and impossible. Nadia was fourteen. A pearl taken from a clam, and you should have seen her dance!"

Alex was crying freely now. She took out a white handkerchief. "We went to the ballet. That's all we did. Katya would not listen to Michael; none of us would listen to him. Nadia and Mara laughed and chattered as we left the theater and we did not even see the three men, but Michael did. He stopped two of them. The third one, a man with red hair, moved faster. Michael managed to pull Mara and me away from the building. I should be grateful and I am, but at the time I wished I had died with them. Vasily's death had always been anticipated. We lived with the possibility every day, but Katya and Nadia?" She shook her head and the tears dropped into her lap.

She looked at Frank. "Have I told you anything you didn't know?"

"You've told me more than I learned in fifteen years. Why?"

"Whoever gave Jared those pictures knew what he was doing. It wasn't one of ours. It had to be one of Jared's."

Frank stared at her. "It wasn't me."

"Verify, Frank."

"I will."

NINETEEN

Alex called one of the pilots from the other room. She unclipped the wire inside her lapel and handed it to him. "Take this out for a walk, will you please? It will be all right; he won't mind. I will take any blame for it. Just walk around the block and come back."

Once the ear and its bodyguard were gone, she turned to Frank. "It's my turn for an answer or two. I understand there was a child involved. Did they... is it... dead?"

"No," said Frank.

Alex drew a deep breath and closed her eyes. She opened them again and said, "When they left after the funeral, they were bent on revenge. Was it Michael who refused? You know, the young one, Misha's son. Did he refuse?"

"No. Mack said no."

"Mack! Misha?"

"Yes."

"He said no?"

"According to our information."

Frank stopped because Alex was not listening. Her head rested against the wall behind her, tears streaming from closed eyes. She opened them and smiled. "When I pray for a miracle, I always give God advice on how to go about it. I'm glad He never listens to me. His solutions are always better."

She sobered; the smile vanished. "But he is operational," she said to Frank. "Michael, I mean."

"Yes."

The pilot with the wire came in through the front door, and as I watched her pin it back on, it occurred to me that I had a question to ask. Something had puzzled me, and I was beginning to piece together an answer.

"Why wasn't Jer... Michael interested in Sarah?" I asked her from my spot by the window. Frank turned and popped his eyeballs in surprise. Alex's guarded reaction added weight to my private theory.

"I don't understand," she said. "Who is Sarah?"

I told her about the double date that was designed to gain access to Sarah's apartment. I watched her as I told her.

It had been bothering me since Sarah's first smile. She was not an easy woman to refuse. The operation made a liaison necessary; why was Michael unwilling? Reasons would have to be compelling. Like love or hate. Hate? Not likely. Sarah was one of the rare kinds of occupational hazards that make people think espionage is a good line to be in. Dottie was proof that things could always be worse.

Love, then. Was he attached, or infatuated, somewhere else?

Alex confirmed it. Her face turned red and she unconsciously covered her lips with her fingertips, as if to hide the memory of a kiss. She played with her wedding ring.

What would it be like to spend adolescence cloistered in the same house with this woman? She taught Michael flawless English. He must have been an eager learner. I would have been. And then a tragic early widowhood....

Michael went home unwilling to use Sara. He came back ready to woo Concordia, all reservations overcome, by death and revenge and....

"You turned him down then?" I asked Alex. "Why?"

The shock on her face answered for her. I never got a verbal reply.

Frank's reaction to my little deduction surprised me. I thought it was all pretty obvious. He twisted around in his seat and stared at me with frog-eyed wonder.

I shrugged. "Just wondering."

Inch came in shortly after that, protesting the rough treatment Alex's men gave his bodyguard as they pulled an unloaded .38 out of his belt. I don't know why people feel safer around empty guns. I don't.

Frank gave Inch a few choice threats, tailored to the whiney little bureaucrat's pressure points. It was a display of tradecraft that made me appreciate both the effectiveness of information as a weapon and the skill Frank possessed in wielding it. I learned a lot about my new job while watching the librarian squirm under the weight of three sentences.

Inch opened his briefcase and handed Frank a folder.

Alex stood by the fire. Frank walked up to her.

"I took two pictures," he admitted. "But I never gave them to Jared or anybody else. You're on the wrong track."

He opened the file and leafed through the loose sheets of paper. He flipped through them, first slowly, then quickly. There were no photos. I could see his profile in the glow from the fireplace. His frog eyes bulged in panic at the woman who seemed rather small and insignificant as she stood silently, grimly staring at him. The sweat on his bald head reflected the flames behind her. It had become suddenly very hot in the room.

Alex took the file from his hand and also leafed through it, while Inch protested feebly. He fell silent at a glance from Frank and only squeaked again once, helplessly, as Alex turned and dropped sheet after sheet into the fire.

"It wasn't me!" Frank squeezed the words through his teeth.

"Prove it," she said.

He spun around and faced Inch. "The logbook! Did you bring the log?"

"Of course," said Inch. "I always...."

"Just give it to me!" Frank snatched it from the briefcase before it was fully opened. He tore through the pages, searching for an entry.

Inch took it from him and found the right page almost immediately. "Twenty-first of June, and there's your signature."

"Not mine!"

Alex crossed the space silently and peered at the handwritten entries in Inch's book.

"It is your signature, Bud... uh, Frank," said Inch in a patient tone. "I'd recognize it anywhere."

"But you know it wasn't me. You had to have been there!"

"I wasn't there. I was on vacation that week. See?" Inch pointed at another column. "Pete Stanick, the new guy, checked you in."

"But Pete... Pete..." Frank was beginning to stammer.

"Pete died in that bad crash in Maryland on the Fourth of July, remember?" said Inch. "They said the fireworks caused it. I remember it because I have a very good memory for details. I've always thought I should be better utilized in the event of...."

Inch could not continue because Frank had him by the throat.

When Frank was calmer and could be released, he shook himself, straightened his tie, and faced the woman in the mourning suit. "I need two things from you, please," he said earnestly.

"Why should I?" she asked. "It's not as if we have access to a court of justice, is it? What gives you the right to an appellate review?"

"You should help me because you call yourself a Christian, and because I am innocent."

"Come off it, Frank. Nobody here is innocent."

"I'm innocent of this!" He put his hands out in front of him, flat, palms downward, as if to physically hold down his emotions. Calmed by force of will, he said, "This you'll understand—he'll understand. It's an incredible false flag. He's about to be conned. Tell him!"

"What are the two things you want from me?" she asked softly.

"Time and a miracle."

"How much time?"

"Twenty-four hours? Okay, six." No answer. "Two?"

"I'll try."

We left the little house off 87th Street with an uncertain grace period of two hours.

"What was all that about a miracle?" I asked as he got into the car. "Don't tell me she's devout."

"What?" Frank was distracted. "Depends on what you call devout."

"She's not then?" I asked, rather hoping, pointlessly in view of both our positions, that she wasn't.

"No. She is, really."

"But she is... was married to a specialist."

"So?" Frank challenged me with this word, and it alerted me to something in him. He stiffened and thrust out his chin, defending himself against attack. The subject meant something to him.

I took up the challenge. "So, the two are not compatible. It has to be one or the other."

Frank looked ahead, but I could see him studying me out of the corner of his eye. He nodded. "Maybe," he said. "But if you're one, then your business is with the other. The problem comes when your god tells you to kill."

"Huh?"

"Did you know that Barabbas was a terrorist?"

"He was?" This was my first ever Sunday school lesson. I didn't know who the hell Barabbas was, but I knew how to pretend.

"Yes, of course." Frank rubbed his hands in the cold. "Blew up Romans all the time." He waved at the steering wheel impatiently and told me to start the engine.

I didn't argue. I was on shaky ground anyway and maybe there was plastique in the old Roman empire. What did I know?

Frank watched my face carefully as I pulled out onto 87th Street, marking my grimace as the Mercedes swung in behind us.

He said, "I hope Alex comes through with that miracle."

TWENTY

We drove around, aimlessly, maybe in the general direction of Edbrooke Avenue, but not directly toward it. There had been no sign of the Mercedes for the last five minutes, but this was not reassuring.

"Where the hell are we going?" said Frank. "We should be heading for the airport. No. Not good. Too obvious. Come on Steve, get your brain in gear and help me, damn it! I have an escape hatch, but I need to get to it unnoticed. Think of a way to get me out of here."

"I...."

"You need to bail out in about an hour. So think quick."

"I'm not bailing out," I said. "Why are you giving up?"

Frank stared at me. He reminded me of Humpty Dumpty teetering on the wall. Round eyes in a round face full of concern. "The setup is perfect," he said calmly. "There are no holes in it. Even Pete Stanick is dead."

"Every possible witness is dead? What about Slavin?"

Frank dropped his chin and rolled his eyes up toward me, all patience and condescension. "First, tell me how you will find him and extract him in one hour. Then, explain how you will break him, and finally, maybe you can tell me how you plan to convince Mack that Slavin's word is worth anything."

"Okay. He's out. Jello?"

He gave me the same look and whistled softly.

"Fine. Fine. I see you're a pessimist, Frank. I'm not giving up."

"Neither am I," he said. "I'm just getting out. I've seen Mack's work, lots of it, don't forget. What about a train?"

"What about Jared's people?"

"You may have noticed them in the morgue."

"His wife is still healthy."

"Healthy and happily ignorant of her husband's occupation."

"So she says."

Frank did not seem interested in the idea, so I dropped it. We did not speak again for several minutes. Frank stared blankly at the door handle. I glanced at him periodically but kept my attention fixed mostly on the traffic in front of me. The snow of the day before was gone from the street and piled on the curbs like a sculpture of a city skyline at dusk, all brown clumps and furrows.

"Frank, what about the little girl?" I turned the car east and headed for Edbrooke.

"Which little girl?" he asked sadly. "The little dead dancer?"

"No. Jared's little girl, Janey. She said she helped him, didn't she? Maybe she helped him on this case. Maybe she saw something. She's an incredible kid, maybe...."

"Maybe she planned the operation," said Frank sarcastically.

"We can ask," I said.

"We don't have time."

"We don't have time to do anything else."

"The apartment's not secure," he said as we pulled up in front of it. "You'll have to bring her down here."

Cordelia Jared came to the car with her daughter. That was fine with me. I was amazed she agreed to the interview at all. Frank did not look at them as they climbed into the back seat. I asked my questions from the front, half twisted so that I could see Janey seated behind Frank, but could only catch from the side the emanations of Cordelia's disgust for Me And My Kind.

We established that Jared often used his daughter to service dead drops and on two occasions as a live drop. The first time had been two years before. The second time was in the past June.

"You're sure it was June?" I sensed that I was on the right track.

"Yes," said the girl. "School was just out. It was June. It was hot, too. I remember because the guy had a suit on and I thought he looked hot. I wore shorts."

"The guy? What guy, Janey?"

"The guy who gave me the envelope for Daddy," she said with a look of *How dense can you be?*

"What did the guy look like?"

"Like a guy." She shrugged her shoulders.

"White guy? Black guy?"

"White."

"Tall? Short? Did he have a mustache?"

"No. He twitched. Besides that, he looked like anybody, I guess."

"He what?"

"He twitched. You know. His face went up and down on one side like he was winking but couldn't do it without moving the whole thing."

Frank turned around in his seat, trying to see the little genius directly behind him. Cordelia glared at him with the ferocity of a mother bear whose cub is threatened. I expected her to growl any second now.

"By any chance, did you look in the envelope, Janey?" I asked.

"Of course I did. Daddy wasn't angry about it, either. He said I should learn to look without making it obvious."

"What was in the envelope?" We could not waste any more time.

"Just some pictures."

"Pictures of what?" I closed my eyes, waiting for an answer that was taking eons too long.

"Pictures of some kids. And a lady."

My next question came from instinct, not conscious thought. "Did you recognize any of them, Janey?"

She did not answer right away but glanced at her mother. I twisted around in my seat to search Cordelia's face. She was puzzled.

"Did you recognize one of the kids?" I asked Janey again.

"Not then."

"But later?"

"Yes."

"Which one?"

"Jerry. One of them was Jerry." She said it quietly, head bowed.

Cordelia shook her head. "Why...why didn't you tell Daddy?"

"I didn't remember at first," said the little girl. "And when I did remember where I saw him before, I liked him too much. And Aunt Concordia liked him. I didn't want to spoil it for her." She sobbed. "I didn't know he was an enemy. I didn't know!"

"One more question," I said to the weeping child. Cordelia opened the car door. "Was this the man who gave you that envelope?" I pointed to Frank.

"No, of course not," said Janey. "He doesn't look like anybody. He looks like Mr. Douglas at the gas station."

"Right. Good work. No. Brilliant. I am truly brilliant," Frank said after Cordelia slammed the car door behind her.

"You!" I started the car as punctuation.

"That's right. I picked the right man for this job. I'm brilliant. Now then, my beamish boy, head for the airport. We have work to do, and when I say we...."

"I know. I know. You don't have a turd in your pocket."

"Nor a mouse. And I hope no other creatures are lurking in this car. You did follow the rules, I hope?"

"To the letter."

"Good. We have to call Alex and tell her where she'll find our star witness. Then we'll call the office and have them put Jello on ice."

"On ice?" I could not believe it. "You're not going to protect him! He nearly got you killed. Let them have him!"

"Like hell. They'll make a hero out of him. I want revenge. If Mack cuts his throat, I'll have to go to the funeral and say nice things about him to his relatives. I'll have to give a eulogy for the man who single-handedly destroyed more than fifteen years of my work. I want him to live. I want him to pay for his mistake."

"Mistake? Frank, you're fucking delusional. This was no mistake."

"Stop at the next phone booth you see," he said, ignoring me. "You followed all the rules? The car is secure?"

"All the rules."

"Nobody got near it?"

"Nobody." I was a little exasperated with his paranoia.

"Nobody's been in it?"

"Nobody. Except...."

"Except? Except who?"

I did not answer. I was thinking.

"It's impossible," I said when Frank began bouncing on the seat. "He's as American as apple pie."

"Who is?" Frank's eyes were bulging.

"Charlie."

"Who's Charlie?" He was sideways in his seat, leaning toward me, his eyes ahead of him by about a mile.

"This guy. I gave him a lift to the terminal this morning."

"In this car?"

Too many impressions crowded my memory at this point. I could not be sure which was real and which came from my dream the night before. I pulled the car over to the side of the road. Traffic roared by us. I heard Rachmaninov. A Santa Claus stood in front of a store on our right. I saw Charlie at the airport. Charlie in the hotel. Charlie in the bar. The Santa rang a bell. I heard Charlie talk about his father.

That was the trigger. I knew what it was that I was missing about Charlie's next-door neighbor. He reminded me of Charlie. It was in the walk, in the way he moved without seeming to. A silence of movement. And the people in Iowa? No resemblance. It was not just the difference in hair color, build, and facial lines. It was the difference in character. The people in that picture would not object to their son working for a tractor company. It was not exactly a fate worse than death in Iowa. Charlie the musician was not their son. He was Mack's son.

Frank saw it in my face and groped around under his seat. He found the device quickly and stared at it. "Bastards!" He rolled down his window and tossed it out, then leaned fully forward against the dashboard, beating his round, hairless head against it like Charlie Brown.

"You realize," he said to me through clenched teeth, "that they are, at this moment, positively rolling with laughter. The Frenchman has tears in his eyes, it's so funny."

There was nothing for me to say, but I said something stupid anyway, trying to draw attention away from my blunder. "There's a phone booth," I said, pointing ahead. "Did you want to call Alex?"

Frank was merciful. He said nothing. Keeping his head on the dash, he swiveled his face upward and looked at me.

"Right," I said. "No need. They know it wasn't you. What now?"

"Airport," he murmured.

I turned north and headed for O'Hare. For the first time since we came to Chicago, we were completely silent, which was odd, because it was also the first time nobody was listening.

TWENTY-ONE

I dragged my feet through the airport. Frank rolled on ahead of me. *Last one to the phones is a rotten egg.* I must have smelled pretty bad by then. Frank hollered over his shoulder as he moved at Mach through the main concourse, telling me to call Jay and put a hold on Charlemagne's airplane. Jay was not in. I left a message with somebody who didn't want to take messages on Christmas Eve. I calculated the chances of my message getting through and smiled.

I was not embarrassed. Well, okay. I did sting some from the thorough hoodwinking I had received from Charlie, or Jerry, or Michael, or whatever the hell his name is. But embarrassment did not make me drag my feet. I figured out that we were not only going to fail to protect Jello, but the mere attempt would irritate the team. Trying to bring Jello to justice would require us to share secrets, WEDGE secrets, talking about them openly, in a secret sort of way, in the black and even in the semi-black world, and none of that would go over big with Mack & Co.

I couldn't explain this to Frank when we traded results from the phone attempts. He was also unsuccessful. No one had seen Jello since he came back from the conference the day before. We dashed—he dashed, I dragged—through the terminal to the observation deck. We had no change for the viewing machines, having used it all on the phones. A business jet took off, but we could not see the tail number.

"You left a message?" Frank had a defeated look. "So did I."

After we returned the rental car and checked our bags, I talked Frank into having lunch while we waited for our flight home. We found a table in a dark corner of a large, empty restaurant in the terminal. Frank told me to order for him while he went to the toilet. I studied the menu, engrossed. After twenty-four hours without a full meal, I was ready for anything this place could offer.

"May I take your order, Suh?" said a scratchy voice over my right shoulder.

It was the exaggerated Southern accent in the "Suh" that started my mind working, but my mouth was already ordering a steak sandwich. When all the synapses had connected, and I knew the bum in the parking lot would not be working here as a waitress, I slammed the menu down in front of me, stood halfway, and stupidly thought about pulling my gun, though he had a good grip on my arm. I looked at him, hoping I might find a weakness, an opening, to strike and run.

The transformation was incredible. The Frenchman's dark, wavy hair was neatly cut, the temples slightly grey. He looked like a prosperous businessman. His beard was gone; he wore a three-piece suit, expensive and impeccable, and a gold watch. He laughed at me with black eyes and a full set of white teeth, then he made me move out of the choice corner seat I was in and set a dollar and some change on the table in front of me, a return on my investment in charity. I sat uncomfortably in another chair with my back to the door.

Charlie sat down next to him. He didn't introduce us. I felt the sting all over again, doubled now by the parking lot bum. Louis thought the whole thing hilarious. I wondered where Mack was. And Frank.

"We thought you were on your way to see Jello," I said nervously.

"He is not at home," said Louis. He leaned his chair back against the wall. He looked very casual.

Charlie was more tense.

I worried about Frank.

"Where is he?" I asked, more for something to say, and not really knowing which man I meant, Jello or Frank.

"He is in Chicago," answered Louis.

"Who?"

"Jello."

"Why?"

Louis did not answer and my mental effort to figure it out for myself was interrupted by the relief I had at the sight of Frank taking the chair on my right.

He was disheveled and subdued. The nap of the short fringe of hair circling his naturally tonsured head had been ruffled. His tie was crooked, the knot squeezed into a little ball at his throat. He played absently with a salt shaker. Whatever words were used in that men's room interview with a man he knew, or attempted to know, for more than fifteen years, they were not happy ones.

But he was alive.

Mack came in with him, also impeccable in a three-piece suit, the bulge of his SIG carefully masked by the cut of his coat. His hair was blond, like Charlie's, with no sign of grey, but his face was more lined. I found it hard to study him as he sat in the corner seat opposite me because he was so frankly dissecting me. His gaze was constant, hostile, penetrating, and it burned holes in me, making me squirm involuntarily.

Louis chuckled. "Brilliant bit of intelligence work with Alex there," he said to me. He looked at Charlie, smiling. "It raised our eyebrows, did it not, Michael?"

"Yeah. Thanks, Steve." Charlie's teeth were cemented together.

Louis' compliment was a great help, but it melted away under the blue-eyed inquisition from Mack. He recessed the silent torture long enough for us to order lunch from a laconic waitress, then leaned forward and began a verbal interrogation in German. I maintained my legend.

"Your German is abominable," he told me.

I had no answer. I was listening to his accent, trying to hear what had so frightened the Czech woman. I could not tell. He spoke slowly; he sounded Austrian. He sounded educated, upper class Austrian.

"How many children were on that airplane?" he asked, boring blue holes in my brain.

Oh shit.

"What airplane?" I tried to look puzzled.

"The airplane you shot down over the Bering Sea."

"I don't know what you're talking about." I wanted to vomit.

"Cut the crap, Steve," Charlie said in English. "No spy verse spy games if you want to deal with us. Make your choice right now."

I looked at Frank. His ping-pong ball eyes were fixed on the salt shaker. No help there. I looked at Mack. The ice in his blue eyes dazzled me. He raised his eyebrows slightly, waiting for my decision. His expression seemed so hard, so controlled, so alien to me, that I knew instinctively my answer did not matter to him at all. He would act on it, one way or another, without another thought about it. The only one to suffer any consequence or enjoy benefit from my next words would be me.

"Seventeen," I said.

Frank rested his head on his hand and turned away from me.

"And how many commissions are out against you?" asked Mack.

"They're all petty two-bit contracts."

"How many?"

"Five that I know of."

"And your family?"

I swallowed. Hard. "All five are inclusive."

"Why are you here?"

Frank had said I would need a reason. I had one, even if it sounded hokey coming from me.

"I was trained as a warrior," I said. "I belong in battle."

"The battle against what?"

"Against the slaughter of innocents."

The waitress brought us food. We were silent as she put a plate in front of each of us. Jay came up without a sound, carrying an extra chair from another table. He put it between Louis and me and sat down on it, elbows on knees, head in his hands, breathing heavily. He had news.

"I found him," he said to Mack when the waitress cleared out.

Mack picked up his knife and fork.

"I found him," Jay went on, "and then I lost him." Each statement came in short bursts, like an SOS. "He met Slavin. Slavin had somebody else with him. Took us half an hour to figure out who it was."

Mack ate like a European, with both knife and upside-down fork. He chewed slowly. "Who?" he asked after swallowing.

"The Barracuda."

Jay expected some reaction. There was none from the team. Frank and I, on the other hand, choked on our French fries simultaneously. Jay took the opportunity to pinch three from my plate.

With Jared dead, The Barracuda became Slavin's top surviving solo specialist. He had a reputation for not being overly picky about his targets.

When my throat was clear and I could speak again, I asked, "Who's the target?"

Louis threw his head back in a long laugh, then leaned forward toward Frank. "How were you planning to prove to your bosses that Jello is dirty?" he asked him. "Where is your verification?"

At first, I did not see the connection. I did not understand that Louis was answering my question with a question. But the synapses connected again and I figured it out before Frank answered.

"I have three proofs," he said quietly to the salt shaker. "Steve Donovan, Cordelia Jared, and most important, Janey Jared."

"There is your answer," said Louis. "Not just one target. Three."

"They will take care of the easier ones first," Mack told Jay. He put down his knife and fork, wiped his mouth on a napkin, and set it beside his plate. "Have your watchers pick them up at Edbrooke, and this time, do not lose them. We will take our opportunity when The Barracuda finishes."

"I'll arrest him," said Jay.

"Fine," said Mack. "But Jello is mine."

A lot happened in the next few moments, but almost nothing was spoken aloud. A casual observer would not have understood it.

My decision should have surprised no one. Ideas confused me; Janey was real. I knew my action could endanger other equally real people in the future, but I counted on Frank's presence as a kind of insurance policy. I hoped he would have the good sense to fire me, but not until I woke from a nightmare in which a pretty little girl with a halo of soft brown hair lay in a cold room at the morgue, next drawer to her father.

My first decision was to rescue Janey myself, if I had to. This was obviously a last resort, since my chances of success made snow in the Sahara look like a sure bet. Janey's only real hope, as I saw it, was with the three men who had almost killed her two days before. My next decision, the one that probably impaired my ability to do my job—irreparably it seems—was to do whatever was necessary to commission an operation against The Barracuda. Within the next thirty seconds.

I looked at Frank. His expression was sympathetic, but he shook his head. "No authorization, Steve," he said.

That eliminated money as a motivator. My own meager resources were laughable; without the government, I had no hope of affording Charlemagne. I considered lying but rejected it on the grounds that I was not likely to be believed.

What about sympathy? Or altruism? I looked for some in Charlie. I couldn't tell. Like Mack, he was watching me, expressionless. I saw no sympathy there, and even less in Louis. His eyes held a hint of cruelty barely concealed. He would not volunteer to risk his life to save the daughter of a dead enemy. Mack would have to decide.

I looked at Jay last. In my last resort plan, I would need his support. He nodded. I could count on him. But I looked at him for another reason. I did not agree with what he had done, but at last I understood. I decided to offer the same as the price of a commission. I looked at Mack.

"For now," Mack said to me before I could speak, "it is enough that you are in our debt."

TWENTY-TWO

"So babysit," said the Frenchman. He waved the barrel of his gun at Sarah's apartment.

I was not sure why they brought me, but I knew it was a breach of the rules for me to be this close to an impending operation. I knocked softly on Sarah's door.

"Be very quiet and come with me," I said when she answered.

She looked surprised, but she complied. I held her arm firmly as we passed between Mack and Louis and walked to the stairway. Her smile was wasted on her former lover. He was busy picking the lock to the Jared apartment. Charlie was already heading through Sarah's flat to the kitchen window and the connecting fire escape.

"Do you have someplace to go?" I asked her as we stood in the doorway downstairs.

"My mother's, but...."

"Good. Do you have a car?" I had no time to enjoy her flirting. I was listening and watching.

"Yes." She pointed across the street.

An old Chevy was parked on Edbrooke, directly across from the pizza parlor. I walked her very quickly to it, opened the door, and shoved her into it.

"I don't have keys," she protested.

I hot-wired it.

"How will I...?"

"Just go. Now."

Instinctively, I stepped back into the shadowed doorway of a boarded-up grocery shop as she drove away. An alien movement caught my attention and made me take cover. It was alien because it did not belong in the place where I saw it, at the time that I saw it, on Christmas Eve. I stood in the shadows and peered across the street into the plate glass front of the pizza parlor. There was a tall shape at the telephone. Joshua Atkinson? Working, no doubt. Catching up after the pre-holiday rush or to prepare for the post-holiday rush. Why on the phone? Talking to his family. 'I'll be home by four o'clock. Tell the kids.' Did a man like Joshua Atkinson have a family? Why did his presence in his own place of business disturb me? Why did his phone call disturb me?

I waited and watched, disturbed.

My instinct was right. He came out of his shop in a manner I recognized. He did not want to be seen. He moved, he slunk, into position to check the east side of the Jared building. I could not see it, but I knew that Charlie should be up there. Was Atkinson acting as backup for Charlemagne? He ran across the intersection diagonally, crossing both streets at once and coming to the left, or west, of the apartment building, out of Charlie's view. He flattened himself against it. No. He was no backup. At least not for Charlemagne.

I pulled my weapon and followed quickly when he disappeared onto the roof of the lean-to at the back of the building. I stood precariously on the same trash can he had used to get up there, straining to hold myself by the elbows on the lowest point of the sloping corrugated plastic roof. There was no time to climb after Atkinson. He was at the other corner of the building, looking up, his gun pointing up toward the street, or toward Sarah's kitchen fire escape. He was ready to shoot.

I was in an awkward position and maybe should have taken greater care, but I did not know how much care Atkinson was taking. I only knew I had to fire before he did.

The bullet hit him in the right hip and spun him suddenly so that he dropped his weapon and slid down the sloping roof toward me. I should have been prepared for it, but the recoil from my weapon overbalanced me and I fell heavily onto my back, with the wind knocked out of me. I was not yet able to breathe when Atkinson launched himself at me from the roof eight feet above. I rolled away in time. He did not wait to catch his own breath before he attacked. His strength and size were superior to mine, but not his skill. I had only luck and better training. I used these.

I lost my gun, which was lucky, because I had been losing the battle for control of it. I gave a mighty heave when I saw the barrel pointing at my neck and felt the pressure of his hand on the finger I had on the trigger. The gun escaped both of us, flew against a trash can and discharged the round in the chamber. His other hand was closing around my throat and I had no way to dislodge it. My empty hand found a broken piece of concrete, flat with a sharp edge. I brought it up against his left temple. It was almost unnecessary; the unguided round from my gun had hit him just below the ribs and he could no longer breathe. He fell heavily, blue-tinged, bleeding and dying.

I looked up when I noticed the shadow. Charlie was standing on the lean-to roof, telling me to move. There was a suppressor on his Glock and my heart was pounding in my brain. I barely heard it as he put a bullet in Atkinson's head.

"Find your gun and get up here," Charlie said.

"The phone rang and things went sour," he continued as I scrambled back onto the trash can. "It's a stand-off. Papa against Slavin, Louis grinning at Jello and Jello quivering in a corner. Everybody's ready to shoot, but The Barracuda has his gun in the girl's ear. So it's up to me and here is what you're going to do."

"Me?"

He hoisted me to an unsteady stand on the roof. His strength was incredible.

"You said it's up to you," I babbled. "I can't...."

"Shut up." He pushed me diagonally up the roof. "Screw your rules. We're talking nanoseconds in timing here. The Barracuda's behind a microwave and some cabinets. I don't have anything lethal to shoot at, so you're going to help move him."

"I...."

"You're going to draw his fire. I'd do it, but he might hit me and that would ruin my aim."

"Hit?"

"Don't worry. He might miss."

"Might!"

"Listen, Steve," said Charlie. He shoved me up against the corner of the building. "Remember, you're on his list. You're a dead man anyway. Don't think we're going to stick around for your sake if the girl goes down."

I climbed the rusted fire escape ladder slowly, trying to be quiet and trying not to fall off.

"What about the mother?" I whispered over my shoulder.

"She's down. Be quiet."

I reached the third floor and crawled toward the front of the building. I cut my hand on broken glass below the Jareds' blown out kitchen window and looked inside from a bottom corner. I could see the Frenchman standing in the dining area off the kitchen, looking down into a far corner, smiling. A counter ran under the window and along a wall running perpendicular from it on the left. Cabinets were attached to the wall about eighteen inches above the counter. A small microwave stood at the end of it, maybe a dozen feet from me. I could see a shoulder in what looked like a tweed coat, between the top of the microwave and the bottom of the cabinet.

"Aim high," whispered Charlie. "But don't hit anything. Shoot at the top of the cabinet, then stay put so he has something to shoot at."

I looked at him. His expression was businesslike. He could have been a broker telling me to buy AT&T. I rose to my knees, faced into the window, and fired.

I heard three shots at almost the same moment. One was my unsuppressed Smith & Wesson booming across the tense stillness that had been. Next came two silenced shots: Charlie's next to my ear, and The Barracuda's. I should not have been able to hear that one, given the chaos of the moment, but I heard it distinctly, because it hit me.

I knew I was hit as I hung below the window, but that did not concern me as much as the possibility that Charlie might let go of my coat. He was not a lot better off. One arm was looped over the window sill; the other held me. The fire escape clanged as it settled in a jagged heap on the ground below us, kicking up a red dust. Through the noise and the ringing in my ears, I heard a man screaming, high pitched and sobbing but definitely male.

Louis and Mack pulled us in through the window. I lay panting on the kitchen counter for a few seconds, half strangled, my left arm strangely numb, until Mack yanked me off, set me on my feet and shoved me toward the dining room table. Under the table, Louis crouched over the still form of Cordelia Jared. Janey sat by her mother's side, holding her hand, rocking and sobbing with an increasing intensity that was growing into hysteria. Already, her cries were replacing the noise from Jello, bruised and bleeding in a corner of the living room. His screams were now mere whimpers.

"Babysit," ordered Mack, shoving me toward the group under the table.

"Tell her," Louis said in German, "that her mother is alive, but she must not move her. Tell her to hold her hand until the ambulance comes. It will be here soon. You stay with her."

Charlie gave me a series of instructions about a commuter flight to Detroit out of Midway airport in the morning. I absorbed his instructions passively, without understanding them, distracted by the crescendo of Janey's screams.

Mack shoved me again, roughly, so that, though he struck the back of my left shoulder, I felt a searing pain in the front, on the side of my neck, bringing me back to an even more painful awareness of everything that was going on. I envied Cordelia her unconscious oblivion.

"Do something about the girl!" Mack shouted at me.

I looked down at Janey. She was now out of control.

Charlie pointed at Jello and said to Mack, "What about him?"

I knelt by Janey and took her in my arms, muttering something soothing. My grip on her was enough to prevent physical damage, but I failed to stop her from seeing Jello die, and I regret that because he died badly when Mack cut him. I don't know why. He should have slumped quietly, but instead, he threw his arms up and his legs out, flailing at the air and spewing blood with a look of horror on his face. I held Janey screaming and I wanted to scream with her. But I told her not to look and turned her face away.

We waited for the ambulance no more than five minutes though it seemed longer, and Janey was calm during the last part of it. We waited in the silence and smell of spent gunfire, spilled blood, and satiated rage.

But what pierced me through more than worry, sorrow, and pain, all of which I felt then, was the knowledge—not the intellectual kind stored in a few brain cells but knowledge organic, permeating every part of me—the knowledge that the hatred in that room would not be buried with the corpses that waited with us.

TWENTY-THREE

Jay met me in the ambulance and gave me a shopping bag with some things in it. Christmas gifts, he said, and a message to please deliver them. I spent the night in a windowless closet of a room at Roseland Community Hospital, contemplating the gifts, unwrapped and without addresses or explanation. *Another fucking test*, I thought wearily. Another logic puzzle. But despite the pain, I was comfortable and the puzzle helped to pass the time until my watcher fell asleep and I could get out shortly before dawn.

I found Janey in another closet-room near the intensive care unit. She was calm, in an adult way, with a maturity that frightened me. Her eyes were badly swollen from crying and her soft brown hair was matted in a wild series of flatnesses ranged about her head like fields on a terraced mountainside. She told me with a hopeful note in her voice that her mother was expected to live, but the music in her tone was flattened, and the hope had a tinny ring to it.

She gazed at the object I held out to her for a long time before looking into my face incredulously.

"You expect me to accept that from him?"

I shrugged. I didn't know what I expected.

"Jerry's my enemy," she said flatly. "He is the worst kind of enemy. He pretended to be my friend."

I was tempted to remind her that it was Jerry who shot The Barracuda, but it occurred to me she might not consider that such a very great favor right now.

She looked again at the gift in my hand. I looked down at it too, searching for something to say. It was an exquisite little music box. I turned the key, and a porcelain ballerina, slender and wearing a tutu, turned in a slow pirouette on a crystal stage.

I looked at Janey, and as if to fill a pause in an ordinary conversation, I said, "His sister was a dancer, you know."

She stared at me for a long time, and I watched her piece everything together silently. I could see her understanding grow and her expression change. It did not comfort me but only frightened me more because I thought she was far too young to share such a history. She took the box from my hand.

"Tell him thank you," she said to me with a steady eye. "But I know we are still enemies."

Then she dismissed me. Without word or gesture, she shut me out. I knew it and accepted it because she was no little girl on the edge of adolescence. She was a product of centuries.

...

I found Sarah at the address she had slipped to me as I shoved her into her car. Her mother answered the door with the same smile, bestowing it on me with equal generosity. Sarah joined in until I was surrounded by smiles. They were happy to see me.

They invited me in. A tin tree in a corner supported a few blue and white bulbs. Christmas cards proclaimed "Season's Greetings" from a table surrounded by a sectional sofa in black vinyl. I was invited to sit down. I declined.

Sarah enthusiastically accepted the bottle of expensive and unpronounceable French perfume I gave her from Louis. It was one of those rare occasions when it's good to be the messenger. She acted as though the gift came from me.

Her mother offered me coffee. I declined again. I desperately wanted a cup of coffee that morning, but the pain around my neck was getting worse and I had to catch a flight. I disentangled myself from Sarah's affection and shifted my left arm painfully in its sling. This only increased their concern, and their sympathy, and their attempts to comfort me, but I fought hard and managed to get out of there with my virtue intact.

...

There was a sad grey light over the city by seven that morning when I approached the little house behind the gas station and entered the backyard from an alley. The miniature clouds I produced by breathing seemed to be the only things hinting at life in the still neighborhood, but when I stood before the back door, I felt a difference here. I heard squeals of laughter in little voices, pans rattling in the kitchen, slippers on the kitchen floor. I knocked.

The door opened. Samantha's face changed as quickly as did comments and questions—delight, concern, confusion. She invited me in.

A small child ran into the kitchen in Mickey Mouse slippers and Batman pajamas. "Look, Gamma!" he said, holding up a toy space shuttle. "Look what I got!"

"Now didn't I ask you to wait until I come back?" She opened the oven door. "I'll be right there. Tell everybody to be patient."

She basted an enormous turkey that was already filling the house with the smell of sage and onions. She closed the oven door, poured coffee in a mug, and stuffed the mug into my good hand, not listening to my polite refusal. It was hot and delicious and very needed, but I spilled a few drops on the spotless linoleum floor as Samantha pulled me by the sleeve into the living room.

"Everybody! Look who's here!" she shouted over the din.

I was cheered at as if I were Santa himself by people who had never seen me before. They cleared away torn wrappings and ribbons from a place on the sofa and directed me to it. It took fifteen minutes for George to introduce me to those of his children and their families who had come from out of town. Samantha elaborated each introduction, so that I knew most of each family's history by the time she was finished. The local children would come later that afternoon, she told me. I wondered how they would all fit in that little house. The room was very full already. The unwrapping had begun again in earnest as soon as Samantha came into the room and continued through the introductions, punctuating them with excited squeals.

I took the little box out of my pocket and gave it to Sam. George looked over her shoulder as she opened it. She took out a small cross of diamonds on a fine gold chain. Her husband helped her with the clasp.

She beamed at me with tears in her eyes. "From Mack?"

I nodded.

"You've seen him? How is he?" asked George.

I did not know what to say. Obviously, these people knew him differently than I did. I shut out the memory of the killer I had seen in action the previous afternoon and remembered instead the cold, hostile man I had met in an airport restaurant. That was no help.

"Tired," is how I answered George.

It was not easy to refuse their invitation to dinner. The house was comfortable and warm. There was something delicious announcing itself from the kitchen. The people were friendly and interesting and their children delightful. But I had my own to go to and I was becoming impatient to get there. As I said goodbye to everyone and walked back to the kitchen with George and Samantha, I understood what it was that Mack had found here at a time when he no longer had his own. This was a world in which every face was a window to a human soul. It must have saved his life. It certainly saved the lives of others.

I remembered one of those others sitting alone in a little room at Roseland Hospital. I told them about Janey and gave them Jay Turner's number to arrange something. As I stood with my hand on the kitchen door, George gave Sam one of his significant 'leave us' looks which I was just beginning to recognize, and turned to me.

"I saw you, you know," he began quietly. "I heard a gunshot and I ran over to see what I could do. I watched you two up there, you and Mack's kid, saw you fall. I was trying to figure out a way to help when the other two pulled you in. I didn't realize you were one of them when you came here the other day."

You can't keep your hands clean if you dig in the dirt. Even if you use a shovel.

I said to George, "I'm not one of them."

He answered me with a look that asked my own question. *What are you then?*

I pondered this on the flight home. *Unemployed* was the first answer I came up with.

...

An artsy-crafty wreath decorated my front door. The minivan was parked on the street and needed washing. My wife met me as soon as I cleared the wreath. I kissed her, held her, and buried my face for a minute in the brown hair that fell to her shoulders in soft ringlet curls. She led me to the sofa and took the shopping bag with the last gift still in it. This constituted my luggage, since everything else had been checked onto another flight at O'Hare the day before.

The solution to the last puzzle from Charlemagne eluded me and I brought it home thinking I'd return it through Frank. It was a pen and stationery set, obviously for a woman, but I had no clue as to which woman. The pen was expensive, chrome with gold trim, very feminine. The paper was also expensive, but it was the pattern around the border that threw me.

It didn't fit any of the women I had met. It was too young for the old Czech lady, and anyway, there was only fear in that relationship. It was too pink and bourgeois for Cordelia Jared. The design was one of those pseudo-country designs with rocking horses done in pink, white and blue, like the rocking horses we had all over our kitchen. It was just the sort of thing my wife would like, I realized, as a frost took a grip on my heart.

I collapsed on the sofa without even asking about my son. Two inches of snow lay on the lawn reflecting the light of a sunny December day over my shoulder through the open curtains behind me. My wife sat next to me and took the stationery set out of the bag.

"How nice," she said.

"No," I said in muted panic. "It's not for you."

"Yes, it is." She opened the box and took out the item that had puzzled me most. It was a small plastic envelope holding a folded piece of carbon paper, business sized, larger than the stationery.

"And this is for you." She handed me the envelope.

Sometimes it is impossible to move in a nightmare.

"They came the day you left," she said carefully. "They were charming. They said they knew you. We had coffee. They said you were waiting for a flight to Chicago and they would be on it with you, but they promised you would be home for Christmas. I knew I shouldn't have let them in when they took off their coats and I saw all the guns. And the one, Michael's father, he really frightens me." She looked down at the box on her lap, then up at me again, biting her lower lip.

I was still speechless.

"They explained a lot," she continued. "They said I had a need to know because it affects me. I'll say it does." There was accusation in her voice.

"The tallest one was unhappy with the locks on the doors and windows," she said. "He put new ones in and said to tell you not to change them. There are no devices in them, he said. There are devices you won't find, but they're not in the locks, so keep them. These are necessary. He said the new locks won't stop him, but they will stop most." She glanced at the playpen in the corner where our son slept.

"Sally...."

"Be quiet and listen," she interrupted. "This is important. I am to tell you that the rules are changed and from now on you follow their rules. Michael said they would prefer no more files, period, but they know this is unrealistic in a bureaucracy. So they decided on a compromise. They want to be on the mailing list."

She paused to see if I understood. I nodded. "He asked me for a picture of us." She paused again when she saw the alarm on my face. "I gave him one. Michael's father said to tell you that he now has a file on you. Anything you write, anything you find, anything you feel you have an urge to steal, needs to be in it."

I stood up and looked at the living room of my home on Christmas Day. The tree was the same, decorated with wreaths and geese saying 'welcome'. The clock on the piano ticked. The sofa was flowery, overstuffed and comfortable. I could smell a turkey like Samantha's, with sage and onions. But for once, I was not hungry.

I walked to the window. There was a new lock on it. Outside I had a picture-perfect view of middle America, safe suburbia. I wanted, briefly, to return to it, but it was only a painting with no space in it for me. I had been painted out. I closed the curtains.

TWENTY-FOUR

Frank gave Jello's eulogy. He said nice things about him, did his gagging privately. It was too secret, they decided, or it was too embarrassing, to publish the truth, and so, for the sake of the family, for the sake of the Section, for the sake of.... Jello's coffin had a flag on it. Frank almost walked out when he saw it. A few of us put on a military display of honorably removing and folding it for Jello's widow. Nobody seemed to notice we were a few hours early. Then we marched Frank up to the pulpit where he delivered a few diluted platitudes with a taut smile. Some people thought the occasional choking in his voice was evidence of how attached he had been to his fallen comrade. Several colleagues told him this, and when he choked again at the word comrade, they took it as proof that no amount of bureaucratic wrangling could come between true friends.

Friendship was a sore topic with Frank after Jello's death because he knew he had lost his friendship with Mack, lost it before he knew he had it. I still don't know what was said in that men's room at O'Hare airport, but it was probably the first time those two ever spoke an honest word to each other in a decade and a half. How they had developed an affection for each other is beyond me, but I am convinced it was this that kept Frank alive when all the evidence was against him.

Frank did not forget my part in Alex's miracle. Maybe as a reaction against the possibility of failing another friend, he stuck by me during the ordeal of the following months.

The aftershocks of Jello's betrayal registered quite a few points on the Section scale. Damage assessment was constant and penetrating. There was even talk about alerting the FBI concerning Jay Turner. This idea was quashed at a higher level, though, where interagency cooperation is unfashionable.

After investigation came retribution, vindictive and indiscriminate. I was an early victim. The board decided that I killed Joshua Atkinson who was, they discovered, a sleeper agent recruited by the KGB in Cambodia and activated for this operation. They decided I killed him because they found an extra bullet of mine lodged in a beam of the lean-to. From this, they deduced that the round that hit his heart was no accident. I don't know how that extra bullet got there. They insisted Charlie's round was not the cause of death. I had to acknowledge that I broke a few rules, and I suppose I was not very cooperative during the polygraph. Anyway, I was sacked.

Almost.

Frank went out on a limb from his new exalted position in the late Jello's office and reminded them of the need for verification. The board tried to contact the only witness to Atkinson's death, the one whose bullet they said could not have killed him. They could not contact him. Frank tried. He failed, too. They asked me to try and as luck would have it, I managed to set up a meeting in a hotel room in Berne.

The main result of that meeting was my retention as an employee and as Charlemagne's American babysitter. I kept my new job, but along with it I took on what seems to be an indelible stigma of suspicion. I became a leper.

Sometimes it can be funny, as it was when I heard two rookies whispering about me by the coffee machine. I popped out at them from around the corner, and they disappeared down the corridor in a flash, leaving me a hot cup of coffee in the machine. Free.

Most of the time, though, my reputation is a disability that threatens my effectiveness. Frank tells me not to worry. He says it was the same when he started. It will wear off, he says.

I wish I could be so sure, but I see too many differences between Frank and me to count on my career following his. One example is my relationship with Charlie. We use the familiar form, *du*, with each other. Mack and Frank never used anything but the formal, *Sie*.

I think the biggest difference between us was implied by Mack during that meeting in Berne. There were six of us in the room, drinking a bottle of Charlie's scotch. I was sorry to see that Frank and Mack did not speak to each other. The chairman of the board that was sacking me asked them about a dozen unnecessary questions, all of them ignored with icy stares. Charlie was a singularly uncooperative witness.

Exasperated, the chairman said finally, "Why did you agree to this meeting?"

"Steve requested it," Charlie said with a shrug.

"Is Donovan the only one who can request a meeting with you?"

Charlie nodded and poured a little more into my glass.

"Why?" The chairman was warming up now that he was getting a few responses.

Mack answered. He leaned back in his chair, relaxed, but still caustic. He smiled half way, maybe from the scotch, or from the joke Louis had just told him in French. Anyway, it was at least half a smile, but it disappeared when he answered the chairman.

"When the Allies liberated Dachau," he said, "they were so appalled at what they saw, that they shot the camp guards on the spot."

The chairman wrinkled his brow, trying to take this in.

"They broke the rules," said Mack.

"Who?" asked the chairman. "The camp guards or the Allies?"

"The Allies. They killed their prisoners. The men they killed had obeyed their orders by killing their prisoners."

Frank and I looked at each other in surprise. This was a virtual flood from a man who usually kept his words to himself.

"I don't understand." At least the chairman was honest.

Maybe that was why Mack explained more without sounding irritated. "Bureaucracies depend on men who follow the rules. Controlling a bureaucracy depends on men who know when to break them."

"But breaking the rules can go too far." The chairman shifted in his chair. "It can be disastrous."

This time Louis spoke. "Yes. It requires the ultimate risk, the risk of being wrong."

"We have many men besides Donovan," insisted the chairman, "who are Allies, not camp guards, who are capable of taking that risk."

"Perhaps," said Mack. He looked at the scotch in his glass.

"Will you be willing to work with one of them?"

"No."

"Only Donovan is acceptable?"
"Yes."
"Why?"

Mack leaned forward and looked at me while he answered. Frank said later it was a threat, but I knew better.

"Because he lives where we do," Mack said to the chairman as he looked into, not at, me.

"Where is that?"

Mack raised his glass to me slightly—a toast. "I believe Frank calls it a room without doors."

[cc: WEDGE]

EPILOGUE

The tall man was the kind who always got promoted. He had a manufactured face, except for horsey nostrils and lots of hair that greyed correctly at the temples, inspiring confidence in the wisdom of his years, until he opened his mouth.

"Are you Leo Vilseck?" He pronounced it 'vile sack.'

Leo nodded. "Yes, Sir."

The man wrinkled his horsey nose and looked at the file in front of him.

"This document refers to a Frank Cardova. Who is he?"

"That's me, Sir. I am Frank Cardova. It's my game name. Vilseck is my real name." He pronounced it properly, not being sufficiently subservient to mispronounce his own name.

"Game name?" The man was truly lost now. The other two bureaucrats on the investigative panel leaned in to him from either side. They advised. They explained a little, too. Only a very little. He favored Frank Leo Cardova Vile-Sack with a solemn look, as befits the chairman of a panel, to disguise the fact that he didn't know beans.

He knew so little, in fact, that he was unaware that Frank had pegged precisely how ignorant he was.

"We are here today, Mr. Cardova, to discuss the recent defection of your subordinate, one Stephen Donovan." He looked at the paper again. "And another subordinate, Daniel Martin Kessler." His nose drew up toward his eyebrows. The bureaucrat to his left whispered to him. "They're what? The same man?" He looked up at Frank-Leo. "Do you have anything to say?"

"He hasn't defected, Sir. He just quit."

The bureaucrat on the chairman's right interrupted. "He joined his own team, Buddy. That's a defection."

"Who is Buddy?" asked the chairman.

"Look, Bruno," said Frank, "Steve is free to quit his job any time. It's the American way."

"Are you Bruno?" The chairman looked to his right. "I thought you were Thomas Stevenson?"

"He can't quit and then carry all his secrets across to his team," said Bruno.

"All his secrets were about the team. Which one do you think will surprise Charlemagne?" Frank's bulging eyes threatened to leap out at them.

"Charlene? Is there a woman involved in this?" The chairman searched the paper on the table.

"There are sensitive sources and methods," stammered Bruno.

"Come off it, Bruno," said Frank. "You met them in Berne. What methods do you think Steve could use that Mack wouldn't know about anyway?"

Bruno shuddered.

The chairman searched for some mention of Max.

The man to his left spoke. "I'd just like to know why, Buddy. Can you tell us that?"

"You know why, Gizmo. The third attempt, when his wife's car blew up and the neighbor's cat died under it—their sixth new neighbor in two months—and the baby almost toddled right into the flames trying to save that cat. That's what did it. He didn't have a choice. He has to protect them somehow."

The chairman put his hand to his forehead. "Gizmo?" he muttered.

"You think Charlemagne did it?"

"Of course not, Giz, you bonehead. Steve's got enough enemies of his own to more than qualify him for the team. He's where he belongs. I should have seen it coming long ago."

The chairman tried to regain control. "We must assess the damage, determine what information has been compromised, initiate corrective action, institute legal action."

"Nothing's been compromised," Frank said flatly.

The chairman looked up from the paper he was reading.

"Nothing?"

"Nothing." Frank swung his round head from side to side.

The chairman looked at Gizmo, who covered his upper lip with his lower lip and shrugged. Bruno sighed and pushed back his chair.

"In that case, I find no cause for further action." The chairman closed the file. He noticed for the first time that the cover was striped diagonally with strips of red tape, and in between the strips, a name was printed in bold letters. "Now who," he groaned, "is WEDGE?"

The End

BREVET WEDGE

Early 1980s

Brevet — *A commission promoting a military officer in rank without an increase in pay*

A spy's worst enemy is another spy...
—John LeCarré, *The Pigeon Tunnel*

PROLOGUE

He wanted to kill her.

Nick tapped the ash from the end of his cigarette into an ashtray on the bedside table. He looked at the straw-colored head lying on the pillow next to him. The blankets were none too clean, the sheets a dingy grey in the morning light, but the motel constituted pure luxury for a thief from the Soviet Gulag. He had come far, but this vile woman made the killers he had known seem like saints. They were all hot, vicious, and effective. She epitomized the cold, thoughtless, and selfish. He would rather die by the hand of the first than live with the second.

"You're not still mad at me, are you Nick?" She yawned and stretched bare arms, awakened by the intensity of his stare.

He had a glimpse of one surgically enhanced breast. "It was irresponsible," he said.

"I know. But I did it so we could be together. You'll see. We'll have the insurance money and can go anywhere we want. David will be in college and it'll be just us."

"The people you hired are dead," he told her, snubbing one cigarette and lighting another.

She reached for the one he had started, so he lit yet another for himself.

"I didn't hire anybody," she said after a long drag.

"The ones you manipulated your husband into hiring."

"Oh."

He wanted to tell her all of it, scream it into her face. He clamped his jaw shut lest he lose control.

She blew the smoke through pursed lips and turned to look at him. "Did they get the guy? Ricky's enemy, I mean. Did they get him before they died? Do you think their friends will go after Ricky now, or should I tip off the FBI to make sure?"

Her single-minded ruthlessness took his breath away. He could not explain to her that her actions would not only kill her husband, which was her desired outcome but also put him in jeopardy. He presumed it was not what she wanted, but he couldn't be certain.

"Why the Chinese?" he asked.

"My uncle.... I thought you would be proud of me."

Proud of her? Admiring of her cutthroat proclivities, her inventive, though imbecile, means of achieving her ends? And those ends were directly contrary to anything that might be good for him. He wanted to tell her about the man whose throat had been cut and also what it meant.

"I needed Ricky alive."

"But you said last night that they failed. So he is alive. You're confusing me."

"Six men are dead, Linda. The people who killed them will come for Ricky. They are smart people."

"You know who they are?"

"Yes."

"Maybe you can get them to finish the job, Nick."

It was a germ of an idea, emanating from an evil source, but if he could entice them to rid him of her as well, it would be worth it.

ONE

As a senior intelligence officer, I can't not make a record, no matter what Mack says. I will lock this up at my bank rather than at work since I now know how unsecure all secret systems are. All the caveats and classifications apply. This is WEDGE material. I'm taping it so I can truthfully say I didn't write anything down.

It began as I enjoyed a brief, rapturous moment pulling into my driveway on Friday evening before a long holiday weekend and the beginning of an entire week off.

Oh, wondrous release from the politics—and by God, my job has developed some political strains—the nagging worries, the inanities, the constant battering I receive from above and below. Goodbye, dungeon-like, windowless office. Hello doting, half-dotty, but loving wife, who holds my martini, shaken, not stirred, ready for my imbibing. Sigh.

Sharp intake of breath.

A car with two blond men in it sat parked in front of my house. It was not the usual black Mercedes, but I know Mack when I see him, and I never wanted to see the cutthroat son of a bitch at my house. He did not acknowledge me, though he was frankly watching me. So was his son.

I marched through my front door with my hand on my Walther PPK, ready to do hopeless battle against the missing Frenchman. *I'm sorry about what happened, you assholes, but my family is fucking off limits.* Dear God, I was beginning to sound like Steve and I was ready to fight like him, too, in whatever way my short, round body would allow it.

I was prepared to take the Frenchman apart. He grinned at me from the corner seat at the kitchen table with what I knew had to be my martini sitting in front of him. Steve stood at the kitchen sink drying a crystal glass for my wife Maryann, because she won't let such things go in the dishwasher. She bustled over to the refrigerator, pulled out the shaker, and poured the remains of a batch into a fresh martini glass. It was already in my hand when she added the olive. I stood quivering and my shaking hand threatened to spill the over-full drink, so I threw half of it down my throat to preserve it.

Only the Frenchman, sometimes called Louis, appreciated the state I was in. I could tell by the way he grinned at me. His black eyes twinkled with that mixture of merry madness that always made me shudder. He had grey hair mixed in the dark brown at his temples. It reminded me that the little bit I still have is even more grey. Maryann and Steve joked and jabbered away as usual, the same way they did when we had the Donovans over for barbecue on the happy day of my granddaughter's baptism.

Louis sat in the corner, leaning back and spreading his jacket open so the leather straps of his shoulder rig, the stock of his gun, and the cases of extra magazines on his belt, all advertised themselves directly to my eyes. Yes, he was saying to me, you are right to worry. But don't be stupid.

"Leo," said my wife, "Sally and little Danny are coming to stay for the weekend. Isn't that lovely?" Maryann did not know my game name was Frank Cardova. She didn't know I had a game name. She was overall ignorant of the game I was in.

Maryann thinks all babies are lovely.

I turned up the corners of my mouth. It was expected of me.

"I have to go get her," Maryann said and turned to Steve. "Are you sure she'll come with me?"

There was always that doubt about Sally.

Maryann went to change into something that would make her look less pudgy as if pudginess would thwart her purpose with Sally, and as if there exists an outfit capable of transforming a pudgy body into a supermodel. I followed her into our bedroom.

"Steve is different, you know," was the first thing she said to me.

She wiggled into the new gabardine slacks with the special tummy control panel in front.

"No, I didn't know. Listen, Maryann..."

"I think they want you for the whole weekend. Louis said...."

"Louis! You call him Louis?"

"That's what he said to call him." She giggled. "He kissed my hand. Isn't he precious?"

"He's a killer, Maryann. There's nothing precious about him."

She stuck a round, magenta earring into her earlobe. It matched some of the flowers printed on her blouse.

"I know he's probably dangerous," she said. "But it's hard to imagine. He's so charming. It seems Sally and Danny are in some kind of trouble. They're helping to protect them. Isn't that sweet?"

"By bringing them here? By having you bring them here?"

How sweet.

"Steve says they must not touch their minivan, you know, the silver one. He says there is information that there may be a car bomb. I had no idea Steve had such terrible enemies. Why do you suppose that is?"

I had not told her about the airliner he shot down as an Air Force fighter pilot. I told her now.

"How horrible!" She shook her head, deploring the world as it is. "When I answered the door, Steve pushed his way in and Louis was right behind him. You will help, won't you Leo? Louis said they will need you to stay at the safehouse. He will give you the address."

She put on her mascara by holding the wand steady and blinking her eyelashes down across it. Next came lipstick. She puckered up and put some of it on my cheek on her way out.

The Frenchman chuckled when I gave a last longing look at the half martini still in my glass. He swallowed the rest of his before he left my kitchen and my home. Then Steve and I had a little talk in the laundry room and he told me the score. As with everything else in Steve's life, it began with a fight.

TWO

Steve Donovan is a pretty medium sort of guy. He's medium height and medium weight, with medium brown hair, maybe too much of that, or am I just jealous? Anyway, he has a lot of brown hair that he doesn't always keep well-trimmed and more than medium brown eyes with eyelashes almost like a girl's. This combination earned him the Section nickname Bear.

The token Woman in The Section, which I run, dubbed him that, and gave him a lot of her attention, as women generally do with Steve. He hates the name, but I don't think he minds the attention.

The point is that you wouldn't expect this middle-roader to be a black belt, multiple degrees, in several different styles of martial arts, but he is. He spends much of his free time at it, as he was on the day off I gave him that Friday. He told me he was attending a class in what he called the dojang that morning, having a normal workout, probably beating up one of those big bags that hang from the ceiling, bags that look soft and moveable but are deceptively filled with cement.

Steve turned on instinct when two men came in through the office and sat down in the spectator section. He didn't hear them, he told me, he felt them. They were, of course, Mack and Louis (the Frenchman). They wore suits with ties that were not out of place in a political town like this but did not belong in a karate studio.

The dobok and black belt Charlie wore when he came in did belong, though, and Steve introduced him to his sensei. Everybody was polite. The sensei asked Charlie who his teacher was. Vasily Sobieski, Charlie replied. The instructor didn't think he knew the name. Would he and Steve like to spar?

"Sure," Charlie said.

"What did you say?" I asked Steve when he told me this.

"What the fuck was I supposed to say? No, thank you, it looks like you're here to kill me? Or how about, no, I'd rather have your father over there spectating quietly slit my throat. Shit, Frank. I said sure. Just like Charlie said."

"You thought they were there to take you out?"

"It crossed my mind. They don't make social calls, do they? My mind ran a fast search through the list of The Families trying to find one that might be able to afford to commission them."

The Families was Steve's name for the relatives and friends of people on the airliner he shot down who had sworn vengeance. Steve had been dodging a few handy accidents lately.

"And?" I asked him. "Could any of them afford Charlemagne?"

"No." He shrugged. "Besides, I beat the shit out of Charlie."

I was surprised. "You mean he's not very good?"

"He's fucking great. I'm just better. That's all."

But that wasn't all. I could tell by his tone. I waited.

"Charlie made me look good," he said finally. "In front of the other two. It's a kind of test, Frank, and I've passed the preliminaries."

I looked at him standing there in my laundry room that Friday evening. It was one of our few opportunities to talk privately. He pressed buttons on the washing machine, punched them like they were the enemy. He knew then and I knew then that death is not the only dramatic change that can occur in a life.

"How do you know you passed?" I asked him.

He smiled. "Mack told me I fight like Vasily."

THREE

I checked my back as I drove to the safehouse, circling the route three times to look for watchers. I never saw them. Steve rode with the team, a fact which even in my then-ignorant state I marked as significant, and he told me later they were behind me the whole time. Watching my back was the excuse—no doubt as preparation for shooting me in it. But I never saw them. Their tradecraft is that good.

The place was as generic as safehouses come. I didn't know who had set it up for them. They have networks I am only dimly aware of, and they carefully hid the local one from me. As generics go, the suburbs, the streets, and the neighborhood of this house, even the late summer day, participated in studied plainness. Green lawns and trees ran to olive drab, showing up against the bleached sky without defining lines. It reminded me of Southeast Asia, where everything melted into the booby-trapped landscape. It was maybe not as hot here, but it felt every bit as deceptive and dangerous.

I walked into the house. It smelled like a safehouse. That is to say, there was strong coffee brewing. I helped myself and thought about that half martini I was missing and all my wife's tales of a harmless (to me, but not to her) day's adventures at the coffee morning, the women's book club, the charity bazaar planning committee. Every event sans the Frenchman and his charms.

The team came in behind me. Louis, as usual, swept for bugs right away, forcing us all to chat mindlessly to keep any devices actively transmitting. There were none and he went outside to set up the perimeter sensors, infrared and motion, and took Steve with him. I had never been allowed to observe the details of their security measures. Steve was not only watching; he was being instructed.

That left me standing by the coffee pot staring at the two assassins who blamed me for the loss of wife/mother and daughter/sister less than a year before. Our conversation was more than a little strained, to say the least. In monosyllables, Charlie told me to shut up and wait for a general explanation when Steve and Louis returned.

I drank my coffee.

We gathered like one big happy family at a wobbly kitchen table with twisted metal legs and a white Formica top. It matched the metal and Formica of the kitchen cabinets. The place looked more than commonly institutional. It must be an FBI dive, I thought.

Mack spoke to Steve. I was being allowed to listen but not formally acknowledged as a participant. I was under the increasing impression I was expected to play a role, that my play in this game would require sacrifice, and it would be more than half a martini's worth. I knew I would never be compensated for it, not even to the extent of a simple thank you, but staying alive would be plenty thanks for me.

Mack's Austrian German was as slurpy as ever and I watched Steve struggle to take it in at least as fast as he sometimes can manage good old *hoch Deutsch*, which is to say, not very fast. A government investigation into government corruption gets quicker results.

I've listened to Mack for almost twenty years, so I was able later, when we were alone again briefly, to fill Steve in on the details he missed due to language.

"We have information," Mack told Steve, "that Five-Fifths has a commission on your family."

Always up on the news, Steve said, "Who the fuck is Five Fifths?"

Where did he get the vocabulary? And in two languages?

Charlie answered. "Five-Fifths is a new team. They got their start in the IRA, but are civilians now, operating privately. Their clients are predictable, all bargain basement payers. The team is not good enough yet to demand high fees, but their bomber shows potential. They are becoming noticed."

Steve took all this in, more or less. Charlie's English is American, but his Deutsch is as Austrian as his papa's. Steve swallowed hard and asked in German which made Mack wince—made us all wince—"Who commissioned them?"

"The name is Lorese," said Mack.

I thought I could see a scroll of names running through Steve's mind's eye listing The Families who wanted him, and his, dead.

"They are not one of the usuals," he told Mack.

"No. They are Creoles, living in Surinam. There was an old and distant uncle on that airplane."

Steve was full of questions, crowded in his throat, clamoring to be let out first so they all stuck in the doorway of his mouth making it open and shut three times before one finally squeezed past the others and made its way into intelligible language.

"What do you propose?"

"We propose nothing. This is your affair."

"But you're here. You saved my life. I saw the C4 in my car's wheel well. My wife, my son...."

Charlie interrupted, "What do you want to do, Steve?"

I watched my subordinate's face. I had to. I was losing friends and associates at an astonishing rate this year and here was the latest. Does one become an operational specialist at the first drop of blood, or before then, when the trigger is squeezed. Or does it happen even earlier, at the point of decision?

"I want to kill the mother fuckers," he said.

There are some sticky philosophical problems here. On the one hand, Steve is hunted. I know that my natural reaction in such a case would be to defend myself. Steve is better at that than I would be, and offense is always the best defense. On the other hand, Steve is guilty as sin of the crime for which he is hunted. I like to think I would pay for such a crime, gladly, but then, I'm guilty of helping, in my own careless, bureaucratic way, in the deaths of Mack's wife and daughter, and I am not asked to pay, except in the stony silence of broken acquaintance. Why should I expect Steve to pay? Under whose law? While I can claim the vagaries of bureaucracy, loyalty, and obedience to authority in my defense, so can Steve.

Sally and the baby should need no defense, but they are targets by association. I still have three children at home. The sight of Mack and Charlie in front of my house sent a convulsion of fear through me. I was ready to run the charming Frenchman through with a lance over one pudgy middle-aged woman who mixes great martinis and puts on makeup before going out to rescue the threatened.

Sure, I can condemn Steve's decision. I just can't say I wouldn't have done the same.

So we sat around the table as Steve metamorphosed into a killer and I caught Mack watching me as it sunk in. He turned away quickly.

"Do you want the family dead, too?" was Charlie's next question.

Steve's brow wrinkled. "Of course not. Is it even verified they commissioned it?"

Louis smiled. "No."

"I didn't think so," said Steve. "It's all wrong. They aren't one of The Families; they're too conveniently far away. The old uncle is not even a close connection. No, I want Five Fifths, not the Loreses."

"But somebody is paying Five Fifths," said Louis, always the first to bring up finances.

"Who?"

He shrugged.

"Let's find out." Steve sounded just like Louis, despite his bad Deutsch.

"And then?"

"And then...." Steve's turn to shrug.

There was work to be done before we could find out anything. I got on the horn and lined up all the green stamps I had saved over the years, preparing to cash them in for a toaster oven that would probably burn down my house someday soon. Not that I'm saying Steve's not worth it, or that I don't owe Mack. He is and I do, but that doesn't make it easier to part with one's life savings in favors for a hopeless cause.

When all my ducks had lined up neatly in a row, I turned to what was going on in our humble safehouse, to the domestic tranquility that might very well be possible when only scotch and black coffee are available, but I doubt it. Charlie and Steve were gone. Where? I wanted to know. To watch Steve's car, I was told. Lucky stiffs, I thought, and they'll be so stiff by morning after such an exciting night that the young bully will no doubt take it out on me. I did not know which young bully I meant.

Louis stayed busy at the green screen of a new personal computer, glaring at me every time I tried to have a peek at what he was doing. I didn't see anything precious in the way he sloshed coffee over the carpet or complained about lousy American food.

I sat on the sofa and knew it was a mistake, but had no excuse to move to the hard, straight-backed chair I would need to stay awake. Mack sat in an easy chair, watching a sensor screen flashing green dots at him from a briefcase on his lap. I stared at him unwillingly, asleep with my eyes open, until little bells going off in what was left of my common sense warned me he was staring back at me.

I guess I closed my eyes soon after that and laid my head half on the back of the sofa and half on my shoulder. My neck froze in that position, stretching one side and shrinking the other so that sitting up became a painful contortion, but I had to get to my feet fast. Mack was kicking me in the shin, not hard enough to break it, but hard enough, and saying something about 'having them.' I heard Charlie's voice coming over the radio, reciting street names.

"Go wake Louis," said Mack. In German it was even shorter, only two words instead of three.

I hit the corner of the wall as I stumbled into the short hallway, bruising my shoulder and making what I hoped was enough noise to wake the Frenchman before I got to the door. People with reflexes like his are not safe to wake up. I reached the bedroom door, knocked, and cleared my throat. I opened the door slowly, careful not to stand directly in the doorway, then looked inside and reached my hand in, feeling along the wall to turn on the light.

The Frenchman was sprawled diagonally across a double bed, completely dressed, except for his jacket. His tie was loosened and his shirt sleeves rolled up. One arm was flung up over his eyes.

Surely the bastard wasn't going to make me come in and shake him. He had to be awake. I noticed the way his shirt and belt met in the middle smoothly, without overlap by one or the other, both looking expensive, and the whole effect being one of well, but not over, fed health.

I'd look like that—well, I wouldn't be as tall—if I worked out several hours a day the way these guys did. But I have a living to make, food and shelter to provide for four other people, college tuition for three more, and I'm still paying for the wedding of another one. That means I have to spend most waking hours in a windowless box reading reports by fluorescent light in between brief episodes of gut-wrenching terror, testing heart-attack theories by drinking whole pots of strong coffee.

I stepped into the room and cleared my throat again. The bastard was being his old charming self all right. I sighed and walked up to the bed, reached a hand toward his shoulder, and stopped when he said, "What?"

...

I never use my vehicles for things like this, mostly because things like this are rarely conducted in my own country, this being another agency's jealously guarded turf, but circumstances dictated otherwise and the three of us climbed into my car after checking for booby traps.

Circumstances are tricky things, and the one that led me to delay buying a new alternator in July was particularly unlucky. Strong prayer got the car started anyway. Mack did not look at me, staring straight ahead through the windshield as I cranked the engine, but his lips were so tightly compressed, they threatened to turn white. I could hear the precious Louis sneering through his teeth at me from the back seat. The car ran fine once it started.

The radio Mack held crackled. He turned up the volume, and Steve gave us directions to the Five-Fifths safehouse.

FOUR

I knew when I turned off the ignition that it was not going to start again. There was nothing I could do. The neighborhood was unfriendly. My companions were unfriendly. Five-Fifths, the most unfriendly of all, had holed themselves up in an industrial complex, between a restaurant supply and an auto body shop. The entrance to their lair was a rolling metal door, truck-sized, in a concrete wall.

I parked on the next block and had to tell Mack and Louis before they left that the car wasn't going to start again. They were checking their weapons at the time, preparing to run to the rendezvous with the other two, and my news was unwelcome. Mack's blue eyes did plenty of cutting into my ego. He told me, in syllables, to go to their car, an ill-fitting BMW, on the other side of the industrial site.

It took me twenty minutes to get there by a roundabout way. It was a humid night and I was sweating. I could not touch the car; the alarms were set in a way only they knew, and if I disturbed them, the car would be unusable. Disturbing them for no reason also would be useless to me. I didn't have the keys. So I shivered in a doorway as the night temperature dropped and condensation formed on my scalp. I had to be careful to stay out of the view of security cameras on the industrial buildings around me. I listened for footsteps.

I had used up twenty minutes in getting there, and it was another twenty before I heard what I wanted: running footsteps, two sets, no, four. How many men were in Five Fifths? I tried to remember. Five, or six? Six. They wouldn't run to the car if they were the victors. They wouldn't know about this car any more than they would know about the broken one two blocks away. And they couldn't care less about a shivering babysitter in a doorway. I shrank back a little anyway. I could see my belt buckle catching the light from a security lamp across the street. It glittered like a beacon.

Charlie threw the car keys at me. "You drive, Frank."

I had to take my hand off my Walther PPK to catch the keys, which is a good thing because fingering my old friend was a self-preservation gesture that could have killed me. Louis had seen my hand inside my coat and I was already looking down the barrel of his Modèle 1935. From my angle, it seemed his night sights were centered just above my nose.

"Where?" I asked as I started the engine.

"It doesn't matter," said Charlie. "Drive around and check our back."

He was my passenger. Steve sat squashed between Mack and Louis in the back seat. The car was not roomy. It was a BMW, not their usual Mercedes, with no armor, and the radios were mounted improperly, sliding around under the gear shift. I felt a little smug as I considered the obvious failings of whomever they had suborned into providing this piece of junk. I always provided more than adequate vehicles.

There was some catching of breath, after their, shall we say, exertions, and then the run to the car. They smelled of cordite. In the rearview mirror, I saw the Frenchman's eyes move constantly under the street lights, watching for bogeymen in the streets. He turned every few minutes to stare behind us. Charlie gave me continuous directions for back-checking and losing tails, and it took all my strength to seal my lips so I would not blurt out—to my guaranteed detriment—what I thought about having some kid teach me my trade. Their tradecraft is superb, but he didn't tell me anything I didn't already know, and if he did, I missed it, as I would not have done if his father had said it.

After ten minutes of turns, stops and starts on a humid night, and maybe there were other reasons, old iron-stomach Steve spewed.

He'd had a few donuts and a lot of coffee. Much of it soaked Mack's pant leg. Louis protested loudly. I swerved to pull off the road, and they rushed to get Steve out of the car, but he was already finished and it was pooled on the floor on both sides of the hump in the back, inching its way forward under the front seats. They put Steve in a window seat then, and Mack made him ride doubled over, saying this would help, but breathing it all in with such close proximity only gave him the dry heaves. We opened all the windows because we were all in danger, and Mack finally let Steve sit up and breathe air.

"Is there anything back at that warehouse that I should be taking care of?" I asked with a casual air.

"Like what?" Charlie gave me an innocent look.

"Like bodies. Evidence. Police. That sort of thing."

"Is that what you do?" asked Charlie. "I thought you just made bad coffee. I suppose there must be a reason for your existence."

I squashed the sudden urge to throttle the brat.

"There is a phone." He pointed to the console between us, where a box slid back and forth between the seats. "Use it."

"I'm driving," I reminded him. "And at any rate, I have to be there, I can't take you with me, and I don't have a vehicle."

There were a few moments of silence, like a memorial to lost babysitters everywhere, and then the Frenchman said, "Your wife has a car."

"How the hell do you know what my wife has?" It was out before I could stop it. Of course, my wife had to take something to collect Sally and the baby, and only a moron would not be able to deduce from that fact that she had her own car, as does any other American woman in our socioeconomic class, another telling fact to the average moron, and of course, Louis is no moron. But he had no business even thinking about my wife. I saw his eyebrows rise in the rearview mirror, and he fired off a significant glance to his side, where Mack no doubt returned it.

FIVE

"Really, Leo, I can't believe you would do such a silly thing." She swabbed the knot on my forehead. "What made you do it?" I looked around. I was in my bedroom, on my bed. My wife was wrapping a washcloth around an ice cube. She put it on the bump. She wore the brocade bathrobe I gave her for her birthday, the one from the sexy lingerie store at the mall.

"Who brought me up here?" I asked.

"Steve and Charlie."

I remembered lunging for the Frenchman. "Did I hit him?"

"No," she said.

"Did he hit me?" I did not remember seeing him move.

"No. He moved away and you fell forward into the washing machine." She went to her closet. "Nobody's ever kissed my hand before, Leo," she called from the racks. "I wish you hadn't spoiled it. I'm not used to such gallant manners. I was enjoying it."

Evidently. "He's very polite when he shoots people, always says *may I*." I took the ice cube off my head and threw it at the closet door.

She came out wearing a magenta jogging suit and wrinkled her little nose at me. "You keep saying that," she said. "But I can't imagine it."

"Try. There are six examples of his work in an industrial park a few miles down the highway. I have to go clean it up. I need to get on the phone with Chief Harkon and then I'll take your keys. My car's dead. We'll pick it up in the morning."

"Louis killed six people?"

"He helped."

I stood up, fought down the spinning sensation, then the nausea, pulled her into my arms, and buried my sore head in her dark chestnut hair. I crushed one side of her 'do'. She impatiently plumped it back out with her fingers, but she smiled at me and kissed my bruise gently.

"I didn't see Pete's car in the drive," I said. Pete is our eldest son still at home.

"He and Michael are staying at the wrestling coach's house tonight. They have a match in the morning." Maryann opened the bedroom door and shepherded me out.

I nodded. Michael is our youngest son still at home. I was glad the boys were not in the house. That left Theresa, my daughter, to worry about. A big enough worry.

From the top of the stairs, I heard voices in the kitchen. "My God! They're still here!"

"Yes, of course, Leo. They're hungry. I told them to help themselves."

Downstairs, I heard the refrigerator door close, the clink of plates and utensils, and a feminine giggle. I counted on help from Steve, but he wasn't there. Mack and Louis sat at the kitchen table, drinking coffee and eating coffee cake. Charlie leaned casually across the counter, smiling at my daughter. He was no more than a foot away from her, as she built a hoagie on a baguette, using everything available in the house, from mayonnaise to my favorite Genoese salami. She giggled at something Charlie was saying to her as I stormed in.

"Where the hell is Steve?" I demanded of Charlie.

I wanted his eyes off my daughter's legs. He had been slyly stealing glances at her thighs. She wore jogging shorts and a cropped college sweatshirt. Her dark brown wedge haircut was messy, but only in the most becoming way. There was mascara on her eyelashes, the little vixen, but nothing covered the sprinkle of freckles across her nose.

Charlie paused and gave me the same blue-eyed X-ray stare I'd had so many times from his father. "Steve is in the garage, cleaning the car." It was a calm, matter-of-fact answer, delivered in a way that heightened the contrast between his state and mine. "Are you going to attack the sink the same way you did the washing machine, Frank?"

"You son of a bitch, she's eighteen!" I probably shouted this. I've been told I did.

Maryann came in behind me saying, "Shhh! The neighbors!"

Charlie answered me with a very cold, "My sister would have been fifteen this month."

Simultaneously, Theresa said, "Dad!" but in a way that it took much longer than a three-letter, single-syllable word should take to be said and heard. My wife, meanwhile, repeated her theories about the neighbors.

"Go to your room!" I told Theresa.

Maryann sounded like a snake with her shushing. Louis laughed. Steve's wife, Sally, came in from the garage wearing a pair of wet rubber gloves and carrying a bucket that stank. She shouted something about some men being beyond all help and tossed the contents of the bucket down the sink drain, which set Theresa off about the knife there that she wanted to use to cut the sandwich. I repeated my order to Theresa. She defied me with a loud "No!" and gave Sally a dirty look.

My wife found her another knife for the sandwich and delivered it with a lecture on manners. Louis roared with laughter. Sally filled the bucket again and sloshed it through the kitchen, then the laundry room, and finally out the door to the garage, which she slammed. Charlie deliberately ran a finger lightly over the skin of my daughter's leg, and if I'd had chest pains then, my sense of doom could not have been greater.

I was shouting at the top of my lungs now, and could feel it, could feel that my eyes were not blinking because they burned, could feel my hand reaching toward the gun I had never used except to qualify once a year, reaching hopelessly I knew, because Charlie was so much faster, so much more accurate, so much deadlier than I am that it was no match. I was going to die. But by God, I had to....

"Michael."

It was said quietly, in German. It made the whole room quiet because, until that moment, Mack had said nothing. He followed the single word with a significant look.

I thought, at first, he was talking about my son, *auf Deutsch*. Had the boy come home? No. Mack meant his own son. Charlie's real name is Michael. Charlie, aka Michael, snatched his hand away from my daughter's leg like it had been burned by dry ice and he couldn't detach it fast enough without leaving behind skin from his fingers. He lowered his eyes, looked away from mine, extinguished the defiance. He took his other hand out of his coat, off the Glock in its holster, and sat at the table, across from his father, away from my daughter, eyes down.

I was impressed. My daughter was still slicing the sandwich. I took my hand away from my gun and grasped Theresa's arm to propel the disobedient child from the room. My wife restrained me. I admit it would have been undignified, but I was shamed into wanting some obedience, even at the cost of a scene.

Mack defused this, too. "You have something to do," he said, looking at me only briefly, only long enough to get the words out and make them imperative.

SIX

"They're all slimy. And he's the slimiest. He looks like a frog, a lumpy, bald frog, and if that's what you think you're married to, that and the sneaky, dirty job that man does, then have at it. I'm not going with you, and neither is Danny."

Sally turned at the sound of the door shutting behind me. I was in the garage now, standing on the little step at the door to the laundry room. The BMW was in front of me, my wife's car parked on the other side of it. Sally and Steve stood between them. She had been speaking with some heat and was breathing hard. He had that blank look that I've tried myself once or twice, never successfully, the external evidence of an internal war against committing oneself to any certain action in an uncertain situation. His mouth was open slightly. He was doing a good job of looking unintelligent.

I cleared the rear bumper of the beamer before they moved. It was a poignant moment. Then, Sally threw a sponge into the bucket between them, splashing Steve's pants, and stomped past him and around the front of the car. She slammed the laundry room door shut behind her.

I might have paid more attention to being called slimy if my mind were not so full of Theresa. Justice where it is due, Charlie is everything a father looks for in a daughter's suitor. He is rich, educated, and intelligent (one does not always follow the other), and he looks respectable. She would find him handsome, no doubt, with his blue eyes and blond hair, perfect build, and he's witty, oh yes, very witty. All of that, except that he kills for a living. He kills bad guys, other killers, society's pathogens, but he kills, and in the end, that's all he does, like a poison called medicine, a human chemotherapy.

I remembered another babysitter's daughter, Alexandra Dolnikov, daughter of my old boss Fred. Now she's the widow of Vasily

Sobieski, the team's dead explosives expert. I wondered about her for a moment, locked up somewhere with her child for safety, protected by Mack, Louis, and Charlie. She was not much older than Theresa is now when she first met Sobieski. I'd been pretty smug when I told Fred the score back then.

"Listen!" Steve and I said it together. Then we said, again together, "You first."

I went first because I'm the boss. But I forgot what I was going to say. "You sure know how to impress a new boss, Steve. I'm glad you didn't throw up on me."

The car door was open. It oozed a sick smell mixed with pine cleaner. Steve's brow wrinkled. "New boss? I suppose so." He played with the door, swinging it on its hinges, like a fan, to dry the wet carpet, as an exercise in futility.

I put my hands in my pockets and shuffled my feet.

"I'm on my way to the scene," I said.

He nodded. "Did you call Chief Harkon?"

My turn to nod. "Was it bad?"

He shrugged. "Pretty gruesome. But fast. And the tangos were all scumbags. There's that at least." He stopped swinging the door. "I never got sick in an airplane."

"Listen, Steve, Sally...."

He interrupted me. "She didn't mean... she's upset."

"No, I know. She'll come with you. Give her time."

He shrugged again. "They don't pick up their brass, Buddy. I tried to pick up mine. It's all U.S.-made, while theirs is Austrian. It's probably not a good idea for me to be linked to this—in my position, that is."

"You resigned your position yesterday, Steve."

"Thanks, Buddy. I knew you'd take care of it. Should I turn in my weapon before I leave?"

"Do I want it?"

He thought for a moment. "No. You don't. I'll dispose of it—later."

My turn to say thanks. "Did you find all your brass?"

"No," he said. "I missed two."

Great. This was going to be delicate. My own hometown, my personal friend the police chief present, and two stray pieces of all-American residue amid dozens of foreign shells to find and dispose of without telling Harkon why. If it's not political, he will say, why worry about it being traced to your office? He doesn't know what my office does. Not many people do. It doesn't function in full sunlight.

"Have they said anything? Have they told you why they're bringing you on the team?" I wanted to ask him if he knew what he was doing. I restrained myself.

Steve leaned over the door window, resting his chin on his forearm. The door squeaked under his weight. "I'm Charlie's project," he said. "Mack approves and Louis is amused. I think it has to do with Alex."

Here was intelligence, juicy, grade-A prime, vitamin enriched, and I'd been dieting too long. I wanted details. I wanted to know how Steve had figured this out. Then I remembered that forgotten thought.

"Speaking of babysitters' daughters, Steve...."

He closed the car door and smiled. "I'll try, but Charlie's pretty fast." He picked up the bucket. "I'd better go."

We both said, "Right" at the same time.

SEVEN

Home again after meeting Chief Harkon.

"Where are they?" I asked.

"They went to the safehouse," said Maryann. "They said you know where it is. The blond man said they couldn't sleep here. The older blond one. The young one kissed Theresa in the laundry room. She's on cloud nine. But then Steve came in and stopped him, said he owes it to a friend who is out on a limb for him."

Maryann took a breath at last as she put a cup of black coffee in front of me, next to the remnants of a miserable sliver of coffee cake left over from her generous hospitality of a few hours ago. I was about to protest the depredation of all my comforts, but she continued.

"So the young one, that would be Charlie—isn't he just a doll, Leo? Charlie told Steve that a woman is a sufficient test of any friendship, and then his father told him something in German, so he sat down and ate the sandwich Theresa made for him. She says she'll never speak to Steve again, for stopping the most wonderful kiss in her life."

"In her whole, long life." I said it to the crumbs on my plate.

Maryann sat beside me at the kitchen table and frowned. "Is that blood on your sleeve?"

"Probably."

I'm not one of those secret squirrel types who never tells his wife anything and then wonders why she blabs significant details to the world, but I've always been careful to come home clean. Maryann knows my job is secret and maybe nasty, but there is a difference between simple knowledge and the full understanding that comes from experience. I watched it begin to dawn on her.

She pursed her lips to pose a question but it didn't come right away. Maybe it began as a who or a what question, but it came out finally as, "Not the young one, too? Not Charlie?"

I nodded.

"But he's so sweet."

I gagged.

She was thoughtful for a moment. "Sally and Steve have some real problems, Leo. I had a long talk with poor Sally. She's such a pretty girl."

Poor spoiled but pretty Sally.

I emptied my pockets onto the table. Maryann watched the brass roll out, handful by handful. She questioned me silently.

"Two of these are Steve's," I explained. "I couldn't very well tell Harkon what I was looking for, or why, so I had him help me pick them all up."

"Steve?"

"Yes."

"But not you, Leo?"

"What? Of course not."

"Thank God."

Even with the fresh memory of six men on their backs staring through their own blood at a factory ceiling, I felt, of all things, not gratitude, but regret. Was I so vain that I thought I should make that grade, too? I am a superb intelligence officer, a competent bureaucrat, a rare enough animal. What made me think I should want Steve's skill and Steve's invitation? I certainly didn't want Steve's enemies or his marital problems.

I tried to smile, to hide the momentary lapse.

"Did Mack say I was to come to the safehouse?" My feelings swung the other way now, toward a desire to be left completely out of it.

Maryann nodded. "He said there is information to sift through."

"I'm not surprised. There wasn't a scrap of paper in the place. Harkon had to take my word for who the corpses were. I told him about their one-time IRA affiliation. He concocted his own theory from that—a nice, plausible story of terrorist double crosses that is completely wrong but will make everybody happy. I let him believe it. The team had stripped away all the intelligence, as well as the explosive."

"Why would they do that?"

"They live on information. They get first dibs on all documents in most cases. It's usually part of the deal."

"But why would they keep the explosive?" Maryann reached for my hand and held it until I took it away to drink my coffee.

"High explosive is expensive." I showed her how empty my cup was. "And Louis is cheap."

"But he dresses so well," she said as she took my cup to the counter.

I mimed her words behind her back while she poured another cup.

"Does this have to do with that Air Force incident?" she asked. "Sally thinks it does. She has never forgiven him."

"A lot of people have never forgiven him."

"Are they the ones trying to kill him? Hiring thugs to blow him up. And Sally and the baby, too? For a mistake?"

"Mistakes can kill, Maryann. Someone has to be responsible. Why not the guy who pulled the trigger?"

"But the baby?"

"I agree that's excessive."

"So one of these families wants to add more atrocity to atrocity? It's atrocious!" She was very angry, rubbing the guts out of her special antique coffee cake dish with a towel, while my fresh cup of coffee grew cold on the counter. I didn't move from my spot at the table, though. It was a ringside seat for watching this performance.

"I don't think it was one of the families this time," I said, because I wanted to stir her up a little more and because I really didn't think it was.

She threw the towel at the sink and missed. It slid to the floor. "Then who was it?" she demanded, hands on hips.

"That's what Mack is trying to find out."

"And when he does?"

I smiled as she picked up the towel. "He'll do what he does best."

I had the satisfaction of seeing her suppress a shudder.

EIGHT

Mr. Sweetie Pie lounged diagonally across the institutional sofa in the safehouse living room. Mr. Well Dressed was not in the room. "Louis will be very upset if you take your eyes off the sensors," Charlie told Steve. "You should not upset Louis."

Steve sat scowling in an armchair against the adjacent wall, watching the green screen on the coffee table before him, monitoring the sensors outside.

"Where are the others?" I asked.

Steve kept his eyes on the screen. "Asleep," he said.

Charlie didn't speak. Steve kicked him in the ankle, showing a whole new level of familiarity. I noted it with dread. "I know. I'm going to," said Charlie.

Going to what, Brat? I collapsed silently in the chair opposite him. I admit, my expression was not friendly.

He could do a pretty good unfriendly face, too. "Did you go home?" he asked me.

I glared.

"Did you see Sally? Did she say anything?"

Sally? I shook my head slowly. Maybe I was too tired to keep up with the thoughts of Sweetie Pie the Lightning Bolt.

"She has to come with you, Steve," said Charlie.

The bastard has designs on Sally!

Steve shook his head. "I'll do my best."

"Do better than that. Show some backbone. My father is after me to produce an heir, but what woman is willing to be locked up for life at Vasily's Carpet? You have an advantage. Sally is already your wife. You can make her come with you."

Steve looked away from the screen, and we both stared into Charlie's light blue eyes, so innocent, so virginal—in the face of certain realities.

"Spoken like a bachelor," said Steve. He looked back at the screen. "Is that what you call the place? Vasily's Carpet?"

Charlie nodded. "I could produce a bastard by Theresa. Do you think that would please my father?"

"Fuck, Charlie!" Steve kicked him again.

"What? Yes. She's delicious!"

"Mack said...."

"Call him Misha. His friends don't call him Mack." Charlie looked at me. "Why aren't you reaching for your Walther?"

"Because this is such an obvious provocation." I impressed myself with my cool tone. I was so far beyond enraged, it had a calming effect.

Charlie sighed. "I am instructed to assure you I won't make any bastards by your daughter. There is no reason for you to attempt suicide."

I looked at him lounging there, without his tie or jacket, the Glock in its holster showing black against his white shirt. His talk was appropriate to the hour, a pre-dawn collection of sleepy nonsense.

"If you're anything like your father was at this age," I said, "I'll need a lot more than a half-promise not to get her pregnant."

He straightened up a little and opened his eyes wide. They were as bloodshot as mine. "If I am polite to you, will you give me details of my father at this age?"

He was a young carnivore, full of mischief.

"Papa is very moral now and has given up his mistress. So has Louis. They are both almost saintly. I find it unfair." Charlie raised his right hand. "I promise and give you my word as a gentleman, that I will not touch your daughter, Theresa, not even a little bit, nor at all, though I find her scrumptious and wonder how she is your daughter."

The fingers of his left hand were crossed. It was the best I was going to get.

He put his hand down and became very still like his father is before he kills. "My promise is good," said Charlie, "as long as you keep yours."

"Mine?

"Yes. The one about not writing any of this down or telling it to another soul."

"But I have to make a report...."

"It need not be lengthy, or true. I shall dream of Theresa."

His meaning was pretty clear.

He looked at his watch and wagged a finger at me. "It's time to wake them up. I will make coffee." To Steve he said, "Be sure you are looking at that screen when Louis comes into the room. Stay on his good side. It is important."

Like any government fixture, the chair was not designed for comfort, but I found it a lot more comfortable than the thought of waking Mack and Louis. I stayed in it. Charlie stood up. "I told you to wake them up," he said.

"I don't take orders from kids."

I expected a blow, an attack of some kind, and would have welcomed the bruise as a badge of ultimate victory. I was disappointed.

He clamped his lips together and stared at me for a full half-minute. No threats, no movement at all, just that same still menace that gives me the creeps with his father. Finally, he said quietly, "In my father's absence, I am responsible. If you disagree, then you must take it up with him."

I made as much noise as possible going down the hall. I banged on the first bedroom door, then on the second, then prepared to enter the first room, carefully, and had my hand on the knob when the door flew open and I was on my stomach on the hallway floor, one arm twisted behind me, the other pinned at my side. The Frenchman sat on my legs. I shouted "It's me! It's me!"

Mack said something from somewhere behind me, and Louis laughed.

NINE

"Your son is disrespectful to his elders." I found myself alone with Mack at the kitchen table and this was my brilliant opener. I'm sure it was lack of sleep that put me off my usual stride.

Mack's eyebrows came up a fraction. "Your daughter should not display her legs in that fashion."

"American boys are taught enough manners to keep their hands to themselves."

"Then your Michael is as much a foreigner here as mine." He pulled a wrinkled piece of paper from his shirt pocket.

"My Michael?"

"He spent the evening with a girl."

"He was at his coach's house."

"I have the report here." He smoothed the paper on the table. "It seems his coach has a porch in front of the house. And a daughter."

"You had them watched?"

"You know my methods." He shoved the paper toward me. "It is a quaint American term, necking."

"You don't have to do this. I have not been able to say it before, but I am sorry about what happened to your family, and I am heartily sorry for the role I played in it. You don't have to make me sorrier by threatening my family."

"I have not threatened your family." He looked positively offended. He needed a shave and his tie was missing, his shirt open at the neck. The leather of his holster was gleaming black, worn over the shoulders and across the back so that his SIG Sauer nestled under his arm. He scowled, disgusted with me. "When did I threaten them?"

"Your very presence. You have to admit...."

"When did I commit such an atrocity as you suggest? In your experience? When?"

"I've heard ...."

"When?"

"Never in my experience."

He leaned against the wall, still scowling. We stared across the table at each other in silence for a few minutes and, for the first time, communicated, though silently. You son of a bitch, he said to me without speaking, why the hell didn't you destroy those pictures?

I ask myself that every day, I told him without words. The regret is unbearable.

So many years! His eyes shouted at me. I saved your miserable neck countless times and could not depend on you to bend one bureaucratic rule to protect my family?

I know, I know. I'm breaking them all now. See? I covered up the killing last night. I fiddled with the computer to release Steve to you. *I'm here, breaking all the rules now.*

"Why am I here?" I asked him aloud.

"When we discover who hired Five-Fifths, you must commission the execution."

"You expect to find him here?"

"Yes, of course."

I'm pretty sharp, brilliant, in fact, but I wasn't following this. "It wasn't one of The Families?" I said.

"No." He took his coat from behind his chair and began going through the pockets, throwing a half dozen passports and a couple of thin wallets in my direction. Then he reached into the corner beside the microwave cabinet, pulled out a briefcase, put it on the table, and opened it. It was full of cash.

"It is one hundred thousand," he said. "And only a down payment. The Families offer as much, but not up front, and not in dollars. This was a big commission for Five-Fifths. Unfortunately, they did not survive it. They were not rogues; they were strictly political. Working without a babysitter would have been unthinkable to them. It would ruin their reputation. They were intent upon building it."

"So there is a babysitter somewhere," I said as I stared at the passport picture of a dead man. "And The Families could not provide a babysitter." It was an American passport, a professional-looking forgery. "But whoever commissioned it used the airline incident as cover." I was thinking out loud, and just let it roll. "Yes," I said. "The commission on Sally and the baby is just a cover for getting Steve. But why? Not that he doesn't have plenty of friends who hate him. What about the FBI man, Turner? Did he give you this safehouse by the way? It isn't one of mine. Turner and Steve never really got along."

"It is not Turner," said Mack. "He is not barbarous enough to kill from simple animosity. Killing like this needs something more: greed, hate, fear, revenge, jealousy, or worst of all, political policy. But like Turner, the killer must know that Steve shot down that airplane."

"That's not hard. It was in all the papers."

"But Steve uses his game name exclusively now. The killer must know both his real name and the new one, his history, and his present."

I put my head in my hands and stared at that nearly perfect American passport. "And he must know how to hire a specialist team," I said. "He must provide a babysitter. He must, in fact, be in my Section." *Oh God, not again.* I looked up. "You're not suspecting me?"

Mack closed the briefcase, irritated. "Of course not."

"Then why? Why do you want me to commission the execution of one of my subordinates?"

He leaned toward me. "Steve learned disobedience through disaster. He must now learn obedience. Blindly following rules is dangerous, but without them we are barbarians."

"He is becoming a specialist." I didn't think that was too far off barbarian.

"He is already operational. I must get control of him quickly, or he will be unmanageable."

"Unmanageable! You guys were never manageable. I don't have any hair because of all the times you made me pull it out. Fred told me he was promoting me when he assigned me to you, but he didn't say I might not live to enjoy it."

"Fred? Feodor Dolnikov?"

"The same. He assigned me to you. Gave me a cigar, the most terrible cigar ever made, to celebrate the occasion. He had a gross of the awful things. They were famous in The Section. He bought them when his kid was born and still had them ten years later because he couldn't get rid of them. People would take one out of politeness and then put it back in the box when he wasn't looking."

"His kid? Do you mean Alex?" There was a smile of sorts, around his mouth and behind the blue eyes.

"Yes. Alex. I still have that cigar, somewhere."

Then a real smile broke out. It is the only time I have ever seen him truly smile. He's got perfect teeth and no dimples, but all the mischief of his son times two. It made me forget who he is and what he is and it disappeared when the Frenchman walked into the room.

TEN

"You know, your English is slipping," I told The Brat. "It's not as perfect as it was last Christmas."

"I have not had opportunity to use it with someone who can corrects me. Alex is too busy since my mother died. She organizes the house now, and the household accounts."

"Can correct. I can correct you and will be happy to be of service."

"I will be happy if you shutted up."

I stared through the windshield at a clump of weeds. It was late morning on a drizzling Saturday. The humidity made itself into water and stuck mud to everything. This was lucky cover for my wife's otherwise noticeably pink minivan. The Frenchman balked at getting into it but was persuaded when he realized he would spend most of his time outside anyway. He preferred lying in the mud beside a telephone junction box. Charlie and I sat dry and ridiculous in a pink car nestled in a clump of weeds. We could see the target mobile home fifty yards to our left. There was a light on in the kitchen even in daytime, because the day was so grey.

Steve and Mack drove by in a jalopy.

"Where's the beamer?" I asked on the radio.

"We left it back there when we stole this one."

Great. I rested my forehead on the steering wheel.

"Household accounts?" I said to Charlie. "Do those contain the expenditures for mistresses?"

Charlie whistled softly. "Papa said you were good."

The jalopy pulled over in front of the target house.

"As I recall," I said, "Alex is not particularly pretty."

"There are other qualities more valuable than beauty." It was not merely a recitation. The kid was serious.

"For example?"

"There is the ability to live at Vasily's Carpet. We are not easy to live with."

"We're going in." It was Steve's voice on the radio.

"I always thought Alex was a bookish girl," I said. "Do you think she'll like Sally?"

He winced. "I think they will fight like cats."

Steve and Mack climbed out of their stolen car dressed in stolen clothes. They both wore torn, greasy blue jeans and black tee shirts decorated with skeletons and guitars and Olde English lettering dripping blood. They knocked on the front door of the target house.

Louis came back to the car, trailing a wire leading to a parabolic mic he had attached to a pole and carrying his equipment under one arm. The drizzle had become rain and soaked him to the skin. His black hair streamed down over his face in waves and ringlets. He climbed in the back swearing. I had been working on my French, so I knew the words he used.

"Testing, one, two, three," Steve said over his wire. He and Mack wore their mics under the t-shirts.

"Be quiet." Mack's wire worked, too.

The door opened and they went in.

The whole morning had been preparation for this culminating moment. We began by fine-tooth combing Five-Fifths' effects, coming across a little personal phone book. Bad form, to keep such a book. It even had phone numbers in it. All the numbers were European, complete with country codes, and Mack kept the book for later but gave Steve the engrossing occupation of reading each and every entry, one by one.

He found a number, without a name, scribbled sideways in a margin, and behold! It was a local number. The Frenchman got on the phone, calling someone—I suspected it was Turner—who broke into the phone company's computer and obtained the address of this one local phone number found on the body of a dead former terrorist turned specialist. We sat in the drizzle and watched that address for two hours. It was this slightly dilapidated single-wide trailer in front of us, past the weeds.

The occupants were a common law couple, man and girlfriend, who inhabited the same house but conducted separate lives. She was a part-time garment worker, discount auto parts store clerk, and temping receptionist. He, on the other hand, had no discernible occupation. From this, we surmised that he must be our target.

Charlie, Louis, and I watched through alternating drizzle and deluge. We would have liked to put a touch inside the house but could not think of a way to do it unobtrusively in daylight on a Saturday. We contented ourselves with wiring the phone and pointing a directional at the place. The television was on. The guy never budged. Unless he talked to himself, a touch on the house would not have yielded anything, anyway.

Mack and Steve had tracked the over-employed female, who was scheduled to be at the discount store that morning. She came home at eleven. We spent half an hour after that wondering where Steve and Mack were.

Mack told me later that Steve had done it all. The clothes came from a thrift store, the car from an apartment lot. Steve caught the lady's attention at her discount store, asking a series of questions about auto accessories that Mack didn't understand. Mack said Steve was flawless in every gesture, every nuance. He rolled his eyes at the ceiling; he snuffled; he even adjusted his pants at the crotch. The lady was captivated. Mack was impressed. *That's our boy.*

Steve told me later he felt he had passed another test.

"Yeah, hi," he said when she came to the door. "You left this." He handed her a wallet.

"Hey, thanks." She took the wallet. "What a bummer if I lost this, huh? You wanna come in? You wanna beer?"

"Yeah, sure."

The boyfriend was there in the living room, Steve told us later, on an old couch in his shorts and a torn tee shirt. The woman led them to the kitchen table, pointing to two unmatched rickety chairs. They sat down. We heard the scrapes on the floor over the wires.

"Yer all guys, so I ain't gonna tell him to put his pants on. I mean, you gotta be comfortable in yer own house, right?"

She was dressed in spandex shorts stretched over thick thighs and a sleeveless tunic that did not travel the same ground as her bra straps. Her bleached hair hung below her shoulders in broken lengths of wavy cascade, except for a tuft above her forehead that had been teased into an imitation of a cockscomb. For what reason, I didn't know. She wore full-length false fingernails painted with pumpkins for Labor Day. The paint job alone probably cost her more than her share of the rent. I can describe all this because I saw her later.

We heard the beers open and a bag rustle. "Try these," the woman said. "I got a good deal on 'em at Save U More. They're vinegar and blue cheese. Pretty good, huh?"

Crunches came from Mack and Steve in stereo. Mack said, in German, "These are the most vile things I have tasted."

"What'd he say?" she said. "That's not English, is it? Is it Spanish?"

"No. It's German. He said the chips are real good," said Steve.

"German! Wow! You speak all that stuff? I can only talk English."

"She speaks English," said Mack, "the way you speak German."

"What's he saying? Can you understand it, really?"

"He says he wants some more of them chips."

"Sure, honey." The bag rustled.

"You help me eat these, Steve, or I will stuff them down your throat."

"What'd he say? What'd he say?"

"He said thanks a lot."

"Yer welcome. How do you say yer welcome? Tell me how to say it so I can say it to him."

"Fick dich."

She practiced it once or twice before saying it to Mack. She shouted it, so he'd understand. It was at this point that I was glad Steve would be Mack's problem from now on. Back at the safehouse that night, he pounded a fist like a tree trunk into Steve's gut a couple of times to teach him respect.

I'm not allowed to do that to my subordinates in the civil service.

The guy on the sofa was the target, and Steve did his valiant best to start a conversation with him. Sonny In Shorts only grunted once or twice, in a friendly way, and watched the game on TV. I was beginning to take an interest in it myself.

We heard another beer can open. "Thanks," said Steve.

"You want a beer, Carl?" The lady shouted it over the TV commercial. "Shit. He's stoned. Look at that. Fucker's asleep. He's always asleep. You wanna go in my room and fuck, honey?"

We presumed she was talking to Steve.

"Bring him, too," she said. "Look at the size of them arms on him. He's kinda old for me, but if the rest of him looks like them arms, I can handle it. You can, like, translate."

There was a pause, then a crash, then a short scream, followed by the woman saying, "What the fuck?"

Steve briefed us later that she'd sat on his lap and reached into the front of his pants where the stock of his Smith & Wesson was digging into his gut. She was on the floor that fast, while Mack covered the sleeping boyfriend. Steve called for Charlie and Louis. I listened over the wires, in quadrophonic now, as they got down to business and worked over the boyfriend while the girlfriend wailed. After the first few blows, the woman made a run for it, but the Frenchman caught her.

The boyfriend said when he had the chance, "I dunno what the fuck you're talkin' about."

The woman was nearly hysterical. "Tell 'em, Carl. Tell 'em about that briefcase you brought to that phone booth."

"What briefcase? What the fuck you talkin' about, Cheryl? I don't know nothin' about no briefcase."

"You do, too. You took that briefcase to that phone booth, just like Brasser told you to, and you gave it to that guy, you know, that guy with the red hair and he said the code words like Brasser said...."

"Yer the one works for Brasser...." His words were cut off by the next blow.

It was Charlie who said, during an eerie silence while the boyfriend sucked air, "Tell me about Brasser, Cheryl."

"Doug Brasser. He works for the guy, the guy... don't hurt me. Please, don't hurt me. He works for this guy who helps my union. I run errands. He pays good. Please,...."

There were some details and then the bang.

The team took Maryann's car and left me with the jalopy. I called Chief Harkon from the mobile home and administered what first aid I could to old Carl wearing his underpants, whose face had been redecorated for no reason. The drugs he was on kept his pain down and his memory in tatters. His girlfriend's brains were spattered on the kitchen wall. There wasn't anything I could do for her.

Steve took his brass with him this time.

ELEVEN

The festivities wanted only alcohol to set things in motion when we pulled up to the picnic pavilion late in the steamy but otherwise dry afternoon. I had napped for an hour and shaved for this without enthusiasm. I kept hoping we'd be rained out. No such luck. The sun was determined to spite me.

Klem and Wringer argued over the tap they were mis-threading into a keg. I remembered Wringer's last operation and the secret little award we gave him for coming home alive. He and Klem were swearing at each other with plenty of vehemence.

I decided they were not my quarry. Both were too low on the totem pole to be bothered by Steve.

Maryann put her casserole dish on a picnic table. It lined up behind chips and dip, a bean salad, three potato salads, and a relish tray. The next table held bags of hamburger and hot dog buns, bottles of ketchup and mustard, pickles, mayonnaise, and sweet relish, bowls of sliced tomatoes, lettuce leaves, and chopped onions. Napkins, paper plates and cups, and plastic spoons, forks, and knives covered the third table. A space had been reserved for the large trays of burgers and hot dogs that would come off the grill when things got going.

In the meantime, Klem shoved Wringer into the table, scattering plastic utensils over the cement floor of the pavilion. Wringer's wife helped him pick up the plasticware and put it back neatly on the table, then pushed him toward the tap.

"Hurry up," she said. "I want a beer."

Theresa brought another contribution from our house, and for the first time, I noticed what she was wearing. I disapproved entirely. It wasn't just the tight fit of her shorts, but the little top she wore did not quite meet the shorts' waistband.

It shouldn't matter, I thought. They're back at the safehouse sifting information. They won't dare show up here. The last thing they need is for a bunch of babysitters to be able to identify them.

Of course, like the sun, they showed up.

I could feel The Brat's eyes on Theresa's bare midriff. He was sitting with the others in the armored black Mercedes I had acquired for them. The one with properly mounted radios and a working car phone. The one with tinted windows that maintained their security in the face of all the faces staring at them from the pavilion.

The entire Section was there with their families. Charlemagne was not blown, the Section was. Everybody knew the legend. They knew who was in the car. I scanned the paled faces of my subordinates. One man almost wrenched his wife's shoulder out of its socket as he shoved her behind him to hide her. I wondered which one of these people wanted Steve dead.

Then Steve got out of the car. Announcements don't get any clearer than that. Whoever commissioned the hit on Steve now knew he was up against Charlemagne. Things would get desperate from here on out.

Steve held the passenger door for me and climbed in the back seat with Louis and Charlie. We proceeded to sit there, facing a subdued holiday picnic, while I named every man sweating in the humidity under that pavilion. No doubt Steve had already done the honors, but for some reason, I was required to do the same again. And they didn't even need bamboo shoots to make me do it. I was gauging the likelihood of each person being the quarry even as I pointed him out. It was this that Mack was reading on my face.

"So, six," he said. "You suspect six of your men. And The Woman?"

He said it with the capitals, the way it is said in The Section. Steve must have told him how to pronounce it.

"She would be a strong seventh," I said. "But she's still in the Amazon. I spoke to her this morning via satellite. I have the coordinates so I know she's there, and the satellite link is the only communication she has. Also, I don't think it's her style. If anything, she would seduce Steve, not kill him."

There were chuckles from the back seat.

"Let us go back to your house to discuss the list," said Mack.

"Why my house?" My voice was pretty sharp.

"We are hungry. The food you provided is terrible."

"I didn't provide it. Whoever you pressed into service on this—I'm presuming it's Turner—is still doing the catering. All I did was get you this car."

"Go, tell Maryann to come home."

"And to bring back the food she brought here," said Charlie.

Louis hissed. He is such a food snob.

I walked up to the pavilion and was accosted by so many agents, I could not find Maryann.

"I thought Steve quit," said Sturgeon. His fishy brother Cod nodded.

"Why is he riding with Charlemagne?" asked Barcode.

"Maybe he got a new car," I said as I scanned the pavilion.

"He got out of the passenger side."

"Maybe it's a British car," said Mole.

"Maybe you're a dumbfuck," said Skosh.

"Are they supposed to be in the country without a babysitter now that Bear quit?" said Beauregard, always a stickler for the rules.

Mole said tsk tsk and it sounded like a twitter.

I spied my wife and daughter talking to a group of women in front of a table laden with salads. The men who were not mobbing me had clustered around newly arrived coolers of beer.

I fought my way through the crowd and told Maryann to pack up and meet me at the van.

"We should leave the food," she said, "It's far too much for us."

"No. All of it."

I looked around at everybody in earshot. Luckily, the initial crowd of senior officers was busy arguing and would not hear me. The juniors would not be as adept at understanding that I meant to feed an army.

Maryann opened her mouth to argue.

"Just do as I say," I said heatedly. She gaped at me. I don't think I have ever addressed her in that way. Theresa stared wide-eyed.

"Give me something to carry," I said, more as a way to cover the moment for the sake of the entire audience.

There was stony silence as we loaded my wife's pink car and Maryann drove us out of the park.

"I'm sorry," I said.

"They're coming over, aren't they?"

I stared at her with new appreciation. "You should have been an intelligence officer."

"I have seven children. Of course, I can figure out something that simple."

Theresa piped up from the back seat. "They're coming over? Charlie too?" The voice was way too eager for my taste.

Maryann gave me a sideways glance. "Honey," she said to the rear-view mirror, "I think it would be best if you do not encourage Charlie. Your father doesn't think it's a good idea, and I think he's right."

"But why?"

"He's too old for you right now, for one thing," said Maryann.

"But that's not why Daddy doesn't like him."

My women were better intelligence operatives than my crew. I took a deep breath and let it out with a hiss.

"Tell me, sweetheart," I said, "when you kiss him, do you put your arms around his neck?"

"Ye-es."

"Do me a favor when you kiss him today," I said, avoiding a sharp look from my wife. "Put your arms around his waist and slide your right hand up his side, under his arm."

"Dad! I know he wears a gun like you do. It's not going to shock me."

"No, just listen. When he stops you, look in his eyes. That's all I ask. Don't be playful; don't keep trying, just look in his eyes. Okay?"

Maryann's jaw was so tight, her lips turned white.

"If you say so, Dad." I couldn't see it, but I could hear her roll her eyes.

The Mercedes was there when we pulled up. They were already inside. Sally and Steve were having a public discussion on the front lawn for the entertainment of the neighbors.

TWELVE

In the general chaos of my household, with the food, the dishes, the noise, the jackets taken off, ties loosened, the sulking of Sally, and seething anger in Steve, I wanted a quick breath of peace in the chair next to the piano in the living room. It was already occupied by the Frenchman. He raised an eyebrow. I guessed it was too much for him, too.

I had forgotten my instruction to Theresa, so when Junior, son of battering ram, hit me square in the gut and pushed me up against the wall next to the sofa, I heard Steve's voice as I tried to breathe, and became vaguely aware of a growing audience.

"What the fuck did you say to her, old man?" said Charlie as he tightened my tie for me.

It is impossible to speak without breath.

"Daddy, I'm sorry! He asked me if you told me to put my hand there. Charlie stop it! That's my dad!"

He loosened his grip and I found sufficient breath to say, "I only told her to look in your eyes when you stopped her. You told her the rest."

This got me the response I expected. What I didn't expect were his words as I struggled again for air.

"Did you tell her about you, Frank? About what you did?"

"Frank?" murmured my daughter.

"Your father," said Charlie. "His game name is Frank. Has he told you? Did you tell her, Frank? I was there, you know. I watched them die that day, you fucking bureaucrat. Don't act like you're better than I."

"Than me," I wheezed. I couldn't help it.

"That is not grammatical," he said.

"It's not if the word 'than' is a conjunction, but it is grammatical if it's used as a preposition and that's what everybody says. Even educated people. It would make you noticeable."

There was a long, silent pause. Being noticeable is a sin. The only sound was my wheezing. The explanation had been expensive in air but paid for itself in time to breathe.

The Frenchman reached his hand over the piano and hit a few keys, just a noise, not even musical, then beckoned to Charlie. The young man took a deep breath, sat down on the bench, and played my favorite, Rachmaninov's second piano concerto.

Louis forced everyone into the dining room where we all listened while the music crescendoed, developed, progressed, and resolved before he and Mack made it clear to Maryann, Sally, and Theresa this was business they were not expected to stay for.

Charlie came in and took a seat at the table next to Steve. Mack opened proceedings.

"We think we know the origin of some of the money," he said. "But first, I want from you a brief description of your six subordinates. Tell us why you suspect them. Tell us also why you do not."

I wanted coffee. I wanted ibuprofen. I needed Maryann. I started with the fish brothers.

"Sturgeon and Cod went through training together," I said. "Sturgeon got his nickname because of his long pointy nose, and Cod because of his wide mouth. Sturgeon is from Wisconsin, Cod from Maine. I can't assign them to operations near each other unless it is a joint project relevant to their teams because they are constantly in each other's business. They socialize together; their families practically live in each other's houses. I suspect them because they whine continually about how unfair everything is. I think if it is someone in The Section, the most plausible motive, aside from some sort of sleeper mole, is jealousy about Steve's promotion. I think these two resented it.

"I don't suspect them because neither one of them would have wanted the job. It would mean breaking up their collaboration or even their friendship. They are comfortable with the status quo. I don't think they would want to change it."

I really needed coffee. I needed comfort, maybe some arnica for my bruised ribs.

"Who is Mole?" prompted Louis.

"He is the quintessential moaner," I said. "I don't suspect him of being a mole. His nickname comes from a character in a cartoon. He looks just like him. Pointy head, no neck, beady eyes. He objected to the name at first, but now he takes it in good part because he doesn't have a choice. He even keeps a fez on his desk as part of the joke."

I received a generalized blank stare all around.

Steve explained, "The cartoon character wears a fez."

Some cultural nuances just cannot be sufficiently conveyed.

"Mole is another one who did not take Steve's promotion well," I said. "He was number two after The Woman. I could not pass her up, though, and just give it to the next man, so I gave it to the last man in The Section and Mole let me know how deeply he disapproved. He also made Steve's life a living hell when he got back from Chicago."

Steve nodded his agreement with this.

"I could exonerate him based on sheer cowardice," I said. "He would never risk his worthless neck, or lack of one, by taking on a team like this. Do you think we can get some coffee?"

Mack sent a pointed glance Steve's way.

For somebody who had spent most of his time at the bottom of the pecking order, Steve was slow to catch on to his more important duties. Mack put an elbow on the table, supported his forehead with his hand, and glared at Steve from under his palm.

Steve left the room and we all sat in silence until he sat down again.

I resumed with the next name on my list. "Barcode got his name because of his pinstriped suits."

The door opened to Maryann and the blessed coffee, except there wasn't any. She came in bearing only the burden of a worried look. Mack stood because Maryann, a woman who was at least technically not a servant, had entered the room. The rest of us stood because Mack did. Steve and I were not used to this. Nor was Maryann.

"There is an African American man at the door saying he is with the FBI," she whispered in my ear.

"ID?"

"Yes, he showed me one, but I don't know how their IDs should look."

"Did you let him in?"

"Of course not. Not with them here," she said through her teeth, using just her eyes to indicate whom she meant.

We were all still standing. I'm pretty sure it was not sitting well with Mack.

"Jay Turner is here," I said. "He's outside. Do you want him invited in?"

Jay was none too pleased about being left waiting on the front step, but what really bothered him was what he had to announce to Mack.

"Your safehouse is under surveillance. I have to move you."

What really bothered me was what he said next.

"It occurs to me you should just stay here. It is a big house, apparently unsuspected, and Cardova has a secure line."

"Who is Cardova?" asked Maryann.

Jay turned to look at her. "And I'm told the food is better."

"The house is not big enough," I said.

"We could ask the boys to stay at the coach's house," said Maryann, "but Theresa's best friend is out of town this week, so she can't go over there."

"If the boys are already out of the house," said Jay, "let them stay out, but don't evacuate anybody. It will call attention to the place." He gestured at the team. "You need to stay out of sight and we will have to do something about the signature Mercedes, which is why I did not provide one in the first place. We must also retrieve your gear."

Steve and Charlie brought the Mercedes back later that night after fetching all the gear and backed it into one side of my garage. Jay Turner provided two teams of watchers to dry-clean their route. Maryann gave Jay a grocery list.

By eight o'clock Sunday morning, the second day of my vacation, I had the houseguests from hell, and Maryann was making pancakes.

THIRTEEN

Theresa passed the maple syrup to The Brat with a smile. It was not the wished-for troubled smile of revulsion and horror. That look was reserved for me.

In the next instant, I forgot my worries about my daughter because my wife was giggling and blushing over something the Frenchman had said to her as she put a platter of sausages and biscuits on the table. She was wearing makeup and looking considerably un-pudgy, and judging by where his eyes were, the Frenchman was appreciating that fact.

The Brat took it all in and grinned at me with malicious enjoyment as I lost my appetite and bit my tongue so hard I could taste blood.

Sally sat on my left, with the highchair to her left and back a bit, then Steve next to her, and Louis to his left, next to Maryann. To my right was Mack, and then his son. Theresa sat down between Charlie and Jay on Maryann's left. I almost caused a scene about it, but Maryann gave me a warning look.

"The more you object," she had said that morning as we dressed, "the worse it will be for you. Even aside from all the physical contests you have no business joining, you now owe us, Theresa and me, an explanation about what Charlie mentioned. You do know that, don't you?"

The memory of my nonresponse to her prodding made me gaze into my coffee, the only thing in that noisy, chaotic room for which I had any appetite. Mack interrupted my reverie of self-pity.

"We must discuss the operation. You need to know about the money," he said.

"Not in German," I said. "My wife speaks German." Not that anything we said at this end of the table would break through the distraction of whatever Louis was saying to her.

"French?" said Mack.

"Frank's French is abominable," said Louis.

"I'll just listen, then," I said with some heat. "I'm really good at listening."

There was a silence, like the kind that inhabits disaster. Even Sally and the toddler paused in mid-argument over the throwing of sausages.

"Hey, pass me the butter, will you please?" Jay asked Steve, and the moment passed.

Louis and I did not exchange gunfire.

Mack began to brief me. "The money may have come from a Chinese source here in the US, since it was all well-used small denomination dollars. We have a description of the contact."

"How did you get all that?" I said, impressed.

"Charlie and Steve visited the man the courier named Brasser. His contact was a short Asian man who did not speak English well."

"When did you do this?" I asked Steve. "And where is Brasser now?"

"Last night before we retrieved the gear," he said as his face hardened. "He met with an accident."

"Your French is worse than your German," Louis told him.

"If that is possible," said Mack.

Sally threw down her napkin, yanked the child out of his chair, and left the room. Maybe she speaks a bit of French, I thought. I made a mental note to find out the languages of everybody's wife in The Section.

"It's been almost twelve hours," I said, looking at my watch. "Should I be calling Chief Harkon?" I had him on speed dial now. "Did you pick up your brass?" I asked Steve.

"No brass," he said. "His neck broke."

"He fell down the stairs," said Charlie. "It was a quiet apartment building. Gunfire would have been too disturbing."

I saw Theresa blanche just a bit at this baldly cold statement from the man she liked kissing, and I remembered vaguely that she had taken French classes in high school. Surely she did not know enough of the language to understand this conversation, did she? I made a mental note to find out all the languages of all the family members of all the members of The Section, and to start with my own.

Jay Turner had no language aside from English, to my knowledge, and blithely allowed Maryann to heap the last of the pancakes and bacon onto his plate.

I had eaten nothing, and my coffee was cold.

The meeting droned on as meetings do. There were too many inputs, too many asides, and too many questions. The Frenchman told too many risqué jokes while ogling Maryann's backside as she cleared the table. Once again, I forgot I was hungry.

Mack brought me back to the meeting by banging his palm on the massively expensive table I had grudgingly bought after Maryann's sustained campaign for it some years before.

"We are discussing your subordinate," said Mack when he had my attention, "the man you call Skosh. He is on your list." We were back to English for Jay's sake.

"He's Japanese-American, fourth generation." Then in response to several blank stares from around the room, I added, "You said the contact was Chinese. They're not the same, you know." My understanding of European geography far outstrips my knowledge of Asia, but I do know a few basics.

"Skosh is on my list because I'm pretty sure he could kill a man," I continued. "I kind of doubt he'd hire anybody to do it for him, though. I did not select him for the promotion because I need him too badly in the Far East. His expertise is considerable."

"Presumably his contacts are also considerable," said Jay.

"True, but he is pretty contemptuous of all non-Japanese Asians. I can't see him getting cozy with the Chinese. He disagreed with my selection of Steve because he thought it was stupid. The reason I have serious doubts about him being the one is that he thinks most things we do are stupid. He spreads his contempt around liberally and without prejudice. I don't think he cares enough about Steve to kill him. And finally, the contact was a short Asian man. Skosh is quite tall, thus the nickname. It means short."

"I should meet him at his dojo," said Steve. "His sensei is a Ryukyuan from Okinawa."

Theresa came in with a fresh pot of coffee and laid it on the sideboard.

"Do you think that's wise?" Jay asked Steve.

Steve shrugged. "He's a black belt. The best way to know a man is to fight him."

"My mom says the best way to know a man is to kiss him," said Theresa, smiling at The Brat to my right. He grinned back.

If I was ever meant to have a stroke, that was the time. I half rose from my seat, flung out my arm, and pointed at the door. "Out!" I shouted with everything in me and then some. Theresa was truly horrified now. She stalked out with the obligatory slamming door as commentary.

It was the first time in years she had obeyed me.

Mack shortened the momentary thrill of victory. "Your daughter is of age," he said quietly. "It is her choice, and my son will not hurt her. I worry that you will make yourself ill. Or worse."

I had a hot reply ready on my lips when my brain engaged with the subtle, ambiguous threat in the last two words that is his hallmark. My lips closed tightly and I swallowed into oblivion something along the lines of 'spoken like the father of a son' before I remembered why he had no daughter and the role I had played in that.

It was the first time I had ever been grateful for one of his peculiar threats.

FOURTEEN

"It occurs to me," said Jay Turner, "that the words 'or worse' may have been a threat."

"Ya think?" said Steve.

He was in the back and Jay rode in the passenger seat of my wife's pink car. I was driving us to Steve's afternoon appointment at Skosh's dojo.

"That's the thing with Mack," I said. "You're never really sure if the words are a threat because they can mean different things, but you are sure you feel threatened."

"What do you think he's threatening you with?" asked Jay.

"I think he plans to cut my throat."

There was silence all around until Jay said, slowly, "Maybe. But I think if he intended that, he would have done it by now."

"I agree," said Steve. "He doesn't waste time between decision and execution." There was another pause at the last unfortunate word, given the topic.

"While death is certainly bad compared to making yourself ill," Steve continued, "there is something worse than both in Mack's book."

"What?"

"Fucking up the operation. I think he's worried you're irrational about Charlie and Theresa and will blow up at the worst possible time."

We rode in silence for the next ten minutes, while I rehearsed a long internal speech I wanted to make about how it is not irrational to want someone other than a killer, even an extremely well-paid specialist, for one's daughter, even if it's just a kiss, and no amount of assurance that he won't hurt her means anything when he's armed to the teeth and I know for certain his intentions are way more than a kiss. We pulled up to the dojo. The plan was for me to stay with the car while they went in.

Before Steve closed the door, he said, "If it makes you feel better, Charlie didn't take out Brasser. He was just winding you up."

I had already checked with Harkon. Brasser's neck was indeed broken. I had thought in the next few days Steve would be either dead or fully operational. Hell, he had just told me he was already fully operational. It didn't make me feel better.

Steve did not look even winded when he threw his holdall in the back thirty minutes later, pushed it over, and sat next to it. Jay climbed in front.

"It's not Skosh," said Steve.

"He was very respectful of Steve," said Jay.

Shit. Skosh knows. "Did you beat him?" I asked Steve.

"Yes, of course."

"And?"

"And he's a really good fighter, but he uses only one style. I surprised him with a move I learned in high school wrestling. Took him down, and that was that."

I swallowed hard, not wanting to ask. Steve glared at me in the rearview mirror.

"For fuck's sake, Frank, we left him very much alive."

"And as I said, very much more respectful," said Jay.

"Something you might want to try, Turner," said Steve.

One arrogant smart aleck in my house was not enough. Charlie had a clone. I pulled Steve aside before we went inside.

"Tell Mack I will behave," I said. "I won't fuck it up."

Maryann handed me an ice-cold dirty martini as I came through the kitchen door. I took a sip and kissed her on the lips. She blushed for me, which I found delightful until I saw the Frenchman sitting behind the kitchen table cleaning a submachine gun.

"We need to talk," said Maryann.

"Yes, yes of course. After I sit down a while."

"You really need to talk to Theresa."

"I will. I will." I escaped to the living room and sat in my favorite chair, pretending this was the end of the second day of a fabulous vacation. Jay joined me, sitting in the matching chair before the fireplace. He also had a martini in his hand. I calculated how long my good vermouth might be expected to last.

"Why aren't you in Chicago?" I asked between sips.

"I saw the traffic come in about Five-Fifths, so I took a few vacation days and came down to see what was up. Took the opportunity to give the local office chief a break. I owe her."

"You alerted Charlemagne?"

"Yes."

I'd like to say we sipped our martinis companionably, but the truth is the atmosphere was tense.

"And brought them into the country? Yes of course you did," I said, answering my own question.

"Look, Frank. I know you believe in the established order and the rule of law, but your very job takes place in the cracks where there is no order and there are no rules."

"I believe in method and procedure," I said. "With authority and oversight so that the cracks, as you call them, don't swallow us unawares. I opt for civilization, my friend. I don't want the denizens of chaos invading my comfortable life. That is why I do this job, to keep them at bay."

Not to invite them into my home with my wife and my daughter. I didn't say it out loud, but Jay knew very well what I meant.

"You know, Frank," said Jay, "my people have rarely fared well under the established order."

"And yet here you are, one of its officers."

"I am," he agreed. "Insofar as that order protects the weak from the strong, I am a card-carrying member. When it fails or reverses the protection, I intervene. I like to think I saved Sally and the baby. I don't give a damn about Steve, but his son did not shoot down that airliner."

"And the woman courier?"

"She was not just a courier," said Jay. "She was a key part of the Five-Fifths US network, she and Brasser. That, at least, is part of my official remit, to keep outside networks off US soil."

"But not by acting as judge and jury," I said.

"Come on, Frank, what jury is going to understand the evidence, even if your bosses ever consented to release the information?"

I wanted a second martini, and so did Jay, but Mack called another blasted meeting and both of us were too professional to walk into the dining room sucking on olives and holding martinis in our hands. There was a pot of fresh coffee on the sideboard. I poured myself a cup as a consolation prize.

"Frank," said Mack, "tell your women we must not be disturbed."

Like that was going to go over well.

It did not go over well.

FIFTEEN

I have to admit that as meetings go, those run by Mack are above average in purpose and relevance. Sometimes he lets people get too creative, like when they discuss scenarios and responses, but on the whole, he makes them stick to the point.

This meeting was about Steve's assessment of Skosh as an enemy. Short answer, in Steve's words, "It's not him."

"Why?" said Mack.

"If he wanted to kill me, he would do it himself. He wouldn't hire somebody. He would not use Chinese money to pay them. His family has been here for four generations but is still very Japanese. They spent the war in an internment camp. They have, or at least he has, a kind of special arrogance against the Chinese. And given the history between the two countries, I don't see them dealing gladly with someone so culturally Japanese."

Mack got an entire cogent paragraph out of Steve with a one-word question. When I asked him a question, the answer was usually a grunt.

"There are two more men on your list," Mack said to me. "Tell us about them."

Of course, I had no business discussing my agents with a foreign specialist in the presence of his entire team, but I had learned some home truths about loyalty and the established order less than a year before and I was committed to this operation in a personal way, completely outside official channels. I had no moral framework like Jay's on which to hang this decision. I was doing it because I felt bad for Mack, for Steve, and even for Charlie. I did not feel bad for Louis, who shared equally in the present danger. I especially did not feel bad for him when he was flirting with my wife.

I cleared my throat and launched a detailed discussion of Barcode and Beauregard.

"Barcode is one of my favorite subordinates and would have made a perfect babysitter for Charlemagne. I did not choose him because without him, we would have lost his team, who are not in your class but are first-rate nonetheless. I don't know if Barcode resented being passed over, but I would have resented it. He lives alone and seems to exist only for the job, is a lifelong bachelor, and practices the most perfect tradecraft I have ever seen. He would be largely undetectable if he were to have a plan to kill Steve. That fact and his pinstripes, which earned him his nickname and are an abomination of the highest order, make me suspect him, but his long unblemished record tends to clear him."

I took a deep breath before describing my least favorite subordinate.

"There is not a lot to say about Beauregard except that he irritates me. Always and in every instance. Beauregard is from the bayous of lower Alabama, just above the Florida panhandle. The self-appointed arbiter of righteousness in The Section, he finds fault with absolutely everything. He is on my list for two reasons. He seems to find more fault than usual in Steve, and he disapproves of Charlemagne. I don't know why. He is not cleared to see any WEDGE material; he has never been briefed on any Charlemagne operation, and to my knowledge Steve has never discussed the team. I know I have not."

Steve said, "He wanted to give me the benefit of his wisdom when I got back from Chicago. I tried to be tactful, but I think he was offended when I wouldn't discuss the op or the team."

"Does he discuss other teams with their babysitters?" asked Charlie. "Or did he single you out?"

Steve considered the question. "It's not just me. He gets into everybody's business, always trying to be avuncular about it."

"Does he succeed?" asked Louis.

Note to self: conduct a briefing about not discussing teams even within The Section. Of course, the answer to Louis's question was yes. Steve did not blab much because he was suspicious by nature and not popular among his peers. He also preferred a workout in a martial arts gym to having a beer with the guys, giving them another reason to distrust him.

"Does either of them, Barcode or Beauregard, have an Asian connection?" asked Mack, just as Maryann came in. He did not stand.

"Please don't mind me," she said. "I'm just going about my duties, fulfilling my womanly role serving coffee." She placed a fresh pot on the sideboard and noticed me shaking my head. "Don't you shake your head at me, Leo. We will discuss this later."

I rolled my eyes. "I was just answering Mack's question, not shaking my head at you. Thank you for the coffee, now...."

"You're wrong, Leo."

"Huh?" Sometimes words evade me. I expected a continuation of the sniping I had experienced earlier when I told her to stay out. Note how she obeyed me.

"You're wrong," she said. "They both have connections."

All the eyes that had been trying to stay out of a marital tiff were now on my wife. When the silence lasted more than a beat, Maryann said, "I'm sorry. I should not have spoken. Silent and obedient, that's me." She picked up the empty pot.

Mack sighed. "Tell us."

"Me?" She put the pot back down and stood with her hands on her hips. "It's not like I have anything to contribute other than food and drink, serving wench, and kitchen drudge that I am."

There was a guffaw from Louis. Mack gritted his teeth and said, "Please."

Mind you, she knew how dangerous he was and did not care. She was that angry. But she answered him. "Barcode's dad was a flamethrower at the Battle of Iwo Jima. He was seventeen. Imagine giving a seventeen-year-old marine a flame-throwing machine or whatever they call it. He attended a couple of our get-togethers and told me he still has demons from the war and not a lot of love for Japan. Not surprising, if you ask me."

She was speaking to a man who cuts throats for a living. But he's not seventeen. Nor do I think he ever was.

When she did not continue, he prompted her, "And Beauregard?"

"His wife's uncle, or great uncle...," Maryann thought for a moment. "She's too young, a bit of a gold digger if you ask me. Beauregard must have been almost twice her age when they married, so it must be her great uncle."

Mack so perfectly controlled his impatience that he was more still than usual.

"His wife's great uncle, then," she continued, "was Claire Chenault's crew chief. They go to Flying Tigers functions every once in a while. She told me there is always great Chinese food at these dinners, and presumably Chinese people as well."

The last words were a bit pointed as was her semi-glare in Mack's direction, and she concluded with, "Dinner will be ready in half an hour and I will need to set this table. If that is all, m'lord, I'll be going about me duties."

She actually curtsied before picking up the empty pot and sweeping out of the room.

The Frenchman exploded with laughter and pounded the table. Jay Turner and Steve shook silently. The Brat grinned at his father, who allowed a half smile to show on his face.

"She is magnificent!" said Louis, pointing at me. "If you do not reward her tonight, I will."

Given what I knew of the Frenchman, I was sure when I was alone with Maryann later, that I had no choice.

SIXTEEN

Before I could reward my most excellent wife, I had to get through another meal with a houseful of unwanted guests. Jay went missing temporarily. His place was set, but if he did not get back soon, he would starve. Maryann had made roast beef with all the trimmings, and most of us were on our second plates when Jay finally showed up.

Maryann tried to wave him into his seat, but he stood in the doorway with a worried look, wondering how to proceed with so many in the room. The longer he hesitated, the quieter the room became until even the baby stopped squawking.

Mack looked up and put his knife and fork down. "What is it?"

Jay drew in a deep breath. "There is another team in town."

"Who?"

"Potemkin Village."

This was an up-and-coming Eastern European team that could someday rival Charlemagne. Someday soon. They often worked for the Soviets but were essentially freelance and specialized in deception schemes. Their explosives expert was considered one of the best now that Sobieski was dead.

Mack shrugged one shoulder and waved to Jay's seat. "Come. Eat," he said, ever the gracious host in my own house. He did allow me to retain my seat at the head of my table and deliberately ignored my pointed stare.

The conversation changed with Jay's announcement. Mack began another meeting, right there among the mashed potatoes and gravy, and in English. He was rude and arrogant at the best of times, but tonight he opted for just arrogant.

"We will go to the sovereign house in this city," he said.

It's actually outside the city, because parking is a problem inside, leaving the half-mile restriction on violence around a sovereign house meaningless when there is no place to park within the limit. Also, when things are too congested, our city streets restrict the possibilities of safe ingress and egress by making ambush too easy. The concept of having a refreshment stand, so to speak, where warring factions could meet in safety was too important to forego in a city where every warring faction in the world showed up regularly, so someone had the bright idea to invade an old clubhouse at a golf course on the outskirts. It was called Chucky's because the concept itself wasn't already scary enough. Occasionally, a clueless politician showed up there to play golf and was escorted politely off the premises.

"When?" asked Louis.

"Tonight."

"Who?" This from Charlie.

"All of us."

Louis wiped his lips on his napkin and sat back in his chair. He looked at me. "We will need a babysitter."

"We will need both," said Mack.

"I am not a babysitter," said Jay.

"I'm not going anywhere," said Sally as she wiped little Danny's hands. "I don't need a babysitter."

Steve put his hands over his face. "I've told you repeatedly what a babysitter is, Sally," he said through his fingers.

"You men and your silly games. It's time you got a real job, Dan." She took the baby out of his highchair and walked out the door.

There was a stunned pause at this strange mixture of delusion and willful ignorance. Maryann raised her eyebrows. Even my daughter opened her eyes wide.

Mack tore his gaze from the retreating Sally and looked at Jay. "You are the domestic authority here. Our presence must seem officially sanctioned. Frank cannot conduct an operation on American soil."

I wondered if the son of a bitch knew my highly classified job description as well as every other fact of my life. Of course, he did, I concluded with a sigh.

Mack addressed me, having read my mind. "Your laws about internal surveillance are public, and your personnel policies are easily obtainable with Louis's skill." Was there a hint of a smile? *I need to take up Zen to empty my mind of all thoughts.*

He then favored me with an unmistakable smile. I shivered. "I've never gone into a sovereign house with you," I said. I did not want to start now.

"You must be there publicly, in the car, so they see we are here officially. Also, you will park your car behind the Mercedes. There are no sensors on the car, and Todor Chilikov is very good with plastique. You should take the FBI car, not the pink one."

"Who will stay here...?" Charlie swallowed the words 'with the women'. Wise boy.

"Can't I come with you?" Theresa asked Charlie.

"No!" Even Maryann joined in that chorus.

"I can add another team of watchers outside," said Jay.

"Someone should be inside." Again, Charlie avoided saying, 'with the women.'

"What about Skosh?" suggested Steve. "He can fight and he doesn't miss much."

I had my misgivings about Skosh, but the man had taken defeat with dignity and Steve did have fleeting moments of good judgment, provided the subject was not female.

"Skosh and Maryann will defend the house very well," said Louis, smiling at my wife. She smiled back.

...

Armed and arrogant as usual, Skosh arrived in good time. Maryann was by my side at the front door. Sally and Theresa came into the hall a moment later.

"Is this some weird job interview or something?" Skosh asked me. "Because if it is, I'm not interested. My team's the best in Asia and that's where I want to stay. I don't know anything about any other continent and I'm content with that."

Before I could answer him, the team walked in, wearing suits, having shaved and combed their hair. By the team, I mean all of them because Steve was obviously part of it. He had the look, the alert gaze, and the tight jaw. I heard Skosh whisper, "Shit," and I knew Steve's judgment was right once again.

Before we left, Mack pointed at Theresa and Sally. "You," he said, "will obey Maryann and Skosh exactly, in all that they say. Am I clear?"

Theresa gulped and nodded.

Sally stood defiant, glaring at him.

One moment, he was standing a few feet away. The next, he was directly before her, his knife in his hand, the blade before her face so that she looked at the edge cross-eyed. Though I had seen its results many times, I had never seen the actual instrument before, never in almost twenty years. For the life of me, I did not see him deploy it. It seemed too large to have come down his sleeve, but maybe that was a trick of a dangerous moment. It moved again so that the tip was under her chin, lifting it so her eyes were locked on his.

"This," he said, "is my game piece in the silly games men play. If you disobey those two at all, in any way, I will use it to gut you like a fish. Now, am I clear?"

"Yes," she whispered through her teeth because she did not dare move her jaw.

The knife disappeared, again seemingly without movement. Mack looked at Skosh and said, "Do not let her out of your sight. Theresa and Maryann will look after the child."

"Yes, Sir."

They walked through the kitchen and out the side door to the Mercedes in the garage. Steve did not look at his wife.

I passed Skosh on my way to the front door. "Fuck, Frank," he said. "In your own house?"

I walked down to the street to join Jay in the FBI car and saw at least one pair of his watchers a few yards away.

"Why are we doing this?" asked Jay.

"They need intelligence."

"About Potemkin Village?"

I nodded. "I think Mack suspects this is less about Steve and more about Charlemagne."

"A trap?"

"Precisely."

SEVENTEEN

We sat in Jay's car watching the Mercedes before us until the gunfire began and we were tempted to run and see. We kept our eyes glued on the Mercedes.

"What do you suppose?" said Jay.

"I suppose they put up some wannabe thug to attempt a distraction for us to leave the car."

"I was thinking the same. Why don't they just shoot us?"

"Because first, that would alert Charlemagne that the car is insecure and second, we're inside the half-mile perimeter, just barely, but inside. Bad form."

"Not bad form for the thug?"

"No. He doesn't, or rather, didn't know the rules."

"Didn't?"

"When he was alive."

"Did Charlemagne kill him then?"

"Charlemagne or any number of others. The rules are enforced by the clientele. I'll have to wait by the body for Chief Harkon. You'll need to follow them back to the house. Do you have watchers standing by to help with the dry cleaning?"

"Three teams."

"Excellent. Here they come."

I noticed the blood right away, and the wheezing peculiar to a man in pain. Steve staggered for one step and Louis steadied him.

"Whose bullet?" I was asking about the bullet that killed the shooter, whose identity was no longer important. I knew he would be dead.

"Louis's," said Mack.

I nodded. "Jay will cover your back as you get to the house. I called Chief Harkon on Jay's car phone and will wait by the body. Where is it?"

He pointed, told me the distance, and after the briefest nod, climbed into the Mercedes.

Harkon raised an eyebrow at me, but that was all. "Who shoots such a weak charge?"

"Someone who is very, very accurate."

"Evidently." The chief looked at the small hole perfectly placed between the man's eyebrows. "You're never going to explain all this, are you?" he asked, shaking his head. "No, no, of course not. Shit. I thought I had a dirty job." He patted me on the shoulder as I took my leave.

I took a taxi and was only a few minutes behind by the time they had insured themselves against a tail. At home, I walked into a world war with venue in my living room.

Everybody was there: Jay and Skosh hiding in a shadowed corner of the room, Theresa watching fascinated, the team standing with stone faces, except Steve, who was leaning on Louis and bleeding on my carpet, and Sally in full throat about the hardships of her life, all of it directed at her fading husband, the sole author of her troubles.

"That man threatened me and you did nothing!" she screamed, pointing at Mack. "He's dangerous! That one, your best friend," her arm swung to Charlie, "is the son of Satan! And the other one is just a clown."

The clown was wearing his most dangerous smile. I am sure if he'd been able to let go of Steve, he would have shown her just how funny he could be.

Sally's diatribe continued into a downward spiral of incoherence but an upward one of volume, when Maryann came out of the kitchen, her arms covered in flour. She faced Sally squarely, drew one flour-encrusted hand back as far as she could, and let fly a mighty open-handed slap across Sally's face.

"Get a grip, Sally!" she said. "You listen to me. Your husband is bleeding on my living room carpet and your son is upstairs screaming for his mama. Pick one and go to his aid. We'll take care of the other one."

When Sally ran upstairs sobbing, Maryann turned to Louis and said, "What do you need?"

Louis respectfully asked for boiled water and the use of the dining room table. Politely even.

Everybody bundled into the dining room, where we laid Steve out on my expensive table and watched as Louis removed his holster and shirt. The holster, or rather, the Smith & Wesson in it, had saved his life. The bullet that would have killed him shattered the gun and traveled a little way through the leather of the holster, cracking a rib and leaving a shallow dent in his chest. It forced a piece of the firing pin into his upper chest just below the shoulder, breaking a minor vein, causing stains on my carpet, and not inconsiderable pain to Steve.

Charlie brought the medical bag in from the Mercedes parked in the garage. Theresa followed with a large bowl of boiled water and a stack of clean tea towels.

"Mom went upstairs. She said to tell you there is a shaker of martinis in the fridge," she said, with an obvious intention to watch while Louis dug out the shrapnel and sewed up the wound.

Skosh took his leave with a wince, as Louis brought out a scalpel.

Mack and I also took the hint and found the shaker. I retrieved a jar of olives from the back of the bottom shelf where I had hidden it, and we made ourselves comfortable at the kitchen table.

"Have you told your wife?" asked Mack.

"No."

"You must."

"I know." I took a large sip of my martini.

"Why am I still alive?" I said. I figured I might as well ask it since we were already on this excruciatingly painful subject.

Mack considered me a moment. "At first," he said, "I thought you would be more useful to us alive. As you can see, I was correct. Then, I learned you had become more thoughtful about your blind obedience to a flawed system. Perhaps you did not deserve death."

"I have never been blind to the flaws of the system," I said.

"Yes, I am aware you and Jay discuss such things interminably. You are Ismene to his Antigone."

He must have had a bug in Jay's car.

Mack continued. "I am locked in a prison bounded by monsters, but most people in this civilized world are at the ordinary fleeting mercy of petty bureaucrats and do not know it." He sipped his martini, savoring the taste of my excellent vermouth, and resumed. "I know what I am and do not pretend to any morality. But there is power in small decisions, and we think nothing of the destruction they cause."

"There is a wide spectrum of guilt," I said, feeling mine acutely.

"Between me killing one man with a knife and another man killing millions with a pen? That is a wide spectrum, but the difference between two discreet instances can be very small. The holocaust depended on the many who thought they were doing their duty, like Eichmann. He was proud of his work."

"Still," I said, "even flawed order is necessary or the need to survive makes killers of us all. It is a paradox."

"When you arrive at the paradox where order meets chaos," said Mack "you only begin to understand the question."

"I believe in the necessity of order," I said, "and yet I acknowledge my guilt within it."

Mack raised his eyebrows and finished his martini. "So do I. And because I did not kill you when you deserved it, the Mercedes did not blow us up tonight. We are alive to drink martinis and discuss the nature of paradox."

...

I climbed the stairs strangely comforted by what I thought might have been a compliment from Mack regarding my steadfast guard over that Mercedes in the face of gunshots and general emergency. I mulled over his words and thought I could make a good case on the compliment side of things, as opposed to the threat side, which was more usual.

As I came near Theresa's door, I was surprised to see Louis come out of her room. He raised an eyebrow at me, lifted his bag of sensors as an explanation, and entered the next room, presumably to install perimeter sensors outside the window there as well. Despite the obvious explanation, the encounter made me uncomfortable enough to knock on her door. She answered me from inside. I asked if everything was all right. She assured me it was.

As I walked away, I heard her giggle and stopped to listen, but there was no further sound. I hesitated in the hallway, reviewing everybody's whereabouts. Jay was downstairs taking the first babysitter watch. Mack was on watch for Charlemagne, wearing a headset plugged into a radio receiver designed to monitor the sensors, supposedly more reliably than the green screen. Steve was sleeping off a low dose of painkillers on the sofa next to him. Louis had not come out of the next room. Sally and little Danny had gone to bed long ago and anyway, Theresa had no use for the woman. Maryann was waiting for me in our bedroom.

My foot stepped forward, drawn in the latter direction, then back in indecision. If I went to Theresa's room and she was alone, had giggled perhaps at something funny she was reading, she would be angry and at a time when I owed her at least my trust. If I went in and she was not alone.... because of course the only one unaccounted for was the son of Satan himself. I had given my word to behave myself, but I knew I would not, could not, because although Mack was right, she was an adult, she was also my last baby, the darling of my life, and I would act without thought and without care and either get myself killed or destroy the op or both. And the op, this unofficial, non-sanctioned op born out of chaos, held my wife and daughter as hostages.

I had an inkling, the merest shadow, of life locked in a prison bounded by monsters.

I continued to my room, where Maryann was waiting.

EIGHTEEN

I spelled Jay a few hours later and spent my watch drinking warmed-over stale coffee with the Frenchman in the living room. Steve surfaced, sore and still groggy, but demanding coffee of any description other than weak.

We were all in the kitchen an hour later that Labor Day morning, the beginning of my third day of vacation, trying to figure out how to brew more coffee, when Maryann and Theresa came in with smiles like Cheshire cats. Maryann's smile gratified me until I saw Louis's sly grin, but Theresa's reminded me about last night, who had been missing, and what I wanted to do about it, when she put her hand on my arm, taking the coffee pot from me and giving it to her mother.

"Dad," she said, "I'm the last in my class to give it up, and the only one to give it so well, to an exciting man I will remember forever. So, I want you to be sensible about this."

If she thought that was supposed to help, she was wrong. I prepared a moon launch, beginning with my blood pressure.

"He did not hurt me, Dad. I will still start college when this is over. I'm not going anywhere, still living here, and I'm not marrying anybody. It was my decision."

Maryann gave me a maddeningly compassionate smile. Louis had the grace to leave the room. Steve stayed, though. He was a born intelligence officer who also needed coffee.

"Louis knows I speak French," said Theresa.

"I didn't know you speak French."

"He read my high school transcripts," she continued. "He placed a sensor outside the window while Charlie sited his rifle, just in case, he said. Have you seen his rifle, Dad?"

I've seen what a sniper rifle like that does to a human body. But I said nothing.

"Then Louis left, and well, Charlie followed his instruction about being gentle." Theresa was doing her best not to laugh out loud, her face adorably full of dimples.

Now I wanted to kill Louis as well.

By the time Mack came in, I had my first cup of decent, hot coffee in my hand and felt more in control of myself. I knew eventually Steve would give Mack the entire story in execrable German. I swallowed hard. It was the first time I was the knowing subject, not the recipient, of prime intelligence. Mack raised an eyebrow and I knew that he knew that I knew.... You get the idea.

...

I had just sat down to a plate of scrambled eggs and bacon in the company of the usual crowd seated at the dining room table—which Steve had bled all over the night before—when Jay waltzed, no stomped in, addressed me, and said, "Come on. We gotta go."

Quite apart from his use of gotta instead of his usual 'must needs', Jay's manner told me this was urgent. I looked at my plate in sorrow.

Jay would have stomped out the same way, but Mack raised his hand.

"Sorry," said Jay. "Here." He shoved a shopping bag across the table at Steve.

Then he turned and tried to head off the man coming through the door. Chief Harkon stood in the dining room and surveyed the scene. Because he was visibly armed and unexpected, the response was immediate. The Chief was covered by three handguns pointing lethally at head and heart. It would have been four, but Steve had just begun to unpack his new Beretta.

"I told you to stay outside," Jay said through his teeth.

The Chief nodded slightly at Mack and lifted his hands into the air. How did he know this would be the one to worry about?

"Come on you guys," I said. "He's a cop."

Mack gave me a withering look, then lifted his chin at Louis, who was closest. He relieved the Chief of his sidearm and patted him down. Turnabout is fair play, I suppose. He found a small pistol strapped to Harkon's ankle. There was also a wicked-looking knife in his belt, which Louis slid across my flawless dining room table to Mack, who put away his SIG Sauer.

I saw Harkon turn pale as he watched Mack open and weigh the knife. I offered him the seat between Mack and Charlie. He declined.

"What is it?" said Mack to Jay.

"One of Frank's guys is dead," said Jay.

"Which?"

"Everybody's here," I said, puzzled.

"No. One of your guys, one of your spooks," said the Chief. "I called the FBI when I knew, and the ballistics match the gun of another one."

"Who?" said everybody ever born, including those at my breakfast table.

"Doyle. The dead guy, that is. Or was," said Jay.

"Barcode?" I asked. "And the match?"

"Steve Donovan. His Smith & Wesson."

"That file is on a secure computer. And the S&W is in pieces on my living room coffee table. When did Barcode die?"

"Last night at about ten," said Harkon.

"I know, I know," said Jay. "Ten o'clock is when Steve was shot. It gets even better. A bullet from a gun registered to the dead guy who shot Steve near the sovereign house was embedded in the door jamb at Barcode's apartment. Registered, mind you, and with the ballistics on file."

"Two-bit thugs don't usually register their guns," I said. "So there was a woolly plan to stage a shoot-out scenario between Steve and Barcode? Did you secure the premises?"

Harkon nodded.

"I expect we'll find something that incriminates Barcode regarding the Chinese," I told Jay.

"This is very crude. It cannot be Potemkin," said Mack, still playing with the knife.

"No. It's not them," I agreed. "It's someone in The Section who wants to get away with killing Steve but is too stupid to know when to quit. You can give back the Chief's weapons. We're leaving."

I had managed to scarf half my plate during the discussion, grabbed the remaining bacon, and ate it on my way to Jay's car. The Chief followed us with no other comment but a low whistle and climbed carefully into his squad car.

Harkon got there before us, having the benefit of lights and siren. Barcode had lived in a third-floor walk-up efficiency apartment. The place was spartan in the extreme, so I wondered how our quarry would have managed to plant the evidence so as to be credibly hidden but still easy to find.

"Those guys in your dining room, Leo," he said as I walked by him. "Are they houseguests, or something?"

"That's about the size of it, Chief."

"Or something," said Jay under his breath.

"And your guy who died here?"

"He wasn't involved. He's an innocent bystander."

"I'd hate to see what happens to the guilty among y'all."

"Yes, yes you would hate to see it," said Jay, under his breath again, but perfectly audible.

"Oh, I saw a bit back in that warehouse the other day," said the Chief. "Six of them, and one of them, who must have been a lookout, had his throat cut." He made a slicing gesture across his neck.

Now I remembered and realized why Steve had vomited in the car. He had been there at the time.

Jay found it; a tiny book full of daily cipher keys tucked almost, but not quite, carefully into the bottom of the phone on Barcode's bedside table. Conveniently, there were no signs of any actual messages. We were supposed to believe he deciphered messages at home and then did what with them? Burned them on a hot plate? Ate them like in a bad spy movie?

I was looking for an idiot. An idiot who had called in the deadliest of Charlemagne's current list of enemies with the help of at least one foreign power, after a failed attempt at killing a colleague with the help of a different foreign power. Steve might be my guy's target, but he wasn't Potemkin's. He and his family were now the bait.

NINETEEN

"You are usually more timely in your perceptions," said Mack. I was back at my dining room table, empty of food, both me and the table. Mack started the meeting with this assessment of my realization that Charlemagne was now the true target.

I could tell Steve's reaction to my observation was a wisely unspoken, ya think? I was prepared to take him down a peg, new gun or not. He had disassembled his new Beretta 92SB and laid the pieces on the bare wood of the table, along with an oily cleaning rag and a leaking bottle of solvent. I took a coaster out of a drawer in the sideboard and slid it down the table at him. He looked at it, puzzled.

"For the solvent," I said.

His puzzlement continued until Louis leaned over, picked up the solvent, and put it on the coaster.

It already had etched a small ring into the finish.

We were all tired, of course, on day three of an op that was as opaque as it had been on day one. Two bystanders were dead, and both for no good reason. One had been duped into certain death. The other died as a too-obvious red herring. We had clues and suspicions, but no hard facts.

Mack did not look pleased, and he was looking at me.

"I have gone over the entire Section roster," I said. "The remaining five of the original six are still the most likely by a mile. I should say the remaining four. Skosh acquitted himself well and I think we can use him again. That leaves Beauregard, Mole, Cod, and Sturgeon. All of my initial impressions hold. Beauregard remains my least favorite person, which is why I distrust my preference for him as the culprit."

"This house is still secure," said Jay. "There are unknown watchers on the safehouse and some freelance watchers on the Donovan house, but nothing here."

"For the moment," said Mack, "we are as secure as we can expect to be in the circumstances. Potemkin's attack is likely to be by explosives. It is their strength. Where is the pink minivan? Can we pull it in alongside the Mercedes? It should remain unknown."

"Done," said Jay. And he made it happen. Good man.

We went back to first principles and decided Potemkin's main attacks would consist of deception and explosives.

"The entire op has been deceptive," said Charlie. "Are the Chinese even involved?"

"I think they are," I said, "or were, but only because they were given an opportunity to suborn one of my guys. They now have him by the short and curlies and are not likely to let go. He has to be getting uncomfortable about it."

"Short and curlies?"

I opened my mouth to answer, but Theresa came in with more coffee. Louis explained, en Français, which I knew he knew damn well she spoke. I glowered at him. He grinned. She blushed. So did Charlie, to his credit.

"I want the personnel files of all four men," said Mack.

"I can't...."

His stare hardened.

"No, listen," I said. "I'm not refusing. I'm officially on vacation and can't go into the office to get any files without calling attention to it."

My relief at this easy excuse was short-lived.

"Then we will retrieve the information and you will tell us how."

His voice was soft as butter and sharp as his knife. He wanted me to compromise the entire Section. The room was silent. Everybody understood. Even Theresa, who was holding hands with The Brat.

"If it helps you," said Louis, "we have most of it already, as do the Soviets."

So many thoughts and arguments went through me. Did I trust them? Of course, I did. I trusted them to look after their interests entirely. Did I have a choice? Maybe a slim one. But this was not the time to add even a small resentment to the mountain of seething fury that sat within this relationship. What made me decide? The word 'Soviets.' I looked at Louis when I said, "Fine."

Of course, I would change all the codes and safe combinations the moment they were done and have the place thoroughly swept for devices.

Of course, they knew that.

But what Louis knew about what the Soviets knew was my quid pro quo, and Louis knew that, too.

I made it clear to Theresa that she should leave. She resisted until Charlie gained the cooperation from her that I could not.

I told them in which office down which hallway they would find the records. There was a pause.

"Is there a computer in the vault?" asked Louis.

First of all, he shouldn't know about the vault. Second, the vault had nothing to do with the original request for four personnel records held in a file cabinet safe in a different room. Third, the computer... *Shit*. The computer.

I just kept telling myself 'Soviets', over and over, as I gave the cipher lock codes, the alarm codes, the combo to the file safe, the combo to the walk-in vault, and finally, the passwords on the computer.

I was now thoroughly compromised, not to a foreign power, but to a team of foreign freelance killers I had known for close to twenty years and to whom I owed an enormous debt of guilt. I hoped it was now paid by this abject surrender to necessity but knew better. I had made only a down payment.

This is how it is done, I reflected, the trade in information. It was my bread and butter and I was swallowing a relatively mild poison with this meal, in comparison to some. So which of my four agents had been exposed in this way to Potemkin Village? We never used that team. They were primarily a KGB asset. Which of my guys would even get close?

TWENTY

"Where the fuck is your car, Frank?" said Steve. "We need it tonight. We can't take the Mercedes. Misha asked me and I had to admit I didn't know. I hate fucking having to admit things like that to Misha."

After my initial irritation at this rich change of deference toward his new boss now that it was no longer me, I noticed the name he was using regularly now for Mack, and the irritable tone typical of an exposed specialist during an operation. How would Sally deal with this transformation? She had not dealt well with the husband of three days ago. What would she do with this new one? Would she understand what had happened? Would she even believe it?

Maryann drove me to the shop for my car in the pink minivan.

"Leo," she said as we pulled out of the driveway, "are we in danger?"

"Yes," I said after a moment's thought. She was never easy to fool, so I did not bother to try.

"Equally? I thought it was just Sally and the baby."

"Not equally, but all of us."

"Because of those men or from them?"

"Both. Again, not equally. The outside danger is far more potent and is directed at Steve and his family and the team itself."

"And those men staying with us," she said, "what do you call them?"

"Charlemagne. It is the name of their team."

"You've known them for some time?"

"Nearly twenty years. I first met them when they were around Charlie's age."

She was quiet while she negotiated a left-hand turn across traffic. As we pulled into the auto repair shop, she said, "Would that man be capable of gutting Sally like a fish?"

She placed the minivan in park and set the brake before I replied.

"I've never known Mack to make a threat he was not prepared to carry out," I said carefully. "He doesn't bluff."

"Oh, Leo." She turned to look at me. "All these years, this is your job? Every time you went away?"

"Yes."

"I've been so comfortable all this time," she said, looking away. As I reached for the door handle, she said, "But I still want to know what they want you to tell me."

My pause was momentary before I made a quick egress. "I know. I will."

Back at my happy home, with my car in the driveway and a pair of Jay's watchers keeping an eye, or rather four eyes on it, I walked into another world war between the usual combatants, Steve and Sally.

"I want to go home! This is stupid! There is nobody trying to kill us. The only threat to me came from that horrible man with the knife and you did nothing! He has a screw loose!"

"You're the one with the loose screw, Sally. Why won't you listen to anybody? Why did it take a knife, his knife, to make you shut the fuck up?"

"You're just playing your silly games, acting all macho instead of getting a decent job and providing for your family!"

There was more, much more, all of it variations on a theme of why can't you be more normal?

Steve's answers were less varied and boiled down to why can't you shut the fuck up about it? He was under massive pressure, still in some pain, and had not slept more than four hours in the last twenty-four. The look he gave her as Maryann pulled her into the kitchen told me a year might be too generous an estimate of their chances.

Mack, Louis, and Charlie had not been in the living room as this went on. I wondered where they were. Probably rifling through my study, I thought, as Steve walked back to join them. When the three of us came into the kitchen, I closed the living room door just in case, because I was about to impart a few home truths and did not need an audience. Maryann began making lunch, and the steam soon overwhelmed our inadequate fan system, so I opened the door into the dining room, checked it, and was satisfied it was deserted. The blinds were drawn, but the extra air was welcome in the hot kitchen.

Sally blubbered at the kitchen table, nursing a cup of tea, no doubt provided by Maryann, but I noticed there were no 'there theres' coming from that quarter. Maryann was as fed up as I was. It is fine to be concerned for the safety of a fellow human being, but it becomes increasingly difficult when the beneficiary of our concern is a ninny, which is the word I knew Maryann would use to describe Sally. I had other words. She was a beautiful young woman. I knew very well what Steve was thinking when he married her. But she would never be a Maryann when they were our age. If they lived that long.

I sat down across from her. "Look, Sally," I said gently but as firmly as I could, "Steve has a job. He has been hired by the number one team of freelance killers in the Western world. I can't put it any plainer than that.

"He lives in a world where everything is vicious and deadly except you and Danny. He is a hunter and is hunted and is himself becoming vicious and deadly. That is never going to change. He will only get better at it. And his name is now Steve. I'm sure he told you that, many times. When you refuse to acknowledge the name change, you endanger him, yourself, and your son even more. Do you understand?"

She shook her head.

I sighed. "At least try to take in what I am telling you. Steve is never going to be normal. He will never hold a middle management salaried job. He will never mow the lawn in a suburban yard on Saturday and play golf on Sunday. He will fight and get badly injured and go do it again as soon as he's healed, even as you saw him last night with the shrapnel in his chest. No doubt, he will die young."

She picked up her head at this and said, "If he dies, can I go home?"

This chilled me more than anything I had ever heard out of Mack. It was a completely unthinking, cold menace that is impossible to counteract. I prayed the Frenchman did not have a listening device in the kitchen. I knew Mack already had no use for the continued existence of this empty-headed woman. That she could be so callous and selfish about the life of a team member, her own husband, would make her life forfeit if he found out.

"Sally," I said through clenched teeth, "every time you cause trouble with the team, and I repeat, Steve is on the team, you threaten me and my family as well. Does that fact register with you at all? Because it is very much front and center with me."

She gave me a scornful look. "This is all nonsense. I don't have to listen to this anymore and I won't."

I got up from my chair so as to have some leverage to shout at her. My arm was ready to point and my mouth open when I saw a long, slim leg, expensively clad in summer-weight grey wool, stretched out on the left side of the door leading into the dimly lit dining room. I closed and opened my eyes. Maryann gave me a questioning look, then saw the leg, then paled. She stood by the counter facing the open doorway.

I went through the door and turned to face them. The Frenchman sat now on my right, Mack on the left, in chairs on either side of the door. Both were in shirt sleeves and shoulder holsters, their weapons gleaming in the dimness. The Frenchman spoke.

"We found something on your computer."

I had pegged it. They had been in my study.

"We came to tell you, but the conversation," he gestured toward the kitchen, "was interesting, so we did not want to disturb you."

Mack leaned forward, resting his forearms on his knees with his hands clasped before him, and looked up at me. "Can we be heard in the kitchen?"

Maryann nodded.

"Yes," I said.

"Vasily enjoyed American women," said Mack. "He said they did not seem to know danger. His American wife understood the most subtle threats, however." He raised his eyebrows. "She still does. She heeds them. This one does neither. She is a danger to us."

He was perfectly still, staring a hole through me with laser-blue eyes. I knew the last sentence to be the deadliest I had ever heard him say. He normally employed only one solution to people who endangered the team.

"I will kill her, but not today. It would not be good for Steve. But she remains a threat."

He sighed and stood up, walking with that incredible stillness into the kitchen where he addressed Maryann. "Your reward nights with your husband must wait. He will have duties elsewhere anyway. I want you to be in this woman's presence at all times." He pointed to Sally. "She is to sleep with you. You will accompany her to the toilet. If she does anything other than care for her ordinary needs or those of her son—Steve's son—you must alert one of the team."

He spoke then to Sally. "Do you understand this instruction?"

She rolled her eyes. "Like that's going to happen."

"If you do not understand my words, perhaps you will understand this."

He crossed the room with that strange still movement of his, yanked her by the arm out from behind the kitchen table like an explosion, and backhanded her face, hard, sending her flying into the refrigerator door. Maryann stepped away from the counter and out of his way because he was already standing over Sally as she gasped for breath and in the next instant lifting her and backhanding her again so that she fell into the chairs at the table.

"I'll call the police," she gasped.

"Do you think you will live until they arrive?"

He looked at Maryann. "Do not leave her."

"Yes, Sir."

I had never seen him hit a woman. I had seen him kill a couple. I mean I saw the results after the fact, but they were enemy killers trying to do the same to him. To my knowledge, he had never hurt a non-operational woman, at least not personally. Threaten with an intention to fulfill it? Plenty. Show pity when the operation went that way and an innocent death was unavoidable, no. All of this I had seen, but I did not think he would strike a non-operational woman. He stalked out of the kitchen.

I had also never heard my wife say 'yes, sir' to anyone. She gave Sally a pack of frozen peas for her eye and a tea towel to wrap it in.

Louis came in looking for coffee. Maryann handed him a cup, shaking. He put his arm around her shoulder. "It is okay, *mon cher*," he said. "No one will hurt you."

"I teased him," she said. "I defied his edict to stay out of the meeting."

"And you were right to do so. You provided valuable intelligence. You have nothing to fear."

"He was so angry just now."

"Angry? Non. He is desperate. We do not know what to do. He had to make her believe his threats. Frank tried reason. She is impervious to both, so Misha tried to show her. She should be killed or otherwise neutralized completely, but we cannot because of the child."

Louis sighed. "No, Misha is not angry. This was a calculated move, like everything he does. I am the one who can be emotional and destructive. I would have killed her long ago."

Maryann registered the businesslike tone, for want of a better word, and opened her eyes wide at the man who had kissed her hand. She turned back to the pan beginning to sizzle on the stovetop.

"I'm going to sue that bastard," Sally said. She sat on the floor in a corner of the cabinets, holding the peas against her eye.

"I think sometimes it is not a good thing to feel too safe," said Louis, smiling wryly at my wife. To Sally, he said, "It is important to remember that men are dangerous, Madame. *Vraiment,* all men are dangerous, but some are deadly."

"Now do you understand why I do not want Theresa anywhere near Charlie?" I said in a low voice.

"Ah, it is too late now, *n'est-ce pas?*" he said. "Theresa is not like Sally. She knows Charlie is dangerous. It is because he is dangerous that she likes him. You have much to learn about women, my friend. I wonder how it is you won your excellent wife. Maryann liked the danger in me also." He grimaced. Maryann did not look up from the pan sizzling on the stove, but I could sense her tension. "Until Misha showed her what such danger can mean." He sighed again.

Louis left the kitchen shaking his head as Sally muttered about lawyers from her corner.

I sat at the table, elbows propped, with my head in my hands.

Maryann made lunch in silence.

TWENTY-ONE

Lunch was not festive. Not subdued either. More like funereal.
We took our usual places. No one dictated where we should sit, but we repeated the pattern we had established at the first meal as happy families do in any house. Maryann and I sat as hostess and host, she near the kitchen door and I across from her. She was subdued. If Sally had received an intravenous infusion of threat medicine from Mack to almost no avail, Maryann overdosed on the fumes. I could see Louis on her right doing his best, but her smiles at him were halfhearted. I found myself regretting it as much as he did.

Five people at the table did not know about the kitchen education session: Jay, Charlie, Steve, Theresa, and Danny the toddler. All of them, without exception, felt its aftermath. Danny was so good, nobody noticed him in the highchair, and he ate all his peas.

Steve, of course, noticed the shiner on his wife's right eye, and the bruise on her left cheek. I saw the questioning glance he sent to Mack, who was as cool as a glacier and gave nothing away.

I was concerned when Sally glared at Mack in defiance. I knew about prisoners who use defiance with their interrogators even while under torture, but those brave people do so with full appreciation of the danger they are in. Sally had no such understanding. She defied a man she considered a liar and a game player, despite the contrary evidence of the pain in her eye. I saw no courage in this, only folly.

Steve noticed the look, of course. It added to the question on his face caused by the sight of her injuries. She put more peas in the bowl before her son. To everyone's surprise, except that of his parents, one oblivious to her danger, the other distracted by it, Danny again ate them dutifully.

"That man hit me," Sally said to her husband, indicating Mack across the table from her.

The table was utterly, completely, fully, profoundly silent. No one breathed. I swear it. I know I didn't breathe.

There was a long eye-to-eye, right across my nose almost, since they were close to me, Mack to my right, Steve to the left, one seat and a highchair down. Steve's query exchanged with Mack's glacier.

"Sally," said Steve softly and kindly, as he began the happy families approved method of uncomfortable public family fights no one wanted any part of. "Your life and Danny's life depend on your cooperation. Can you see that? When I got back from Chicago, you understood it. What happened?"

"Our future depends on you coming to your senses, Dan. You should have stayed in the Air Force. You were going to be a general one day and you had to go and give it up for no reason and now you have this stupid job with the frog man and these nasty people and that man hit me!"

Nobody ate. Chewing would cause noise.

"I was never going to be a general," said Steve. "It was never in my nature to toe the line that well for that long."

"But you went to the Academy. Daddy said those people become generals. I was raised to be a general's wife."

"Most of us never become generals, Sally. Jay over there was much more distinguished than I was, and he is not a general."

Jay did not seem to appreciate the attention. He dropped his eyes onto his plate.

"Of course not," said Sally. "He's not as handsome as you are. If you can't be a general, then you should get a good job so we can buy a nice house and Danny can go to a good school. I'm not unreasonable, Dan."

"We've talked about this, Sally. I have the best job I can get and we have to move or people will come and kill us."

"I'm not listening to this nonsense anymore. I'm going home. I will not be made a prisoner in this awful house!"

She stood up and tried to take Danny out of his highchair. Steve stopped her. She turned on her heel and moved behind me heading for the door at the other end of the table that led to the living room. Mack was in her way. He leaned back in his seat and, almost casually, grabbed her arm as she tried to sweep past him.

"Let go!"

He said nothing.

"I need the bathroom."

"Maryann has been working all morning and has not finished eating. You must wait for her," said Mack.

I noticed Maryann put her napkin beside her plate and open her mouth to say it was quite all right, but Louis put his hand on her arm and gave the slightest shake of his head. She subsided and picked up her fork, though like everybody else, she did not eat.

"This is stupid! You can't make that old woman my jailer!"

I could feel the disapproval in the air. Maryann was universally esteemed. Of all her provocations, this disrespect of my wife was the thing that lost Sally the most sympathy from everyone in the room. The Mack-induced bruise and shiner were forgotten, even by my daughter.

"Sit down." His voice was at its most menacing softness.

"Make me."

He obliged.

She sniffed and looked at her husband from her usual seat at the table.

"You make this necessary, Sally," said Steve.

His manner was as glacial as his boss's. He picked up his fork and ate, as did Mack, now back in his seat. Everybody, except Sally, had lunch. I don't know what her expression was as she sat there. I kept my eyes on my plate.

Danny ate more peas.

TWENTY-TWO

I was helping Theresa clear the table after lunch when Mack came back into the dining room and with the barest sideways movement of his head, summoned me. Theresa saw the summons and took the stack of plates from me.

Mack turned and walked toward my study. I followed, as I plainly was expected to do. Once in the room, he sat in my chair at my desk, which disturbed me not a little. Louis sat on a corner of the desk. The younger men of the team sat in chairs that had been brought in from the back patio. There was a third chair empty. Mack pointed to it. I sat.

Why am I here? I thought with alarm. This was a team meeting, with listeners unwelcome in the extreme, held in my study and chaired by Mack sitting at my desk. I did a mental inventory of everything that might be in the desk drawers, the small filing cabinet, or the credenza behind the chair which held the secure phone and the home computer. I'm pretty careful as a rule, but complacency can create egregious lapses. I have been guilty of that from time to time, usually whenever fate calls for maximum damage out of minimal mistakes.

"You are here," said Mack, reading my thoughts as usual, "because we will be discussing matters that concern you."

Technically, every op concerned me. It was my job. But he meant the word concern in a slightly different context that suggested something personal, the very worst connotation of the word. I was duly concerned.

Mack pointed at me with an open palm. "If you write any of this down, Frank, I will slice your carotid and require Theresa and Maryann to watch you bleed out."

I swallowed hard. "I give my word."

I figure there is a difference between recording privately and securely for one's own memory and writing for file. This will never be in any file. And it's not written.

Nonetheless, I swallowed hard again, especially at the way he indicated my family by naming the ones present in the house. A piercing look from those blue eyes made me swallow hard a third time.

He looked at the others. "Do you see that? He gives a reasonable response to a known threat!"

"You are not a monster, Papa," said Charlie.

Steve and I exchanged a quick look regarding the irony here. Slapping a woman rated the monster scale, but other, um, things didn't?

"Then why does it feel otherwise?"

Louis answered, with an acerbic tone. "Because Alex will disapprove."

Tension and warning bounced around the room with an accompanying pause to allow everybody to keep his temper or prepare to intervene as the case might be.

I presumed Alex disapproved of a lot of things. She was also very familiar with what Charlemagne did, not just for a living, but to continue living. She had been naive once upon a time, but never a fool and was disabused of her naiveté early on. Would slapping a particularly obtuse woman who threatened everybody's security qualify one as a monster while threatening, with obvious sincerity of purpose, to gut her like a fish did not? These were heavy questions and I was glad Steve still saw them as such. I could see them going through his mind. I suspected he would soon lose the faculty of recognizing such ironies.

I also knew in that instant that trouble was brewing in Charlemagne. The Frenchman's sharp jibe and Mack's razor-thin answering look suggested a rift. The name Alex indicated the reason. The unspoken communication I saw between Charlie and Steve confirmed why Charlie was desperate to have him on the team. I felt smug about my deduction for about a nanosecond before Charlie saw it on my face and afforded me a silent and additional virulent threat to his father's of a moment ago with just an ice-blue stare. I was swallowing hard a lot lately.

Mack returned to the business at hand. He directed a discussion of Potemkin Village.

"Jay says they're still watching the safehouse," said Steve, "or somebody is, but now not as heavily as they are my house. He says they have hired or otherwise acquired an army of watchers and a few rent-a-thugs, all of them concentrating on my house. The Potemkin team itself is probably based within the neighborhood. There are quite a few houses for rent nearby so it wouldn't be difficult."

"Why?" asked Louis. "Do they think you will go back there with a woman and child, alone? If so, why the army?"

"They do not expect him to be alone," said Mack. "We have announced he is one of us. The army is for us."

"But so obvious? What is their plan?" asked Charlie.

"They hope for an unexpected event to draw us," said Mack. "which brings us to the mole in Frank's office. There are too many suspects, too many clues, and none seem applicable to anything." He pushed his hair back from his forehead and looked at me from under his fingers.

This was my moment, it seemed, and I had nothing. Desperation called a few things to my mind and I practiced a little out loud brainstorming with them.

"I still think the mole, at least, is after Steve and it's personal," I said. "He must be a bit of a coward, especially since Steve is tough to beat in any fight, so he had to seek funding for a contract. Also, maybe he needed help making arrangements outside our normal channels." I paused, feeling my way through this line. "The Chinese took him up on his offer first but bowed out when it went sour and they lost an entire team. Ever the opportunists, the Soviets acquired the option and decided to exercise it, using Potemkin Village, which is known to have its own agenda regarding Charlemagne. My mole did not set out to compromise himself. He just wanted rid of Steve. But he's probably desperate now. Compromise is easy to acquire and impossible to escape."

I knew this last bit of wisdom too well.

"Which brings us to another reason why you are here, Frank," said Mack.

Was he rubbing it in? I had begun to think I had given my two cents and would be dismissed to repair to the kitchen and be rewarded with a martini, but Mack thought differently.

"If we live through this operation," he said, "we will take Steve and his family with us. Once your mole knows they are gone, he will come for you. He will learn that you and your family harbored us and Steve. He will want your family as well. He has shown he has no ordinary scruples by targeting Sally and the child. Maryann and Theresa will never be safe. You will enter the black without skills and without resources."

I was absolutely speechless because he was absolutely right.

"When we find the mole," he continued. "it is essential we receive a commission on him. You must not depend upon your orderly system to keep you safe. It need not be a large commission, but we must have it and execute it before we get on the airplane. Do you understand?"

I nodded dumbly.

"Can you acquire it within eighteen hours?"

I gave another dumb nod. I knew he wanted a proper commission as part of his quest to bring Steve into line, but he was wrapping me up tight in a straitjacket of obligation and implication that would last the rest of my life.

The other revelation in his last question was that he expected to be wrapping up the operation itself the next day. I had no idea how that could be; it was still such a woolly mess.

The meeting was not over; there was more to come and none of it involved a cold, dirty martini. Mack looked at Louis, who addressed me.

"Your computer is infected."

"My computer?"

"This." He indicated the home computer sitting on the credenza behind my desk.

I was becoming an expert at dumb nodding. He rolled his eyes. "I have traced it to this game." He held up a disk. "The virus collects everything you do on this computer and deposits the information on this disk."

"It's a good thing I don't do anything on the computer, then," I said, a little resentful of his condescending tone. "Maryann uses it for recipes and Christmas letters. The kids play games on it. I never touch it."

"Yes. This is a game. One or more of your children must play it. The information stored here began to be gathered just before we came."

I nodded, not quite as dumb for a change. "If it's a shooting space game, it belongs to the boys, otherwise it's Theresa's. She likes those word puzzle games."

Louis nodded at Charlie.

"I will speak to her," said The Brat.

"You will not!" I snapped. "I will."

"Charlie will," pronounced the judge sitting behind my desk.

I seethed as the topic changed.

TWENTY-THREE

"Steve," said Mack, "I am afraid that until Sally decides where she will stay and under what terms, we cannot allow her to know anything about Vasily's Carpet. We will instruct the pilots to land at night and will blindfold her on the approach to the house. Alex will arrange rooms for you, Sally, and Danny within Vasily's Carpet, but Sally will not be permitted to leave those rooms until you and she can negotiate a reasonable solution. As she is now, she is a grave risk to us, and we cannot allow her to know anything at all."

By this point, I had replaced seething with being as still as any fly on a wall can be, praying nobody with a fly swatter would notice me. This was detailed inside information.

"I don't get it," Charlie said to Steve. "When we were at your house while you were on your way to Chicago last year, all we did was open our jackets and let her see the weapons. She understood right away. She was tight-lipped about it, and nervous, as she should be, but she understood and did as instructed. What changed? What has unhinged her?"

Steve threw his head back and slumped in his chair, legs stretched before him. "I wish to God I knew."

Louis asked it. Of course, he would ask it. "She is beautiful. Do you make love to her frequently?"

Steve narrowed his eyes, rejected the possibility of not answering, and said, "She won't let me."

"How long?" said Mack.

Steve paused to remember. "Maybe a month."

"Someone new has come into her life then," said Louis. "A man?"

Again, an intensely thoughtful look wrinkled Steve's brow. "Noooo," he said, stretching the word and shaking his head slowly. "Not a man. She doesn't go anywhere except to coffee mornings with the Section wives, and she even quit going to those."

"When?" Mack and Louis said it together.

Steve opened his eyes. "About a month. And she's always on the phone." I could almost see the creaking machinery in his head creating steam as he searched his memory for facts he never before had any intention of paying attention to. "Linda!"

"Linda who?" This time I joined the Mack and Louis chorus.

"I don't know. I don't know any of the wives."

After all, what could be more inconsequential than a bunch of middle-class wives? To my shame, I didn't know any of them, either. I always left that to….

Three of us stood at the same time. Louis sat further back on the desk laughing. Mack said, "Sit down. We are not finished. When we are, I will ask her while Steve stays with Sally."

"Um," I said, expecting the fly swatter any second, "I think I should ask her."

Please don't make me explain why you are the last person who can expect a coherent answer from my wife right now.

Mack's eyes dropped fractionally then looked at me. "Very well," he said, "but I must be with you." He raised a hand to stop my interruption. "I must see her face and hear her voice as she answers. Maryann will cope with my presence if you are there."

"Tell us about Sally," Louis said to Steve, as serious as I have ever seen him.

"I met her in Colorado Springs during my senior year at the Zoo." He saw the question on our faces. "The Academy. I was in my last year. She was a waitress. She had a degree in something from Colorado State, but she was waiting tables when I met her. To tell the truth, I was pretty desperate to get in her pants, so I proposed. She accepted, and we had the big deal military wedding in the Academy chapel right after graduation. After that, pilot training at Reese in Lubbock and F-15 lead-in at Luke in Phoenix. She hated every minute of both. She spent a lot of that time at home with her parents in Colorado. Danny was born there."

"Then you went to Alaska?" prompted Louis. "Was she happy there?"

Steve closed his eyes momentarily. "No. She hated that, too."

I began to understand where the Frenchman was heading.

"Does Sally like to travel?" I asked.

"Fuck, no," said Steve. "The only thing she hates worse is moving. It took months each time just to unpack the boxes and by then we were packing again."

"So she doesn't dream of a romantic trip to, say, Venice?"

"Venice? You've got to be shitting me. You may as well suggest Mars."

Mack picked up the thread. "Has she ever traveled to Europe?"

"Hell no."

"Did you tell her you will be moving to Europe?"

Steve stared at Mack, pausing, swallowed, and said, "I told her yesterday."

Mack raised an interrogatory eyebrow.

"She went ballistic," said Steve. "She said Linda told her that would happen and that she would never see her family again and Danny would grow up talking in some strange language, and more like that."

"She fears change," said Louis.

"Yes."

"Her passport has no stamps on it?" asked Charlie, unable to believe the concept.

Steve's brow furrowed. "She doesn't have a passport."

I have to admit, I was part of the room-wide shock at such a concept. My kids had passports from birth.

"And the child?" asked Louis.

Steve shook his head.

Mack sent a very pointed look Charlie's way. "I'll have them delivered to the airplane," said Charlie.

"In eighteen hours?"

"In twenty. It will be that long before we can take off. What? They need not be authentic. They will not be required for US entry."

There followed a long-winded parental stream of criticism and blistering heat about Steve's irresponsible choice of such a wench, and now he had a son by her, his firstborn, and she would always be in his son's life and his, no matter what happened. Even if she were to die, his son would be damaged either by the association, the questions, or the lack of a mother.

After a while, I had the feeling that much of this speech was directed at Charlie. A glance in The Brat's direction gave me verification of the theory. He had the tight, sullen jaw and rolling eyes I have seen on Theresa's face any time I've tried to impart a few home truths.

I found myself reluctantly agreeing with every word Mack said and having no sympathy for the two blistered young men in the room. Louis was suppressing a chuckle.

I reflected that Mack did not like Sally at all. Not a good omen for Steve's marriage, but I was not sure Steve himself was all that invested anymore.

TWENTY-FOUR

We descended upon a peaceful kitchen like a murder of crows, dividing the women, taking Maryann and Theresa to other rooms, and neutralizing Sally's ability to overhear or even realize there was an interrogation going on, though little Danny provided all the cover anyone could want. He sent up a wail the minute Mack walked in the door. Steve held his son and Louis struck up a conversation about baby food with Sally.

Mack and I led Maryann to the study. On the way, I saw Charlie and Theresa sit down together on the living room sofa. Charlie held the computer game disk in his hand.

We sat in the three patio chairs still set up before my desk. Maryann glanced uneasily at Mack but was otherwise her usual composed self, maybe a little more on the somber side.

I considered my words carefully. I did not want the question to affect the answer.

"Maryann," I said, trying not to be the protective overbearing husband I so wanted to be, "do you know if any of the women connected with The Section is named Linda?"

She furrowed her brow. "There are no women in The Section," she said, "except Millie and her name is, well, Millie."

"Women connected to the men, I mean, like mothers, sisters...."

"You mean wives. Why not just say that? Though there is one sister named Linda. She lives in LA. She came to dinner once with Barcode. He wore those awful suits, poor man. What was his real name? Del, Dale?"

"Doyle."

"That's it. She happened to be in town and agreed to even the numbers at a dinner party for me, but that was three years ago. He was a bit odd, I think, but it's a shame he died. Besides his sister, there are three wives named Linda."

"Which three, my dear?" I asked.

She named them. One was very junior. Another was support staff, and the third...?

"Bartok? Bertrand?" She was concentrating hard, too hard, on French names, I thought.

"Bertram!"

I did my best not to react. "Have you seen her with her husband?" I asked.

"Yes, of course."

I raised my eyebrows to urge her on.

"He's the one, you know, the one who looks like a bloodhound. They're from Alabama, I think. You call him...."

"Beauregard," I said to Mack.

I noticed he needed a shave and realized their usual sartorial precision had deserted them hours ago. Mack had rolled up his sleeves displaying forearms striped by scars. Circles under his eyes told me he was already functioning on adrenaline. We were getting close.

He leaned forward in the chair and asked Maryann, "Has Sally taken any calls from Linda Bertram?"

"I wouldn't know. I've only been her keeper since this morning."

My wife was becoming a bit more belligerent than I considered healthy under the circumstances, especially given the increasing stillness in Mack. Always a bad sign.

"You would know," he said. "You know everything that happens in this house. Has she?"

"Why? So you can hit her again?"

"As I recall, you also hit her."

"That was different. I had a good reason."

"What reason?"

"She was acting like a ninny."

"I hit her because she was becoming dangerous. Which is the better reason?"

"Don't fence words with me, mister."

"I dare not. But I must ask the same from you. I am the foreigner here. You have me at a disadvantage with your words."

"You're never at a disadvantage in anything, I would wager."

"I try not to be. What is your answer so that I may not need to hit Sally again?" said Mack, but with no smile.

"I don't believe violence ever solves anything," said Maryann.

"Yet your husband deals in violence every day."

"My husband is not violent."

"That is correct. He does not commit violence. We do that for him. Now, again, how do you answer me?"

"If I don't, will you hit me, too?"

"No. I will hit him." He pointed to me. "For failing to control his over-intelligent wife. Now answer my question."

The last sentence was an order, not a request, and I hoped she understood that.

"She has not had any calls."

"Did she make any?"

"Yes, but I don't know who she called."

Mack stood and held out his arm. "Come, I will return you to your duties as Sally's keeper."

I opened my mouth to protest, and he pointed at the secure phone on my credenza.

"You have something to do. How long before you will receive the authorization?"

"At least until morning," I said. "It's Labor Day. And there are only two very circumstantial proofs."

"There will be more before tomorrow." He pointed again at the phone.

A knock on the door interrupted us, followed by an impatient Charlie. "Bertram," he said.

"You now have three," said Mack.

I called my boss.

TWENTY-FIVE

Dinner was subdued. Two people were missing entirely. Louis and Steve had been sent to get some sleep. Jay popped in and out, grabbing what he could from the breadbasket, showing Mack various telex messages, and disappearing again. Charlie looked like he wanted to provoke something. Theresa was reading a book at the dinner table, a family mortal sin, but she had a dispensation from her mother. We all wanted to escape. No one begrudged her descent into innocent fantasy. At least it was more rational than Sally's mythology.

"So Sally," said Charlie. His father looked up sharply. "Tell me about Linda. Is she a fun person?"

"How do you know about Linda?"

"You mentioned her." Which was a lie. "Isn't she one of your friends?"

"She is. We laugh a lot, mostly about our sons."

"She has a son?" asked Charlie.

Theresa stopped reading and gave him a narrow look.

"She does," said Sally. "He's a lot older than Danny, of course, but still all boy. He knows about computers. I hope Danny will learn all that stuff. I'm hopeless with it. So is Linda. She's older than me, but we're very much alike."

"How old is her son?"

"Seventeen going on seventy, Linda says. He's always telling her about all kinds of dangerous things in the world."

"Does he? What about her husband? I'll bet he knows a lot about danger with the job he's in."

The Brat was a born interrogator. We heard a lot about Beauregard, his high opinion of himself, his low opinion of his colleagues, his family's strengths and shortcomings, and the sad state of the world. Mack was looking thoughtful.

"I only asked for the one," I said to him in a low voice.

"The woman may be a dupe," he said, "but the boy will cause you trouble later."

I think Charlie was campaigning for a package deal.

...

Acutely uncomfortable is how I would describe that night. Charlie had guard duty, you might call it, staying at my house with the women and assisted by occasional visits from Jay as he had time.

"My son knows better than to become distracted when he is responsible," said Mack. It did not make me feel better. I was driving my car with Mack up front and Louis and Steve in the back. They were going to burgle my office while Mack and I waited in the car. So many disaster scenarios ran through my brain that I ran up a curb while making a right-hand turn.

"Fuck, Frank," said Steve.

We drove to about half a mile away, let those two out, doused the lights, and crept up to just outside the perimeter sensors. Then we waited. The moon did its part by being new as opposed to full, but the facility was lit like daylight. Still, I did not see them go in. They were that good. Of course, they had the benefit of having extracted all my knowledge without having to torture me for it.

"So how do you figure tomorrow's the day?" I asked, making conversation.

"The FBI has intercepts from Potemkin and the embassy."

That no doubt they are not sharing with us. "That's right," I said, "Jay is your creature, isn't he?" I was a little piqued.

Mack turned his head to look at me. "You also are my creature, Frank."

Touché. Too-bloody-shay. "You did it very neatly," I said.

"I did nothing but accept the opportunity. Your guilt did most of the work."

"I said I was...."

"Sorry. Yes, yes. They are dead and you are sorry. And all your vaunted loyalty is plundering your computer system as we speak. Do you enjoy the irony?"

Why was his grasp of irony always so dark?

"You know damn well I'm not enjoying any of this."

I could feel him smiling and sought a change of topic. "Don't you think you were a little hard on Steve today? Did you know his parents died in a car crash during his third year at the Academy? Declines in both grades and behavior soon followed. That is one damaged young man."

"Of course, I know his history. If he does not learn judgment, especially with women, he will not live to be a damaged old man," said Mack. "My son was with them the day they died, Frank. Like Steve, he has very little family, a burning desire for vengeance, and damage. The two will be formidable by my age. If they live."

"As I recall," I said, "you were already formidable by their age. And damaged."

"Do you think anyone who does what we do is not damaged?"

Maryann had packed a thermos of coffee for me, with two mugs. How did she know? She did not know where we were going or why or for how long. She only knew we were an odd assortment at a weird hour of the night and in my heap of a car. Why not four mugs? Somehow, she knew it would be me and Mack.

To my surprise, he accepted the offer. We drank silently for a few minutes.

"You and Maryann have been married for thirty years."

"Yes."

"Longer than I have known you."

I nodded.

"Do you…?"

"Yes, we do."

"You do not know what I was going to say."

"Yes, I do. I learned it from you. And the answer to your next question is we work on it. To keep it fresh. Both of us. I don't have a mistress."

"I know that," he said with scorn. After a few more minutes and a refill, he said, "My marriage was arranged by our families. If you…."

"I won't write it down."

He sighed. "My wife gave me two children and it was over. We were civil. Sometimes fond. Like Sally, she was beautiful to look at, but also like Sally, she refused reality. It frightened her too much."

I thought about the brave young woman I suspected was now under consideration for the post. Alex was my old boss's daughter and not so beautiful, also not much older than Theresa was now, back when I met her in Chicago a dozen years ago. She would have to be very brave indeed, I thought, to marry this man. I took another sip of my coffee.

"You didn't dislike your wife as much as you do Sally, though, did you?" I asked.

"No. She disbelieved, but she grew up understanding the need for security. She was not a danger. She was just not... there. Sally is worse than a danger. You were present when she said she does not care if he dies. She is malignant. And she has access."

I nodded. "I was the one who explained that concept to Alex."

"Her father explained access to her, because of Vasily's father."

"Yes. He explained what it was. I told her what it meant. I told her she would have to go with Vasily."

I poured us another cup. I knew what he wanted, and I gave it with the coffee. "Alex understands access. She knows reality, loyalty, and responsibility. The religion thing strengthens her; it doesn't weaken her like it does some. She is not squeamish about life."

"She was squeamish in Chicago."

I was in the dark here. I badly wanted to know what he meant, but I could not ask. Instead, I said the first thing I could think of. "She was very young, Mack."

"She was," he agreed.

"Louis told a witness in Chicago last year," I said, "that you cried over your wife's coffin."

It was an incongruity given our current conversation and I am too much an intelligence officer to let such things go. I feared I could almost hear that dangerous stillness settling in him, but to my surprise, he answered.

"No," he said. "Not Katya. Nadia, my daughter. Louis also was not himself that day and so misremembered. Nadia was everything a father could wish, dutiful, kind, obedient, beautiful, a talented dancer, and not too intelligent. I always thought a touch of stupidity in a woman helps to make her compliant. Until I met Sally."

"Too much of either can have the opposite effect," I said.

"But your women are very intelligent, and they comply well enough."

I wondered which women he meant. "With you, yes," I said. "They have a fair amount of common sense. Sometimes they even listen to me."

I thought he was having difficulty processing this latest admission of my inadequacy as a man controlling his women because he paused the conversation for so long.

"I am sorry there will be no marriage between Theresa and my son," he said finally with some reluctance.

There were so many ways to unpack these words, my mind could not decide on a favorite, so I thought instead about how happy I was by their practical import. Theresa would not wed a young, reckless killer and womanizer like I knew his father had been at his age, and then be locked up in some mountain fastness on the other side of the world with three other killers, one way more reckless and two-way more experienced, and all three of them too interested in women and not in a platonic way. I found I was delighted with this news and did my best to hide it.

"It's not a problem," I said.

"But if she is pregnant...."

"She won't be. Maryann had the doctor put her on the pill more than a year ago."

"But she was a virgin. Louis...."

Of course, Louis would know this. I so wished I was physically capable of killing him. Mentally, I was quite capable.

"We were not about to let biology derail her career," I said. "She is heading for medical school."

I think he was honestly shocked.

"It is a different world," he said finally.

"It is," I agreed. "I rather like it."

TWENTY-SIX

We were home shortly before four on Tuesday morning, and I hoped it was the last morning. Maryann had fresh coffee ready and greeted me at the kitchen door wearing her oldest bathrobe and a patient expression. Her luxuriant chestnut hair with its merest touch of grey stood out at all angles. I greeted her with total gratitude, and not just for the coffee.

"Almost over," I murmured in her ear as I hugged her. She smiled.

Jay sat at the kitchen table, eating.

Mack pushed his way in, looked around the room, and said, "Where is Sally?"

Jay swallowed his food and told him he had put a watcher on her door.

"In the house? A watcher in the house?" Mack nearly shouted it. For him, I mean. It registered just above normal conversational volume.

"He is not armed and he will stay inside until it's over," said Jay through a mouthful of biscuit.

Mack allowed himself to be mollified with bad grace, ignored the proffered mug from Maryann, and pushed me through the living room door ahead of him. I heard Louis and Steve enter the kitchen behind us.

My daughter, the future doctor, was sitting in a chair before the sensor radio console, wearing a headset and listening for signals denoting intruders. Charlie came in from the hallway. He had a silent communication with his father that manifested itself in the merest chin lift and meant Sally was where she should be because Mack visibly relaxed.

O-four-something is the perfect time for a meeting, especially if nobody has slept, everybody is armed, and most are facing at least the possibility of death in the next few hours. Mack took my seat at the head of the table for the first time. I took his seat on the right. Things had changed.

Maryann provided coffee, biscuits, and bacon, piled on trays. Nobody used plates. The time for niceties had passed. Crumbs were swept to the floor to make room for the plan of Steve's house and neighborhood to be unrolled across the dining room table. Theresa and the sensor console were brought into the room so that all she had to do was raise her hand to get instant attention. Maryann was asked to stay, to her surprise and evident mistrust. She sat opposite Mack, near the kitchen door.

"Beauregard, or Richard Bertram, has a seventeen-year-old son named David," said Louis, beginning a discussion of the personnel records.

Heads swiveled to Theresa. She was busy filing her nails and could not hear what was said because of the headset. The Brat walked over to where she sat near the living room door and snapped his fingers. She looked up. I knew better than to launch myself at the arrogant son of a bitch. He was so like his father. She took off the headset.

"That nerdy friend of yours, with the computer games, what is his name?" said Charlie. The emphasis he placed on the word friend told me something. Was he jealous? Also, where did he learn the word nerdy? From Steve?

"David. I told you. David Bertram. He's very smart. He graduated with my class, but he is a year younger."

Lucky for him he is still a minor, I thought, or he'd get no older.

No one else in The Section had a seventeen-year-old son named David. The other two Lindas had no sons at all. Compelling, but not conclusive, as far as evidence goes, I thought. Then Louis moved on from personnel to the computer, describing in detail how he had accessed each compartmented file.

Luckily, those files were only summaries. I had moved all details and sources away from the central system in The Section when I got back from Chicago. I wanted to make it as difficult as possible to access certain critical information.

"Unfortunately," said Louis, "those files were only summaries with no details or sources, but I was able to locate the file for last year's CETUS WEDGE operation on a separate server, and I was not the first to do so." He looked me in the eye as he said this, telling me how useless that little security measure had been. It inconvenienced no one except those who legitimately needed the information.

"The file is located on a server in another part of the building," Louis said, "but both the server and the terminal in the vault communicate through a mainframe computer in another building on the campus. All communications are secure. There is no communication off the campus unless it is manually uploaded from a physical storage medium.

"The Cetus Wedge file contained the ballistic signature that was determined to belong to Steve's Smith & Wesson at the end of that op. That information was changed two days ago. The change was accomplished on the terminal in the vault, according to the history files of the terminal."

Louis paused, like a judge about to pronounce sentence, which in a way he was. I noticed that Theresa was all attention, with her hand holding one earpiece of the headset to her ear, leaving the other ear free to listen.

"There is a logbook just inside the door of the vault," continued Louis. "An electronic record is made any time the vault is opened. If there is no signature on the log matching the time of the electronic record, it will trigger an investigation. Steve explained this to me and signed your name to the log."

"Thanks, Steve." I meant it. I had forgotten this bit of minutiae.

"Two nights ago, at almost the same hour, Richard Bertram signed the log," said Louis.

"I can't believe he would know how to turn a computer on," I said, "let alone change a file."

"He did not," said Louis. "I gained access to the video files of the hallways that are kept in the system. They are on a sixty-hour loop. The video of Bertram opening the vault door has not been erased." He held up a video cassette. "His son is clearly with him as he enters the vault. You will need this."

Louis handed me the cassette. Evidence does not get much more definitive than that. I set it on the table before me and stared at it.

"It should be both," said Jay, ever the cop. I looked up sharply. He raised heavy eyebrows at me.

Maryann's eyes widened and I realized she knew we were talking about death.

"He's seventeen," I said.

"Old enough in some states," said Jay.

Mack was looking at me. "He will come for you later," he said. "He will come for them." He pointed to Maryann and Theresa.

"To hell with later," said Jay. "He's an accomplice to murder right now."

Must be nice to be blind to ambiguity.

"What? No!" said Theresa. "He's my friend." So she knew, too. I was rather proud of my intelligent women.

"Do you have enough to gain the commission?" Mack asked me.

"Yes." I sighed, then admitted, "For both."

"Will you ask for both?"

"Dad, no!"

"You say he is just a friend?" said Charlie.

Theresa froze. She heard the menace, the tinge of jealousy, and instinct told her Charlie would not worry about Jay's desire for justice or Mack's insistence on the sanction of a properly constituted commission, or my propensity for moral deliberation.

"You wanted a dangerous man," I mumbled.

"It appears she has two," said Louis, chuckling.

Mack spoke to me again. "You must tell them now, and you must decide."

"There is no question about the older Bertram. I will ask for that commission. There is sufficient evidence for the son as well...."

"Dad, are you judge and jury? How can you? It's not even a fair fight. And he's seventeen and a friend of mine."

"Do you want me to give him a fair fight, Theresa?" said Charlie. "Do you think he will win?"

His tone was soft, but his words held all the venom he intended and Theresa aged a decade with that new understanding.

"Tell them," said Mack.

I took a deep breath, moved down the table to a chair next to Theresa, and looked at a blank spot on the wall before me. I began a full and truthful confession, publicly, to everyone in the room. All but two already knew the story, because they had been there. For my wife and daughter, it wasn't just a confession of my part in the deaths of Charlie's sister and mother, Mack's wife and daughter. It was a revelation to them of my real occupation, of what I had been doing all my adult life to put a roof over our heads, of the dirty universe I had fought to keep as far away from that roof and my world as I could and which was presently sitting at my dining room table discussing a thing called a commission.

Maryann closed her eyes, opened them, and said, "And now you are asked to make a judgment that may affect the lives of your wife and daughter." She sighed and hung her head for a moment. "For myself, Leo," she said looking up at me with the directness I knew and loved so well, "I would rather face a danger in the future than kill a boy in the present. But I want to protect my daughter as well. I am tempted to say at any cost."

"Dad," said Theresa quietly, "I would help you if you committed a murder, even if it made me an accomplice."

I sighed and hung my head "Then be an accomplice in a non-murder, and, I hope, to multiple non-murders." I took her hand and turned her to face me. "I'm sure you know better than to blab about the people you've met this weekend, but I want more than that. I want perfect silence about how you spent the holiday, down to every little detail. No references to 'someone said,' no descriptions of anything anywhere anytime. Describe a fantasy novel as far removed from this as possible, but nothing else. That includes not one mention or even an oblique reference, no knowing smiles, no blushes, and I know this will cost you considerable cachet among your friends, but there must be absolutely nothing about Charlie."

I felt the room stiffen, and it was my turn to look at each of the team and smile, especially at the Frenchman.

"You guys didn't know that was one of my duties, did you?" I said. "I'm the guy who neutralizes the pillow talk and cleans up the information sieve you invariably leave behind."

Louis shrugged. "Who has time to talk? Misha especially has no conversation."

Misha threw him a sharp glance.

"The SIG in his holster speaks volumes," I said and turned back to Theresa. As my eyes swept across the table, I did not miss the sly looks exchanged between Charlie and Steve. *Donovan is not going to miss Sally very much, after all.*

I continued. "All of this is vital, sweetie, but it goes a thousand percent for David. You must never, ever speak of this to him, and you must stop speaking to him at all, casually and gradually, but very soon. None of us will attend the funeral because we will be out of town on a previously arranged trip to somewhere. You will start college as planned but transfer elsewhere next semester. We'll discuss that later. Can you abide by everything I've said?"

"You know I can, Dad, I'm not stupid."

Maryann also nodded, with a slight smile for her daughter, whom she then pulled from the room to help her with Danny, upstairs crying for his breakfast.

I picked up the disk on the table and looked at Mack. "I will call my boss," I said. "It will be only Beauregard."

He acknowledged this with a single nod. "And Potemkin Village," he said.

"Of course."

It was just after five o'clock.

TWENTY-SEVEN

It took about two minutes to secure the commissions. That was a minute and a half for one rogue babysitter and thirty seconds for Potemkin Village. Uncle Sam is not fond of hostile specialist teams who show up on American soil uninvited.

I nodded at Mack as I entered the dining room. He was leaning over the plan Steve had drawn of his home and the cul-de-sac that surrounded it.

"For fuck's sake," said Charlie. "Where did you learn to draw, Steve? Your son would have done a better job with a sharp crayon."

Charlie was learning some new American idioms from Steve. These were markedly different from those he heard from Alex. I had to admit the criticism was apt though. Drunken rectangles lined a crooked street that ended in even more inebriated squares connected in a row of four. An X marked the second square from the right. Rough circles tried and failed to depict rows of hedges and bushes between each of the townhouses and surrounding the front and back of Steve's unit.

"How tall?" said Mack, pointing to the row of circles to the right of the house.

"About seven feet."

A pause, a stare, and Steve looked at the ceiling while he calculated. "A little over two meters," he said.

"And here?" Mack pointed at the squiggles to the left.

"Uh, I can see the top of the guy next door's head, and he's shorter than I am."

Neatly done, I thought. Steve left the conversion to Mack. I wanted Mack to ask him how much shorter the man was just for the pleasure of watching Steve convert inches to centimeters.

"These?" Mack was asking about a row of circles clustered along the front of the house.

"They reach to about halfway up the front window."

"What were you thinking, Steve?" I couldn't help it. He had been in the game for only about a year and had some really good instincts, but this house was boneheaded.

"I like the privacy," he said. "You can't see in from the street."

"And you can't see out to find who's hiding in the bushes," I said. "Curtains will give you privacy, for God's sake." I suspected Sally had something to do with it, but she was already not a favorite person in Mack's eyes, so I let it drop. So did Steve, with a grateful look. I had saved him from another calculation.

Another large paper was unrolled and the china cabinet raided for four fine crystal goblets to weigh down the corners. This chart illustrated Steve's inability to draw the inside of a house. He had the sofa roughly drawn in at one end of a room that served as both living and dining room.

"Where do you eat?" asked Mack.

Steve waved vaguely toward the other end of the ground floor room.

"At a table?" said Mack, as still and as quiet as I had ever seen him. I wanted to slip out but dared not move. Neither did anybody else.

"Um. Yeah. I...."

Mack's fist hit the table hard enough to topple two glasses over onto the polished surface, chipping one, and a third completely off the table and onto the floor, where it shattered. There followed a blistering stream of German invective listing all of Steve's inadequacies, from the choice of Sally—a point that still rankled, it seemed—to the house covered in bushes, his inability to understand so simple a system of measurement a five-year-old can do it, his impudence, his sloppy care of his new weapon, the state he keeps his holster in, his despicable table manners—I wondered about the materiality of this one in the lifestyle of a specialist—and his utter inattention to details.

I realized Steve was standing like a statue, glanced to my right, and saw Jay in the same stance. They were both Air Force Academy graduates, presumably accustomed to this sort of thing. Jay didn't speak the language, but he knew a dressing down when he heard one.

Mack sat down again and spoke in English, reasonably calm given the topic. "We must know every detail of a space we enter, as accurately as possible, or we die. Things go wrong. The more we do not know, the more things go wrong. Get that into your brain. Let it become part of your spine. Ignorance kills!"

Steve pulled the paper toward him and took out a pen. "I'll..."

"No," said Mack. "There is no time and they will blow it up anyway."

Steve stared at him open-mouthed, a silent "How...?" dying on his lips.

"Why have a man like Todor if you do not use him? He is a slow fighter and a mediocre shot." Mack looked at me. "If we had Sobieski, we could save the houses. He would also tell us how they might detonate. And he could fight."

I gratefully counted this as mild criticism compared to what had been dished out to Steve. I had been partly responsible for Sobieski's death as well as those of Mack's wife and daughter.

To Jay, Mack said, "Did you move the people out of the houses nearby?"

"I moved everybody out of the cul-de-sac. There are three single-story houses backing up to the rear fence along the townhouses. I moved those people also."

I wondered if I could steal Jay from the FBI. It was not fair they had somebody like him and I didn't. He was compromised, yes, but oh so competent.

"Watchers?" asked Mack.

"I have mine in the house directly behind. I can neutralize Potemkin's watchers out on the street. We know who they are."

"Do so. They know we know." He stood over the first diagram and looked over his shoulder at Louis seated behind and to his right. Louis stood, looked down at it, and murmured something to Mack, who indicated the blank area on the left side of the cul-de-sac and asked Steve, "What is the terrain like? What is here?"

"The ground slopes up from the street," said Steve, no doubt in approved military fashion. "It's quite steep, about forty degrees, covered in waste brush, scrub trees, loose baseball-sized rocks, grass, and weeds. There is a street at the top, about thirty feet higher than the street in the cul-de-sac. Distance from street to street I would say is sixty-five feet."

That was a first-rate answer, detailed, precise, and knowledgeable. He had to do it over in meters. And then define baseball-sized.

Mack and Louis spoke quietly.

"Michael," said Mack, "where will Dani Suta set up his rifle?"

Charlie thought for only a moment. "On the high ground directly across from the house, so he will slant northeast, with morning sun at the earliest time at the front. He can hit a fly on a wall at two thousand meters, so he will not understand the need for cover from so close a range."

Louis chuckled. "He will lug all that long-distance equipment for no reason. Misha will take care of him in a few seconds."

"Back up?" asked Mack.

Charlie considered. "I'd say one on either side, some seven meters down the slope. And there will be a radio. He is famous for answering with a grunt."

This level of precision intelligence astounded me. In that instant, I learned a dozen truths, the foremost being the sheer volume and detail of information these guys needed just to stay alive. Next was their consummate skill in gathering the intelligence. Finally, I knew in my gut that in accessing a server by going through our main frame, the Frenchman had vacuumed the main frame. Gathering everything available would have been impossible, but he took anything we produced about operations conducted by other teams or terrorist organizations, first the hostiles, then friendlies they had their doubts about.

It must have registered across my face. I realized no one was speaking and all were looking at me.

"Do you have a complaint?" asked Mack.

"When one has been well and truly fucked," I said, "there is no use in complaining about the last stroke."

"If it is the last," murmured Jay next to me.

"Now you know what we require," said Mack. "That is why we invited you and Jay to this meeting, so you will understand what we require for the future, if we live, and for the present, which we will address now."

I had wondered why Jay and I were there. I never before had been privy to their planning, but usually was just ordered to perform this, that, and the other thing now, in the next ten minutes, and an hour ago, depending on urgency.

"What are the numbers, Jay?" asked Mack.

"Four fighters, including Suta, from Potemkin Village, plus Todor Chilikov and four rentals who are at best mediocre, but can fire an AK-47."

"Is this information good?"

"The best. The man who rented them out to them is an acquaintance."

"How?"

"We grew up in the same neighborhood. He is now a gang leader here. He does not lie to me."

"Can he call them back?"

Jay shook his ponderous head. "He wants them gone. That's why he rented them out. You are doing him a favor."

"Are they black?" Mack's brow was furrowed. It would be an easy way to identify them in this neighborhood.

"No."

"You will need another babysitter, perhaps Skosh, for cleanup," Mack said to me.

I opened my mouth to protest.

"Unless I am dead, you will have other things to do."

Arguments die under the weight of some statements. "I'll call and put him on standby," I said.

There were more increasingly detailed and rehearsed instructions. Steve was made to repeat his instructions three times.

"Your strength is in unarmed combat," Mack told him. "I do not want you to be near enough to use it. Shoot. Fast. Relentless."

Steve nodded.

"If they plan to blow up the house, and you are the targets," said Jay, "how do they plan to get you in there?"

After a general, uncomfortable silence, Steve said, "My wife."

"How can they use her?"

"Through fear and deception," said Mack. "Have you made arrangements to take the child?"

Jay nodded. "Just as soon as they're awake."

"No," said Mack. "Now. Take the child now."

But it was already too late.

It was just before six o'clock.

TWENTY-EIGHT

Theresa found her mother when she handed the headset to the watcher and went to the kitchen for coffee. Maryann lay sprawled under the table, her head toward the refrigerator, a significant bleeding gash at her temple. A can of green beans lay beside her. Theresa raised the alarm.

In forty-five seconds, the dining room was in chaos and unrecognizable. If a gun existed that could scratch my table, it was doing so, with help from high-capacity magazines, suppressors, belts, knives, radios, and other paraphernalia.

Maryann regained consciousness, pointed to the key rack, and started another pot of coffee. The keys to my car were gone, along with both Sally and the baby. The mess of Danny's breakfast had not yet congealed on the high chair tray. Louis disinfected and bandaged Maryann's temple. He offered her a questionable European pain reliever, but she took a couple of ibuprofen from a small kitchen drawer instead, then ran upstairs and threw on a t-shirt, jeans, and a pair of sneakers.

The team got dressed without undue modesty, despite Theresa and Maryann, now bandaged, streaming in and out of the kitchen door with more biscuit, egg, and bacon sandwiches, heated in the microwave, so almost fresh, and pots of coffee.

Maryann stopped to stare once until I cleared my throat. She put the hot coffee pot on the unprotected table, something she normally never would do, and scurried back to the kitchen. I put a placemat under the pot. Theresa's eyes were wider than I had ever seen them and no amount of throat-clearing made her avert them.

She stood with a platter of biscuits until Maryann called her from the kitchen, then placed it on the table between two MP5 submachine guns and backed to the door before leaving and returning with more food.

The Brat took a beautiful Ferlach custom-made sniper rifle from its case, checked the mounts on the scope, inserted a magazine, screwed on a suppressor, chambered a round, and sited the scope before he noticed Theresa watching him. She held the now empty coffee pot in her hand. He gave her a somewhat rueful smile, donned his magazine-laden belt and Glock, then shrugged on a black jacket.

I was given grunting lessons by Louis, who had heard an actual sample of Suta's radio discourse. How I was to come into possession of his radio was not explained to me until they were just about to leave.

"If they have the woman," said Mack, evidently unable to force her name through his lips, "they know now about you, Maryann, and Theresa. You will take them with you in the pink minivan." He gave me instructions for a rendezvous point on the block beyond the ridge road, behind a convenience store. Jay and his watcher were to meet us there. My house would remain undefended.

The scratches on my dining table became trivial.

The team all wore close-fitting black clothing, with enough stretch to allow full range of movement, sturdy boots, and looser-fitting jackets. The automatic rifles and submachine guns were slung over their shoulders or across their backs. Charlie carried his rifle.

They filed through the kitchen, past the sink full of dishes, around the open dishwasher, through the garage door, and into the Mercedes parked inside, pausing only to put spare gear into the trunk next to the first aid kit and another radio set.

My family and I followed them, in t-shirts, jeans, light jackets, earplugs, and worried looks. I wore a shoulder rig with my Walther PPK under my jacket. We climbed into the minivan, and I clicked the garage door opener. Jay and his watcher were already on the road waiting.

We all took different routes to the convenience store and rolled in at about six-twenty. The front passenger, back, and side doors of the van opened. Jay replaced Maryann as my passenger. She moved next to Theresa in the back, with Mack on the floor across their feet. The other three arranged themselves in the very back, staying low, with comments about the crap allowed to live there, like a beach umbrella and a tennis bag, both of which were passed to Maryann and arranged somewhere on the back seat. Maryann lost her reserve and became herself again, so she gave as good as she got, telling them what she thought of beggars trying to be choosy. The watcher, a junior special agent, stayed in Jay's car to manage radio traffic, a couple of jamming bursts, and the FBI car phone. He was also responsible for the security of the Mercedes.

Mack directed every turn from the floor behind me and had me park slanted-in toward the curb on the side of the road above the cul-de-sac, nose pointed at the townhouses below. Despite an abundance of scrub trees and low brush, the view was excellent. My car was parked below in front of Steve's house behind his silver minivan. When the hell had Mack checked out the neighborhood sufficiently to be this precise, I wondered, and how did he do so without the thousand and one watchers in the area noticing?

"What about their babysitter?" I said, staring straight ahead. "Have we accounted for him?"

"He will not be here. Babysitters do not participate," said Mack.

"What the fuck am I doing here then?"

"You are learning the bad speech habits of Steve. It is good I am taking him from you. Now listen."

There followed detailed and minute instructions to govern me for the next sixty seconds, followed by the least welcome of all strictures.

"If we fail," he said, "you must take Maryann and Theresa to your safe place and contact Alex. She will get you out of the country."

He knew about the safe place. He knew I could contact Alex. "My government...."

"You are your government, Frank. If we fail, you will have failed. No one can repair that. Get out."

I thought he meant out of the country. Before I could put up another argument, he hissed, "Now!"

I complied. As casually as possible, I climbed out of the driver's seat and meandered down the side of the van, watching the ground near the edge of the road, searching for something that must have fallen out some thirty feet back—otherwise expressed as ten meters. I made a great show of spotting something and picking it up. Satisfied, I turned and headed back, still watching the ground, spotted another something at the edge of the brush after about two and a half meters, bent to pick *it* up, and saw Mack take out Suta, the sniper.

It was fast, absolutely silent, and horrifying.

The next thing I knew, he was stuffing a pistol into my belt, a firing pin in one hand, and a radio up the sleeve of my other arm. It's not like I hadn't seen the results of his work a bunch of times. I was just never present to see the process, that's all, and I never want to be again. My paralysis lasted less than a millisecond though, so I was able to stop the radio falling out of my sleeve, shift the pistol to a more secure position, and saunter seamlessly back to the car.

Once in my seat, I reached behind Jay to give my wife the things we wanted any watchers to believe she had dropped and I had retrieved.

"What is this?" she asked, holding out the firing pin.

"Just keep it, I'll explain later." I had turned forward again by this time and in my side mirror saw a long rifle barrel resting on the seat back behind Theresa and past her ear, its suppressor extending a few inches through the open window.

"I thought you were going to take Suta's position," I said quietly.

Charlie snorted softly. "He was accustomed to being further back. He knew nothing about effective cover. The place is completely exposed."

I would not have said completely exposed, having walked past it in total ignorance, a state in which I would have happily remained had I not followed the instruction to pick up a stone just where I did. I suppose cover is in the eye of the beholder.

"Daddy."

"Yes, baby."

"I'm scared."

"I know sweetheart, but Charlie is very, very good at this and will be careful. You will hear it, but it has a suppressor so it won't shatter your ears."

"I have two in the hedge on the right and a third on the left down below. I think Papa will take down the one on the left when he gets there."

"What about the other two on the slope?" asked Jay.

"He will have taken them out by now," said Charlie.

"Todor?" I asked.

"I do not see him. With him, that makes three not visible. He will not be in the house. That means there are only two in the house with Sally. They are rentals. Easy for Louis and Steve. Todor will be in a place where he can detonate by radio."

It occurred to me that Louis and Steve must have exited the van while I was walking behind it. I never heard a thing.

There was a squawk on the radio I held, asking for Dani. I grunted into it. The radio seemed mollified and quieted, but not for long. Jay watched a stopwatch for three more seconds, then shouted into his radio, "Now!" and the most unholy blanket jamming of all transmissions in the area made us both squelch our radios at the same time. It lasted thirty seconds, during which time gunfire erupted below us.

We could not pinpoint the suppressed MP5s in the din, but the AKs boomed in long bursts from inside the house and from our left. Sally ran out the front door, dragging little Danny by the hand. One of the tangos in the hedge on the right emerged and grabbed her arm, putting the muzzle of a handgun to her head. She let go of Danny's hand and he ran toward the silver minivan on the street as fast as his stubby little legs could carry him. He was chasing the neighbor's cat, which ran under the car. I heard the whizz-boom noise of the large suppressor behind my right ear and the skull of the man holding Sally exploded, forthwith.

Theresa said, "I'm going to be sick."

"Not yet. Hold still," said Charlie.

The house blew up and Danny was still on his way to the minivan as it also blew up before him in sympathy. A gun battle developed on the right between Steve and the hedge. As the child moved closer to the now burning car, Louis streaked from behind Steve on those long legs of his, tackled the boy, and covered him with his body.

The shooter in the hedge moved just outside his cover for a fraction of a second, which was enough time for Charlie. The man went down, not before hitting Louis at least once. Theresa threw up. Maryann held steady, though a little green, but she did not have the straight line of sight Theresa had.

There was no more gunfire. There was the crackling of the houses that were now all alight, and the cars, both the minivan and my car behind it. There was the eerie silence that always accompanies death. And of course, there were smells: of smoke and gasoline and cordite and blood.

I saw nothing more because I was speeding down the road and into the cul-de-sac. Jay was busy on the radio, asking for the standby surgeon to meet us at my house, asking Harkon to set up a perimeter, calling off the many sirens we could already hear from emergency vehicles, explaining they were not needed. He handed me his radio and I was patched through to Skosh. He would be here in four minutes to meet Harkon. I would be gone in less than three. An FBI watcher pulled up alongside us and took Maryann, Theresa, Sally, and the baby up to the back of the convenience store where they transferred into Jay's car.

We folded the back seats down and the team arranged itself along Louis's prone body, taking turns keeping pressure on a bullet wound that was too far up his leg at the back and inside and bled too much for my comfort. Louis lay on his stomach cracking bad jokes.

We stopped at the cars where Steve and Charlie took possession of the Mercedes and led us to my house.

There was no shortage of hands to carry Louis into the dining room, and I suddenly didn't give a shit that the magazines in his belt were scratching the hell out of my once fine table.

TWENTY-NINE

Sally tried to have a snit the moment she got in the door. Steve shut that right down. He tried to make her help the surgeon alongside Theresa, but she had a fit of the vapors. All that blood and stuff. Then we suggested she help Maryann fetch and carry whatever the doctor needed but had not brought with him. She did so with enough bad grace that Maryann gave up asking. Little Danny needed attention. His hair was singed and there was a blister on his forehead. The doctor gave Sally a salve for the blister and she took the boy into the kitchen, tended him, and fed him. She was competent to do that much.

Maryann washed Louis down after we stripped him and determined how we would hold him. Anesthetic was not on the cards. It was against the team's policy to be unconscious during an operation—their kind of operation, that is, not the medical kind. As far as they were concerned until they were out of US airspace, they were still operational.

Theresa set up a tea trolley with clean towels and the doctor's instruments, still sterile in their wrappers and laid out neatly, and assisted him throughout the ordeal. The rest of us held Louis still. He is a powerful guy. It wasn't easy.

I had seen them shot up, burned, hobbling on broken bones, vomiting blood, and peering through beaten faces. I had never seen them endure the treatment necessary to put them back together, not for something this serious. That usually took place on their well-equipped airplane where I was not invited.

Louis said nothing. He had been given the proverbial strip of leather to bite down on, cut from one of my best belts, which Maryann brought downstairs for the purpose. There were a few grunts and the veins stood out on the straining muscles of his arms, shoulders, neck, and legs.

The femoral artery was unaffected, but just barely. The damage was deep and though no bones were broken, the torn muscle would be painful for a long time. It took the doctor an hour to staunch the bleeding, remove the bullet, disinfect the wound, and suture the layers of tissue and skin. The team allowed an antibiotic but took it from their own medical kit in the trunk of the Mercedes.

Louis had begun to drift in and out of sleep by the time the last stitch was knotted. Maryann folded a clean bath towel, put it under his head, and covered him with a blanket. Mack sat in a chair, legs splayed out before him, filthy, disheveled, and exhausted. I sat next to him, in better physical shape, but mentally destroyed.

Charlie and Steve came in having washed and changed into clean shirts and sport coats. "We'll take care of it, Papa," said Charlie. "Steve must do it."

"Yes," said Steve.

Mack agreed with the merest nod.

I gathered my wits and said, "I'm going with them. I have to debrief him first." He raised an eyebrow. "Charlie and Steve will be there," I said. "They'll brief you," He gave a half smile.

On our way out to the garage, we met Jay in the kitchen, in the refrigerator actually, pulling out a platter of leftover biscuit sandwiches from breakfast. Sally glared at her husband from a chair in a corner, holding his sleeping son in her arms.

"We picked up Todor on his way to the airport," said Jay. "We had to put him on the airplane home. Turns out there is no law against carrying a radio."

"Ah, that is where your people and my people diverge my friend. Can I convince you to come over to the dark side? We offer good pay and benefits."

"Like hell you do. I'll stay on this side of the law, more or less."

"Sometimes it seems more less than more by your own choice."

"Choices can be tricky, but at least on this side, I can sometimes sleep at night."

I rode in the back of the Mercedes after Steve took my PPK and patted me down. We argued about how we were going to manage this. Steve wanted to just go in and blast away. Charlie was sympathetic but more receptive to my reasoned approach.

"Don't be such a fucking cowboy, Steve," I said. "This is not the OK Corral and I'm not Wyatt Earp. You'll end up getting me and my family killed if you don't listen to me, and I take exception to that. I'm glad you're alive and I hope you'll be comfortable in the blackest of black worlds, but I have no desire to join you. As somebody who should know told me recently, I have neither the skills nor the resources to survive there. Go with God, my boy, but leave me behind in some semblance of safety. Love, Frank." I kissed the air.

Charlie turned to look at me with a furrowed brow and a skeptical expression. "What do you suggest?" he said.

"One of you should go up to the front door and ask him to come with you. Bring him here. It's important that David, especially, does not see me. He must not associate this with Theresa." I knew that point would register with Charlie.

"What if he's armed?" he said. "It's not like we can pat him down in the street without inviting comment."

"True. Give me back my Walther and I'll cover him."

"I'll turn around and cover him," said Steve.

It was like I never knew him; he was so completely one of them.

Charlie went up to the house, no doubt with his most winning smile, and poured on the charm to Linda, but would not come in, with the best manners imaginable I was sure. When Beauregard surfaced, Charlie asked him to step outside, which he did with curiosity all over his face, having never seen this guy, who was too young to be one of Charlemagne. They were halfway to the car when he noticed it, blanched, faltered, and tried to turn. Charlie was ready for this and kept a firm grip on his arm, his Glock poking a hole in Beau's ribs. He opened the back door and shoved him in.

Beauregard found himself seated next to me, which surprised him, but not as much as the Beretta staring him in the face with Steve behind it with his finger in the trigger guard.

"I never meant...."

Charlie pulled the car away from the curb.

"It doesn't matter what you meant, Beau," I said. "I want to know what you did. Tell me about the Chinese."

He had dropped a bug in somebody's ear at one of his wife's great-uncle's dinners and was shocked, absolutely shocked, when he was contacted by somebody, some Chinese guy, with a briefcase full of money. He never meant....

"Cut the crap," I said. "What did you do then?"

The guy who gave him the briefcase also gave him the name and number of a guy. Really, he didn't expect the guy to try to blow up Steve's car. "I mean, my God, the baby!"

"Yeah, yeah," I said. "Why? What were you after?"

"I wanted Steve out of The Section," he said, trying very hard not to look at the Beretta. "He has no business there. He's not suited and he has no desire to learn from more experienced men. I thought I'd just scare him off. I've never been fully utilized in my opinion...."

His use of the word utilize was almost reason enough for the commission in my book, but I am an extremist.

"Linda agrees I'm under-appreciated," he continued nervously. "I worked so hard all my life and I'm never going any further. I'll retire soon and then what? I just wanted to scare him. Honest, that's all."

"Who suggested the Chinese?" This was a shot in the dark. I have no idea why I asked it.

"Linda said I should ask her uncle."

Steve and Charlie did not even raise an eyebrow at this prime intelligence. I made a mental note to call the guy on the China desk from a secure phone. I also sincerely hoped Charlie took Linda's involvement as just that of a silly woman trying to help her husband.

"And when it went wrong?" I said.

Beauregard's hands were shaking. He had been approached by somebody who knew all about it. Said to call him Nick. He could see Beau was in a bad situation, said Nick, and he had the surefire solution. He'd take care of the China problem and the Steve problem in one simple operation, and he asked nothing in return, absolutely nothing. Beauregard didn't think he had any choice, especially after Barcode. Nick knew about Barcode, too.

"Why Barcode?" I asked. "Why'd you kill him?"

"David thought it would be good to give you a different suspect, so we came up with a plan, and he's a genius with the computers, did you know that, Buddy? I'm so proud of him."

Theresa had said she'd help me if I committed a murder, but I don't think she would ever suggest it. I had a sour taste in my mouth about a lot of things right now.

I extracted a complete description of Nick and told Charlie to drop me off at a gas station. Steve gave me back my Walther. I took a taxi home. The Mercedes was already back in the garage and the last bags were being stuffed into the trunk, along with a diaper bag. The pink minivan was pressed into service once again, as Louis, dressed in a black warm-up suit he must have hated, was gently helped into the back, where he lay on his stomach for the ride. Mack sat next to him. I drove. Charlie and Steve took the Mercedes. Maryann, Theresa, Sally, and Danny rode with Jay.

I didn't know why my wife and daughter had been invited to the airfield, but I was glad they were staying in my sight. I could not bear to think of them alone in the house. I resolved then to find a place that is smaller, less conspicuous, and more easily secured.

At the airfield, it took some time to load all the gear and the injured man and to impart last-minute instructions and threats to me and Jay. I saw Charlie trying to take Theresa's hand. She pulled away. I recognized the hardening face of his father as he had been at that age and shuddered.

Sally sobbed all the way up the steps. Steve held Danny and talked airplanes with him as they went inside.

...

The house was quiet when we got home like it was sighing. The dining room table was a write-off and the crystal goblet still lay in pieces on the floor. Beds were all unmade, bathrooms filthy. The kitchen won the nightmare contest hands down, with dirty dishes everywhere, the dishwasher overflowing, and the refrigerator decimated of food, but no shortage of the baby food that had dried and stuck to an abandoned highchair. Maryann handed me a very dirty martini, made one for herself, and we sat on the sofa in the living room, the only relatively unscathed room in the house.

"Leo," said Maryann.

"Yes, my most beautiful girl," I said, slipping an arm around her shoulder. The martini combined with the sheer volume of relief gave me ideas.

"I don't understand Sally at all. I understand better the violent men you had here. We're all capable of some of that, more or less. But Sally is almost more dangerous, wouldn't you say? To not believe anything that's said to her and to put everybody's life in danger because why? For no reason."

"She was afraid, Maryann, but you're right. Mack said it best. Fear and deception have robbed her of common sense."

"Do you think Mack will kill her?"

"He wants to, but I don't think he will because of Danny. There is only so much trauma a child can handle, especially one that young. Mack won't take his mother from him, at least, not yet."

We sipped companionably.

"Leo," she said again. "I have a confession to make."

I held my breath, waiting for some mention of that damned Louis.

"All those years," she continued, "you would go off for days or weeks and come home exhausted and you wouldn't talk about anything. Sometimes you did no more than grunt for hours. And often you wouldn't eat, even when I made your favorite dinner. I thought it was an affair. I was so hurt. There were times I didn't ever want to talk to you again, but we had young children and you were a good provider. Most important, you came around in a few days after each time and then you were right as rain until the next trip."

She took a healthy sip of her martini. "I'm sorry I ever doubted you. I'm sorry I was not more supportive during those times."

I took a deep breath. "You supported me, Maryann. I was always knee-deep in blood and filth and treachery and terror. It just took me a few days to surface again as a human being. It never would have been possible without you. Even Charlemagne thinks you are the best thing since sliced bread. I think they're a little jealous."

I didn't mention the Frenchman. I figured if I'm her type, he can't be, so why bring it up? Besides, she was sucking on her olive in a way that drove Charlemagne completely out of my thoughts.

...

They found Beauregard in a ditch not too far from his home. He had been shot execution style by someone who accepted instruction from a more experienced man.

"Family says he went off in a Mercedes," said Chief Harkon, as we looked down at the body. "They say a young blond guy came to the door and they started talking and just got in a black car. That's the last they saw of him."

We stood and contemplated the mystery.

"I just can't seem to shake the memory of a Glock 17 I saw from a very unhealthy angle," he continued. "Was that yesterday?"

"Yes."

"Seems like it was a long time ago. Anyway, the guy behind the Glock was kind of young, I'd say. Kind of blond, too."

"Very blond," I said, correcting him.

"You want me to do anything special about this dead guy? He's another one of your employees, I think."

I nodded. "Can you just let me have the ballistics report when you get it?"

"Sure. Mind if I ask? Is this the last one? I mean, is it over and are they gone?"

"They?"

"The killers you were hosting at your house."

I took a moment to answer, deciding on a touch of truth. "Yeah. They're gone, and it should be over." There are no guarantees in the black, I wanted to say, but I kept my mouth shut. I suspected he knew it, anyway.

"I'm thinking this guy," he used his chin to indicate the body before us, "killed the other guy from your unit."

"That's about right."

"Some workplace dispute, maybe."

I gave a half nod, half shake.

"When you say it should be over, I'm guessing it's not over for everybody. Maybe it's not over for you."

I closed my eyes. "No."

"But it's over for him." He looked down at Beauregard.

"Yes," I said. "It's over for him."

...

I put the Beretta's ballistic report in the Charlemagne file and sent a copy via FedEx to the accommodation address I had been given in a teeny tiny country in the Alps. The following week, I picked up from my own accommodation address a packet with all the information the Soviets had on The Section, as promised by Louis, and began tightening up our filing procedures, because nothing is ever over for us bureaucrats.

EPILOGUE

A servant led Sally silently down the hallway, along its strange eastern carpet, and opened a door at one end. Without making eye contact, he indicated that she should enter, then closed the door behind her. She stood in a bare room, high ceilinged like all the rooms in this place, and windowless, again like all the others she had seen.

Misha sat behind a large mahogany desk at the far end of the room. His chair, the desk, and a plain, straight-backed kitchen chair in front of the desk were the only furniture in the room. There were no decorations anywhere. The bare floor made an echo of her footsteps as she acquiesced to his gesture to sit in the kitchen chair facing him.

He looked at her through bloodshot eyes. His face held three days' growth of a beard, blond like his hair, with hints of grey blending in almost imperceptibly. He wore all black and reeked of blood and vomit. There was dried mud on the belt that held his SIG Sauer semiautomatic. His sleeves were up, exposing powerful scarred forearms. He placed his palms flat on the polished surface of the desk.

She summoned defiance. He gave her contempt.

"What do you want?" she said. "Who do you think you are locking me up like this for the past week? I don't even know your real name."

"You may call me Satan. As you see, we have returned from England." He remained still and silent after this, until she began to fidget.

"I am told you have not asked to see your husband." His blue eyes seemed to pierce her skull.

"So?"

"You may be gratified to know he is expected to live."

She shrugged. "Great. Then we can go back to that hovel you put us in before. At least Danny can play outside there—when there isn't six feet of snow."

He continued to regard her silently.

"Why did we have to come back to this prison?" she demanded.

"While we were away, we needed to ensure your safety. This is the safest place. Were you not well cared for by the staff?"

"I don't believe you."

"That is your choice." He continued to stare at her.

It began to unnerve her. "What do you want?" she demanded again.

"I want to know what you want."

"You know what I want. I want to go home."

"Steve cannot go back. You know that."

"I know nothing of the kind. And his name is Dan. Get that through your thick skull."

Misha became very still and it unnerved her again. She did not know why he had that effect on her but elected to maintain her defiant return stare. Finally, he said, "Steve Donovan is his name. He is in my employ. Everything he has, everything you have, belongs to me and you will do me the courtesy of calling him Steve simply because I say you will!" The last word was accompanied by a fist pounded onto the top of the desk, making her jump involuntarily.

His voice became quieter, but she could not make herself relax. She fidgeted on the chair, trying and failing to find a more comfortable way to sit.

"I have a proposition for you," he said.

"I'm not giving up my son."

"He is Steve's son as well, but I will not ask you to give him up. Will you listen?"

She hesitated, suspecting a trap. "Ye-es."

"You cannot go home." He held up his hand as she opened her mouth to protest. "Unless you want your parents to participate in your danger."

"I'm not in any danger." She rolled her eyes.

"Very well, then. Go home to them, but the boy will not go. I will allow you to place your parents in peril, but not the child."

"It's no use talking to you, mister. You are a liar."

"A few months ago, a man held a gun to your head; your house and car were destroyed by explosives, and your son was nearly killed until my friend risked his life and indeed, took a serious bullet wound, saving the child. You were present for all of that. You saw it, you heard it, you smelled it. What part of it was a lie?"

She had no answer. She would have said it was all playacting, as she knew it was, but the brains of the man with the gun had splattered against the side of her head and there was all that blood and.... She closed her eyes at the memory and tried to close her mind, comfortably, safely, but could not, which allowed his next words to enter.

"You may go anywhere you like, but not home. You will be able to call your parents as much as you wish. I will give you a telephone number to call that will keep them and you safe. Understand that I do not care about your safety. I care about the child. To that end, I will give you a house, a car, a modest income, and will cover all the expenses involved with raising the child, such as food, clothing, and school fees. You may pick any place east of the Mississippi River. There are stipulations. Are you prepared to hear them?"

"Yes."

He listed them, like items on a grocery list.

"You will do nothing to endanger the child. I do not mean that you will do nothing that you think will endanger him, but nothing that I think will do so. My opinion is the only one that counts. If you endanger him, Steve will take the child. You will never see him again, and all support will cease.

"If you elect to voluntarily allow the child to live with his father at a future date so that you may resume what you call a normal life, you will continue to receive the same support minus the child's expenses.

"You will resume your maiden name and call Danny by that name. I will provide the documents necessary to satisfy schools and other authorities.

"You will tell your parents, whom you may call as often as you wish, that you cannot say where you are because Dan, as you call him, works for the government in a secret job. You may give your parents the accommodation number I will provide so that you can receive calls, and when he is old enough, you may allow the child to speak to them, but you will never visit them nor give any hint of your location. If you do, Steve will take the boy and all support will cease.

"You will not disclose to anyone, at any time, Danny's true name or any of the details concerning the separation from your husband. You may say you are divorced and leave it at that. Is this clear to you?"

She nodded. "When can I leave?"

"Where do you wish to go?"

She thought. Geography had not been a strong subject for her. "Texas," she said.

"It is west of the Mississippi."

"Tennessee."

"No."

"You said!"

He raised an eyebrow.

"All right, all right. North Carolina?"

He considered it and nodded.

"When can I leave?" she asked again.

He opened a drawer on his right and drew out a small number of large papers, elaborately captioned and densely printed. He pushed one page toward her and offered a pen.

"What's this? I can't read this. What are you asking me to sign?"

"Your divorce," he said. "It will be granted by a court in Vienna before the end of the month. Sign where I have marked an X."

"I can't read it. It's written in some kind of gibberish; how do I know what it is? I don't trust you."

"You may trust me to kill you if you give me any more trouble."

It was the stillness in his manner, in his voice, in his staring blue eyes, that pierced the fog of her delusion just enough to make her act in her own best interest. She signed.

He took the paper and the pen, and said, "Go. Pack your things. You leave tonight."

The End

A LIGHTER SHADE OF NIGHT
A Charlemagne Short Story Collection
Mid to late 1960s

INTUITION

Louis demonstrated the technique again. For such a smart guy, Misha was taking his time learning the simple thing he was trying to teach him. He remembered Uncle Bertrand showing him the maneuver just after he had reached adolescence. He learned it on the first attempt in this very gymnasium in the basement of Misha's house.

"Again," said Louis. "Do it again. The dummy now. Your knife comes uncomfortably closer to me each time. Go for the dummy like he is real."

A teacher faced with a precocious pupil, whose excessive talent becomes suddenly evident, can react in any number of ways. Pride, jealousy, disbelief, and finally dismissal will run through the pedagogical mind in quick succession. Louis was usually well aware of his emotions, allowing them almost complete freedom of expression on his face, in his words, and through his actions. He stood transfixed as Misha opened the neck of the dummy in a move so fast as to be almost invisible.

His student raised an eyebrow, asking Teacher for a grade. What could Louis say?

"You will do very well if you do not mind the blood," he said.

It was what Uncle Bertrand had said to him. It turned out he did mind the blood and concentrated on keeping a bit of distance from it. Louis was a superb marksman.

"I do not mind blood," said Misha.

"You have not done this before."

"I have killed twice."

"You shot them. It is different."

"I will not flinch."

Louis looked into that impossibly still stare. Misha's nineteen-year-old blue eyes had watched his parents and siblings die by car bomb a month before. The murderers responsible had done their best to annihilate him as well, to their own destruction.

"You are first born, Misha. You should not fight. Marry the girl they picked for you and raise an heir. I do not mind helping you survive, but you were not trained for this like I was."

"My family's enemies chose this occupation for me, Louis. I will marry her and beget as many heirs as possible. How do you suggest I protect them? Build a castle? Hire an army? This is not the Middle Ages. I must know where our enemies are and bring the fight to them. It is the only way to survive. You need not tie yourself to me."

"Of course I am tied to you—by more than blood. We have been friends since our infancy. Of the three of us, you always saw furthest. What do you propose?"

Misha picked up a strop and ran his blade over it before putting it away. He looked up at Louis.

"We must find Vasily."

...

After a week-long journey to a desolate place in search of their friend, Louis trained his binoculars on a decrepit Gdansk manor. Its exterior rendering had peeled away from the underlying brick, giving the house a diseased aspect. He could see barred windows at the basement level.

Misha returned from his inspection of the other side of the house. "It seems the only working entrance is on this side. I have checked again. There are no intact staircases to the main doors."

Louis pulled a damp roll of paper from his jacket pocket and handed it to his friend.

"What is this?" asked Misha.

"A plan of a similar house three miles away. I got it from the old man I drank beer with last evening while you disapproved and told me to stop. I did not stop after you left, and so we have an idea of what the layout may be like in there." Louis nodded toward the house.

"Which may or may not be accurate."

"But is nonetheless better than nothing." He met Misha's steady blue eyes.

"Where is the sentry likely to be?" asked Misha.

Louis took the chart from him, unrolled it, and pointed. "Here. If he hears you on the stairs, he will turn to face you."

"He will not hear me."

Louis suppressed a guffaw at what, at first glance, seemed unwarranted overconfidence until he remembered all the games requiring stealth they used to play as children. Misha always won. He nodded instead, reinforcing his courage through Misha's confidence.

"In that case, he will be facing toward the prisoners," he said.

"There will be more guards with the prisoners, I imagine."

Louis nodded. "At least two, that is KGB procedure."

As Misha studied the basement drawn on the plan, he said, "Initially, I will hold the body to direct the spray, but the floor will be slick with his blood. Be careful as you move past me. I will be able to follow within moments."

Louis wondered about his friend's unnaturally accurate grasp of the job. "You have never...."

"I can read."

"We should use suppressors. Though not silent like your knife, they are at least quiet." *And will provide backup if you balk.*

"Of course."

"And check for keys before you let the body drop."

"Good advice, I will."

Louis knew his lifelong friend came from a cold family, but this calculating stillness in the face of fear unnerved him. He suppressed an urge to shake a morsel of humanity into Misha.

"There may be more of them staying upstairs, like in a barrack," he said.

Misha agreed. "Then we must be very quiet. Do we know their habits? Will they be drunk by a certain time?"

"By one o'clock, according to another source I met last night, but they have high tolerances and can be deadly until nearly comatose."

"While you were gathering your intelligence last night, I watched this house," Misha said with just a hint of a smile. "There were no lights on the ground floor, but a few on the northeast side of the first floor. These were dark by two o'clock, confirming your source's information. The basement lights stretched along the western wall to the left of the door. They were dim, probably coming from a lit hallway."

Misha pointed to a room drawn on the plan and continued. "Near this kitchen will be the interior staircase to the cellar from the upper floors. See, it is indicated here, very much like in my house. We must be wary of sounds coming from that direction."

Louis refrained from pointing out that, because Misha's house was vastly larger than this one, comparisons could be dangerous. But he did bring up the next thing on his mind. "Do we know Vasily is here?"

"Yes."

Louis paused. "Is there additional information? That Vasily has an interest in making bombs, and that the local communist party headquarters was blown up, does not mean..."

"And there was a press report that the perpetrators are being held here."

"Yes, but no names or descriptions were released."

Misha stared at him. "He is here."

Louis said nothing, expressionless, and Misha added, "Yes, I am risking our lives on my intuition. What was her name, by the way?"

Louis narrowed his eyes suspiciously. "Who?"

"Your other source."

"How did you know...?"

"I know you."

Louis sighed. "When do we go in?"

"Tonight, after the lights upstairs go out."

"So soon? More reconnaissance..."

"This morning at dawn I heard a shot coming from the basement. They carried out a body just before you arrived from your... intelligence gathering."

Louis's eyes opened wide.

"It was not Vasily," said Misha, smiling. "Intuition," he continued, in answer to Louis's next unspoken question.

"But you fear he will be next."

Misha nodded. "I will be back after sunset. I recommend the small, dark copse to the West." He pointed to their left. "There is a mossy hollow under the trees, where you will hear any movement from the house but may rest when there is none. What was her name again?"

Louis ground his teeth and glared. "Bronya. She may be a little old for you."

Misha grinned, turned, and disappeared through a wilderness of brush. He was gone before Louis remembered to ask him how he planned to get the three of them out of Poland, assuming they survived to need a way out.

A soaking rain, light but steady, lasted all afternoon. Despite interference from the dense canopy of branches above him, by sunset Louis was wet enough to wish he could catch the streams of water dripping from his chin to quench his thirst. His black curls plastered themselves to his forehead and cheeks, and his jacket did little to delay the thorough saturation of the inner layers he wore. His boots held the line, though; he was grateful for dry feet.

Misha's arrival brought with it an end to the rain. He was comparatively dry, but only because he wore a better coat. Bramble branches and cockleburs decorated it. He must have crawled for some distance, judging by the caked mud on the front of his legs and torso.

"Bronya's uncle has a boat with a motor and also a petrol supply," Misha said.

Louis indulged himself by curling his lip into a snarl as he glared at his friend. "Did you engage it?"

"Yes, but we will not use it."

The snarl gave way to confusion. "Why?"

Misha shrugged with only a maddening smile.

They stood in the gloom of fast-falling night, well covered by tall grasses and brush, and watched the lights go on upstairs in the house-turned-prison. Louis marveled at the stillness that characterized his friend. Not only his stance, he thought, but even his movements are economical in the extreme. He opened his mouth to ask how he liked Bronya, to show he had forgiven his friend's poaching, when Misha spoke first.

"Instead, I bought a rowboat."

The injury over Bronya renewed itself. "Did you hire someone to row?" The flash in Louis's black eyes was invisible in the dark, but his voice held a touch of venom he was sure Misha could hear.

"No," came the smooth reply. "You and I will take turns. There is only one set of oars. If Vasily is able, I am sure he will want to contribute as well."

"Does your intuition tell you that I am about to pummel you?"

"Yes, but you will not. You know that I have judged correctly. And yes, Bronya was very nice indeed."

"I am sure I will come to value your judgment, Misha, and even rely upon it, but I will never appreciate your ability to read my mind. Stop it."

When the time came to move, it was a relief, a welcome journey from wretched boredom to adrenaline-fueled terror. Louis fretted, his back plastered against the wall beside the door Misha had entered. They had crept down the crumbling cement steps in their socks at Misha's insistence, making Louis's feet join the rest of his body in cold clamminess.

He counted slowly to thirty, doubting for a moment that Misha would be able to perform but suddenly sure he would. The man—still a boy, really—must be the last of a host of peculiar ancestors, he decided. Thirty seconds reached, he entered, turned left down the dim hallway, and passed Misha, who held the dying sentry so that the lessening spray from his carotid hit the wall silently.

Louis's stockinged feet now squelched through blood.

Sounds of blows against a body leaked through the door at the end of the hall. Louis waited as Misha unlocked it with keys he had taken from the sentry. Two men, in the process of beating a prisoner, turned at the sound. Louis's Modèle 1935 dispatched them rapidly, with finality and precision. He was pleased with the new suppressor he had fitted. The sound was no more than a soft pop-zip.

Finding Vasily in one of the cages to the left took only a moment despite the dim light. He stood when they entered and tilted his head toward the prisoner in the cage next to him. "He is an informer," he told them in French.

Louis eliminated the spy as Misha unlocked Vasily's cell and shackles, and supported the eighteen-year-old—nearly carried him—from the cage. Louis took the keys and unlocked the others on their way out but used a few choice threats to make the inhabitants cautious about moving too soon. There was no sound from the basement as they emerged into a moonless night and disappeared into the brush.

...

Surveying a small wooden house with consternation, Louis wondered if he knew it. They had reached it by a circuitous route through a semi-rural suburb of Gdansk and were viewing the place from the back, but it seemed eerily familiar to him, or perhaps the neighborhood was. He couldn't be sure.

"I do not understand why you insist on this delay, Vasily. We must hurry," he whispered.

Instead of answering him, Vasily asked Misha, "Did you secure a motorboat?"

Louis hissed with exasperation and answered for Misha. "He did but then bought a rowboat. If you must delay us like this then you can help us row, despite your poor hand."

He winced to himself when he remembered the mangled mess he had seen in the dim light of the basement.

"May I borrow your gun, Misha?" Vasily asked. He took the old relic Misha proffered him and held it in his left hand, the hand that was still whole.

Louis winced again.

Vasily stood and crossed the five meters to the back door of the house. Louis tried to follow, but Misha held his arm, stopping him, and shook his head. They watched from their places concealed under an evergreen tree on the left of the open space. Vasily moved back from the door after knocking and waited.

When Bronya stood in the open doorway, he stepped into the light from her kitchen.

"Vasily!"

"My uncle was not involved, Bronya."

"I don't know what you're talking about." She said it too quickly and with too much vehemence.

"They took him because he was with me when they came for me. After you met with them. After you made love to me."

Her eyes searched the darkness. "Are you alone?" Her voice held notes of rising panic.

"They shot him at dawn yesterday." Vasily raised the gun.

"Vasily, please, I didn't mean…"

Louis was unable to learn what she did not mean because she died before finishing the sentence. But he could guess. The hastily contrived suppressor on Misha's gun was not as effective as the one on Louis's Modèle, but it was quiet enough. There was no sound from within the house either, because her uncle was waiting for them with several other men at his motorboat.

The disappointed ambush stood stomping and smoking under the lights of the quay as the three friends rowed silently past them in the pre-dawn darkness with muffled oars.

Louis took his turns each time that day, rowing without complaint, watching the gruesome work of the night before show itself in Misha's hardening gaze.

"How did you know she was dirty?" he asked.

Misha's answer explained more than usual. "I saw something in her eyes and wondered why she feared me."

They reached Gdynia after nightfall and stowed away on an empty trawler bound for Kariskrona. The hold stank of bilge and rotting fish. They lounged on a large pile of canvas, dry and alone but for the occasional curious rat.

"I propose we go into business," said Misha.

"What business could we possibly go into?" asked Louis. "I am trained for only one thing."

"Precisely. I propose we go into the business that Vasily's father made such a success. But instead of being solos, we should form a team. No country wants to risk another world war, but governments will continue to need quiet solutions. My intuition tells me that in time, if we live, we will be very successful. We are younger than the aging partisans of the last war and can employ more modern skills."

Louis nodded. "The combination of these with more traditional methods can be formidable."

"I agree," said Vasily. "We will need a trade name to shield us from our clients."

They contemplated names for a time until Louis spoke again. "I have been considering our more peculiar ancestors. The name we choose must sound formidable, like them."

"I say it should conjure the ghost of a warrior," said Vasily. "A feared barbarian."

Misha broke the next long silence. "Then let it be the warrior we all share. Let the name be Charlemagne."

COLD CUNNING

"Misha, we are surrounded."

Vasily's low voice held no hint of panic or any other emotion. It was a bald statement of fact meant solely to inform. He watched one of three sides of the perch where they had taken refuge. The roof and parapet of this square keep in a ruined castle had miraculously survived time, war, and weather. The cliff face forming its fourth side intermittently dropped clouds of snow onto their heads.

Louis felt more agitated as he trod through fifteen centimeters of snow, tamping down new pathways from aperture to aperture in the crenelation. He moved in long strides, anticipating the violence to come. Besides sex, he could find no better way to feel alive than to risk death.

Misha's cold, still countenance did not change. He stood like a snowman, his hatless, blond head well on its way to matching the landscape. One of the drawbacks to his habit of stillness, thought Louis. You risk turning into an ice sculpture. He smiled at the idea. The snow made it harder to see Misha against the white sky, like an effective camouflage. Louis shivered at the cold and became more careful about showing his dark head between the apertures.

He marveled as Misha displayed an even more deliberate economy of movement than usual while watching the scene below through binoculars. The AK-47 Louis carried would easily reach the men on his side. Louis peered carefully through an aperture on Misha's side to see what could be so fascinating. The man below them, just inside a curtain of trees, held silent communication with someone to his left, judging by the hand signals he gave.

Misha shifted the binoculars to his right, and Louis's eyes followed the movement, finding the other half of that conversation also within range of their AKs. This meant they must be in range of their enemies' weapons.

It seemed Charlemagne was trapped. This was the name Misha, Louis, and Vasily had given themselves when it became clear they needed to earn the cooperation of friendly governments to defeat their enemies. The name gave those governments a team they could hire without attribution. It gave the team a name they could use to conceal their identities.

Initially, Charlemagne accepted commissions from small governments for increasingly large sums and access to the information they needed to stay ahead of an expanding list of operatives seeking to kill them. Their business was growing. So was the number of their enemies, though they were only in their twenties.

"How many?" Misha asked, not taking his eyes off the man he suspected might be in charge, the one in his binoculars signaling to either side, often emphatically.

Louis moved to a different aperture. "I have two in this view and one more in the next aperture to the west."

"I have three," said Vasily. "The entrance is below me."

Eight. A bit excessive for the elimination of three young men on a hiking holiday in the mountains. They had been careful to hide their weapons. Misha had even forbidden Louis the enjoyment of a willing young woman at the hostelry they stayed in the night before.

"You will not be able to hide your gun from her," Misha said.

"It has never been a problem before."

"It will be a problem here. These are small, poor villages and it is winter. They have nothing else to do but talk."

And make love. Perhaps my refusal caused more comment than my gun would have, Louis thought. She was both delectable and willing. But he kept his mouth shut and obeyed without an audible grumble. He and Vasily had come to realize their survival depended on Misha's judgment. It was superior to their own. But as in this instance, it could be constraining, and constraint was against Louis's nature.

Misha wore a snow blanket at least a centimeter thick by now. Louis noted that it did not melt. *So his body temperature must be as cold as his manner.* He moved back to the aperture on Misha's side of the keep to discover what could be so enthralling.

The man below signaled frantically—emphatically—arguing with his hands. He was easy to see even without Misha's binoculars.

His black jacket and waving arms stood out against the pristine white of the snow around his position, both on the ground and in the trees, weighing down the branches of the pine he stood next to.

"There is disagreement among them, Misha," Louis murmured.

Misha also kept his voice low. "It appears a few loyalties have become more fluid. We must find how best to exploit it."

"They all are in range," said Louis, "and not well covered. I can take at least one, probably more before they scramble to conceal themselves."

"It is the same on this side," said Vasily.

Misha dropped his binoculars and picked up his AK. "We will each kill only one. Mine is the commander. One on each side, then silence. If they attack, we will respond, but I do not think they will." He paused. "On my word..."

"Now."

Misha's modulated voice never changed.

The commander had drawn his arm back but died before he could sweep it forward to order the attack. Two other men, one on either flank, died in the same moment. Three more ran. The two who remained were in Vasily's view at the front of the keep. They stepped out from under the trees, holding their weapons by the straps out to their sides at arm's length. Then, dropping the guns to the ground, they stepped away, arms raised, and waited.

Both Vasily and Louis reported no other movement. With a gesture, Misha sent them below, while he covered the approaches to the door.

Vasily covered Louis as he checked their prisoners for more weapons and gathered the two AK-47s from the ground. He tied their hands behind their backs, prodded them up the stairs to the roof, and forced them to kneel. Misha began the interrogation.

...

"He is a brute," said the taller man, Milos. He shook his blond curls in contempt for the target. "He beats his wife. He beats the servants. Ask Blago here. He will tell you."

The smaller, dark-haired man with a pinched face nodded. "He hit me many times for a minor mistake. A very small mistake."

Misha regarded him silently. "Tell me about the small mistake."

Blago paled, perhaps at the memory of the beating, more likely at the quiet purr in Misha's voice. He swallowed and said, "I spilled some wine."

"What kind of wine?" said Misha, still quiet, still purring.

Another swallow. "Lafitte."

Blago could not tell if his interrogator knew the wine. The man betrayed nothing. His stillness made Blago shiver involuntarily.

"How much did you spill?"

Somehow, Blago understood it would be unwise to lie. "I dropped the bottle."

"A full bottle?"

Misha did not need a verbal answer; the man trembled. He reflected that he would have hit him also. His father would have disapproved of such an act when dismissal might be more appropriate. But he was not his father. He would have hit him. Perhaps not repeatedly.

"How many times did he hit you?"

Again he saw the answer before the man spoke. "Only once."

So far, the target was behaving as he would, including the attempt at ambush. Misha's attempt would differ, however, by succeeding.

The shadow from the wall behind Misha had begun to creep over the other man. It would be dusk soon, a good time for another ambush. They must move. He knew Louis would prefer to execute these two before moving on, but he suspected they had more information to give.

He remembered a shallow cave they had passed on their way down to this valley. The narrow entrance to the cave would be easy to defend against anything other than overwhelming force, though the climb would be arduous in the snow. He led the way, with Vasily and Louis prodding their charges, none too gently, to move quickly.

Misha gave each man a sip from his canteen before separating them to opposite sides of the cavern and setting a guard schedule. He considered continuing the interrogation but decided he would rather have enough light to see their faces as they spoke. It is easy to be deceived by the mere voice of a man who believes his own lie.

...

Vasily bound their ankles and gagged them. The team took turns on watch while the other two slept. Dawn streaked in, leaving a bright narrow strip on the back wall of the cave and plenty of light outside to continue their questions.

Vasily could smell it and so knew where to look and find it in the wet trousers of the servant. He had been in this position and understood that pity would be neither useful nor appreciated by the recipient. Instead, he helped Misha continue the interrogation, each taking one of the men outside to relieve himself while Louis enjoyed another hour of sleep. They stood knee-deep in snow on a wide rock ledge overlooking the white sagging treetops of the forest.

Vasily left Blago, tied and standing, on a narrow ledge, making sure the sunlight fell on Blago's pants to dry them. He crossed the ten meters to where Misha had begun the morning's questions with Milos.

"How do you know he beats his wife?" Misha asked as he retied the fair-haired man's hands behind him. The man's shoulders stiffened during an almost imperceptible pause. "Do you know her?" he prompted. Again, more stiffness and another pause.

"I have spoken with her on occasion," came the careful reply.

"If her husband is so reprehensible, why did you join the party he sent to ambush us?"

The man's mouth opened and closed twice before he managed to produce sound on the third try. "I hoped to sabotage it."

"Did you succeed?"

"No, the commander was about to order the attack when you shot him."

"But there was dissension. Did you lead the dissent?"

The man looked at his shoes and shook his head. "Blago did."

"Do you mean the servant?"

He nodded, head low.

"Tell me how it is you are able to speak to the wife."

After much rambling, clarifying, evading, and admitting, Vasily understood the target's wife was from the same village as this man, that she was very beautiful, and they had grown up together.

"Does she have a child?" asked Misha.

The man looked up with the suggestion of a smile. "Yes."

"A boy? A son?"

"Yes. A son," he answered with a pathetically easy-to-read expression.

"Your son," said Misha.

The man's eyes opened wide. "You are a devil!"

Vasily and Misha left him shivering on the ledge and walked to where the other prisoner still blinked in the brightness reflected by the snow.

"What was the disagreement you engineered against your commander?" asked Vasily, prepared to loosen the man's tongue, but hoping he would not have to. Funny how the simple human disaster of peeing one's pants could call up his sympathy. Perhaps it was because he had been in the same condition not very long ago until Misha and Louis pulled him out of that hellhole.

Blago shrugged. "Somebody suggested the commander wanted many dead so he can take over the province from Stefan."

Stefan was their target. The servant had Vasily's attention. He squirmed under it.

"Who suggested it?"

There was no answer.

"To whom did you suggest it?"

Another wide-eyed stare, but this man did not call Vasily a devil.

"I told a tree. I pretended someone was behind it."

"Why?"

Another silence. Vasily moved in close, using proximity to make the man feel his menace like a creeping cold.

Blago shivered in the sun. "She paid me."

"Why would she do that?"

"To protect him."

"Him? The other man with you?"

"Yes, Milos. When the shooting started, I tackled him and made him stay down. Then I forced him to surrender with me."

"Why not let him run away with the others?"

"Because..." Blago looked at his boots. "Because he is sure to say the wrong thing to the wrong person. He always does."

"You judged it safer to be with us?" Vasily wondered about these people. "Why?"

"Because we hired you."

"A man calling himself Alfrid hired us."

Blago nodded. "He is the intermediary. We sent a man to the city to find what we needed. He found Alfrid. My brother-in-law raised money for the fee. He is head of the next village over, across the river. Everyone contributed. Stefan took almost all the harvest this autumn and sold it. We are hungry. We had to do something."

Vasily wondered what additional tactics helped create such universal generosity to commission a murder, though he knew how powerful a motivator hunger could be.

"And the wife?" he asked.

"She will marry Milos, and he will take charge."

"You just suggested he is stupid."

"Yes. If he were any smarter, it would not work, you see. He would know that she is actually in charge. This way, he will be happy; she will make him think he is the boss, and we will eat."

"And you? What position will you hold?"

The servant looked away before answering. "I will be her advisor."

"And lover," Misha murmured later as Vasily relayed the conversation to Louis.

...

Blago's intelligence was key to the success of their task. They killed seven bodyguards before reaching the target. The guards died without much pain, having consumed the better part of three bottles of very fine whiskey, probably provided by the servant out of Stefan's cellar. Misha and Vasily each took out a sentry silently. With surgical precision, Louis dropped the first two men who turned towards the door as Charlemagne entered. An unlucky three more fell to a single automatic burst before the rest fled or surrendered.

The woman appeared, finally, as they prepared to leave after they had selected several files from her late husband's office as part of their payment. She wore an embroidered sash, and her blonde hair curled like a crown around her head in a tight braid. Her young, dark-haired son held her hand tightly.

"Do you not think, Misha," asked Louis as he opened his rucksack, "that the woman would be better off marrying the servant? He is more intelligent."

He stuffed their fee, paid in gold, into the bag and hefted it onto his back.

Misha considered for a moment before answering. "But she and her village will be safer this way. She has the gift of cunning, and it is always best to disguise it."

AVARICE

"*Mon Dieu*, Vasily, I wish you would stop worrying."

The man who says this cannot be seen but can be described. His name is Louis. He is French and in his early twenties, tall with spider limbs, handsome in a wild way, with dark hair that tends to curl over his ears and at the collar of his filthy shirt. He wishes he could scratch and interrupt the dinner of the biting lice, but his hands are in chains. His eyes are blacker than normal, from the dark and from concern.

Louis's companion in the dark is Vasily, a friend from childhood, as different in looks as he is in temperament. Vasily's worried grey eyes and sandy hair are also invisible in the cramped cell. He is smaller than Louis but more physically powerful, a fact he has proven many times.

Vasily moves, making his chains rattle. "I think I have cause to worry, Louis."

"We all have cause."

"Then I am justified in worrying."

"All right. Then stop worrying me with your worrying. You are driving me demented."

"You are already demented. You insisted we do that extra job."

"They paid so well," says Louis. "I have two hundred gold Krugerrands in those bags."

Another rattle. "Hear that noise, Louis? Those are not Krugerrands. There are no bags here, only chains. You were mad to lift that woman's veil. You knew it would infuriate their chief."

Vasily moves again, but it does not help. He will find no comfortable position in their cell. Also, no light, no water, no hope of escape without help. They huddle together, hoping for rescue but not talking about it. Whatever Misha may think of to get them out should not be foiled by broadcasting it to eavesdroppers.

"I had to see," says Louis. "I cannot believe a woman can be so beautiful that she needs the protection of all that cloth. She looked like a funeral gift, wrapped in black, shaped like a coffin. I had to know what was inside."

"Was it worth this?" Vasily lifts his hands, rattling his chains again.

Louis whispers his answer. "No. She was ugly."

The door scrapes open, making them blink in the light of even a meager torch.

"Listen," says Misha. "I have negotiated your release, but you must cooperate."

Misha has not suffered three days under a black boulder. His blond hair is clean and combed; he is clean-shaven. His desert utility trousers still hold their usual crease. He carries his gun in full view under his left arm. There is no need to hide it here; everyone knows who he is, knows what he is.

Louis closes his eyes tightly against the painful light that comes in with Misha.

"Cooperate with what? Why don't you kill the guards and let us fight our way out?"

"Do not listen to him, Misha," says Vasily. "He is delirious. He has been this way for two days. The dark has blinded his mind."

"I am perfectly rational," insists Louis. "I do not like the word cooperate."

"Too bad," says Misha. "You must cooperate."

He crouches to look at his friends' closed eyes and explains the agreement.

"Cut off what?" cries Louis. "What did you say?"

"I talked them out of that, and we were almost settled on a hand."

Louis squints one eye open and looks at his hands in their chains. "A hand!" He squints at Misha.

"They were determined to have some part of you."

"Listen to you," says Louis. "As if you were bartering for hay. Oh, yes, we'll give you five fingers supplied by my friend here…."

"You committed a crime in this society, Louis. They say you must pay for it."

"With my flesh?"

"Eye for an eye," intones Vasily calmly.

Louis is not calm.

"You will be happy to know I talked them out of the hand," says Misha. "I have been quite successful—beyond what I expected."

"What are we down to now?" asks Louis. "A few teeth? I have plenty to spare."

"Do not be sarcastic. You are in a bad position."

Louis shakes his hands, sending a ching-ching through his prison. "No!"

"What are the terms, Misha?" asks Vasily. "When do we get out of here?"

"As soon as Louis agrees to marry the woman whose veil he lifted."

"What? Never!"

"You must make an honest woman of her, Louis."

"You did not see her."

Misha sighs and stands as straight as he can in the low cubicle. "I have done my best." He turns to go.

"Wait!" says Vasily. He jabs Louis with an elbow. "Congratulations, Louis. I hope you have many happy years with your bride."

"I'll die first," says Louis stoically.

Vasily jabs him again, hard, and looks up at Misha. "When is the wedding?"

Misha smiles. "Tonight."

...

There are preliminaries before the wedding. Louis needs more persuasion; Vasily provides it. Louis needs a religious conversion. Vasily provides that too. His fists are persuasive.

"Ow! Cut it out! Whatever else I may be, I am an honest man. I cannot lie about a thing like that. What if it is true, and I find out... after... Stop it Vasily, you are killing me. You're breaking my back. Ow!"

"There is no God but Allah," Louis tells the desert chief. "Mohammed is the Prophet of Allah."

Rejoicing and dancing last most of the night, with no woman in sight. Louis's long limbs are cramped and stiff after three days folded like a pretzel. He joins the party for the exercise.

"When do we escape?" he murmurs to Misha during a lull in the festivities.

"We do not." Misha concentrates on the rice he is eating and curls his nose as Louis's three-day-old smell intrudes on the saffron and cinnamon. "You will not please your bride smelling like that. You should wash."

"I am not going to have a bride." Louis speaks through clenched teeth, keeping his voice low and his meaning clear.

"You already have a bride." Misha looks up at him finally.

Louis is arrested by the cold blue in Misha's eyes and waits for an explanation.

"Her father and I signed the agreement immediately after your conversion," says Misha. He raises his chin toward the far end of the camp. "It is there on display in your father-in-law's tent."

"You signed?"

Misha nods. "I told them I am your father."

"And they believed you? You are younger than me."

"Yes, they believed me. Your bride has already retired, you know. She waits for you in that tent there."

Misha lifts his arm to point to another tent, and the party roars its approval at what is being discussed. There are grins all around. Even Vasily manages a smile. Joy fills every face but Louis's.

He crouches to face his friend. "You cannot do this to me. You cannot make me suffer like this. For what? For one peek?" His face is a picture of misery.

"Suffer? Since when have you suffered with a woman?"

"She is not a woman; she is a wife!"

Misha sighs. "If she does not please you, perhaps you should divorce her."

"Yes! Wonderful! Can I do that? Will you arrange it? Your Arabic is better than mine."

"I will see what I can do."

Misha goes to Louis's new father-in-law and sits cross-legged next to him. Louis watches their faces as they discuss his salvation.

"What did you work out? Can it be done?" Louis is full of questions and agitation when Misha returns.

"There are problems," says Misha.

Louis's face falls. "Oh."

"But they may be overcome."

His eyes brighten. "Yes?"

"Your father-in-law cannot bear the thought of his daughter cast out into the desert without support."

Louis's eyes narrow suspiciously.

Misha continues. "But there is a rich man willing to take her as third wife."

"Who would want three?" murmurs Louis after a long sigh of relief. "So let him have her."

"She has no dowry. Her father is a poor man, and she is the third daughter of his second wife. He has nothing to give her to satisfy a rich groom."

"He did not worry about satisfying me." Louis's brow is so low, it shields his blazing eyes. "How much are we talking?"

"A hundred Krugerrands is a respectable dowry."

It takes Louis a moment to agree. "All right," he says. "I still have the other hundred."

Misha says nothing.

"I do have it, correct? Or did they steal it?"

"They do not steal," says Misha. "The Sharia holds severe penalties for thieves."

"The Sharia?"

"The law of Islam."

"So I still have the Krugerrands?"

There is no answer from Misha. Louis presses him.

"I had to pay a bride price for your wedding," Misha says finally. "It is not refundable."

"Bride price? Dowry? Wait a minute! Which is it? Who pays for what?" Louis goes on asking such questions while Vasily brings up three camels.

"Your father-in-law gave you these fine animals as a wedding present," says Misha. "Thank him."

He puts a bag of gold coins into Louis's hand and shoves him toward the waiting father. "And pay him."

...

"I thought you managed him well this time, Misha," says Vasily, as Louis trails after them, muttering. "And for once we have escaped without blood."

Misha turns in his saddle and looks at the slouched figure on the camel behind them.

"I am not sure Louis would agree," he says. "I think I see his pocket bleeding."

"A grievous wound."

"Grievous."

And they laugh about it until they reach the border.

VASILY'S CARPET

"I am being eaten alive, Vasily," mutters Louis. "In which rubbish tip did you find these rags?" He shifts his weight to scratch and momentarily takes his eyes off the entrance they are watching.

Vasily does not move his gaze, and so sees their target leave the building surreptitiously and without the usual bodyguards. Right on time. He nudges his friend.

"I bought them in a market. Near the Sabra Camp. Let's move."

They stagger to their feet, limbs stiff from waiting. Louis scratches the back of his neck.

"Thinking about it will only make it worse, Louis."

Louis gives his reply in so low a voice, Vasily cannot distinguish the words, but he can feel their meaning.

"You need too many luxuries," he replies. "It makes minor hardship difficult."

"The absence of itching is not what I would call a luxury," says Louis. He lifts his chin toward the target. "He is checking his back."

He pushes Vasily into an alley. The two shed their outer layers, stow them in a holdall, and step out onto the street in different colored clothing. Vasily stoops to pick up a pebble and puts it in his shoe. He proceeds with a limp. Louis picks up an empty can from the gutter and tosses it down the next alley they cross. Misha is somewhere among the rubbish, but they cannot see him.

The target turns right. Louis turns left at the crossroad, then takes a position on the other side of the street. Misha catches up to Vasily, who has lost the pebble and with it, the limp. They turn behind the target, who checks the street and appears to see nothing amiss.

"I hesitate to involve the woman," says Misha, "but I see no other way. His bodyguards are with him at other times. If there is a gun battle, the target could be hit and we lose the fee."

Vasily nods. "Louis is an expert with women. But why not just pass the target in the street? See, the man brushes against people as he walks to the woman's flat. Louis could easily be one of them. He is deft with a needle."

He is not sure why Misha does not answer. Probably considering all the ways such a simple plan can fail.

"Then what would we do?" Misha asks finally. "Call an ambulance? Carry him down the road ourselves? And after that, how to bring him across the border?"

Misha is thinking out loud. Vasily knows better than to interrupt, and so waits quietly as they watch the target enter the woman's apartment building. Louis is already inside.

"The clients gave us well forged documents to help us get him across," says Vasily.

"That is the riskiest way. Checkpoint guards will see immediately that he has been drugged. I wish they wanted him dead."

"Louis likes the extra fee."

"We have not done a live extraction before. Louis should remember before he says yes to such commissions that if we fail, all fees will stop."

Misha becomes pensive as they find their backpacks in a narrow space between two buildings. They take turns watching while the other discards another layer, revealing a white shirt underneath. They are both sweating as they add ties and light sports coats from their bags. Louis joins them, also looking like a businessman. They follow their quarry to his headquarters, then walk to their hotel a few meters down the street.

...

"This is truly delicious," says Louis. He breaks a bread roll from the basket on top of the room service trolley and scoops up the last of the gravy on his plate. "Let me see. I taste cumin, certainly cinnamon. Is that cardamom?" He closes his eyes as he chews.

Misha has ordered the same meal. "No, it is nutmeg."

Vasily mechanically chews a bite of plain boiled lamb.

"How can you be so indifferent to fine things, Vasily?" demands Louis. "You miss all the beauty that makes life worth living. Your food is so plain, you don't even use salt. I have never seen you admire a luxury, let alone buy one."

As he swallows, Vasily puts down his knife and fork. "That is why you suffer more whenever we are captured because you indulge too much when we are not."

"But you cannot say that a vase of flowers in your room at home makes you suffer more in prison. The housekeeper told me you refused to have it."

"If I get used to it, it will. You are always moaning in lock-up."

"Because I like to complain! It reminds me that I still live. You don't complain only because it requires talking."

Misha places his napkin beside his plate and leans back in his chair.

"Why did you hire watchers tonight, Vasily? Not to give us the luxury of dinner together, I think. Are they trustworthy?"

"I trust them, and the target never moves at night."

Vasily studies the faces of his friends. This request will be difficult. He will be required to explain. How can he explain what he does not understand himself? He settles on four words and pushes them past his throat into the air, never to be called back.

"I have a request."

Louis and Misha wait.

Now he must use six words.

"I have something to show you."

An hour later, they stand before an empty loom in a barn outside the city. They feel exposed and nervous in the large, brightly lit space. Vasily has decided to let the thing explain itself.

They stare down at a magnificent carpet stretching to the far wall.

"How large is it?" asks Misha.

"Three meters by twelve," says the proud proprietor of the shop.

Louis looks sharply at Vasily. "Those are the dimensions of the corridor outside our rooms."

"This gentleman requested the size," says the proprietor, saving Vasily the trouble. "And also the colors."

"When?"

Vasily must answer now. He can no longer depend on others to explain.

"When we were here last year," he says in German. "You remember the job?"

Misha nods, but Vasily can tell he is reviewing every moment of that past commission.

"A simple commission," says Misha. "Not a complicated extraction like this one." He pauses and smiles at Vasily. "It paid for the cipher locks we installed on the doors to the hallway."

Louis turns over one corner of the carpet and is counting the knots.

"It is excellent workmanship, Vasily, but the colors! There should be more red."

"There is red. It is mostly red."

"If you insist that almost-brown is red."

Misha chimes in. "I would have chosen a warmer shade of cream, with more yellow in it. Also blue rather than black."

Vasily expected this. The three of them coordinate perfectly in a firefight but can never agree even on a restaurant. He broaches the difficult subject haltingly, expressing himself badly as usual.

"It is difficult for us to enter this country."

Louis and Misha nod, expecting more.

"The carpet is ready now."

He hopes they will read his intention and translate it into words for him. After all, Misha has already connected the newly locked doors at home to Vasily's only ever purchase of any kind of luxury.

But it is Louis whose mind leaps ahead to what is needed. Switching to Arabic, Louis asks the shopkeeper, "Does the price include shipping? Has it been paid?"

They have reached the essential difficulty. It is compounded by the number of voices and languages bombarding Vasily's ears. The shopkeeper has a brother-in-law, in Arabic. Louis is displeased, in French, with such a complication in the midst of a difficult but lucrative commission. Vasily nurses his automatic opposition into full-blown obstinacy.

Misha sighs as he watches Vasily set his jaw and tells him quietly in German that he will handle it. Switching back to Arabic, he asks the proprietor, "Will your brother-in-law sell us the truck?"

They spend the rest of the night arguing and cleaning their semi-autos. The activity calms them. From this point to success or failure, there will be no rest. Even Louis foregoes a leftover glass of very good wine. They clean and discuss.

"Our timing must be perfect," says Louis. "It will be daylight. The street, crowded. It would be quieter in the woman's flat."

Misha pushes a solvent-soaked patch through the barrel of his new SIG Sauer.

"Sometimes a noisy street will absorb things better than a quiet apartment building. Especially one that requires a three-story climb."

"With a drugged body," adds Vasily. He polishes the stock of his Makarov.

"Someone is bound to see," says Louis.

"But not to understand," Misha replies.

Vasily buckles a belt holding his holster and spare magazines under a loose shirt.

"And not likely to care," he says.

"Timing must be perfect," Louis reminds them. "That rust bucket you bought had better start, Vasily."

Misha buckles his holster-laden belt around his waist. "I checked it, Louis. The truck is sound."

Louis is back in itch-inducing rags. He twitches, glaring at Vasily's smirk.

"Waiting will be an eternity," he says. "Something will go wrong. I should stick him before he goes inside."

Misha rolls his eyes. "We discussed this. If he does not come to her on time, the woman will seek help. You must do it as he is leaving. It will take his bodyguards a while to realize he is late. You said yourself that she is more intelligent than all his guards combined."

"And that is why you don't think she will cooperate," adds Vasily. "They are in love."

"I could explain to her that we will not kill him," says Louis.

He sighs as the others try not to laugh at this.

The target checks his back repeatedly as Misha swelters less and less under successive discarded layers of different colored shirts. He carries a rucksack containing two dark wigs and changes them frequently. Louis wears an eye patch and holds a cracked bowl as he sits with his back to a wall. The target drops a coin in the cup.

Misha, wearing a black wig, greets the driver of a rusted brown truck as the target steps out of the apartment building and turns down the street. The beggar's cup sits unattended on the pavement.

The target slumps in the stream of pedestrians, and two good samaritans catch him and lead him gently away. He is settled comfortably on a large folded carpet in the back of an old truck. One man sits with him, and as the other climbs into the cab, its driver puts it in gear.

By the time the truck reaches the outskirts of the city, the carpet has been folded gently over the target, and only one man is visible in the bed. Vasily presents the proper export documents and pays the duty in cash at the checkpoint. Everybody's papers are in order. The border guard compliments them on their choice of carpet.

...

"Your rug is very beautiful," says Louis as he pours more wine into Vasily's glass, "but the corridor is too quiet. It absorbs sound. I cannot hear footsteps, like those of the servants."

"Or like interrogators?" asks Misha quietly.

Vasily nods and sips his wine.

From this day, everyone except Vasily calls the place Vasily's Carpet.

He calls it Not Prison.

THE SURVIVOR

"What's wrong?" says Louis. He watches Vasily dejectedly move the rubble at his feet with the toe of his boot. When Vasily shrugs, Louis insists, "Tell me what makes you so pensive."

"That." Vasily points to a small section of wall still standing among the debris of what once was a significant villa near the Adriatic shore.

Louis struggles with wooden boards and concrete blocks, shoves these aside, and trips over mortar and bricks. The older portion of the building was built of brick. This remnant of wall, standing only a few feet above the surrounding devastation, must have been in the oldest room of the house.

"So what, Vasily? Everything else is flattened. It is a triumph of your skill."

"An incomplete triumph then," says Vasily. "There should be nothing standing. I will examine my calculations again."

Misha reaches them, wiping plaster dust from his face. "Is there a problem?"

Louis indicates the miscreant piece of wall with a tilt of his head. "That wall refuses to obey Vasily's mathematics."

Misha's royal-blue eyes widen. "Vasily, everything is destroyed, and the terrorists are dead. I counted body parts. We are undamaged, and the fee will be exceptional. There is no reason to be unhappy about a small section of wall."

Vasily looks up at his friends. "There should be nothing standing. Do you understand? Why is it standing?"

Louis snorts in exasperation and struggles up the small mound of debris no larger than the size of bocce balls to inspect. It is an ordinary piece of brick wall. The blast has denuded it of plaster, much of it still hanging in the air as a choking dust. This remnant stretches no more than two meters and stands only a meter and a half above the rubble that buries its base. Louis's long spidery legs crunch and slip as he circles this errant testament to the builders of antiquity.

He catches his breath.

"What is it?" asks Misha.

Louis does not answer. He stands staring at the other side of the ruin as Misha scrambles up toward him. Vasily sighs and follows.

"So?" says Vasily.

The three men stare into a wall niche. It contains an ancient wine pitcher, an oenochoe, whole and undamaged except by time.

"So," says Louis, "it is at least two thousand years old. It is lucky. You never miss, Vasily, but you missed this. We must keep it."

Vasily shakes his head. "How can we do that? It was treacherous getting here. We are on foot, and it is almost winter in the mountains. How do you propose to carry that thing? It will shatter on the first slide down an incline."

"It will not. It is lucky."

Louis raises a dark eyebrow at Misha, waiting for his opinion.

"Louis, I have never known you to be superstitious."

"I am not being superstitious. This is evidence." Louis sweeps his arm over the devastation around them. "Some things, especially some ancient things, set an example of survival."

Vasily snorts. "Don't ask me to help you carry it."

Louis carefully lifts the artifact from its niche and cradles it in his arms as the three men slither down the pile of rubble. He takes extra care and is the last to reach firm ground.

"How will you carry it and be able to draw your weapon at the same time?" demands Vasily. "If you cannot draw your gun in time, your lucky jug will not help you survive. It will not fit in your rucksack with the MP5s, and I have no room for them in mine."

Misha pre-empts a nascent argument when he sees the flash of temper in Louis's black eyes. "You must find a sack to carry it in until we reach the mountains. Then we will sling the MP5s over our shoulders, and the thing will fit in your rucksack.

Vasily is not to be deprived of a chance to goad his friend. "If you fall, be sure to land face down or you will ruin two thousand years of survival."

Louis fights an urge to cuff him. "You are very funny and have no taste."

"But I know how not to behave in a brothel. If you were not wanted by the police after that fracas in Naples, we wouldn't have to cross the worst of these mountains to get out of here. We could take a train from Trieste. You are too hot-headed."

Louis grinds his teeth and looks to Misha in hope of support. He finds no quarter there either.

"When you find a sack, be sure to carry it in your left hand, Louis, and keep your right hand free to shoot."

It takes an hour to locate a large enough bag for the pitcher. Louis spots it, a burlap feed sack half-buried in manure behind a cow barn. It is not long before the smell permeates his skin, but it is an improvement over carrying his find cradled in his arms. Vasily makes faces at him, holding his nose and grinning.

Misha spies a clothesline at another farm and cuts out a portion of it, leaving the ends dangling and the drying clothes on the ground. After they evade the farm hands and scramble a significant distance up the first real slopes away from the coast, he calls a halt and fashions a sling for the sack.

"I am perfectly content to carry it all the way in my left hand, Misha."

"I am not content to pick you up when you tumble down a mountain because you cannot crawl. Some of these passes are treacherous in snow."

"It is not so very far." Louis is conscious of a whiny note in his voice.

"We are not eagles. Half the distance we travel will be on the inclines."

"Remind me to explain the hypotenuse if we get home," says Vasily.

Louis snorts. "Spare me your mathematical superiority, Vasily. I know the Pythagorean Theorem."

"Our feet will know it intimately in twenty-four hours."

The sack gains weight over the next half-day, but Louis is quiet. They are approaching a steep wilderness where they can carry their MP5s. He does not need any more of Vasily's teasing before then.

"Misha," says Vasily, "the jug has general magical powers of stoicism as well as survivability. Louis has not complained once in at least two kilometers."

Louis does not speak while they eat their afternoon rations. He struggles to fit the pitcher in his rucksack as they shoulder the submachine guns. Vasily helps him stuff a dirty shirt around it to make the shape less awkward and unstable across his back. Delighted to lose the stinking sack, Louis says a sheepish thank you.

Misha divides the boxes of 9mm cartridges equally among them. Louis's share fits snugly around the neck of the artifact. He hopes the boxes will not shift and crack it.

The snow begins within an hour after they set out again. "I am uneasy," Vasily says as they toil up a particularly steep trail.

Louis's teasing jibe dies on his lips when Misha answers, "So am I." Vasily responds to life in general with suspicion and paranoia, but if Misha feels that way, there must be a reason. Louis takes his MP5 off his shoulder. The slope here is even more steep and slippery with snow, and he now has only his left hand to support his scramble upward. He notices Misha doing the same.

Vasily spots it first. He crawls to the side of a boulder and cautiously peers around it. His sandy hair, plastered to his head by wet snow, blends into the surrounding rocks. They are on all fours now, staying low on a severe gradient topped by the boulder. Vasily signals for a stop and tells them with hand signals that he sees a muzzle. He peers again, his left hand telling them one, two, three muzzles—waiting. Waiting for what?

Bandits? signals Louis.

Vasily shrugs.

Ambush, says Misha's hand.

Louis watches his blue eyes sweep the terrain, taking in the details of their situation. The snow has dampened sound and is accumulating quickly. Their enemies most certainly have notice of their approach but might not know how near they have come. He and Misha join Vasily in the shadow of the boulder and quietly put down their rucksacks under a short overhanging ledge. They stuff extra magazines into every pocket.

Misha makes his dispositions. He sends Louis to the left, Vasily to the right, and allows the enemy to give the order to begin the fight by showing himself boldly in the center. The surprise allows them to find and remove two snipers who fire at him immediately. Misha's covering fire keeps the third busy until Vasily throws in a small grenade of his own design. Louis ends the career of the commander from behind, as the man takes potshots at Misha with a revolver. It is one of these rounds that grazes his side and starts it bleeding.

Despite his hunger and fatigue, Louis agrees with Misha's decision to climb on into the night. The enemy's shallow cave would make a commodious shelter, but none of them relish sharing it with the corpses they have hidden there.

"You see, the wine pitcher helped us survive," he says, as he shifts his rucksack, trying to ease a sore spot on his shoulder.

"No," says Vasily, "our intuition did that."

"Intuition is just as mysterious a force as a lucky ancient relic," Louis retorts.

Misha allows a note of exasperation into his voice. Or is it pain? It sounds irritable.

"There was nothing mysterious about Vasily's eyesight, Louis. He spied the muzzle, and we were able to surprise them because we were quiet as we climbed. I suggest we continue that way."

Exposed beside a snow-covered rock, they eat in silence at midnight, then shoulder their burdens and stumble on. Misha calls a welcome halt as the sky lightens. The wind has cleared the snow off most of the larger rocks, leaving indeterminate drifts on their lee sides. He uses his knife to cut a twisted branch, two meters long, from a tenacious tree growing out of a rocky incline.

"This tree is a survivor," he says, grinning. "Therefore, my new staff is a worthy artifact."

Louis narrows his eyes at him, though the joke means Misha must be feeling better.

Misha uses the staff to poke through the drifts that cross what once might have been a path. Most of the drifts are no more than knee deep, but when the stick sinks completely up to Misha's hand without striking ground, he looks at Louis. "Which artifact deserves credit for this, the jug or the stick?"

"Your intuition gets all the credit, Misha. As always." Louis is suddenly too weary to maintain his usual resentment.

They huddle on an exposed slope with a spectacular view of mountain shadows running from the dawn. The wind blasts them, but it also blows away the snow covering them before it can melt and make them wet as well as cold. Louis is grateful. One discomfort at a time is enough.

They doze—sitting up against a rock— for the morning hours, two at a time, with the third man responsible for watching.

"We have food for only one more meal," says Misha as he wakes.

They stand, looking down the crevice his stick warned them about that dark morning. By noon, the snow is entirely gone, revealing its length and depth. It takes them half an hour to find a spot narrow enough to jump over it.

Vasily grabs Louis by his jacket when he teeters on the edge, overbalanced by his heavy rucksack. "The jug seems tired of surviving, Louis. Do not follow it," he says, impish mischief in his light eyes.

Louis is too intent on his rumbling stomach to care about Vasily's jibes. At this point, he could eat the pitcher itself if it were edible.

When they sit down at last in a pine forest, sheltered from the wind on this side of the mountain, Misha's next announcement is as welcome as the stale rations he hands out.

"We will cross the Austrian border in an hour. I know a place that will be safe, but we should not have weapons visible—just in case."

Louis sees the wisdom in this but knows the disappearing food supply has not left enough room for three MP5s.

He waits. Misha and Vasily say nothing—apparently unconcerned.

He sighs. "Will there be farms on our way where I may find another feed sack?"

Misha grins. "And clotheslines? Yes."

...

They had blown up a terrorist cell, killed a four-man ambush that awaited them, crossed a mountain in the snow, and evaded a plunge down an unexpected crevice, but a conductor on the train from Villach threatens more misery within just a few kilometers of home.

Louis cannot keep a sneer from showing on his face, the little man is so full of his own importance, questioning their lack of credentials (they never carry any on these excursions), their disheveled appearance (not worse than usual, in Louis's estimation), and the origin of the cash with which they buy their tickets (in gold, as provided under the agreement with the government that had hired them).

What the man really objects to, Louis knows, is the smell coming from the feed sack wrapped around the artifact. People stand at the other end of the crowded car to avoid it, allowing the three of them to lounge over more than their share of seats.

When the officious man threatens to put them off the train at the next station, Louis's hand feels drawn to the inside of his coat, reaching toward the holster there.

"You see, Sir," says Vasily with exaggerated politeness. "We are archeologists returning from a dig near the Adriatic. We bring an important artifact and have not had time to clean up. We are so excited to have found it."

Louis raises an eyebrow and arrests his hand before it reaches his weapon. Vasily is faking a Polish accent. The only language he normally speaks with an accent is English. He speaks German like an Austrian.

The conductor wears a skeptical look. Vasily reaches for the clothesline draped over Louis's shoulder and removes the sack. He opens it, releasing a waft of redolent barnyard that permeates the car. Drawing out the oenochoe, he displays it for the conductor, dusty, substantial, and surviving. Louis allows his face to show his pride in finding it.

The man cannot apologize enough, calling them each 'professor' and 'doktor' and asking them to please, please resume their seats and enjoy their ride home. They thank him with smiles.

Once home, rested and washed, Louis looks forward to dinner. Cook has a special genius for preparing grilled fresh trout in a light cream sauce. She invariably adds something French to the menu, just for him, ever since his regular visits to Misha's house as a boy, and spoils him still. When he is at home, he receives a special treat at every dinner. It helps, of course, that the others in the household also like French food, but he knows she does it just for him.

He walks into the dining room with high expectations; his starched shirt and dinner jacket need filling after several days of meager rations.

Louis nods to the old man sitting across the table. "Good evening, Professor." His mood cannot be dampened. So what if Misha insists on giving their old tutor a comfortable retirement? It has nothing to do with him and will not spoil an excellent meal. Even the memory of the canings the professor applied to his youthful backside when he did not memorize the monarchs of England fade when he thinks of grilled trout. *Monarchs. Pfah! Parvenues! Especially the Saxons.*

"I see you have returned with an artifact," the professor says to Misha as the soup is served. "I am anxious to see it."

"It is Louis's find," Misha replies.

The professor looks at him with surprise. Louis knows the man does not think him capable of any intellectual sensibility at all let alone the capacity to spot an ancient artifact. He does his best not to let his smile be overly smug. A little bit smug, yes, but not excessively so.

Forced to conceal the exact location and circumstances of the find, Misha artfully steers the conversation away from the oenochoe each time the Professor brings it up. Louis busies himself with the superb meal before him and hears none of the old tutor's disquisition on the rarity of such a find of that size.

When the cloth is drawn and an excellent port served, Vasily brings Louis's jug to the professor. Louis has eaten too well to listen much until he hears the word, 'reproduction'.

"What?" He stops his glass midway to his lips.

"It is a reproduction. Don't you see?" says the professor, turning the pitcher on its side. "Here. I must say the quality of Japanese manufacturing has greatly improved."

Louis leaves his seat and peers over the tutor's shoulder at the bottom of the jug. Vasily's eyebrows rise with surprise and delight. No one speaks as Louis reads the words printed there. "Made in Japan!"

Perhaps it is the excellent port enjoyed on a full stomach that makes him treat them all to the heartiest and most joyous laughter—a specialty of his personality. He slaps the professor on the back in gratitude and congratulations for the joke.

The episode of the jug becomes Louis's most popular story. People especially enjoy the way he mimics Vasily telling the conductor, in an impossible Polish accent, "It is most definitely the very vessel from which they poured the wine they made for Socrates!"

PICTURE WINDOW

The first time I realized Sobieski wanted to kill me, I was leaning into a double-paned window twenty floors up from a New York street. I rested my forehead on the glass, my eyes on the stream of lights at the bottom of a skyscraper canyon, and my psyche in the movement and freedom of people and cars. It was the briefest respite from the newly heightened tension of an already stressful job.

Sobieski destroyed the moment with a shove and an expletive, pulling the curtains closed with a powerful yank.

He said some other words, but those were in Polish. I'm sure they were all unfit for polite discourse. He never says much, so I figured the earful he was giving me had to be significant. He emphasized his point by shoving me again.

I heard my boss trying to calm the situation. At least I think he meant to sound soothing. I didn't have any Russian at the time, so I don't know what he said. I understood the words the team leader used, though, because they were in German. Simple. Direct.

"Hör auf!" Stop it.

I didn't even know the name of the team then. We called them WEDGE, because that was the highly classified code name for the file we kept on them. The file held precious little information, and there was no time to read it anyway before my boss pulled me out of my new office and dragged me to the airport for the short flight to New York.

He briefed me on the way.

"How do you like your new office?" he asked.

"It's nice, good. I've been meaning to thank you for the promotion, Fred."

I was grateful for the promotion. I had a growing family and a mortgage. But the first part of my answer was a lie. I hated the tiny cubicle of a room in which my desk barely fit, and the painted cinder-block walls reminded me of a cell. There were no windows anywhere in our building, but the blank mass of cement made me yearn for the transparency of glass. The ops room where my desk had been didn't have any windows either, but it was large and noisy and usually full of men coming and going. I had been promoted out of it.

I work in the secret world, but when it comes to living, I prefer normal spaces of light and movement.

"Buddy, I think it would be wise to give you a new game name," said Fred. "You're now Frank Cardova."

He pulled a manila envelope out of his coat pocket and handed it to me. It contained my new 'shoes', the usual driver's license and passport in my new name, and to my surprise, a charge card as well.

"The card is live and in our budget," said Fred. "Be careful you don't lose it. I'll be there for incidentals this trip, but you'll be on your own in the future. I promoted you to save Jello's life. I hope it doesn't cost you yours. I know you guys are friends, so I'm sure you're happy that I won't be letting him kill himself. I think you have more of what it takes to stay alive.

I nodded. I did not give my boss the details of my 'friendship' with Jello. During our service as advisors in SEA, he had given me survival skills by continually doing things designed to get me killed.

Fred continued, "This specialist team concept is new and, I think, practically invented by the guys you're about to meet. Each of them is formidable on his own. Together, they are nothing short of awesome. They have been making a name for themselves in Europe and the Middle East, and I am determined to secure a working relationship with them for Uncle Sam. The problem is, I have a history with one of them, so I can't be their babysitter."

I widened my eyes. I knew Fred had been around just about everywhere in the black world, but he was pretty senior to have formed an acquaintance with an up-and-coming twenty-something foreign specialist. He saw my surprise and explained.

"I am hoping Sobieski will not remember me, but I must handle this op myself. I tried appointing Jello last spring. He created a disaster that almost killed them all. They were seriously displeased, and it took everything I had to convince them to do this new job for us. I promised I would be there to handle logistics.

"You will be my assistant—my silent and unobtrusive assistant—to get them used to your presence. Then, on the next op that comes up, you will take over as babysitter. Sobieski was four years old when he met me, and it was for no more than five minutes, but memories are tricky things when trauma is involved, and I don't want him connecting me with that particular event."

No doubt my face betrayed my continued ignorance. He sighed and spoke more quietly, maybe so our driver might not hear.

"His old man was the deadliest solo specialist working against the Soviets shortly after the war, and I was babysitter on the op that got him killed by the two things all specialists fear, cunning and treachery. I managed to get the boy to safety but couldn't save his mother. The KGB killed her shortly after. The kid was sharp for four years old. He knew what was going down. He had a stony, serious way about him even then. No noise. No drama. Now, he's already better at killing than his dad was."

We did not talk about the team or the operation during the flight to La Guardia, for obvious reasons, but as we walked into the terminal, Fred muttered, "Remember, once I introduce you, stay strictly in the background. Don't be noticeable."

He met the team at their gate while I picked up the car and waited outside the international arrivals door. At first sight, they seemed unremarkable. Only the one with dark hair and black eyes topped six feet. The other two had lighter hair and eyes. All three wore their hair a little long for my taste, but I chalked that up to youth. It was in the sixties, after all.

Anyway, who would be dumb enough to make a fashion objection to guys who were so professional their suits had been perfectly tailored to fit wide shoulders while disguising the bulges of the weapons at their sides? Not me. I had seen plenty of action and dealt with killers of all stripes. Fred was right. These guys were all business.

I kept my mouth shut and merely nodded when introduced.

The blond one had the bluest eyes I've ever seen, and he fixed them on mine until I dropped my gaze. The tall guy said something in French that made old blue eyes smile. I didn't know any French then but put it on the list of things to correct without delay. The one with sandy hair regarded me silently and with utter indifference. I don't know why I knew this was Sobieski.

The promotion would help my mortgage payment and start a few college funds. It would do nothing for my blood pressure.

I drove. Fred briefed. The team rode in back.

"The target is Kazar. I'm sure you've heard of him."

There was no response from behind us. Fred turned his head and pressed on.

"Do you remember the KGB major who defected to us last year? Well, he has agreed to help us eliminate the threat Kazar represents to others like him. Would-be defectors know the KGB will send their best specialist to impose vengeance. This has a dampening effect on our ability to attract more of them. The major will play bait to Kazar, who is your target."

After a pause, the blond one said quietly, "Such a target does not require a team."

"He's very good. Legendary, even. We want to make sure," said Fred.

"You want something else. What?"

I wondered what Fred would come up with besides the unmentionable truth which was that we wanted a lasting business relationship with these new up-and-comers, or perhaps we needed to fix the disaster of our first try. To my surprise, he had yet another reason.

"Kazar always carries a document, the actual order from Moscow. It's his trademark. He leaves a portion, the clear language portion, near the body every time, but not the torn-off encrypted part of the message. That part won't be on him, but it will be with him, in his luggage, maybe. We want that. Without his people knowing that we have it." He paused as we turned into the underground parking at the hotel, then added, "Also, we'd like the major to live. Others need to know we will protect defectors."

We were booked into a suite that could accommodate five, but frankly, none of us expected to sleep. The press conference to announce the major's new book (actually written by his case officers) was to take place at ten the next morning in an event room on the third floor.

As the silent and unnoticeable assistant, I was sent out for food. The details of the op had taken us past sunset and everybody was hungry. My mood lightened the minute I stepped out onto the sidewalk from the front doors of the hotel. It was New York City, after all, and that meant a noisy, busy celebration of life. I needed it after hours of discussions concerning death.

I took my time, looked in shop windows, listened to buskers, and gave loose change to panhandlers. A sidewalk art display caught my eye. For ten minutes, the artist and I exchanged views on the nature of beauty. He quoted Keats: "Beauty is truth, truth beauty." I countered with Tolstoy: "It is amazing how complete is the delusion that beauty is goodness." The man's work impressed me though, so I accepted his card. I still have it.

I'm sure I wore a delighted grin as the Frenchman met me in the hall and let me into the suite. I don't know where he had been, but he was wearing fresh aftershave. My sojourn had soothed my soul. The food I bought from a street vendor smelled delicious, and I couldn't wait. I laid it all out on a long coffee table and told them to dig in. There were hot dogs of every description, from plain old franks to kielbasa with all the fixings including onions, peppers, relish, cheese, chili, chili-cheese, and sides like coleslaw and potato salad.

Blue-eyes, the one they were calling Misha, stared at the food and then at me. I felt uncomfortably visible. The Frenchman was more demonstrative. He wrinkled his nose and curled a lip. Sobieski chose plain kielbasa on a hoagie bun and ate it quickly while the Frenchman told us what he had been doing with his time. Well, some of what he had been doing.

"Kazar has a room on the fifteenth floor," he said. "The housekeeper told me he checked his briefcase into the hotel safe. I asked a young woman who works with the consigliere. She verified this for me and showed me a copy of the receipt given to Kazar recording the deposit."

Sobieski swallowed the last of his kielbasa, and the three of them walked out the door. Just like that—no explanation, their holdalls still in the suite. We figured they would be back.

Fred and I dug in.

We were replete and groaning, well, I was groaning—too many onions have that effect on me—when they returned the first time, demanding coffee. I ordered a large tureen from room service and understood not one word of the French they used in a long discussion, sometimes animated, always softly spoken.

Fred snored in an easy chair.

The team left again just as I was nodding off. I drank more coffee. I did not want to be asleep when they returned, which they did an hour before dawn. The Frenchman woke Fred by kicking his shin, then placed a tiny microfilm canister in his hand. Fred wrinkled his forehead trying to understand.

"The document," said the Frenchman, taking a pen from his jacket pocket and revealing its true purpose as a camera.

It was at this point that the team's leader stopped Sobieski from punishing me for looking out a window. Then he threw the hotel's room service menu at me. They were becoming wired for the big event. I was already plenty impressed by the microfilm. I could tell Fred and I were of one mind on that. He considered the message to be the most difficult part of the job. Any yahoo can kill. It takes finesse to act like a ghost and copy a document locked in a safe.

I busied myself ordering breakfast.

The team took off their jackets and used the waiting time to clean their guns, rummaging through the holdalls for supplies. They were done by the time we heard the knock on the door and disappeared while I took delivery of the expensive, and to me exotic, breakfast that I had ordered at their direction.

It did not appeal to me, but then, I was not offered any.

Five of us needed to clean up and shave. There was one pants press. Naturally, the Frenchman took the first turn. I was last. By 9:45 we were assembled and sporting forged press credentials as we rode the elevator to the third floor after stowing the holdalls in the car in the basement. The team scattered in different directions.

Fred and I entered the room late enough that it was standing room only, which suited us perfectly. One of the major's handlers stood at the podium. He wore a wire, and his suit was not as well cut as the team's, or even mine for that matter. I knew what that bulge was. Our divisions are compartmented so though I didn't know him personally, I knew what he was; he didn't even know I was there.

Fred and I stood on opposite sides of the room, watching the crowd. We knew when Kazar came in at the center, sporting a camera and press pass, because we'd seen an artist's representation. The blond WEDGE leader was not far behind him. The Frenchman appeared on the left side of the room. Sobieski stood on the right, near the podium. I moved to the back with Fred fifteen feet on my right. Kazar positioned himself on the other side of the podium from Sobieski.

The handler introduced the major, who bravely stepped out from behind a partition.

Describing a sequence that happened in what seemed no more than a second can be difficult, though time courteously slows down when you're in the thick of it like I was. I had a perfect view of everybody, so I'll try to recount it, move by move.

I suppose the catalyst, the very first action, had to be Kazar drawing his weapon and beginning to sight it on the major. Simultaneously, Sobieski flew into the major, bearing him to the ground and covering him with his body. The handler wearing the wire drew his weapon. The Frenchman had nearly sighted on Kazar when he saw the handler trying to form a sight picture on Sobieski's back. The Frenchman's round went into the handler. The man's finger discharged his weapon as he went down, and his bullet crossed the room, hitting Fred in the hip.

Kazar turned to leave, and I drew my Walther PPK. I held it at my side and was still deciding what to do when Kazar's white shirt front showed bright red spreading from an object embedded in his chest.

He went down.

WEDGE's leader walked to the body and retrieved his knife. I calculated the distance thrown at thirty feet. In a crowded room.

I waded through pandemonium and knelt by Fred.

"Get them the fuck out of here, Buddy. Now. Give them the car keys. Payment is in the trunk. Seal the room; expose all film; take down names and addresses. Get those useless handlers to help you. I'll see you in the office tomorrow."

He pressed the tiny microfilm canister into my hand.

Two days later, I was busy memorizing present tense conjugations of irregular French verbs when Fred called me to his office. He looked spent and sat in a wheelchair. He shook his head slowly in resignation.

"Jello struck again, Buddy. The guy who drew on Sobieski, and whose bullet found me, had not been briefed. Jello told the guy's boss he wasn't cleared. I can't fire the idiot for overzealous application of need-to-know."

Fred retired two months later, and I was given a bigger office because I am now babysitter for WEDGE. Odds are, Sobieski still wants to kill me. No doubt, I'll find out for sure during our first op together in the next few days.

I commissioned a picture from that New York street artist and hung it behind my desk. It's a depiction of the view from a window showing a park with people walking, running, and playing in the sunlight. I installed a curtain rod with curtains over it. I close them only when I discuss WEDGE. The people who sweep our offices for bugs hate it.

I find it beautiful.

ON FIRST ACQUAINTANCE

It was a new thing at the time, the idea of contracting out wet operations. It took off in the seventies with the Church Committee hearings, but we were ready before then. When I got back from Southeast Asia, after my colleague Jello failed to get me killed despite his best efforts, our boss took the team away from him and gave them to me.

"If they live, they'll be the best," he said.

What he didn't say was, 'Here's hoping you live to see it happen.'

I did live, and I saw it happen. They were, are, the best. Back then, they were just kids. At least that's what I thought when I saw them step out onto the platform at the Gare du Nord in Paris. Each differed from the others. The blond guy was their chief, of sorts, with remarkably blue eyes and a knack for not seeming to move even when he walked. The tallest was French, a trait he let you know right away, with curling dark hair, long legs, and laughing countenance.

The third, the youngest of the three, looked at me with old grey eyes that had seen too much and done too much. He brushed the sandy hair from a Slavic brow and seemed to decide just how he'd like to kill me. I noticed he was missing two fingers on his right hand. I didn't think it would hold him back from his decision regarding me.

I now know that old grey-eyes was weirdly connected to my boss, whose wife had spirited him out of Russia at age four after his father was killed. Now that's a story worth telling. I wish I knew all of it. I don't, but I know this. Vasily Sobieski was every bit the killer his father had been. I could see it in all of them as their feet hit the platform, but especially in Sobieski.

He was also the only one whose name I knew. They called their team Charlemagne, no doubt for some esoteric reason important only to themselves. The other two called the Frenchman Louis, but after I felt the blue-eyed stare of death freeze my blood when I called the blond one Misha as they did, I decided on simple direct address with eye contact and no names given. More polite than 'hey you' but not by much. I have always referred to the Frenchman as just that, and by the end of that first op, dubbed the blond guy Mack for reasons you shall see.

I led them to a less than luxurious Fiat I had rented.

"This is unacceptable," said Mack.

We spoke German. I spoke the hoch Deutsch, he, an Austrian form with an accent I had never heard.

"It is a good car," I said.

"It is not what was agreed."

"I could not find a Mercedes to rent."

"Then you should have bought one."

Looking back, I confess he was right. It was a drop in the bucket compared to what we were paying them, even then.

I suppose silence was better than the grumbling I was used to with other teams, but I was conscious of animosity from the driver next to me, Mack, and the desire to kill me from Sobieski behind me. The Frenchman's amusing chatter should have lightened the mood, but it's hard to relax when you're sitting in front of a killer.

Mack's lip curled when he saw the safehouse. The Frenchman became silent. Sobieski never said anything anyway, so no change there. I got the impression they were unhappy with me. It was an upper-story flat above a cafe on a busy street in a fashionable area. I had a rented room in the apartment next door for myself. It was a sty. My landlady was a single mother with a twelve-year-old daughter and not big on housekeeping.

Gear stowed, refrigerator declared inadequate, chairs scraping across a torn linoleum floor in the kitchen of Charlemagne's safehouse, we sat down for my briefing.

I began with the name of the target. I even had his address.

"He's an American, one of ours," I said. "The counterintelligence division has determined he has been turned. Here is the verification."

I handed Mack the document. It was another stipulation in the contract. I hoped he would be happier with CI's work than he was with the car.

"What are you looking for?" he asked. He passed the verification to the others.

"We want any couriers you can spot, dead drops, his route past possible live drops, alarms, and signals would be very nice. We would like him to go… accidentally. The French are interested in his case officer, and we intend to share some of this information with them, so his KGB handler should not suspect a termination."

"When is sunset today?"

I didn't know. The Frenchman helped me out.

"18:36."

Mack addressed me again. "Bring the correct car by 19:30. We begin at 20:00."

"Also food," said the Frenchman. "It should not be difficult to find." He pointed down, meaning the cafe.

I felt dismissed, which I was, and should have been a little put out, but I wasn't. I couldn't wait to get out of there, and a Mercedes was not going to fall in my lap without hustle, so I made tracks. By the time I entered my own rented accommodation, it was past nine o'clock that night, and the landlady was out. I unlocked the door and turned on the light. Her daughter stood by the hallway entrance, big brown eyes staring wide, brown curls on her head quivering.

"Are you okay?" I asked.

She nodded very short nods, fast like she wanted to cry. I closed and locked the door, and she ran to a room at the back. I heard a television turn on.

I was so discouraged and weary, I did not undress. I slipped off my shoes, hung up my coat, and lay down on top of the bedclothes in my room fully dressed. Had my bozos scared the girl? They seemed all business to me. Would they go in search of entertainment if time permitted? I later learned that indeed, they would, even if time did not permit, but never with children.

I consoled myself that she was safe now. I was there and had locked the door. In a state of ignorant bliss, I fell asleep.

Still dreaming about other things, my mind incorporated the noises into the dream so that I was completely disoriented when I reached full consciousness. Screams, a man's shout, and the sound of blows came so clearly through the thin wall my room shared with the next, that I thought the emergency had come to me. I leapt off the bed, drawing my Walther PPK and searching for the light. My room was empty, but now my head had cleared. The noise did not stop, so I manfully opened my door and went to stop it.

Barging into the next bedroom, I was in time to see a man backhand the girl. She fell on the bed, only partially dressed.

"What the...?" I said.

The man turned. He was a good six inches taller and considerably broader—I was a bit more trim back then. He clocked me immediately, and I fell against the door frame. My gun was still in my hand so I stepped out of the room, used a two-handed stance, and sighted on his heart. He was only a few feet away and there was enough of him. I was bound to hit something.

"Get out," I said.

To my disappointment, he raised his hands and scooted past me. He slammed the door shut on his way out. After I made sure the girl was okay—if anybody can be okay in such a situation—I showed her how to make it difficult for anyone to get in. It seemed the man had a key.

I spent the rest of the night waiting in the team's safehouse next door. I never did figure out what their alarms were as I came in. I was only sure that I had tripped them all and would probably wind up shot as a natural consequence.

It was the smell of gun oil and bacon that woke me. I lifted my head from the cradle of my arms on the kitchen table. Sobieski was pushing a dry patch through the barrel of his Makarov and staring at me with those expressionless grey eyes.

"He is awake," he said quietly.

The Frenchman turned from the two-burner stove, a spatula in his hand.

"Misha," he said, "our babysitter has had his eye redecorated by a fist."

Mack inspected it and waited. They all waited, giving me the ultimate open-ended question. I could say anything I wanted, but I had the impression silence was not an option. I suspected also that lying would be unwise. So I told them.

"He had a key?" said Mack.

"Yes. My French is not very good, but she said he had a key. She would not tell me who he was."

"Describe him again."

I did.

"You must stay here. Do not go back."

"I should tell the mother."

"She will not thank you for reciting words she already knows to be true but has chosen to ignore." Even as a twenty-something youngster, Mack could pinpoint human character with uncanny nicety.

Of course, he was right, the first example of many I have received from him over the years. My landlady sent me away with a flea in my ear.

That night I could not be on hand to protect the girl but had to listen from next door as the alarm I had taught her to make to stop an intruder came crashing down. I left it to other neighbors on the floor to intervene and quell the screams. They did not. The male voice ran down the cafe steps shouting invectives, and the screams subsided into sobs. I heard the girl re-stack the plates and pans on the chair under the doorknob. At least I had taught her to fight.

I woke to the sound of chairs scraping the linoleum around me, lifted my head, and beheld three very tired young men with red eyes and heavy stubble. It was dawn, and they were hungry. I could tell by the pointed glances toward the empty refrigerator. The cafe downstairs would not open for another hour and a half.

In slow, deliberate movements, Mack brought out from his pockets three film canisters, several handwritten notes, and an up-to-date cipher book. The Frenchman drew a notebook from his inside coat pocket, in which were detailed directions to every post office location the target's cell used and the signals for occupied drops.

Sobieski said nothing and produced nothing, just regarded me with those light eyes of disapproval and calculation.

He was the one I addressed. "Where is he?"

It was the Frenchman who answered. "Montmartre. Very unfortunate."

They were the last words I heard in that room. Charlemagne was gone before I could blink twice, payment in gold in the Frenchman's pocket. I locked the door behind me and slipped the key through the letter slot of the cafe. I could hear the chefs behind the door beginning their day, firing the stoves and whisking omelets.

At Montmartre, my counterpart from the French Secret Service, Guy, stared down at the dead American lying on a bottom step.

"Very unfortunate to break one's neck at the end of so many shallow steps," he said.

I agreed.

We pondered the corpse. The cipher book was timely and of no use other than immediately, so I handed it to him after making a copy. I also read to him the locations and signals of various dead drops around the city while he took notes, but I kept the films to myself. My bosses would decide whether to share those.

"The Sûreté has told me of another unfortunate, shall we say, accident," said Guy. "Would you like to see it?"

Did I have a choice? I am at least smart enough to know when I do not. He led me to a narrow street not far from the Tuileries. At the end of a cul-de-sac off the Rue de Archives a familiar, though very pale, corpse lay in a large pool of blood, already heavily populated by flies, its carotid neatly nicked.

"He appears to be the brother of a woman who lives above a cafe near here," said Guy. He regarded me calmly, letting me know how thoroughly his service had tracked us.

"How unfortunate," I said in bad French. "Would that be the woman who has a young daughter, often left alone at home with no one to protect her?"

"*Vraiment,*" he said. "We have heard the same." He paused, then resumed with quiet emphasis, "My superiors are concerned only that Mackie Messer has not come to Paris to stay."

...

I saw them again a few months later. I do not remember in which city. But I do remember the food. I made sure it was delicious and plentiful, and that the Mercedes was new.

BLACK SHEEP

"It is only just past the border. I attended the gymnasium there, for a little while. My uncle…"

Misha interrupted. "Vasily, you are under a death sentence because of what happened in Gdansk."

The balding American they called Frank who sat with them in a dark corner of a seedy restaurant, spoke up. "What happened in Gdansk?"

Vasily and his two friends responded with a malignant stare. He debated switching to Polish for privacy. Louis and Misha were fluent, but Frank studied too much and had added both semi-competent French and basic Russian to his repertoire. Vasily did not want this American to take up his language. He contented himself with an unmistakably hostile glare.

Misha set his empty glass on the table.

"If you will not wait here, then wait in Prague if you can avoid the Czech secret police, but do not come with us to Krakow. It is too dangerous for you, Vasily. This commission is simple. We will kill the target and be back within the day. Frank will wait with you if you stay in Vienna."

At the last words, Frank's already bulbous eyes opened even wider in alarm. This made Vasily smile. Sweat formed on Frank's forehead.

"It is not simple," insisted Vasily. "He is very high-level KGB, First Directorate. He will have bodyguards, an armored car, and a classified route."

"I will know the route within an hour of arrival," said Louis.

"But your rounds will not penetrate a ZIL-117. He will not stop, and his entourage will annihilate you."

"Then prepare a charge for us that will stop the ZIL, and we will use it. You need not be there."

"I must see the route to find where best to place it without detection and the most effective method to detonate. You will need me. I must go."

Misha signaled for more beer before answering.

"You are wearing your most obstinate face, my friend. I concede you are persuasive, but you do not become stubborn like this without a reason. What makes you so determined to risk summary execution?"

Vasily drained the first third of his new glass of beer before answering. They had a right to know, he mused, but then they would feel obligated to help, and he could not bear to endanger them for this. But they should know, he decided finally as he licked the foam from his top lip because this is what it means to be a team.

"I have had a message from my uncle Henryk in Warsaw. My great-uncle Mateusz is under suspicion. I must convince him to leave."

"How many uncles do you have, Vasily?" Louis asked with a furrowed brow.

Vasily did not answer because he sensed Frank's interest. The man would put the number in an American file to be stolen eventually by the KGB.

Louis did not press the question. His glance at Frank told Vasily his understanding had caught up, and he now regretted asking.

"Where is Mateusz now?" asked Misha.

"In Krakow. He is a professor of medieval history at Jagiellonian University. I lived with him when I was fifteen."

"Your presence could put him in more danger."

...

Great-uncle Mateusz repeated Misha's argument when they arrived.

"Your presence puts the entire family in more danger, Vasily. Why are you here?"

The three young men stood uncomfortably in the professor's cramped quarters surrounded by books and boxes of papers, spilled coffee mugs, and the dank smell of old beer. Vasily had difficulty expressing his thoughts at the best of times. The old man's glare robbed him of what little speech he might have had, and he welcomed Misha's rescue.

"Sir, we have had a message from Henryk in Warsaw," said Misha. "He says that you are in particular danger and must leave Poland. We are here to help you do that."

"Leave Poland? I cannot leave Poland. I do not wish to leave. I have my work...." His scrawny arm swept over stacks of books and boxes in the narrow space. He dropped the arm and frowned, then pointed to the top shelf of one bookcase.

"And I have a cat. I cannot leave her."

The cat blinked slowly down at them with yellow eyes.

Misha's face showed no reaction, but Louis blanched. Vasily ventured a question.

"Uncle, why are you under suspicion?"

"Because it is well known that you are my great-nephew. That is why. When I let you shelter with me, I did not know you would become a killer. I am ashamed. They say you killed a young woman. What kind of monster does that?"

The mixture of truth and injustice in this speech left Vasily momentarily silent, but the injustice spurred his voice.

"She killed Dominik, Uncle."

"The KGB shot him. It was reported in the newspaper. He blew up a building...."

"I blew up the building. Dominik was not involved. The woman knew that but arranged his death regardless. She was arranging our deaths when I shot her."

Louis's eyebrows rose in surprise at both the length and the vehemence of Vasily's explanation. Great-uncle Mateusz dropped his gaze in defeat.

"Then what they say about you is true," he whispered. "I hoped it was the usual lies."

"It is like always, Uncle, a mixture of both. There is some other reason why you have been threatened. What is it?"

The old man hesitated.

"My latest book has been published."

The three young men waited quietly. Mateusz spoke again after a few seconds.

"By the underground press."

During another long pause, the old scholar tidied a stack of papers from a haphazard pile on a small table. He looked up at his still audience and sighed.

"I wrote a strong criticism of Soviet revisionist history. I understand they are quite angry. My presence has not been requested for a ceremony to unveil a statue of Felix Dzerzhinsky in the Courtyard of Modern History. I have been disinvited."

Misha threw a significant glance to Louis who nodded. This must be the destination of their target. What better reason could a high-ranking Russian intelligence officer have to visit Poland than the unveiling of a monument to the Polish founder of Soviet intelligence?

"Do you have a basket for the cat?" Misha asked the scholar.

"Yes, but...."

"Make it ready and pack one small box with your current work. You will leave before the unveiling."

Louis pulled a set of survey maps from his rucksack, swept a table clear of books and coffee mugs, and laid out a chart.

"Show me where they will put the statue."

"I do not agree that I am leaving. I do not agree with whatever it is you are doing here. I protest your presence and ask you to leave."

"Uncle," said Vasily, "you will like living in Misha's house. Our old tutor has retired there. You have much in common."

"Not to mention our regrettable common acquaintance with you," said the old man sourly.

The four men got in each other's way for the next two hours as the young ones devised a plan of escape and another plan they carefully kept from Mateusz. He grumbled at volume as he discarded text after text, sometimes with tears, and filled two boxes with essential documents. Misha stood adamant, and after an argument, the old man tediously examined all, discarded some, and overstuffed a single box, wrapping it with twine to keep it closed.

"I cannot move quickly," he whined. "Even if I am not burdened, I will be a danger to you. I should stay here."

It was a new tactic in his argument, equally ignored as had been the others. He watched Vasily shape and prepare a charge of plastique, his face registering profound dismay.

Louis answered the old man, "Do not worry, Professor. We will find a car and drive to the frontier, then obtain another after we cross."

"Obtain? How obtain? You mean to steal one, don't you? Not only are you murderers, but you are also thieves. I cannot go with you. I will not be associated with such people."

He crossed his arms and stood staring up at the cat. When there was no answer from the young men, each busy cleaning a gun, planning a route, or making a bomb, the old man spoke quietly.

"I have an auto. It does not run, but it is not stolen. I can ride in an auto that is not stolen."

"How can you ride in an auto that does not run, Uncle?" asked Vasily.

Nonetheless, they made it run. Louis picked the lock to a ramshackle garage down the street. Vasily stole the parts that Misha said he would need. They siphoned no more than half a liter from every car they could find during the night, some of them parked behind locked doors easily defeated by Louis, others on the street, until they had filled the tank. They saw no reason to burden Mateusz with such details.

The task they were hired to perform took as much or more ingenuity, tedious research, and planning. Louis broke into the college provost's office and examined his correspondence. Misha climbed onto suitable rooftops along the route to the courtyard where the unveiling would take place. Vasily stood in the deepest shadow of a cloister on the north face of the Courtyard of Modern History and contemplated the shrouded statue in its center. After an hour, he moved silently to the spot he had chosen, lifted the canvas covering, and placed the charge he had devised, shaping it to resemble a portion of the raised wreath that decorated the plinth.

They breakfasted on black bread and black coffee to the sound of a running litany of complaints and recriminations from the old man. He did not know where the box had disappeared to. Had they stolen it? Surely one book would not create too heavy a burden. They were young and strong. Just one book.

Vasily bundled his uncle and the cat into the roomy front seat of an ancient German-made relic of the war. He took the wheel, drove to the rendezvous, and waited.

"What are we waiting for?" asked his great-uncle. "Where are your friends?"

"They are on the roofs."

"Why?"

"In case."

"In case what?"

"In case my work fails."

"Your work? What work? You are a disgrace to this family. To every other vice you have adopted, you add the crime of kidnapping an old man. I will escape you and return to my home. See if I don't."

Vasily set his jaw and said nothing. Between his querulous relative and the wailing cat, he longed for the peace and certainty of a gun battle.

He had already put the car in gear the moment they heard the boom that told them his work had not failed. Louis and Misha poured into the back seat within seconds, wearing clothing as grey as the sky and carrying long rifles. By the time sirens began, the car had already crossed the Vistula River and was headed southwest out of the city.

They skirted the mountains as they made their way in an unhurried manner so as not to draw attention. Misha and Louis stayed down in the back seat. The cat cried for almost three hours. Ditching the car near the Czech border, they shouldered their burdens, rifles, ammunition, climbing gear, hard black bread and canteens of water, a box filled with papers and books, and a cat in a basket. Vasily carried a backpack containing his tools and the box of papers. The professor carried the cat.

The cat accepted its fate, finally, and fell asleep in the basket—a lucky thing during times when they were at risk of detection. Great-uncle Mateusz required more persuasion to be quiet during tense moments. Vasily remonstrated, not always gently. Louis tried unsuccessfully to explain their peril. It fell to Misha to solve the problem.

"I cannot walk another step," said Mateusz. "The basket is too heavy. Be careful with that box, Vasily. One of my papers threatens to escape it because of your rough handling. I am thirsty. Can we not find a comfortable pub along the way?"

Misha stopped and placed the point of his knife under the professor's chin.

"We will soon cross into Czechoslovakia. If you endanger us with your noise, old man, I will solve the problem silently. It is a talent of mine."

Mateusz's eyes widened, and he spoke through his teeth. "And I will be required to live in your house?"

In answer, Misha raised the knife higher and with it, the professor's chin, making it impossible to utter another sound. They exchanged glare for glare before Misha withdrew the knife.

"Now I understand how you acquired your obstinacy, Vasily. It is a family trait," murmured Misha.

Vasily was too stubborn to admit relief when they hot-wired a roomy sedan and began the drive to the next border. After nearly three hours on foot, he discovered that a box of paper gains weight over time. Eventually, the string he carried it by had cut into his good hand.

They ditched the car in a remote area west of a tiny village and picked up their burdens for the last trek. Either Misha's knife or the rugged path they followed to a river crossing kept Mateusz's litany of complaints at bay. The old man concentrated on his feet as they climbed and slithered their way to a remote border crossing into Austria.

Frank met them with a car and their payment. It was past midnight before Great-uncle Mateusz and his feline companion, Nada, had been fed and settled into their new quarters in Misha's house.

The main difficulty of having two scholars in the same household became evident the next morning at the breakfast table. The two old academics responded enthusiastically in unison any time someone said 'professor'. It was Louis who devised a shorthand method of address. Professors Graf and Sobieski became Professor G and Professor S.

The solution mollified Mateusz and turned his expression minimally less sour. The plate of eggs and sausages placed before him with an accompanying basket of warm bread made him fight a smile.

Vasily had no small talk to give, but he caught his great-uncle's almost smile as he reached for a slice of bread. It seemed the perfect time to bring it up.

"Uncle, do you still plan to return to Krakow?"

The old man arrested his knife on its way to a pot of jam and narrowed his eyes at his brother's grandson.

"You know I do."

"I know nothing of the sort. It may be the height of folly since you are implicated in the bombing of the Dzerzhinsky statue, and you are no fool, Sir."

"How am I implicated? I cannot be accused merely because we are related. I will tell them you kidnapped me. I do not answer for the black sheep in my family."

"You will if one of your lambs leaves incriminating evidence behind."

"What evidence? Behind where?"

"An ounce of explosive on your desk?"

The knife clattered on his plate; his mouth opened in an 'oh' and he slumped, dropping his eyes.

Misha cleared his throat.

"I beg to differ with you, Professor S. The authorities in your country are perfectly content to accuse the innocent who bear the burden of unfortunate relatives. I have been contacted by your nephew Henryk."

Turning his eyes to Vasily, he continued, "More members of the family have experienced difficulties, and Henryk is asking you not to visit or communicate with them. I told Frank not to offer us any commissions in Poland."

Vasily sat back with a stunned expression. These were the only things in his life that could be considered normal: his vast, hidebound, gloriously passionate country and his irascible, complicated collection of relatives.

"If I am no longer Polish, what am I?"

"You are a Sobieski, I am sad to say," said Mateusz. "Every bit your father's son.

THIRTY-EIGHT HOURS

He stumbled over the slightly raised metal plate on the threshold between the garage and the laundry room. Perhaps he gauged the distance incorrectly. Or maybe his foot refused to rise high enough to clear it. Understandable after a day that lasted two days, almost an entire full-time workweek, but all in a row. Thirty-eight hours. He counted them while sitting on the long web seating along the side of the Air Force C-130 that gave him a lift home.

The airplane also brought flashbacks to that time when a Combat Talon extracted him from Laos, back in the day. He counted the hours he had been awake in a futile attempt to fall asleep. Sleeping requires you to close your eyes. When he closed his eyes, all he saw were the corpses. Not the ones in Laos, though they would always be present. No, these were from just a couple of hours ago.

Maryann met him at the door into the kitchen, holding an ice-cold martini, shaken not stirred, made with his best Vermouth, he knew. He tried to smile, but like his foot, his lips disobeyed his brain.

She looked at him, puzzled. Maybe concerned.

"Sit down, Leo. I'll bring it to you. You look like you'll spill it."

He collapsed in a kitchen chair, wondering at her puzzlement. A spare corner of his brain reminded him he had not washed. It was his habit to wash the job off before going home. He might arrive tired, morose, and uncommunicative, but he did his best to keep the business trip fiction alive. Until now. There were no facilities in the Gunship for washing up.

...

Maryann watched him stare at the olive in his glass until she noticed he had tracked something onto her clean kitchen floor. She looked at the rag she used to wipe it up. Flakes that resembled caked blood. Glancing at her husband, she took note of the usual indications that he had been on a business trip, like the coffee stain on his white shirt. Not so white. *He is wearing the same shirt he left in.* He always came home tired but not shattered like this. Usually, she suspected he had an affair during these trips, but that would not explain blood on the floor. Blood he must have stepped in.

"Leo, while you were gone, the builders wanted to know what color bathroom fixtures they should order. I said white. I know that's out of style, but I think I would get tired of an avocado bathtub. Debbie has one in pink. I'm already tired of it, and I've only been in her bathroom twice."

She glanced at him as she dried the dishes. There had been no answer. He took a sip of his martini, still concentrating on the olive. Maryann was fully aware that her husband had a secret job with the government. She and the other wives in The Section were repeatedly informed, cajoled, and warned about the need for discretion. They were accustomed to last-minute absences and sudden, unexplained reappearances.

But she had never seen blood.

...

Leo? That's right, he thought. *Time to become myself again.* Leo Vilseck, husband of the estimable Maryann, father of six—make that seven. Debtor in an enormous mortgage acquired to build a house big enough to fit them all.

No longer Frank Cardova. *Leave that behind with the corpses.*

He contemplated the olive until it resembled the bloodless head of the man who lost a knife fight against Mack. He looked away, but his mind projected the image of the victor walking to his airplane with that frightful, deep, bleeding cut from the base of his neck to below his shoulder. Frank had brought a doctor who would fly with them until their first refueling stop. Good thing too, because all three members of Charlemagne, the team he hired for this op, were more injured than usual.

Not Frank, he reminded himself. *I'm Leo.* He took another sip. Leo liked this vermouth. Frank could not taste it.

Sobieski had squelched blood from a long gash in his calf as he supported the Frenchman up the steps and into the aircraft. The latter took a round in the abdomen, which could be lucky or fatal—take your pick.

...

The new house will have a dishwasher, thought Maryann as she put away the plates. No more fights over whose turn it is to dry. *What nirvana*. She wondered why Leo didn't even grunt. He always came home without a word in his head, but he could acknowledge the speech of others. Maybe he didn't have an affair this time, or perhaps the woman is such a horrible person, she left him speechless. Maryann felt ashamed of the glee the thought gave her and put it aside.

"I wonder if the boys will stop fighting so much when they have their own rooms," she said, refilling Leo's glass and adding a fresh olive.

There was no answer.

The girls were more widely spaced and so could be civil to each other on occasion, though she heard them say vicious things on the phone to their friends. Still, they never rolled on the floor, breaking the coffee table like her four boys, who had been born back to back in two sets. Even the younger pair had communicated by using shoves before they could speak.

She wondered how such a peaceful man could beget such hellions. Of course, the girls inherited their acid tongues from their mother. Maryann rarely sweetened her words to make them more palatable. But why were her boys so unruly?

The man drained his second martini. As she mixed another batch, Maryann wondered how she would get him upstairs to bed.

...

Leo Vilseck, Leo Vilseck. It would have been handy if it had taken this long to stop being Leo when he met Charlemagne thirty-eight, make that now thirty-nine, hours ago. Then maybe he wouldn't have reacted as Sobieski inevitably pushed him up against a wall. Leo was trained not to respond to the violence in the specialists he controlled. But Frank got belligerent, registered the glee in Sobieski's eyes, and took three ramrod blows to his ribcage before Mack pulled the young killer off him. It still hurt to breathe. No doubt, at least one rib was cracked.

He wanted the team to be capable of extreme violence when facing an impossible situation like this one had been, targeting five experienced killers with four hostages and a lot of very sophisticated explosives.

Frank was too close to the scene, close enough to watch through binoculars as the terrorists shoved an old woman out the door, evidently telling her to run, which she did. Then one of them proved his manhood by shooting her in the back. Now there were three hostages. He was so busy watching her fall, he nearly missed seeing the team enter the building through a side door.

There was remarkably little gunfire. Charlemagne took extra care because of the explosives. Also the hostages. Maybe. Frank held his breath as he waited for an explosion.

In five minutes, three hostages walked out, hands in the air. Frank nodded to his local counterpart, who deployed police to collect the traumatized—but alive—innocents. The team stayed inside while Sobieski disarmed four bombs.

...

"The baby cut another tooth this morning," said Maryann. "She was up most of the night, poor dear, but it came in eventually and by seven o'clock she was smiling to show it off."

It gratified her to see his lips turn up in what must have been an attempt to smile. The doctors had finally allowed her husband to be present for the birth of this one, an enlightened modern development that she applauded. It could have been that experience, or it could be this child had something special about her that touched her father. Either way, Theresa was his acknowledged favorite.

Now that he remembered his most beloved child, it was time to move him upstairs. Maryann did not think he needed a fourth martini.

"Leo, take off your shoes."

He raised an eyebrow at her, a welcome sign that expression was returning to his face.

"Your shoes are muddy."

She avoided the word 'bloody'.

"I don't want it on the carpet," she insisted.

He complied, slowly. She noticed he had difficulty bending.

...

Frank had crept into the building after he saw the team on their painful way to their airplane. His local counterpart waited for him, keeping the scene cordoned and sanitized. The counterpart vomited at the sight of so much blood. They had no choice but to stand in it. Frank noted what happens when you lose a fight with Mack. This guy had been bigger than Charlemagne's knife expert, but in the balance, size proved insufficient.

Leo looked up the carpeted steps to his bedroom and wondered briefly, achingly, if Maryann could carry him.

Three of the tangos were shot, which was odd, because he did not remember hearing more than one shot—aside from the old woman, that is. Then he recalled the supremely effective suppressor on the Frenchman's Modèle 1935, and indeed, the neat holes in the most lethal spots on each corpse explained whose weapon had been busiest.

The broken neck must be Sobieski's work, he surmised. It was not easily achieved. A machete lay on the floor nearby, explaining the sliced calf muscle. Several other bones were broken on this man before the skewed neck made him into another corpse. *Brave young man. But dead nonetheless.* Leo didn't know why—maybe because he had fought so well against Sobieski—but Leo doubted this was the man who shot an old woman in the back.

He remembered Theresa when they reached the landing. Maryann led from ahead of him now, instead of pushing from the back, and pulled him into the bedroom. He stood blinking, remembering the miracle of his daughter's first breath.

As she unbuttoned his shirt, Maryann's rich auburn hair glistened in a tightly bound ponytail. He wanted to free it. He wanted to do more than that, but none of his body was going to respond to his wishes, he knew. He thought about the anguish and pain he had seen on her face during the hours before Theresa screamed for the first time, similar to the grim, tight-lipped set of Mack's jaw as he staggered to his airplane. The Frenchman's expression confirmed for Leo that belly wounds could be the most painful of all.

Maryann gave birth seven times. It was not long ago that even once could be, and often was, fatal for a woman. What would Maryann feel if one of her four boys took a bullet to the belly? For that matter what would his own mother think of his job if she knew? And what of the mothers of the dead in that gruesome room? Surely, the old woman, shot by somebody else's grandson, had given birth at least once. It was a common enough occurrence, despite the shocked look some time ago on his pre-adolescent eldest boy's face when Leo had explained the origin of babies.

He would have thought Sobieski was a direct spawn of Satan but for a comment long ago from his old boss that he had met the man's mother when the killer was no older than the current age of Leo's third son. What of that? What if one of their sons turned into a

Sobieski, or worse, a Mack? Leo shuddered at the thought and at the despair it triggered in him regarding his species.

...

Maryann snapped him out of this latest dark tunnel.

"Leo, step out of your pants."

She had pulled them down to his ankles and held his arm to steady him.

"Lie down."

She took this opportunity to examine the black bruising over his right ribs, touching gently and watching him wince. This had not been a lover's tryst, she concluded, relieved and horrified at once.

"Should I call a doctor?"

He shook his head.

She took out the beautiful quilt that had been a wedding present from her grandmother and spread it over him.

He smiled, making her hope there would be no nightmares this time. She remembered when he came home from Southeast Asia.

Before he dropped into the welcome unconsciousness of sleep, he grasped her hand and whispered so low she had to bend her ear to his lips.

"Maryann, I love you."

COUNTING COSTS

The only belt-tightening I can unequivocally get behind is my own when a particularly satisfying dinner does the tightening. All other uses of the phrase are false flags designed to trap some poor schmuck in the hierarchy or divert much-needed funds into somebody else's favorite promotion scheme *du jour*.

'Less is more' is a close cousin of the tighter belt and can be summed up as somebody with less understanding making a decision that causes more death, with at least some of the victims innocent and all of them far removed from the decision maker.

The kid delivering the champagne is a case in point. He's dead, and both my competence and veracity as an intelligence operative have been permanently besmirched among the very people who have the power to kill me in an instant. Worse, I still have to deal daily with the guy who made that decision and also, on occasion, with the guys who wanted to kill me because of it.

Let me set the scene.

Just before I flew to Berlin for the usual life and death part of my job, our boss took a vacation. He appointed as acting head of The Section a nincompoop colleague of mine, nicknamed Jello, who had finagled the gig with some fancy political footwork. Within twenty-four hours of the boss opening a beach umbrella in a distant paradise, I confronted Jello about his latest bone-headed edict limiting message traffic between The Section's vault and agents in other time zones.

"You're creating a disaster waiting to happen, Jello."

"Besides the cost savings in scheduling, Buddy, it's necessary for security. We can't have all kinds of messages floating around the world for the enemy to pick up anytime they want."

"Cost savings? Security? Information is our bread and butter, and everything is encrypted!"

"So was Enigma."

"We have procedures. Single-use and all that. I always need background when I'm out. You're cutting my throat here, figuratively, at a time when I'll be dealing with somebody who specializes in it literally."

He gave me the condescending beatific smirk that always makes me want to hit him.

"Read up on people in the area before you go, Buddy. Inch will give you all the files you request—in the vault. Nothing leaves here in any form."

"We're talking about Berlin, Jello. How many Warsaw Pact operatives do you think might be there at any one time? I don't know who we'll come across until I get there, and Inch closes the reading room down promptly, no matter what, at four-thirty. I take off at seven tonight."

...

I landed in the capital city of Cold War spooks with no access to the treasure trove of information back home, so I immediately sought help from the station chief. He was on compassionate leave back in the States because of a death in the family. I was referred to a deputy.

"You should get the information you need from your people," he said. "We send it back there to your office as soon as we get it. I have no proper established procedure for releasing it otherwise."

"But surely, you can make an exception in this case." I tried to sound self-assured and persuasive, but it's hard when you've been on the road and in the air for twenty hours and the spaghetti they served during turbulence over the Atlantic decorates the front of your shirt.

"I don't have the authority to make an exception."

"But you're in charge."

"I'm only the acting chief. It's a named authority and my name's not on it."

Somehow separation by an ocean had given two different definitions to the word 'acting' within the same government department.

I provide operational support for a team of specialists, the term sometimes used for those who specialize in tricky situations that involve death. I am called a babysitter, and the trade name of the team I support when they are working for us is Charlemagne. Their business was booming. They had bought themselves one of those new private jets that were becoming popular among the well-heeled in the late sixties and flew into Tempelhof in style. I knew they worked for other governments as well as ours, and as I watched the shiny new thing land, I caught myself wondering if foreign babysitters had to deal with crap decisions by the Jellos in their organizations. Of course, they did, I realized. It is in the very nature of any human endeavor subject to bureaucracy.

I pulled up next to the airplane and opened the trunk of the car I had rented. Nobody spoke as they stowed their gear. I did my best not to let on that I was more uncomfortable about this op than usual. Being in their company always made me nervous, so I figured a difference in degree shouldn't register. But, of course, it did. Their point man reads minds.

"What is wrong?" Mack said.

The cut-throat son of a bitch knew my thoughts again. I would never get used to that. The other two young men sat in the back seat. Louis, whom I usually refer to as the Frenchman, chuckled as I stammered. Vasily Sobieski, the talented son of another legendary assassin, sent me silent waves of disapproval.

"N... n... nothing that will affect the operation," I said, "just some political shit in my organization. Don't concern yourself."

"I always concern myself about things that may kill me. Tell me."

I did not name names and kept it vague. I could tell Mack was not satisfied by my evasion, but he said nothing more.

At the safehouse, we went over the plan for that night, with Sobieski being more silent than usual, which means he remained creepily quiet, and the Frenchman acting somber, something I've rarely seen. I guess it would have been poor form to be his usual joking self when his friend Vasily faced the lion's share of peril in this plan. They had rehearsed each move ahead of their arrival and informed me how it would go down without need of my opinions, only my obedience to Mack's flawless direction. I was expected to show up on time at precisely the right spot. The usual 'or else' was implied.

Sobieski's skill made the plan just possible. He would scale a wall, set a small diversionary charge, slide down, detonate, and try not to stop flying masonry with sensitive parts of his body. After following Mack inside and slinking past the bleeding sentry Mack would have taken care of in his customary silent way, Vasily would lead Louis through the labyrinth of holding and interrogation cells to our guy before his next session of intense questioning and, we hoped, bring him out of there alive.

The Frenchman's perfect marksmanship and nearly silent semi-automatic would take the prisoner out if they found they could not get him out. That was the order. I wanted to vomit when I read it. I'm sure our guy had no illusions about what his capture might mean in the end.

Sobieski would lead this effort because he knew the building intimately, the same way he knew most of the worst KGB hell-holes in Eastern Europe—through experience. I had never trusted him and knew he did not like me—if he could harbor any such emotion as liking—but I had to respect him.

I promised to bring the car to the rendezvous without fail. I had managed to obtain stand-by medical help through the deputy station chief as well. Even if none of the team were injured, the prisoner would undoubtedly be in bad shape, assuming they were able to save him. I had arranged a place to meet an ambulance.

After the briefing, I offered the team ham sandwiches and potato chips. After suspiciously turning it over, the Frenchman took one bite of a sandwich and spit it out. I have to admit it was a bit dry.

They wore all black clothing and pulled on balaclavas before getting out of the car at the departure point, where they vanished within a few feet of the doors. I know I could no longer see them by the time I counted to three when I drove away with the lights still doused and began dry-cleaning the traffic behind me before heading for the rendezvous.

The coffee I sipped from a thermos kept me awake and, I thought, alert until a pounding fist on the window next to me told me differently. I was hoping for four men and so counted them as they climbed or were helped or pushed into the car. They were all there. The murderous energy, the smell of blood, and once we were rolling, the stench of vomit coming from the back seat indicated that all four lived.

I stopped by the parked ambulance and handed over our guy to the deputy and the medics. Charlemagne stayed in the car.

"A heads up would have been nice," said the deputy, clipping his words.

"Need to know. I should think my request for an ambulance on stand-by indicated something might be going down."

"Yeah, but this particular extraction is going to need round-the-clock protection. Do you have any idea how many people want him dead?"

"I was ordered to hand him to you and that's what I'm doing. Do I need a receipt from you? I'm also taking one of your medics with me. I got a guy bleeding into the front seat upholstery in there." I nodded toward the car.

His glare expressed his views about me and my guys enough to stop me from asking him again about the raw intel I knew I might need before the night was over.

As Sobieski limped into the safehouse and the other two began stripping off their reeking clothes, I hoped for a fleeting moment that the adrenaline high was winding down peacefully without a need for that special comfort provided competently only by female company. No such luck. While Mack showered, Louis gave me the name of a fashionable new bordello complete with an accomplished chef and accommodating women. He even knew the name of the madam.

The message center was a few blocks from the safehouse. Fresh air had become essential to me by this time, so I walked to it and was back in half an hour. I had sent home for any raw intel on the bordello and its employees, giving whoever might be on duty the names and addresses of the madam and the restaurant. Knowing Jello, I did not expect a reply, but you do your job even in the face of insurmountable obstacles and bad decisions in the workplace. Miracles have been known to happen. Besides, I consoled myself, an absence of a reply might mean no information existed.

Forty minutes after my return from my private mission impossible, Sobieski's leg had been stitched up, and the team were all three spiffed up and ravenous for dinner. Dinner and other things in the case of the Frenchman. We took a taxi, the car being too gruesome for habitation.

I stopped to check for answers to my message on our way. There were none.

The meal was delicious. Louis made sure I knew that because of the now-stitched leg injury, he had carried Vasily singlehandedly through the labyrinth of cells and up and down steps to the entrance where Mack could lend a hand. He made a point of reminding me that he did this without having eaten anything since lunch. Sobieski just stared at me with those expressionless, chilly grey eyes of his. My food choices always rankled them.

Madam introduced the woman she had handpicked for her 'most handsome customer'. The Frenchman ordered a bottle of champagne to be brought up to the room before he put down his napkin and followed his shapely diversion, sparing no more than a glancing smirk to his friends. A few minutes later, I saw a very young waiter inexpertly head up the stairs with a bottle in an ice bucket. He tripped on the bottom step and nearly dropped the bucket. Probably his first day in the world of work, I surmised. He looked too young to be shaving yet.

Not twenty seconds after the kid disappeared, the sound of a gunshot blasted into the dining room. Madam reassured her concerned guests, some of them on the verge of panic, that it was just a champaign cork, but we knew better and were already heading up the stairs, weapons drawn.

Louis opened the second door on the left as we topped the staircase. He had removed his jacket and holster and loosened his tie. He held his Modèle with its suppressor attached and struggled to buckle his belt with his left hand. He stepped aside and we entered. His lip curled at me in a sneer as I strode past him.

The waiter lay on the carpet just inside the door, blood pouring from a missing piece of his frontal lobe. The woman lay on the bed, fully dressed, with a neat little low-caliber hole centered perfectly between her open eyes. Her hand held the unsuppressed .38 revolver that had interrupted everybody's dinner downstairs. It had also taken the kid's life.

In terse, expletive-filled French, Louis told us he had laid his holster and its weapon on a bedside table (as you do in such situations) and was busy enjoying the woman's enthusiasm, when she suddenly reached for it. He grabbed it before she could get a grip, but she had the .38 in her other hand and now raised it to fire at him. Louis ducked and brought an arm across the back of her neck. Her finger continued to squeeze the trigger, the bullet finding a random target in the head of the hapless young man just coming in the door with a bottle of champagne.

I ushered them downstairs in a hurry, found us a taxi, and took them straight to Tempelhof, leaving the mess in the bordello to the overtaxed acting chief of station.

Back across the pond at my own office the next day, I found all the raw intelligence the Berlin station had sent to our vault. It detailed the madam's extensive connections with East German intelligence, including a brother-in-law in the Stasi. It even mentioned the dead assassin by name.

...

Aftermath

Our boss returned from vacation, and the prohibition against message traffic to the field was rescinded.

The madam was arrested for espionage and her establishment closed.

The Berlin station threw darts at a picture of me (illegal —I am covert after all) in their break room because the closing of the bordello ruined a rich and no doubt enjoyable two-year collection effort that had already led to the discovery and arrest of three complete minor cells and was about to ferret out the top guy in a major one.

The deputy was posted somewhere unpleasant.

The rental car company charged me for an entirely new interior because of the damage to the seats and carpets and refused my government credit card. I had to pay the charge, in cash, out of my own pocket. Reimbursement took six months.

The Frenchman developed his own procedures for checking an unknown woman. I fielded the consequent complaints each time we went out.

From that day forward, none of the team believed I ever had any intel about unknowns and never again listened to me when I did.

Charlemagne went on to greater and greater feats of doing the impossible and is now the premier specialist team in the West. They bought a bigger, faster jet.

I'm still their American babysitter.

The rescued man lived, had his identity changed, and retired someplace nice.

Jello received a step promotion.

The kid with the champagne is still dead.

QUENCHING THIRST

1968

"It is the worst thing we can do, Vasily. It exposes us. We must wait for our airplane." Misha did not hide the exasperation in his voice.

"It does not make sense to sit here and wait for hours when we could be at the airplane the moment it is repaired." Vasily's voice was not accustomed to such long sentences. It became hoarse toward the end, but he forced himself to continue. "Staying here will make us sitting ducks."

Louis weighed in. "But you propose to make us flying ducks, Vasily. There are reasons why we spend so much money on our own jet. Frank has assured us we can remain in this safehouse for a few more hours. When Misha told him your idea, I thought he would have a stroke."

Vasily rolled his eyes. "I never concern myself over Frank's health. It would save time to fly east on an American airliner, and I would find it interesting."

"You want to meet American women. Be honest."

"Very well. That is true, but more than that, I want to understand what it is like to travel like an American. This is the perfect opportunity. We have no gear and are only lightly armed. They cannot object to us. I have no explosives packed in my duffel bag. We should fly to Maryland to meet our airplane there."

"Those sentences contain more words than I have ever heard you say at one time," said Misha. "I think you will find it more uncomfortable than you imagine, but we will do it if Louis agrees."

Louis agreed with a great show of reluctance and a few pointed jibes. They bought three first-class tickets from a travel agent.

"Flying coach would be more instructive," said Vasily.

"I will not fly coach." Louis stretched his long legs before him on the safehouse sofa as the others packed. "There is no place to put my feet."

"Frank is flying coach. It is the same but a bit more crowded, I think. Six across instead of four."

"The stewardesses are prettier in first class," insisted Louis.

"That is a myth," said Misha. "They do not make assignments based on prettiness."

"But they do not hire them at all unless they are young and pretty."

"They can work in coach one day and first class the next. But I will concede that the food is likely to be better in first class."

There could be no answer to this. Vasily's stomach rumbled in agreement. The op had not presented any challenge beyond tolerance of tedium, but they had been working in the cold for too many hours, and Frank still did not understand the importance of good food. Louis shoved the man up against a wall when he walked in with a bag of hamburgers from a fast food restaurant. Frank's choice of safehouses was improving, though. This one was more private, had secure locks, and a functional coffee maker.

"Also," continued Misha, "there are fewer people in first class. I have requested seats at the back of the section so that there will be no one behind us. Louis and I will take seats A and B, and you will be slightly forward across the aisle in seat E with only a coat closet behind you. There will be plenty of Americans around for you to study. Your curiosity must bow to security, Vasily."

Vasily wore his dark brown suit because it contrasted well with his light brown hair. The suit had been tailored to fit perfectly, with a hint of sheen and flat lapels that were wide enough but not foppish. In contrast, his hair never laid flat. He had yet to find a barber who could tame the thick, straight mane. The suit trousers flared with understated perfection, and the two-button coat closed smoothly over a shoulder holster bearing his Makarov. The mirror showed him a young and prosperous businessman with quiet good taste. He approved the reflection and looked forward to meeting those stewardesses.

The smiles began immediately after Frank dropped them at the departure terminal and drove on to turn in the car. Two pretty young women wearing airline livery and standing behind an information desk gave them directions to the first-class check-in counter. Even Misha smiled back at them. Vasily hoped for opportunities to spend more time with such women—beyond asking directions.

He saw Frank standing in a long line waiting to board the back of the airplane. The worried look on his face made Vasily smirk at him as he walked past the line and through the jetway to the front of the Boeing 707 that would take them across the continent. Perhaps it was a good thing they were flying in first class. Frank made them promise to keep their jackets buttoned but remained jumpy and unhappy about the plan. Vasily never missed an opportunity to make Frank nervous.

His ticket placed him in seat 5E, across the aisle and slightly ahead of Louis in seat 6B. Misha had the window in 6A. Only a curtain separated their backs from the cabin behind them, but it was dark, opaque, and kept closed most of the time. A coat closet stood behind Vasily's seat. He glanced into the back of the airplane before the curtain closed and saw how they had squeezed two extra seats onto each row. Misha was right again. He would have been uncomfortable in that crowd, though he would never admit it.

As he prepared to sit down, he noticed with pleasure a young woman sitting in the window seat next to his. She was reasonably pretty and very American, wearing a miniskirt, white boots, and pink lipstick. Her hair had been teased at the back, and light blue eye shadow matched her eyes. She smiled briefly at him, then returned to the magazine in her hand. He thought she might be a few years his senior, but still, she attracted him.

Vasily felt Louis stiffen behind him. They had been a team long enough now that they could almost read one another's thoughts. He was busy looking at the girl when Louis reacted to a large man blundering down the aisle toward them. Warned by the readiness of his friends behind his left shoulder, Vasily released his seatbelt before the man addressed the woman next to him.

"Dottie, I insist that you sit with me. You are my wife, for God's sake."

Vasily decided on an upward thrust to the chin, two knuckles to the windpipe, and a knee to the groin. There was no space for a kick.

The woman replied to her husband without looking up from the magazine.

"No, Bill, I'm not sitting next to you while you flirt with the stewardesses. You want one of them? Go for it, and I'll hire a lawyer when we get home."

Vasily debated whether he should stand to give himself more options against this much larger opponent, but though the man had bulk and height, he appeared to lack strength. Appearances were easily disguised, though.

The man looked at someone standing behind Vasily's left shoulder. *That will be Louis.* Vasily glanced at the woman next to him. She coolly turned a page.

A stewardess walked up behind the man towering over them and asked him to sit down. He smiled at her.

"Sure thing, honey. You can order me around any day."

He went back to his seat; Louis sat down. The stewardess resumed preparations for takeoff. Vasily relaxed his fists, and the woman next to him turned another page. After a series of very fast side glances, he could see she was looking at a woman's magazine and the article that engrossed her had to do with one of the many mysteries women seemed to care about, something concerning cosmetics applied around the eyes.

On one of his glances, he saw she was looking at him. He returned her gaze frankly, she smiled at him.

"Do you travel often?" she asked.

"Yes." So far, the content and speed of her language were within his competence. He had no trouble understanding.

She continued talking, but her speech became more rapid, so that he missed occasional words, but these seemed nonessential. He learned about a sister in Los Angeles with a new baby and a husband superior in every way to her own. He glanced at her bare knees and imagined sliding his hand up between her thighs. The thought pleased him.

"What happened to your hand?" she asked, indicating the missing last two fingers of his right hand on the armrest between them.

"It was injured," he said.

The clunk of the landing gear folding up into the fuselage beneath them masked her sympathetic cluck. The seat belt and no smoking lights went out and after rummaging in her handbag, she pulled out a packet of cigarettes. She offered him one.

Vasily shook his head. He had spent most of his youth in spartan conditions, in and out of prisons or under interrogation, and found it hard enough to miss important things like women and coffee without burdening his ability to survive without luxuries. He did not smoke, drank very little alcohol, kept his rooms in Misha's house free of decorations, and dressed without ostentation.

She hesitated before retrieving a cigarette lighter from her bag. Vasily remembered he had once seen a man light a woman's cigarette in a cinema and wondered if she expected him to do the same. He added it to a list of things he must ask Louis, the acknowledged expert on how to behave in the company of polite women. He was well enough versed in how to act with the other kind.

She blew out a puff of smoke with a look of contentment. "Where are you from?" she asked. "You don't sound like you're from L.A."

He considered the question. Vasily was Polish, but most of the time he had spent in Poland involved prisons or living rough while doing secret work against the communist government.

"I live in Austria," he said finally.

"With kangaroos and koala bears?"

"No. That is Australia. I live in Europe, in Austria."

"What's it like there?" She stubbed out her cigarette in the ashtray set into the arm of her seat. Before Vasily could formulate an answer to one question, she asked another. "What language do you speak? Is it Austrian? I can tell you have an accent. I wish I could speak a different language, but I was never any good at it in high school."

They had another four hours, including lunch and an afternoon cocktail to spend in this way. Vasily resolved never to admit to Misha and Louis that they were right. They should have waited in the safe-house for their jet to arrive.

He distracted himself by fantasizing about what she must look like, feel like, naked, but he said very little. She seemed not to notice that he never answered her deluge of questions. He watched her face and listened to her talk about her family, her friends and enemies, and most of all, about herself. His quiet attention sufficiently satisfied her without the need for words.

He knew he wanted to sleep next to such softness on a permanent basis, to wake up with unlimited privileges. He contrasted Misha's cold, aristocratic wife with this chatterbox and decided neither would suit him permanently, though he would not turn down an opportunity to bed this one. Misha kept a mistress, so he also seemed less than satisfied with his stunningly beautiful wife. But at least she could hold her tongue.

Lunch was indeed delicious, though silence would have improved the experience. Vasily ordered coffee rather than a cocktail. The woman ordered a concoction called a Mai Tai. He remembered seeing small umbrellas like that in drinks served at a Bangkok brothel. She requested and was granted a second one. It did not slow her speech, but it may have slurred it. He could not tell because he was no longer listening to her, though he continued to watch her, fascinated.

Touchdown came as a relief. Louis stood up before the airplane reached the terminal and handed Misha his hanging suitcase from the coat compartment. He ignored the stewardess who told him to sit down. Another stewardess countermanded the first one and looked past the two men toward Frank, who now stood on their side of the curtain.

"Your airplane has arrived, Sir," she said to him, "and there is a message that a car will be waiting at the bottom of the front stairs."

Frank nodded, looking relieved.

Vasily stood in the aisle and reached for his suit bag from Louis when a hand clamped itself to his shoulder. He whirled, aiming his right elbow at the face behind him but had no room to extend his reach with a kick. The man stepped back just in time to save his nose.

"What the hell, punk," said the woman's husband. "I heard my wife talking to you the whole time, even over the engine noise. I'm gonna teach you to leave her alone."

His wife stood up from her seat. "Bill, you're drunk. Shut up."

"I know he must have pestered you the whole ride, Dottie. Don't worry, I'll make him sorry."

"Bill, don't...!"

The man deserved no less than Vasily's most insolent stare and responded predictably when he saw it. Dottie's husband never connected against his more agile opponent, but both of Vasily's blows landed effectively and dangerously on his jaw and nose in quick succession.

The woman watched, speechless and wide-eyed, as her husband went down backward in the aisle, his face motionless and bloody. The two men to her left took their hands out of their coats but not before she saw their holsters. They pushed the man she had been talking to for the last five hours, the man who had laid her husband flat just now, toward the front of the aircraft, where a stewardess opened the primary door. The seatbelt sign remained lit.

"Go!" said a man inside the curtain. He had bulging eyes and a receding hairline.

The three men stepped over her unconscious husband and disappeared through the open door.

Everyone in the compartment remained perfectly still, the stewardesses stood frozen until the man with protruding eyes cleared his throat and said, "Call an ambulance."

As the wheels came up and their jet headed home, Vasily sat back with a glass of mineral water in his hand. He enjoyed the luxury of the water being *mit Gas*—sparkling—reminding himself of the English appellation—but even more because he was being allowed to drink it in silence. Misha and Louis shared a half-bottle of a very nice claret.

"Tell me what you are thinking, Vasily," Misha said with a smirk as he drank his wine.

"This is unworthy of you, Misha. First, because it is Louis who likes to tease, not you. More importantly, you already know what I am thinking. Leave it be."

"You are scowling, Cousin, glowering into your mineral water. May we surmise the experience did not satisfy your thirst for knowledge of Americans?"

"You know very well it has drowned that thirst." *In a deep lake of English words*

"Maybe," said Louis raising his glass in a mock toast, "but not, I think, your thirst for American women."

KEEPING SECRETS

USA, 1969

A tiger sleeping, a shark submerged, a fighting man in suit and tie, Vasily kept his nature hidden, kept everything hidden because that was his nature.

Nadine saw him in the beverage aisle but paid no attention. She shopped for groceries. At checkout, he put three cans of cola and three bags of potato chips on the conveyor behind her. She reached for the divider stick and placed it after the last of her vegetables.

She glanced at the good-looking man behind her, wearing a suit —*a suit mind you!*—in a grocery store. His sand-colored hair looked unruly and the pale grey eyes did not smile. He paid with a twenty-dollar bill, giving it to the cashier with a right hand missing two fingers. She paid attention to that.

There was no sign of the prison years in Vasily's face, only in his right hand.

It took a while to organize her checkbook and find her keys. By the time Nadine hoisted the last bag into her cart, he was walking ahead of her out of the store. She still had the bank to do, then the post office, and if the weather stayed cool enough not to melt the frozen food, she might fit in a stop for gas. She reached her car and saw him climb in the rear of a black Mercedes backed into a spot in the next row, directly behind her. She opened the tailgate of her station wagon and took the bags from the cart, using each turn to surreptitiously inspect the car behind. The outlines of two more people were silhouetted in the tinted windshield. *Why don't they drive away?* He's probably handing out the colas and chips.

The Mercedes driver touched the gear lever on the column.

"Not yet," said Vasily. "Follow her." He made no move to open the bag of snacks.

Both men in front turned to look at him. The taller one in the passenger seat, Louis, glanced at the bag on the seat next to Vasily. He was thirsty.

They left their question unspoken but fully understood.

"I want her," Vasily said by way of explanation. He still did not open the bag.

The gaze from the driver's royal blue eyes demanded more. Misha wanted a fuller explanation.

Vasily shrugged. "Just once."

Misha sighed and started the car without comment. They tailed the station wagon to the bank, then the post office, and finally a gas station. She asked the attendant for eight gallons of gas before going inside and handing the cashier a credit card. Louis saw the number on the card while he waited to pay for the few drops he'd put into the Mercedes. He examined her unobtrusively while she explained a pinging noise to one of the mechanics and wondered what Vasily could want in her. Nice enough, he decided, but a bit too ordinary for his taste.

The mechanic called in his boss and the woman explained the ping again. This was taking a while. Louis went back to the car where he was delighted that Vasily had opened the bag. He popped the can of cola Misha handed him and drank greedily.

Vasily sat behind Misha, legs stretched across the seat, his back against the door, an open bag of chips balanced on his lap.

"Aside from the moral implications...," said Misha.

Louis swallowed and interrupted; whatever the conversation had been, it begged for interruption. "Moral implications? Are we philosophers now? Theologians even?"

He got the long blue stare from Misha. He countered it with raised eyebrows.

"She is quite obviously married," Misha said finally.

"Yes. She has her husband's credit card." Louis opened his bag of chips.

Vasily stopped eating momentarily. "I would never dare to touch your wife, if that is what worries you, Misha. You know I have too much regard for you." *And for your skill with a knife.*

"Marriage has never mattered to any of us before, including you," said Louis. "If you want to discuss philosophy, let us decide if it is ethical to shoot the target tomorrow before he enjoys his breakfast. Perhaps he should enjoy one last meal."

"That is not what I am saying." Misha's face had reddened, a rare occurrence.

"Leave him alone, Louis," said Vasily. "He is tense."

"I am not tense because of tomorrow." Misha caught himself too late; the words were already gone. He corrected, lamely, "I am not tense at all," then recognized a lost cause and turned caustic. "I wonder how you will get the woman to agree, Vasily? Or will you add rape to your list of ethical grey areas?"

Misha got away with the snipe because it would be his turn the next day. The other two were treading lightly.

Vasily shrugged. "I will ask her."

Discussion turned to ideas on how to get Vasily into a position to ask her. They dismissed as over-dramatic Louis's suggestion that they lean from a car window and shoot out her tires on a lonely road.

"A flat tire would be convenient, though," said Vasily.

As the woman jabbered and gestured, trying to convince the mechanic there was a ping, Misha walked up to the candy machine near the shop entrance. He pulled a handful of coins from a pocket, letting a few slip through his fingers. They landed chink, chink on the pavement next to her car, some under the car, beside a rear tire. He bent to retrieve them and stood again as she turned. He did not smile.

That was the best looking one of the set, thought Nadine. No doubt about it, nothing could beat him, the blond one at the candy machine. She had now seen all three out of that Mercedes and this one won her private beauty contest—*or should that be handsome contest?*—hands down. Except, she didn't like his eyes. *Too blue, too cold. That man is dangerous.* She shuddered.

The dark one had his own attraction. Tall. That's always a plus in a man. Well, not always. Neil's brother was tall, and a real nerd.

The thought of Neil made her ache. She started the car.

Back to the tall one. Hello, my name is Nadine and my husband has several mistresses, so I am taking applications for the post of sugar daddy. Would you be interested in applying? You look like you could afford me, and you look like I would enjoy all the attention you care to give me.

She thought about the slightly wide mouth, slightly, but not too much, thick lips, just thick enough to show that his kiss would be inescapable and unforgettable. The car seat got warm.

Her mind bounced again, stuck like a record scratch, on the missing fingers of the first man. How did that happen?

She wanted to know. Wanted to know him.

Maybe he ached the same way.

Rats. She'd lost them. They weren't following her after all. Maybe that was good. Could be they were related to Neil's scummy buddies, the ones who would kill him someday. Oh, she was sure of that, but Neil didn't listen to her. Would he listen to one of his girlfriends? She wondered.

Nope. These guys are way too classy for Neil. She had enjoyed their company behind her car, sparking small fantasies. Or big ones, as the case may be. It was probably good they weren't following anymore. The chances of three sophisticated men developing a passion for a short middle-class housewife whose husband was a philandering bum.... The chances of that happening in a healthy and wholesome way—Nadine knew what she wanted and what she shouldn't want and these two things matched exactly—those chances were slim. Very slim. Slimmer than she was when Neil announced his latest love and she went on a two-day depressive eating binge. Five pounds made her favorite slacks tight. Cleared the complexion, though. She checked her face in the rearview. No wrinkles yet. Neil's latest was thirty-five.

My husband is going out with an older woman.

She re-focused past her new haircut—straight, smart lines at the side, a bit of fluff on top—and checked the road behind. No Mercedes. Rats. She shouldn't have bought the double Dutch cream fudge. It was calling to her from a grocery bag in the back.

No, it was not the ice cream calling. A different noise, clang, clunk, clang made her slow. The noise slowed. The car shuddered. She pulled off the road onto a forest preserve parking lot. No one sat at the picnic tables. A pale blue sky floated far above the circling trees, but the tables around the little parking area stood in shadow.

The tire was flat, all right, and the groceries blocked the way to the spare. She began unloading. It was easy to hear a car coming because the forest was so still. Even the birds seemed to be off work today. Would they be back in the nest at five? Or would they have to work late with some thirty-five-year-old slut?

She looked up before the approaching car rounded the last curve. Should she catch the driver's eye? Should she accept help? No, she could change her own tire. It would be safer. She finished unloading, ignored the sound of the car, and tried to look nonchalant about being stuck alone near a deserted forest. Not creepy at all. She adopted the body language of I do this every day, strictly routine and I'm expecting twenty people for a picnic any minute now.

Please don't stop. Please don't be a homicidal maniac.

She froze at the sound of a heavy vehicle's tires grinding over the gravel behind her.

Other than the lump in her throat and the nagging suspicion that she'd put a streak of dirt across her nose, she had no feeling when the back door of the Mercedes opened and the first man, the one missing two fingers, walked toward her and offered to help.

"I will be here only one night," the man said as he loosened the lug nuts on her wheel. "Will you meet me for a drink?"

She told herself she said yes because she wanted to ask about his hand and his accent and she wouldn't let it go any further.

O God. Who am I kidding? What about my stretch marks?

...

This had to be the stupidest thing Nadine had ever done, agreeing to meet a man at a bar. She should have stayed home to eat ice cream. She had crammed into her short black skirt and the fifty-dollar cream-colored blouse her sister sent at Christmas. Make-up—perfect. She used the evening setting on her make-up mirror.

So did every other woman in this hotel bar. Many showed off bits and pieces of themselves, all of which looked a hell of a lot better than most of her bits and pieces.

O God. He's not here. O thank God. He's not here. Oh God, he is here.

She had forgotten the powerful attraction in his eyes. What color were they? A mixture, or none at all. Interesting enough to be remembered, but she couldn't figure out the color. Light, but not blue. His hair was the same way, light, but not blond. She wanted to comb it for him. He wore it a little long, longer than hers, but it behaved less or he'd lost his comb. Like Neil was always doing. How many hotel rooms had he left it in?

When the man reached her table, she noticed he had a quiet smile he didn't seem to use often. He bought her a drink and asked her about herself. Where was she from? Did she come from a large family? He was careful not to ask too much, not to pry, but his attention was undivided, all of it devoted to her.

Nadine told him more than she intended, including the children. Surely that would not scare him away from a simple drink at happy hour. She didn't want to know if he had kids.

She searched his left hand.

"What is the matter?" he said. "Why have you stopped talking?"

"Are you married?" She blurted it, like an accusation.

"No."

It seemed to be the truth. He waited for her to go on.

"I... I don't even know your name."

"Vasily Sobieski." He did not ask hers.

"Where are you from?"

"Poland."

Wasn't that one of those communist countries? Is he a communist? Is it bad if he is? What would Neil say? What is a communist, anyway?"

"Are you here on business, Vas...?"

He helped her pronounce his name but did not answer the question.

They moved to another table in a dark corner where the other two men from the Mercedes sat close by. A short, round man with thinning hair and a nervous manner was with them. *Which of these does not belong?* No contest.

She had no chance to ask about his hand. He kept the conversation on her, which was not hard to do once she started talking about Neil. She began at the beginning. It took another drink and a half to finish. By then, the band started, and talking became difficult, limited to the less noisy spaces between songs. He suggested coffee someplace quiet and took her out of the lounge to the elevator. *Is there a coffee shop upstairs?*

He put his room key in a slot in the elevator panel marked 'E' and turned it. The elevator moved through all floors without stopping.

Nadine stood in a speeding elevator with a man she didn't know, on her way to have sex with him. *What the hell am I doing? I know damned well what I'm doing.*

He leaned casually against the back wall, hands in his pants pockets, coat bunched up at his wrists, watching her decide.

"Is there a time when you must be home?" he asked.

"I... I have a sitter. I told her I'd be home by midnight."

"Your husband is not home?"

"He's working tonight. He said."

The penthouse was magnificent. So was Vasily. He took his time. Patience seemed his strongest virtue. Nadine had limited experience. There was her high school sweetheart, then the frat brother in college—more of an almost, really—and finally, there was Neil. None of them had patience like this man. His kiss was slow and long and deep and included an exploration, muscle by muscle, hand to body, until she shook where she stood and let him draw her into a bedroom of the suite.

He continued there, past the buttons, past the bra. She sat on the bed, while he stood before her. She could hear the other men come into the next room. It was the thought of running past them with bare breasts bouncing that kept her from leaving when Vasily took off his coat.

It wasn't a physical deformity; it was a gun. Neil would know what kind. He knew all about such things, even had some locked up in the attic. She shivered when she thought of them being in the house at all and shivered again when Vasily unstrapped the holster and told her to be careful not to reach toward the gun. He laid it on a bedside table.

"What kind is it?" she asked to make conversation, to stall, to give herself a chance to cool down and regain her common sense.

Vasily smiled, chuckling lightly. "A Makarov," he said before kissing her again. Then, he did not let her cool down.

...

"How did you hurt your hand?: She felt she had a right to ask as they lay side-by-side in the sheets, after.

"I did not hurt it. Someone hurt it for me." He turned his head to look at her.

The light was still on but had long since ceased to worry her. Vasily did not seem to notice the stretch marks. She also forgot about them as she looked into the stillness behind his eyes. It was not a peaceful stillness, not the kind that comes when all is done, but the kind that reigns before all is about to be done. It was the ready kind.

"I don't understand," she said.

"My fingers were torn off under torture, in a prison." He smiled. "They did not know I am left-handed. I don't miss them much."

She stared at him. There were other scars, on chest and abdomen, some round, others jagged. She had the same sensation as in the elevator. She did not know this man. She'd had sex with him, but he was a stranger."

"We inhabit the same planet," he told her quietly, "but different worlds."

While they dressed, he explained about the short round man so she was ready when they walked out into the other room. She guaranteed her silence with a shaky signature on the government form he offered. As if she ever told a secret in her life! The guns now in plain sight on the other two men unnerved her, though. She signed quickly and did not stay for coffee.

Nadine was up when Neil came home that night, because she couldn't sleep. She took a bubble bath, drank hot chocolate, ruffled the bed with a few tosses, and finally turned herself out and sat in the kitchen to stare at the coffee maker and think about Vasily.

She heard two sets of footsteps coming from the garage and expected a leggy blonde thirty-five-year-old to follow her husband into the kitchen. She tensed for confrontation. Behind Neil came a short, round, balding man with bulging eyes, and presumably, a government form bearing her signature in his pocket.

This was something so new she had no breath for it.

Neil pretended concern at her being awake so late. He introduced the man named Frank, saying he was a colleague. Frank shook her hand and said "How do you do?" as if they'd never met.

Nadine started a pot of coffee, struggling for enough breath to be minimally polite.

Frank sat at the kitchen table and in a jovial, full voice continued the conversation they must have been having in the car. "So why does the Makarov make you nervous, Neil? You've been in this job long enough to know how to recognize an ally."

Nadine froze, spoon poised over the coffee basket. She stared wide-eyed at her husband. He was glaring at Frank, shaking his head vigorously, and waving both hands, palms down.

Frank repeated the gesture. "What does this mean?" he asked innocently.

Neil's face turned red. "This place is not secure," he said through clenched teeth. He tossed his eyes in the direction of his wife.

"What? It's just us." The round man's eyes bulged further in disbelief. "Don't tell me you don't tell your wife anything at all when you're working?"

"I don't."

"It's unwise, you know. She needs enough information to know what not to say to people. How do you explain... like tonight... What did you tell her?"

Nadine answered for her husband. "He said he had a girlfriend."

"You what?" Frank was incredulous.

"I did not. I said I had to work late. That's all."

She wasn't about to let that stand. "But the phone call, the picture! You let me know... You let me think..."

She began to see the deception clearly and did not like it. "You tortured me!"

Neil answered shout for shout. "I had to. It was the only way to keep you from snooping and then blabbing."

Nadine's mouth moved, but only every other word could make it out of her throat, like a faucet full of air, spluttering. "I—never—you—secret—me."

Neil, evidently thinking he had the upper hand, decided on an official approach. "Security is essential since they moved me into the new section. Did you think I got that raise for nothing? I can't afford to have you running around asking questions."

Nadine threw the spoon at him. It caught his attention. She reached for the coffee mug and weighed it in her right hand. Neil began explaining.

"They moved me to anti-terror." He dodged the mug. She picked up another. "You don't know the killers I have to deal with." This mug shattered on a cabinet behind his ear.

Frank raised an eyebrow but remained a spectator.

Neil dropped his voice, forced words between his teeth, truthful, straightforward words for the first time, the only words that might stop the third mug from flying.

"I spent tonight with a guy who could cut your throat and go back to his breakfast without washing his hands and he's on my side. You don't know what I see."

The couple stood in their kitchen, red-faced, trembling, but silent. Frank got up and turned on the coffee pot.

...

"Why do you think he led his wife to believe such nonsense?" asked Louis the moment they left American airspace. He handed Vasily a gin and tonic.

Vasily put down his newspaper and took the drink, glancing at Misha in the seat next to him. The operation was over, the adrenaline gone, and Misha had not even finished his whiskey before falling asleep. Their jet hit a pocket of turbulence and the whiskey in the glass he still held sloshed over his wrist, running over the blood that dotted his cuff.

Louis took the glass from Misha's hand, put it back in the bar, and sat opposite Vasily.

"What is your theory, your deep thoughts? Why did he lie to her?"

Vasily took a long sip and leaned his head back against the seat before answering.

"To keep her ordinary."

...

Neil never learned how well his wife could keep a secret.

PRIMER CHARGE

Florida, 1970

"There must always be a primer charge," Vasily said to the blackboard at the front of the small classroom. "The primer ignites the main charge. We calculate the force required by...."

This was an anti-terror course, taught by a specialist in bringing terror to terrorists.

His audience sat at a long table facing him. They wore uniforms displaying the insignia of various Army Special Forces units and Navy SEAL teams.

The two men in civilian suits on each end of the table divided their attention between the room's occupants and the door at the back. They were Misha and Louis, the other members of Charlemagne, the famous specialist team—almost as famous as its indispensable explosives expert. They watched his back while he imparted, with a thick East European accent, an incomprehensible bomb-making syllabus to handpicked Green Berets and Seals.

A round, balding man sat on a plastic chair next to the door. He used the game name Frank Cardova and was Charlemagne's American babysitter. He hired them for the job, lying about it. Knowing full well that he lied, they agreed for their own reasons. Frank's responsibility was to house and feed them and keep them from contaminating the innocent citizens they came across.

A bell sounded the end of a fifty-minute hour.

"Will you be covering the advantages and disadvantages of different detonators in the next hour?" asked one of the men. Vasily had no answer ready. The man blocked his way to the door and a much-needed cup of coffee. Vasily had taken last watch the night before. Coffee was essential.

"I was looking for more detail on computing a primer charge," said the man called Martinez on his left. Too close on his left. He tensed, glaring.

"What about the condition of the main charge?" said a third. "We can't always assume it's top quality, can we?"

Lt Col Tom Keoughke, acting commander of the group, rescued their instructor. "You have the syllabus in front of you, gentlemen. Let the man get a cup of coffee." He led Vasily out of the room, parting the crowd by sheer bulk, his graying crew-cut head leading by force of weight from the top of a massive neck and shoulders. Misha and Louis followed.

"There's coffee in the faculty room," Keoughke told them as they exchanged badges with the guard in the hallway.

"I like the stuff in the machine better," said Vasily. He ignored Keoughke's incredulous look and spoke to Misha in German. "My English has become very good. That sentence was American colloquial."

"I like the coffee in the faculty room, Vasya," Misha said with a weary smile. "We will meet you back here."

Vasily found the coffee machine in the vestibule. A small crowd filled the space near the front door of the building, noisy, smoking, and laughing. He waited his turn at the machine, watching them. The man in front of him dithered over making a choice.

"Come on, Sergeant. Decide already. The bell's about to ring."

The voice, young, female, and somewhat breathless, came from a hallway on the left. Vasily turned. She was pretty, wearing her Air Force uniform rather well. Her name tag said MCullough. A pair of dull brown barrettes pushed back the unmilitary red-gold ringlets trying to frame her face.

Vasily smiled. "Please, go ahead of me. I can be late for my class."

"Thank you." She smiled back.

He watched as she walked toward the unsecure wing of the building. The bell rang and she rushed to class, holding her coffee at arm's length.

"Where have you been?" asked Misha when Vasily reached the hall guard. "We were about to come looking for you."

"Getting coffee."

Two breaks later, Charlemagne—this time, the entire team—stood together at the machine in the vestibule. Ahead, the large double doors leading to the main auditorium stood open. The hall could hold four hundred people during primary lectures of the school. To the left of the doors, most course attendees broke up into smaller discussion groups in classrooms in the unsecure wing of the school.

Vasily taught his course in the secure wing, to the right.

"I would like to attend this lecture," he said as he sipped a fresh cup of machine coffee. "It looks interesting."

Louis raised an eyebrow. "Dynamics of Socialist Ideology?"

"I wonder what it is that looks interesting to you, Vasily," Misha said as he noticed the pretty red-haired young woman in uniform standing in a small group gathered at the double doors. She spoke and laughed with her group, but glanced frequently at his friend.

"She told me she would save me a seat," said Vasily.

"I'm so glad this is the last hour of the day. Aren't you?" Annette McCullough asked him as he sat next to her ten rows down from the back.

He nodded.

The room emptied and filled during the break. Military people in uniform invited friends for coffee, shouting across rows. Civilians in suits and ties stood in gaggles. School staff, some in uniform, some not, strode up and down the aisles with purpose, no time to chat.

She gave him her name, her life's history, such as it was, and a description of her sister's dress for an event called homecoming, interesting to her, incomprehensible to him. But he was not bothered by a need to understand and settled back in his seat to enjoy the sound of her voice and the face and manner with which she spoke. She was lively and happy and seemed to like him. He had never come across this combination before.

She asked his name. He told her. She mispronounced it. He coached her in the pronunciation and she settled on calling him Vaz.

He didn't know what he thought of that.

A paper airplane hit the back of the seat in front of him. He picked it up and threw it back at Louis, who sat next to Misha in the back row.

"Are they friends of yours?" asked Annette. "I saw you talking to them by the machine."

He had to admit it then.

Her questions ran like beads on a string, patterned but different, and no space between in which to answer. "Are they in your seminar? Which seminar are you in? Where's the classroom?" He gestured vaguely to the secure side of the building. "Are you in the secret wing? Are you a secret squirrel type? Like James Bond? I've never met a James Bond before. Is there a gadget in your watch? Can I see?"

She reached over him, almost spilling his coffee, took his right hand, and looked at his watch. He imagined himself as Bond, comfortable, respected, and admired by a beautiful woman. Memories of pain, prison camps, and torture cells, of numbing fatigue and gangrenous fear faded. No one had ever created such a space in his mind before, altering, if only momentarily, the way he looked at his life.

"How did you hurt your hand?" She touched the remaining knuckles of his two missing fingers.

Reality crept back, snarling. "Accident," he mumbled as he snatched his hand away.

"Scuse me!"

The voice came from above them and to the right. Vasily ignored it. Annette looked up.

"Scuse me!" the voice said again. "Students are not allowed to bring beverages into the main auditorium." An arm reached toward Vasily's coffee.

He looked up then, tensed, and glared a warning at an officious captain in black plastic government-issue glasses. The man did not catch on but continued to reach for the styrofoam cup in Vasily's left hand.

"Maybe I can help here. I'm sure I can help." The words came in rapid fire from Frank as he sidled up between the seats. "Just let me help you there, Captain. Don't touch... the coffee. It may burn you. You never know."

"He can't bring coffee in here."

"I'm sure we can straighten this out. Mr. Sobieski is a guest instructor, you see. There are some privileges.... He probably wasn't aware...."

"I don't care what he is. He's aware now." The captain had committed himself and was not backing down. "Give me that cup." He reached for it again.

Frank grabbed the man's shirt and yanked him backward.

"Hey!"

A crowd gathered. Louis stood clear on one side, Misha on the other, hands in their coats. Frank pulled the captain, unwilling and complaining back to the aisle and out of the room, smiling and saying, "I'm sure we can iron all of this out with the school commandant." And under his breath, "Shut the fuck up. I'm doing you a favor, bub."

"Who was that little bald man?" asked Annette.

"My babysitter." Vasily smiled at her. "I require much looking after."

She tilted her head, puzzled. "He said you're an instructor. What do you teach?"

Everybody sat down and the lecture began, saving him from having to think of an answer.

...

At the end of the day, Louis pulled off his tie, threw himself on the sofa in their VIP suite, and rambled in his native French. "So when will you finish with her—I want to know. Close call today, eh? I thought we agreed the only lecture we would attend is the one by the defector. What is his name? Godinsky. This unannounced interest in academe will get you in trouble, Vasya. There were two hundred people there today. You cannot quietly beat a man to a pulp in front of two hundred people and call it inconspicuous. I say you call the girl tonight, feed her, maybe, and bed her definitely, and then we will be done with that and I can get on with finding a little of my own or just sleeping." He yawned and threw one arm over his eyes. "Vasily?"

There was no answer. Louis took his arm away. Misha stood over him, silently offering a mug of coffee, and said, "It appears we have a date for dinner."

"Misha, I don't want... I want..." Vasily turned away to pour his coffee and find the words he needed.

As usual, Misha understood, even when Vasily did not.

"Perhaps it will happen someday," he said, "but not this girl. You are a curiosity to her, no more. When that curiosity is satisfied and she realizes what you are, she will have no more to do with you. She is too American."

"I like her for that reason. She thinks the world is fair and friendly."

"You cannot have her without showing her the truth. You cannot show her and still have her. You have a dilemma."

Vasily drank his coffee and hoped Misha would be proved wrong.

Louis combed his dark curly hair in the mirror on the wall over the sofa. "You know this is taking too much out of us, out of Misha and me, don't you Vasily?"

Vasily sat slumped in an easy chair, holding his empty mug. "I am sorry, Louis. I find teaching to be very tiring. I am grateful for your indulgence. Am I doing well, do you think? I mean the teaching? Is it adequate?

"That is not what I mean, Vasya. Taking your share of the watch so you are rested to teach will be dangerous if we lose judgment and reaction speed. Already, I sense something else is going on, but I am too bleary-eyed to know what is making me uneasy. Why is Frank so nervous? The Americans are up to something. I would bet my mother on it. I can tell Misha thinks so, too. And now there is this girl to distract you further."

"You don't think they hired us because my English is excellent?"

Louis raised one eyebrow. "No."

"My skill as a teacher?"

"Um. No."

"My expertise, then?"

"Now there is the question, n'est-ce pas? Think about it. It is like asking Monet to teach kindergarten finger painting. A bit of overkill, perhaps. Excuse the pun."

"So who do the Americans want us to kill? Who will die? And why are they lying?"

Louis shrugged.

...

When they took her home after dinner, Vasily walked Annette to her quarters and kissed her good night at the door.

Mon Dieu! said Louis from the back seat when he returned to the car. "You did not try, Vasily. What is going on here? No sleep! Three hours to prepare for dinner, eat dinner, and return from dinner. Three hours of sleep time and you did not even try."

Vasily did not answer.

"You are not thinking...." Louis threw his head back against the seat as it dawned on him. "You cannot. There is no way, Vasily. What will you do? Blow up a headquarters, gun down a KGB assassin and go home to your American red-head asking what is for dinner, darling? Bring me my pipe and slippers? My uncle Bertrand is correct. You cannot mix the two worlds. You should have spent more years with my uncle like I did. You would not have these delusions. You cannot have both."

"Misha does."

"Misha does not."

Misha was driving. He said nothing.

Louis persisted. "You know that Katya lives a fairy tale. She thinks he is a farmer. Remember when he took that bullet in his thigh? He told her it was a bullet and she did not speak to him for a week. Last time, when his ribs were broken falling against a boulder, he had to tell her he had pneumonia."

Misha nodded.

Vasily leaned forward. "And she believed you?"

"She had no choice but to accept it," said Misha. "Our marriage was arranged. You ask too much of this American woman."

...

The next morning, Vasily noticed it because teaching had required rest. He was alert; the others were already impaired by fatigue. During the first break, he took his coffee from the faculty room with Misha and Louis.

"Something is wrong," he told Misha. He used his native Polish because it was not one of Frank's languages, though the man did try. "Frank is watching the wrong people. He watches the students, not us. He searches them."

Is this what made you finally stop talking to the blackboard?" asked Louis. "Because you were watching Frank?"

At the second break, Vasily followed three of his students to the coffee machine.

"I didn't see you last break," Annette said as she approached.

Vasily was too distracted to notice her smile. Instead, he watched the Navy SEAL team commander behind her, the blond one named McElroy, standing in a circle of people. Vasily's eyes swept the lobby, searching in all directions. *There*. A civilian watched McElroy from beside the soft drink machine. Vasily concentrated next on

Keoughke, the class commander, who had emerged from the secure wing.

Annette spoke again, and Vasily turned to face her. Out of the corner of his eye, he tracked Keoughke's bloused boots, green fatigues over mirrored black leather. The boots entered the men's room on his left. Other feet walked in after them, mostly creased Air Force blue with Corfam low quarters, all except for one pair of civilian gray tweed.

"Will you have lunch with me?" Annette asked uncertainly. "My treat." There was a note of pleading in her voice, a puzzled look on her face.

"Yes. Yes, of course."

One more student. Martinez, another Green Beret. Same buzzed haircut as Keoughke, but no grey. Same attention being paid him by a man in civilian clothes.

Annette said goodbye, sounding wistful. Vasily went back to class to report the little he had learned.

"Those being watched are all military," he told Misha, "and the watchers are civilian."

"Stop recruiting," Misha told Louis. "Drop the project. We do not need new people under these conditions."

"We should leave now. Frank has put us in danger, or he would not be so careful to hide it."

"Undoubtedly, but I want to deal with Frank before we go."

Lunch with Annette was strained. Vasily hardly spoke except to introduce her again to his friends and to Frank. The tension at their table was more than noticeable, making silences profound and awkward. Vasily did not know what to say, so he said nothing. He barely looked at her as he concentrated on the sandwich in his hand.

She tried conversation, but every attempt sputtered. "Oh look!" She waved to a man sitting at a corner table. "There's my boss, Colonel Mark. Do you know him? He seems to know you."

He studied the man.

"He's been around absolutely forever," she continued, encouraged by Vasily's sudden attention. "He's the oldest Colonel in the Air Force, they say, and they must be right. When I told him your name he acted like he knew you and asked how old you are. I said about thirty. Was I close?"

Vasily nodded.

"And then he said, oh he's too young. Imagine that, thinking you're too young for me."

Keoughke entered the dining room and was waved over by Annette's ancient colonel. Both men exchanged solemn pleasantries that felt longer than necessary for a simple hello.

Louis muttered in French, "Wish I had an ear at that table.

...

"What bad omen do you bring this time, Keoughke?"

"Just going to school, Markie. That's all. The redhead's a little young for you, don't you think? I noticed you eyeing her. You always did have exotic tastes."

"She works for me. I heard a big name and I'm concerned for her. That is the only reason I invited you to my table. Have you heard about a Big Name in the area? Should I worry about her? Or is it just a coincidence that I see you and hear the word Sobieski on the same day?"

Keoughke turned and looked at the table where Annette sat with four civilian men.

"You talkin' about the company she keeps, Markie? Is that what's botherin' ya? That guy's my instructor and those are his... associates."

"And the subject he's teaching?"

Keoughke smiled.

"I presume he's well qualified?"

Keoughke leaned back with a knowing smile. "Let's just say Uncle Sam cares enough to send the very best."

...

"He tells great stories." Annette wrinkled her nose in an effort to remember. "Here's one I recall. Just after the Korean War, Colonel Mark was in a counterintelligence unit and a Soviet defector told them there was what they call a sleeper agent, a spy who's so secret, he doesn't even do any spying until he's told to, so there's no chance he can get caught until he's right up there where the best secrets are. Do you understand?"

Vasily ignored Louis's snort and nodded.

"They had to find the sleeper," she continued. "They knew about where he was but not which office he was in. To catch him, they found the biggest juiciest secret they could get hold of and gave a copy to every office. Then they watched them all, hoping it would be too much temptation. It worked! They caught the sleeper stealing the document. Wasn't that clever?"

She looked at Frank. It seemed the thing to do. The others were staring at him.

"Are you ill?" she asked him.

Frank's eyes bulged from his round face. Sweat glistened on his bare scalp. "No," he croaked.

Misha looked at his watch, then at Frank. "You have until one o'clock," he told him in German, "to get approval to double our fee, or we leave."

Frank stood, nodded, and walked out of the lunchroom at top speed.

Annette's brow wrinkled as she watched him go. "Did I say something wrong?"

...

Frank could not get to the message center fast enough.

"Listen, Buddy," Bruno had said, "I know he's a friend of yours but the guy's got the ears of my bosses about the money thing and they're driving me nuts. Your team charges way too much of the green. Jello suggests we pay less this time by disguising it. You know they'll react as desired the minute a weapon is drawn. And then, as the Brits put it, Bob's your uncle."

Jello was not a friend. Back in the early days, Jello's bad judgment had given Frank the thrill of dangling from a winch hanging out the back of a C-130 Combat Talon over a jungle in Laos. Under fire. It could have been worse. He could have been dead on the ground. But the experience killed any feeling of friendship.

Frank brainstormed Bruno's idea, then explained the chances of success. *Nil.* Bruno didn't understand how smart these guys were. Jello didn't understand anything. Frank left home leaving it to chance and hoped he wouldn't end up burned—in the final sense.

He hired the team's explosives expert, the light-eyed Vasily Sobieski, who he knew wanted to kill him, as an instructor at the special ops school in Florida, subject: how to construct a primer charge. It involved math. It pleased Bruno. It confused Jello.

The teaching fee would barely cover the cost of the team's jet flying in from whatever unfortunate location on the planet harbored them. So, he was not surprised by Mack's (he didn't dare get familiar enough to call him Misha) lunchtime ultimatum, only worried. If they left, it would make everybody look bad. If it made the team look bad, they would take it out on him.

He stood at the message center window looking at the blank form before him on the counter and began a missive to Bruno, hoping he would understand it.

```
F 081709Z JAN70
FLASH FLASH FLASH
TSECRET/WNINTEL/NOFORN/NOCONTRACT/SPECAT/WEDGE
OBJECTIVE UNATTAINABLE DUE TO OVERHEAD COSTS AND
NEWLY DETECTED RISK.
```

Frank paused to chew on the pencil. How to put it?

```
INCREASED FEE IMPERATIVE. IRREPARABLE DAMAGE IMMI-
NENT AT THIS PAY LEVEL.
```

Being as how death would be pretty irreparable, especially if it was his, he signed the form and handed it in, then spent an anxious hour pacing the hallway, contemplating the impact of time zones—no problem, same zone—and lunch. The team's break had been early. Bruno was probably still feeding his fat face, not that Frank should criticize.

He was saying a Hail Mary when the comm clerk called him over and shoved a message through the window.

```
R 081812Z JAN70
TSECRET/WNINTEL/NOFORN/NOCONTRACT/SPECAT/WEDGE
MODIFIED FEE APPROVED AT ROUTINE LEVEL. SATISFAC-
TION OF CONTRACT REQUIRED. FUNDING SOURCE CODE AD-
JUSTED REFLECTING ALTERED OBJECTIVE. SUCCESS AN-
TICIPATED. EMPLOYEE SAFETY ENCOURAGED.
```

Aww, Bruno was concerned for his safety.

When Frank returned to the team with additional funds, he volunteered (after appropriate coaxing) a few snippets of information. Like the fact that the recently defected Godinsky reported a military sleeper.. Godinsky thought this wet-ops sleeper would be activated to teach other would-be defectors a lesson, with his body as visual aid number one.

"So what?" said the Frenchman. "You must have squeezed every drop out of him by now. Let them have their revenge."

"Yes, but..." Frank choked momentarily until Mack loosened the grip he had on his tie. "Yes. We have, but we can't afford to lose a defector. It's bad for the travel brochures."

"You have another in line, then?"

Frank nodded after an additional sharp tug. "He's big and he'll bolt if something happens to Godinsky. Nor will he travel while the threat lurks."

"Do you think they will spend a sleeper on one used-up defector?" asked Sobieski.

"No. That's why we sweetened the pot." Frank struggled to breathe between words.

"With us. With me," Sobieski said with a low, flat tone.

"Yes." Frank's rapid reply was cut off abruptly when Mack hit him in his ample gut.

...

Vasily and Annette attended another lecture together, by a speaker from the US State Department, who explained predictions of future geo-political trends. They took the same seats, ten minutes early.

"I don't like your friend Misha. He was nasty to that little round guy, your babysitter...." She snapped her fingers in an effort to remember the name, "...Frank."

Vasily wanted to tell her Misha agreed to remain, despite their danger, not for the extra fee, but to give him a chance to court her. There was no better friend.

He said nothing.

"Why are you so serious, Vaz?"

"I am not serious. Tell me about your briefing. I am listening."

"I can't tell you the actual briefing." She giggled. "It's classified. Oh, but there was something interesting Colonel Mark told me this morning before class. I think he was talking about you."

Vasily became still. She continued.

"The colonel said, 'Lieutenant, allow me to explain intelligence with an allegory. You work up at the peak, where everything is white with snow and visible, up there above the clouds. I've spent most of my career further down the slope, where all is fogged grey—hard to catch details. Underneath the mountain, in the lowest levels, life is very different. That's where the goblins live who eat dirt and ooze slime. I've done some checking, Lieutenant, and your new acquaintance hails from that region. Do you understand my meaning? He does not visit there. He was born there."

...

That evening, Vasily stretched out on the sofa, tie askew, hair more than usually mussed. "So, the Colonel heard of my father. He did a better job of telling it than I could. She took it well, don't you think?"

Louis plugged in a hot pot of water. They were reduced to instant coffee. Frank became even more unpopular.

Misha answered. "His words were very pretty, Vasya. She did not understand any of it."

"She did."

"No. You are as invisible to her as any fairy tale."

"You have had too much wine," said Louis. "Are you sure you can take the middle watch?"

"I said I could," Vasily said flatly. "A target does not need so much sleep as a teacher."

The next morning, Vasily took his coffee, steaming and black, from the faculty lounge in a twelve-ounce styrofoam cup. He caressed it, worshipped it through red eyes created by the middle watch.

Annette met him a few feet down from the top of the center aisle in the main auditorium, near the double doors to the hall.

"Hi." She beamed at him.

He managed a return smile as he swept the room noting the locations of five of his seven pupils taking seats for Godinsky's imminent appearance, wondering which of them had 'kill' on his class schedule.

"I never know what to say to you, Vaz. You don't seem to pay attention."

"I do pay...."

"Scuse me!"

The officious captain, not cowed by Frank, remained determined to keep all coffee out of the main hall. He touched the coat sleeve of an armed man exhausted and on edge. The captain's 'scuse me' was the last thing he would be able to say for months.

Vasily's right hand held his coffee. Given the threat he faced, he preferred to keep his left, his shooting hand, healthy. He chose a roundhouse kick to the face, his toe connecting under the left jaw of the unfortunate Captain, breaking it, scattering teeth and blood, and sending him sprawling backward into the seats. It was the rigid back of one of these that gave the man a hairline skull fracture.

Reactions varied. Louis laughed. Frank buried his face in his hands. Misha watched the room. Most people gasped. Vasily's students admired him. All seven were present. McElroy at the main entrance, Keoughke in the far aisle near the podium. Two others discussed Vasily's technique. Martinez brought out a pen and notebook to ask for an autograph.

Vasily focused on Annette's fear, disgust, and condemnation. They saw each other for the first time in mutual disillusionment. Her glamorous James Bond became a violent creature that ate dirt and oozed slime. His adoring American required too much evidence to see reality.

His stare lasted only seconds, disturbed by an anomalous movement behind her. Keoughke's grey head moved between the seats, his massive shoulders turning to face first the stage, then the seats as he threaded his way down the row. More movement near the podium caught Vasily's attention. The guest speaker had arrived.

Keoughke's movement was wrong, too slow, too deliberate. Vasily recognized him in that fraction of time, watched the draw, saw the body through which the bullet must travel to him. He threw down his coffee and grabbed Annette by the front of her shirt.

She resisted, horrified. He had no time to return fire, instead using the moment to try pulling her away, out of the sights on Keoughke's muzzle. She stood firm and angry until the bullet brought her down.

Keoughke fell under fire from Misha and Louis.

In the rush to kill the threat, no one but Vasily watched the girl die. Keoughke's bullet, meant for him, had nicked the aorta. She bled quickly, internally. Death drained her face to a translucent white, framed in the fire of her hair. An angel with a halo.

Vasily did not talk about it.

...

Frank had no choice but to talk about it—before an investigative panel of executives in his organization.

The chairman, a handsome man with no understanding of Frank's world began the interrogation with, "Why the high fee?"

Frank repeated his report but questions continued.

"Don't you think the fee is excessive for the simple protection of a defector?"

"It wasn't simple."

"Would some other category be more appropriate?

"I suppose, if you must, you could put it under the category of education."

Frank was joking. The chairman brightened.

"Wasn't that the original contract?"

Frank nodded. "Until his fee doubled when he found out he was playing a part in a trap—as the cheese."

"But he did teach. That settles it. The expenditure comes under education and the reason for this inquiry no longer exists. Adjourned."

Frank rose, dumbfounded. One man on the panel paused on his way out and asked him, "Out of curiosity, what exactly, did we learn for all that money?"

Frank answered mechanically, "How to calculate and set a primer charge."

A LIGHTER SHADE OF NIGHT

Vasily took his position in the deeper shadow formed by the corner of a building near the path. The struggle going on under the weak beam cast by a decorative pathway light bothered him. He gave a questioning shrug to Misha standing a few yards away.

It was not the team's policy to play knight in shining armor, but the last few days had been too much like that other time, that other American girl, the one that.... Vasily tried to be as still as Misha but could not help clenching his fists. Even the gloom was the same this time.

They had followed the guy who called himself Nick to the campus, briefly lost him, and now found him trying to rape a co-ed. Vasily saw the flash of the man's knife at the same moment his friend did, but Misha was quicker and already responding.

"Cut her and I cut you," Misha told him. He made him stand, chin up, with the blade at his throat, then nodded to Vasily and withdrew the knife.

Working over this incompetent took no more than a few minutes, a richly deserved lesson in the inadvisability of crossing the professionals who hire you to do a simple job tailing one man. The small-time hoodlum would be more reliable in future. After his bones healed.

Louis helped the girl up and dusted her off while Vasily prepared his attack, so he did not recognize her in the murk of a cold Chicago dusk until he caught up with them where they waited on a bench near the parking lot. The light was better here. Her wild, curly brown hair moved wisp by wisp in the light breeze. She wore a singularly unflattering skirt and carried a large bag filled with notebooks.

Gazing at her, Vasily was struck by both the differences and similarities between this one and that other one. What the hell was her name? She had been pretty. This one was compelling rather than beautiful. But both were Americans, with that innocent faith in the safety of their world, or so it had seemed that other time.

Louis and Misha walked ahead.

"I will not be here on Saturday to take you to dinner as I promised," Vasily told her. "We will leave before then."

She looked disappointed. He marveled that even now after it had been explained to her by people she trusted, now that she knew what he was, she did not have the sense to be relieved at this news.

He wondered how he could soften her disappointment. "I never had any intention of having dinner with you," he said, hoping to cause a healthy disdain for him.

Her eyes fell, studying the yellow circle of light at her feet from the lamp above them. He led her out from under the direct beam into a soft shadow where he was more comfortable and where she could hide the tears dropping to the pavement until she gained control of them. He could see his words failed to repulse her. He said them for her good, but they were painful nonetheless. He could not bear it, not when he remembered... What was her name?

He gave in to regret. "But I would like to have dinner with you," he told her. "It may take time, though. Your government does not often welcome me."

The trusting smile disturbed him, but the lips that formed it were irresistible. He kissed her and discovered how much he wanted her.

"When will you meet this new watcher?" asked Misha when Vasily climbed into the car.

"Tonight."

"Does he know Nick?"

"Yes."

"Make certain he knows what happened to him and why, so that he does not repeat Nick's mistake."

"If he is any kind of decent watcher," said Louis from the back seat, "he will hear about it soon enough."

Misha pulled the car over as an ambulance turned onto campus. He looked at Vasily.

"We do not have time to depend on your new watcher's network to inform him. Tell him immediately. Tell him in a way he will understand."

The new watcher called himself Colt, probably in reference to the old handgun stuffed in his waistband under a dirty flannel jacket of green and black plaid. The jacket blended well in the alley where they met. Shadows of skittering animals flitted through trash and dirt, moving in and out of occasional jagged breaks in a wall or fence. The only illumination came from distant rectangles of light in scattered windows overlooking the alley and the ambient glow of the major city around them against a cloudy night sky.

Vasily began the interview by shoving Colt against a wall and divesting him of the ancient revolver. The man protested when he opened the cylinder and emptied its contents into a pile of rotting garbage. After a quick check for other weapons, Vasily spoke for the first time, still holding the watcher against the wall and increasing the pressure.

"You will not come into my presence carrying a weapon, or you will die. Do you understand?"

It took a bit more duress to get his point across and elicit a satisfactory response. Vasily continued his instructions.

"You will tell me immediately when the man you are watching moves. Nick failed in this. You should visit him at the hospital to appreciate the consequences. I put him there."

Misha had warned him not to be ambiguous.

Vasily explained the procedure for contacting the team. Unlike Nick, this watcher repeated the method precisely and with apparent understanding. That fact and the man's excellent choice of subdued jacket gave Vasily hope that the series of bad luck and obstacles keeping them far too long out in the cold might, just might, end soon.

"Is this one more promising than Nick?" Misha asked when Vasily returned to the safehouse.

"I think so, yes."

Louis pushed a cleaning patch soaked in solvent through the barrel of his Modèle. "I am certain you provided motivation, did you not, my friend?"

Vasily responded with a half smile and asked Misha, "Do you think this guy, Grayson, will be able to broker the deal for the tangos?"

"No."

That was all he said. Flat and starkly pessimistic.

"What then?"

Misha sipped his coffee slowly. "We must find their safehouse. They are soft and lazy, but they know their business. They have an army of watchers and six fighters."

"I am close to finding it," said Louis. "Their excessive number of watchers is a weakness. One of them will lead me to the place, no doubt. They are no better skilled than the ones we have been able to hire, like Nick."

Vasily poured coffee into a cup and sat opposite Misha. "And then? Three against eight?"

"Besides the AKs," said Misha, "we may need explosives."

"Of course, but they have sufficient plastique to bring down a skyscraper, and their bomber is good with it."

"Not as good as you are, Vasily."

Vasily began first watch as the others slept. With more coffee and the challenge of the puzzle presented, he had no trouble staying awake despite the galloping exhaustion of the last ten days. How to design charge configurations, if needed, that would be effective, targeted, versatile, and above all, satisfactory to the Americans? Or, how to dismantle the enemy's placements before they could be detonated, assuming the enemy got what they needed in the end? There was a reason Americans felt safe and were willing to pay his team's high fees. Their government had no patience with large explosions. Such things were bad for business.

Despite incomplete knowledge of the threats they would face, Vasily already had an idea of how he would approach the problem when Frank arrived.

Frank was the American Vasily had least use for. He was their babysitter, providing food, shelter, and transportation on behalf of his government while shielding that government from association with the likes of them. Vasily could feel the nervousness of the man increase, if that were possible, when Frank realized Misha was not present to protect him from his fists. The agent practiced good tradecraft, but not always, and that other girl… that was Frank's mistake, much like that time in Berlin, when another woman tried to kill Louis.

He had come with news. "There's been a message. Grayson's moving."

Vasily told him to wake the other two members of the team and opened a foot locker. He laid out three AK-47s in their cases, then rummaged for magazines and belts. Frank still stood as if paralyzed. Vasily looked up at him and said quietly, "Now."

That was a peculiarity of this man, thought Vasily. The best way to make him obey was to whisper.

They left the equipment and the AKs in the car and made their way on foot to the location in time to see the girl walk through the main entrance of the apartment building. Vasily reminded himself this one's name was Alexendra. He still could not remember the other. He wondered, was Alex dirty after all? Was Frank wrong again?

Louis followed the girl up the stairs like a shadow. Misha and Vasily climbed more slowly, clearing hallways before proceeding. When he reached the second-floor landing, Vasily could hear Grayson's voice above them. There was but one more flight to climb when he heard the soft zip-pop of Louis's suppressed Modèle 1935. Misha took the last few steps two at a time, swearing softly.

The discussion began in French when they were safely inside the girl's tiny apartment. Grayson's body lay in the bathtub.

"Fool!" said Misha. "We will never flush them out now. Grayson was our only link to the tangos. Why is there no connection between the trigger and your brain?"

Louis's face formed a recalcitrant sneer. "He was about to shoot the girl!"

"So what? Let him! Maybe then he would have led us to the targets."

"She is important to Vasily," said Louis. "I saw him kiss her."

Misha's rage made him more still than ever, always a warning sign with him. Before he could speak again, Louis switched to English and said, "And she knows where the icon is. The one Grayson wants."

Vasily wondered again whether Frank was wrong about her. He looked at her carefully. She stood trembling under Misha's penetrating glare. It meant she had good sense, and her occasional trusting smile was for him alone.

"You know where the icon is?" Misha asked her.

It was time to interrupt. Vasily used Polish. "Do you think she is dirty, Misha?"

"No. But she is unusual."

"How?"

"Too intelligent and too ignorant at the same time. Also, she pushes her luck."

"That is what attracts me." Vasily met Misha's stare. "This one must live. If she is not dirty, that is."

"She will not thank you for interfering. It will cost her."

"Nonetheless."

"She may blame you. You cannot force her to live when a quick death may be her preference."

"It is my preference that she live."

"The other one was dirty, Vasily. You had no choice. It was not your fault."

"But it was my bullet. I thought she trusted me."

"She was sent to kill you," said Louis. "These things happen. You never regretted such necessities in the past."

Vasily knew Louis was right, but he could not explain how this girl was different. She knew what he was and did not fear him. The situation touched perhaps the only romantic corner of his heart. Though the other girl had turned out to be dirty, she created a mythical world of safety around him. He wanted to keep the myth, not see it die again—this time with Alex. He lowered his voice and said, "Misha, I am adamant. She must live."

The night did not go well for Alex. Misha did what was necessary to give her a chance, while they fulfilled the commission from her government. It began with tears. Vasily did not doubt it proceeded with screams. He was well acquainted with the levels of pain the enemy would have caused her in the time it took the team to reach her. His AK took out the three fighters closest to her. Louis and Misha accounted for three more, but the leader grabbed the girl and ran, pushing her before him with his knife against her neck. Misha pursued them.

Vasily concentrated on the job at hand. He found and quickly dismantled packages of plastique installed at key structural points in the basement of the huge building. Louis ran in search of the enemy bomber who held the detonation device. He returned, dragging Alex with him.

When Vasily reached the last placement high on a crossed girder above them, he had come to a decision. The girl sat collapsed on the floor, a puddled mess. He needed to know, even at the cost of his own life, though with Louis covering him, it would more likely cost hers. But he must know if she had been sent to kill him. He handed her his Makarov in its holster.

"Please, hold this."

Then he turned his back to her, registered Louis's questioning look, shimmied up the slanting beam, and completed the job. The building and its occupants were now safe, the tangos dead and the team's fee payable. And for Vasily, the myth remained intact as he retrieved his gun. There was a living girl, an American raised in safety, who knew all about him and who still liked him.

"Thank you, Misha," Vasily said as they drove to the airport. They had taken Alex to her parents' home, bloody but alive. Louis picked the front door lock quietly and she slipped inside.

"I hope she will not blame you, that's all," said Misha.

"She told you no, so she must blame me despite your intervention, but at least she is alive." *And with her, the myth of possibility.* He looked out at the lightening sky of a grey dawn over the city.

"She said no to my question, Vasily. You have not asked her yours.. Give her time to heal and try putting some words together for a change."

"But we are leaving." Vasily paused, then said more quietly, "And she said she would not come with us when you asked her."

Louis chimed in from the back, using his long legs to push on Vasily's seat. "That is not the same as coming with just you. Make your offer plain to her. I think she will accept. She likes you."

"How? When?"

He knew he sounded cynical, but the words 'she likes you' had already changed the color of this dawn. Others might consider it a cold gloom, but for Vasily, the clouds were dispersing.

As Misha turned the car toward the FBO where their jet was parked, he added even more sunlight by saying, "We will find a reason. We will force Frank to let us in. Then, you must not waste the opportunity."

Vasily chuckled, feeling the delicious sensation of being alive after an op. "Louis, you must give me lessons on what to say."

...

"The fee barely covered our expenses, Misha," complained Louis from the back of the car six weeks later. "And the tangos were hardly worth our time. Amateurs. Dead in five minutes."

"I thank you, Misha," said Vasily. "I know you arranged it by charging so little." He looked out onto another grey day as they approached Alex's neighborhood. Was Chicago perpetually blanketed by clouds? His only experience with the city remained a memory of various shades of night. He silently rehearsed the words he would use.

But all words deserted him as he stood next to her. He noticed a slight limp, though she seemed otherwise recovered. Her family and friends were busy making Misha and Louis uncomfortable with questions and small talk, but the world had shrunk to a bubble surrounding just the two of them, a bubble lit by an escaping sunbeam from the high window above them.

She smiled at him.

He remembered two of the many words Louis had taught him. He whispered them without the recommended question mark.

"Marry me."

TWO PAIR, ACE HIGH

"I cannot believe you allowed that fortune teller to take your money, Louis," said Misha. "You are usually more careful." He laughed at the thought of Louis parting with so much as a sou on such nonsense.

"You should try it, Misha," said Vasily. "She told me many intriguing things."

Vasily would not say what these were, but then, he rarely disclosed anything concerning himself.

"I agree," said Louis. "She is an interesting old woman, flattering and insulting at the same time, talking in riddles and contradictions. I am to be well loved despite my despicable nature. How is that for a future?"

The young Frenchman laughed out loud, his black curls waving in the warm breeze of Misha's perfect wedding day. Puffy white clouds floated over tents and marquees with pinnacle flags fluttering and guests taking their fill of only the best food and drink.

Now twenty, Misha had avenged the car bombing of his parents, sister, and little brother. The sights, sounds and smells of that day were seared onto his mind, a permanent scar on his psyche. The scenes of his revenge were likewise indelible, but failed to assuage the horror of that day. He had bowed to his relatives and accepted the girl his father chose for him before he died, because he was a dutiful son, and because he didn't know what else to do.

"You will rebuild your family with your beautiful bride," said Louis, always capable of putting his finger on Misha's mood. "Celebrate the fact that you have lived to see this day. Go. Talk to the old woman. She will tell you what a lucky son of a bitch you are."

Misha allowed his friends to shove him toward one of the many entertainment tents peppered across the extensive lawns of his family's estate. He entered the fortune teller's lair chuckling and took the chair before a painted low table without waiting for an invitation.

The woman stood when he entered. She knew who he was but said nothing, her wrinkled face a studied blank, and inclined her head in greeting. A few wisps of grey escaped the drab scarf she wore. Despite the heat of this summer day, she wrapped a dirty tasseled shawl closer about her as she stared into Misha's blue eyes. She shuffled a stack of playing cards and indicated that he should cut.

"This is not a full deck," he said as he broke the pile in half.

"It contains only aces and face cards, my lord. You have no interest in servants."

He did not bother to correct her inaccurate address. This was all in fun, after all.

Gnarled hands turned over the new top card. The ace of diamonds. She placed it before him on the table. The queen of diamonds came next. She set it in front of her on the other side of the little table. Two kings surfaced and found places halfway between the diamonds: clubs on Misha's left and hearts on his right. He found it difficult to keep a straight face as the crone pretended great solemnity in forming a cross with the last card, the queen of hearts, at the center, but it became easier to fight laughter as he watched her face.

She studied the cards, registering puzzlement and dismay, fear and sorrow. He hoped she would not try to flatter him in this charade and glowered at her to make sure.

Her black eyes held his for a long moment before she spoke.

"You are the ace of diamonds, my lord," she rasped, "well practiced at cutting your enemies."

Where did she get this information?

He lowered his brow. She did not flinch.

"Your bride is the queen of diamonds. Also cold and sharp but without your violence. Your families think they have arranged the perfect match, but though she will give you an heir, she will cut you."

This was probably the favorite topic of speculation throughout the neighborhood. All the old woman had to do for this intelligence was listen. No matter how sharp and cold his bride might be, he intended to thoroughly enjoy his exquisite new wife and raise a legion of young heirs to plague the bastard who tried to annihilate his name.

"These," she said, indicating the kings, "are your friends, your champions. One light, one dark." She pointed a crooked forefinger at first the king of hearts, then the king of clubs.

Misha nearly snorted in derision. *Is there anyone who does not know we are a team?*

Her bent frame rocked forward on her seat, as the old woman used her chin to indicate the last card, the queen of hearts, in the center.

"There is the woman you seek. She is not well formed in my mind. I cannot tell you much. She is connected in some way to the light king, and the dark king will fight you for her."

Preposterous. He wanted to shout his scorn, but she raised her eyes to his and arrested the words in his throat.

"Time and hardship will erase this day until you draw again the ace of diamonds. When you see the card and remember my words, look at the woman before you. She is the queen of hearts. She will save your life. Then, after more time and more grievous loss, you will win her."

The witch sat back with a sigh. "And... she will save your soul."

...

"I am adamant," said Vasily in Polish. "She must live."

The girl trembled as they stood in her tiny efficiency apartment arguing. Now a seasoned operative approaching thirty, Misha had caught the twenty-year-old student lying repeatedly but doubted the chit understood Polish.

"Vasily," he said, "there are too many coincidences with this girl. Both of her parents are connected to us in some way, to you in particular. She may be dirty, no matter how many assurances we have been given."

"Nonetheless, I want her. I want her to live."

Misha knew that blank face carved of stone. Vasily would not budge, but he tried one more argument.

"We must use her as bait, Vasily. The operation comes first. Always. She will give the targets what they need from Grayson so we can find them. They will check her and discover she cannot be his lover because she is a virgin. You know they will realize that she is mere bait and will kill her outright, no matter what we do."

Their discussion, sometimes heated, other times analytical, began sketching out a plan that might—only might—appease Vasily but kept circling back to the main obstacle, which Louis summed up in English for her benefit.

"She must not be a virgin."

Misha looked at the insignificant young woman. The tangled brown curls that ranged around her face only highlighted her blanched reaction to Louis's words.

"Choose," he demanded.

Of course, she will choose Vasily. Her preference for him was as obvious as his for her. Louis found it amusing; Misha, mystifying. She wasn't even all that pretty. He waited for her to name her necessary lover.

"No," she said.

This is where she chooses to stand firm?

Misha marveled as arguing voices filled the little room. She agreed to help them kill a band of terrorists. She lied to them repeatedly—when not withholding information outright. The girl even violently smacked a neighborhood enemy in the face with a heavy bag of books. Misha had seen the bruise.

But having sex with the man she quite plainly loved in order to give herself a chance of survival was a moral bridge she would not cross? Had she been older and less ignorant, there would be no problem. But then, if she were older and less ignorant, she might not be a virgin.

Louis found a pack of playing cards in a utensil drawer next to the tiny stove at one end of the room and handed them to Misha.

"Choose, or we draw cards," Misha said to her as he shuffled.

She refused to cut the deck. Louis drew the jack of clubs and smiled. Misha hoped her shuddering reaction would bring her to her senses and make her name her favorite, but when Vasily turned over the king of hearts, Misha wondered why it bothered him. *Surely she will relent now that luck has given her the man she prefers.*

As he drew his card and stared down at the ace of diamonds in his hand, he remembered with a clarity that mimicked the reality of that day in a tent on his lawn a decade before.

He remembered every word.

How could this obscure nothing of an American girl in Chicago have anything to do with his past or his future? It was true his wife had given him one heir and then cut him thoroughly, taking not only to a separate bedroom but to an entire suite of rooms in another wing of the house. His current mistress, installed in a nearby village, might be more willing but only in an equally indifferent way.

"Choose, or we go by the cards," he said to the girl who stood trembling before him.

She shook her head.

He appreciated the irony of having his soul saved by adding yet another crime to his already vicious resume.

...

She dressed again before the other two returned, but the free flow of her tears made Vasily meet Misha's eyes with no more than a questioning glance. The two friends understood each other perfectly. No matter how much Vasily might fantasize about American girls, he knew the necessity they were under.

A little animosity, a hint of blame, would be easier to bear. *Stop forgiving me!*

The operation was fraught with coincidences and obstacles that delayed them at every step. They had become visibly exhausted and noticeable to their enemies. Survival depended on Misha's judgment, and the girl's rescue could not be a factor in his calculations. Only the deaths of the targets counted here.

But Vasily wants... And Vasily had been like a brother from his earliest years.

As the team approached their task that night, it looked more likely the deaths would be their own.

With one bad decision, I have killed my only friends.

Vasily's girl swallowed a tiny sensor Louis gave her before her ordeal began. The targets dragged her through the basement of the skyscraper they planned to destroy, threading their way along a labyrinth of girders, packing crates, and ventilation machinery.

Louis carried a small radio and wore headphones as he led the way. He held up a hand on the second turn, pointing to a sensor that had been placed by the enemy. The radio picked up the sensor as the girl passed it. They would follow it into a trap, but they would be ready.

That old woman would say the girl has saved my life in this way. Misha suppressed a snort. *Nonsense.*

It took time to avoid the sensors and achieve an element of surprise. By then, the girl had suffered considerably and could barely walk when the largest of the tangos dragged her back through the labyrinth. This was the so-called knife expert and thus Misha's natural target, so he pursued them.

He caught up to them in a cul-de-sac of crates and machinery. He knew better than to try grappling with a man twenty kilos heavier with a reputation for skill in a knife fight. The logical thing to do would be to shoot him. Misha was ready, but the man held Vasily's girl so that he could not get a clear bead on anything lethal in the dim basement light.

Without hesitation, Misha slid sideways instead, kicking the girl into a wall and out of the target's hands. He lost his gun in the process and had just enough time to pull his knife from its sheath.

There, Crone. It is I who saved her life, and it has cost me mine.

It was the slowed time of disaster that allowed him the luxury of an imaginary conversation with a fortune teller in the past. He grappled with his enemy on the floor. Each man held the other's right wrist in his left hand.

Death became more certain as Misha's position worsened with every minuscule advance of the larger man's knife. He refused to bow to inevitability, instead straining on, knowing it was futile, watching the glee grow on his opponent's face, which is why he saw the shadow and then the brown curls.

She had crawled to them, her feet being useless, and lifted something above the enemy's head. Misha recognized his SIG Sauer semi-auto handgun. The foolish wench held it by the barrel and brought the stock down on his opponent's skull with all the picayune strength of a mouse.

To an observer, there would have been no indication that the blow changed anything. But Misha and his foe existed in the slow time before death by disaster, and Misha saw the blow coming. He was ready for the enemy's momentary distraction, the infinitesimal transfer of attention from the hand holding Misha's wrist to the tap on his head.

Misha twisted his knife hand as the grip on his wrist softened, thrust the blade it held into the enemy's lower abdomen, and pulled. As he rolled the body off himself, he sat up, panting and stinking of blood and vomit. The girl sat within arm's length, stricken with nausea. Misha held out his left hand for his gun.

"Do not ever touch it again," he commanded.

She handed over the weapon, just managing not to shoot him—or herself—accidentally.

With ignorance, incompetence, and wrong-headed interference, the wench had saved his life. He cursed the old fortune teller.

When the girl refused to come with them, he advised her to stay quiet, using threats to make his point and keep her safe—for Vasily's sake. She glared at him.

He dealt with Vasily's dejection by finding an excuse to return to Chicago six weeks later, where they found her at church, for heaven's sake. Louis supplied Vasily with flowery words designed to woo a bride, most of which he forgot in the moment. But it did not matter. She was as infatuated as he was, saying yes almost before the last syllable of his halting question and knowing nothing at all about her groom. Louis and Misha stood in supreme awkwardness in a crowd of people who did not mask their disapproval.

The besotted couple married in Capri on their way home.

...

Misha sat in a wingback chair before the fire the night of his best friend's honeymoon with the queen of hearts, a glass of single malt Scotch on the table next to him. He pulled the ace of diamonds from his wallet, meaning to throw it in the flames, but stared at it, remembering the closing words of that cursed old woman.

"I have no soul, old witch," he sneered.

The woman spat at the ground, disgusted.

"Then she will give you hers."

He returned the card to his wallet, drained his glass, and sought much needed rest in his empty bed.

The End

If you enjoyed this Volume of the first four books in The Charlemagne Files, please consider leaving a short review at your favorite bookstore.

Join the Charlemagne Files newsletter for more stories and information about the series, its world of covert operations, and the lives of the characters on the team. Sign up at charlemagnefiles.com/contact.

CHARLEMAGNE AND THE SECTION

The fictional world of The Section follows a few conventions. It may help the first-time reader of The Charlemagne Files to know some of these.

Who/what/ where is The Section?

The Section is a department of an intelligence agency of the United States. Its employees are civil servants. It includes support staff members who provide identity documents, financial controls, and physical and document security. The offices are near the East Coast, maybe Virginia.

The operational agents are called babysitters. They arrange on-site logistical support for freelance specialists during operations. Most operations are not conducted within the United States, with some exceptions.

Babysitters themselves do not carry identity documents in their names during an operation and never carry any official identification from their organization. Their purpose is to allow the organization to deny any association with them or their mission.

Nicknames

Babysitters in The Section receive nicknames from their coworkers when they join the office. These names are often undesirable and used mercilessly among the members of the office. It is part of the team-building process in a stressful occupation.

Coins

Challenge coins are traditionally stamped with symbols or mottos that designate the intelligence unit of their owners. The tradition is that when members of the unit are present at the bar and one produces his coin, all must produce theirs. Anyone failing to show their coin is responsible for the bar tab. If all produce their coins, then the challenger who first produced his or her coin is responsible for the tab.

File designations

The highest classification of information is Top Secret. Beyond Top Secret, more sensitive information is strictly controlled in a number of ways including designation as Sensitive Compartmented Information (SCI). This requires an additional clearance and often a named clearance based on Need-To-Know.

In The Section, files on specialists or specialist teams receive a one-word code name, printed across the file and restricted to very few people. When a solo or specialist team is employed on an operation, another designator word will refer to the operation and will be used for funding, reports, etc.

The Section's file name for Charlemagne is WEDGE. Thus CETUS WEDGE (second book of the Charlemagne Files) means an operation dubbed CETUS using the team called WEDGE.

Specialist

A team or solo operative used by Western governments for black operations conducted without fingerprints in high-risk situations expected to involve death.

GLOSSARY OF USEFUL TERMS

(GUT)

AC - Aircraft Commander. The pilot who flies from the left seat of the cockpit and is in command of the aircraft, its crew, and any passengers.

AGE - Aircraft Ground Equipment. Air Force term for what is sometimes called ground support equipment in civilian contexts. Includes things like ground power units, air start units, dollies, jacks, lights, tugs, and tractors.

AFSC - Air Force Specialty Code, also called a career field in casual conversation. Designated by an alpha-numeric code that identifies a person's specific job and skill level.

Babysitter - term devised by the author to indicate those who provide logistic cover and support to the more dangerous operatives.

Bear - NATO name for the Russian TU-95, a strategic bomber used by the Soviets for reconnaissance missions at or over the boundaries of US airspace. Fighters, especially those from Alaskan or coastal bases, intercepted these forays regularly, a mutual game played by US reconnaissance platforms and MIG fighters near Soviet airspace.

Bring-Up Investigation: An expansion of a security investigation to add information because of a time-lapse, usually five years, since the last investigation, or to require additional details for a higher level of clearance.

Class B's - (Air Force) Blue uniform with shirt and tie but not the more formal blue coat.

Class B bachelor - person on temporary duty away from his/her home unit who removes his or her wedding ring for reasons not having to do with safety around the aircraft.

Cockroaches in the car - Okinawa's climate is hot and quite humid. Americans stationed there often buy their cars very used, somewhat rusty, and if not already home to the local insect wildlife, eventually infested. It is advisable at night to shoo them off the seat before sitting down.

COMSEC - Communications Security.

HUMINT - Human Intelligence. Not a comment on the thinking power of Homo sapiens. This refers to the gathering of information and leverage through the use of human relations, manipulations, and interactions.

Kadena Air Base - Large U.S. Air Force base on Okinawa, Japan. Known as the Keystone of the Pacific, it is home to the 18th Wing. Twenty thousand military members and federal employees and their dependents live or work on the base.

Making regular - Only graduates of the Air Force Academy are commissioned as regular officers when they become second lieutenants. All others, such as ROTC and OTS graduates, are commissioned as reserve officers even though they are on full-time active duty. Approximately four years later, a promotion board decides whether such officers should be offered regular commissions, usually when they pin on captain. It is the first real mark of successful career progression for a non-academy grad, though nothing tangible goes with it. One's boss knows one made it, and that means everything.

MREs - meals, ready to eat. Modern successors to K-rations and other attempts at field rations.

O-6 - A full colonel, as opposed to a lieutenant colonel. Also popularly referred to as a full bird colonel, because of the eagle insignia of rank.

Okuma Military Resort, Okinawa - Beach resort on Okinawa for use by armed forces personnel, federal employees, and their dependents.

Q - colloquial term for the BOQ or VOQ, bachelor officer quarters (for permanent duty) or visiting officer quarters (for those on temporary duty).

Škorpion - Czech-made submachine pistol.

Skoshi KOOM - Iconic restaurant on Kadena Air Base, now called Jack's Place after the man who made it the favorite haunt of so many, including the author. Skoshi is Japanese for small and KOOM stands for Kadena Officers' Open Mess.

Squadron Officer School - a military education course for company-grade officers (lieutenants and captains) held at Maxwell AFB, Montgomery, AL. At the time of Captain Nolan's attendance, it would have been 12 weeks long. Selection for in-residence attendance was somewhat competitive.

Tanker - An aircraft that refuels other airplanes in flight. A tanker of the 909th Air Refueling Squadron is a Boeing 707 designated as the KC-135. At the time of this story, the crew of a 135 included the aircraft commander, co-pilot, navigator, and boom operator.

TDY - Temporary duty, usually requiring travel away from one's permanent duty station.

UCMJ - Uniform Code of Military Justice - legal foundation of military conduct. All military members are subject to its jurisdiction, regardless of their location.

Zoomie - Graduate of the United States Air Force Academy

GLOSSARY OF GAME NAMES

Frank Cardova: long-time babysitter of Charlemagne; later, head of The Section; his real name is Leo Vilseck; Section nickname is Buddy.

Jay Turner: FBI counterintelligence agent with a private agenda; no aliases.

Mack: so dubbed by Western babysitters because he uses a knife at times; leader and decision maker of Charlemagne; called Misha by other members of his team; probable real name is Michael; last name is unknown.

The Frenchman: marksman and technical expert of Charlemagne; real name is Louis; last name unknown.

Vasily Sobieski: deceased explosives expert and martial artist whose father was a noted solo specialist; no aliases.

Charlie Taylor: marksman; son of Mack; probable real name is Michael; last name unknown.

Steve Donovan: recent new member of Charlemagne; martial artist; former fighter pilot; abandoned real name was Daniel Martin Kessler.